Andrey Kurkov was born in St Petersburg in 1961. Having graduated from the Kiev Foreign Languages Institute, he worked for some time as a journalist, did his military service as a prison warder in Odessa, then became a film cameraman, writer of screenplays and author of critically acclaimed and popular novels.

ANDREY KURKOV

The Milkman in the Night

TRANSLATED FROM THE RUSSIAN BY
Amanda Love Darragh

VINTAGE BOOKS
London

Published by Vintage 2012

2 4 6 8 10 9 7 5 3 1

First published with the title *Nochnoi Molochnik* in 2009
by Alterpress, Kiev

First published in Great Britain in 2011 by Harvill Secker

Vintage
Random House, 20 Vauxhall Bridge Road,
London SW1V 2SA

www.vintage-books.co.uk

Addresses for companies within The Random House Group Limited
can be found at: www.randomhouse.co.uk/offices.htm

The Random House Group Limited Reg. No. 954009

A CIP catalogue record for this book
is available from the British Library

ISBN 9780099548867

This publication was effected under the auspices of the Mikhail
Prokhorov Foundation TRANSCRIPT Programme to Support
Translations of Russian Literature

 transcript

The Random House Group Limited supports The Forest Stewardship
Council (FSC®), the leading international forest certification
organisation. Our books carrying the FSC label are printed on FSC®
certified paper. FSC is the only forest certification scheme endorsed
by the leading environmental organisations, including Greenpeace.
Our paper procurement policy can be found at:
www.randomhouse.co.uk/environment

Printed and bound by CPI Group (UK) Ltd, Croydon, CR0 4YY

1

Lipovka village, Kiev region

Deprived of human attention, the lonely Milky Way was languishing in the winter sky. The night was utterly still and quiet. Not a single dog was barking, as though the low, starry sky had somehow sedated them all. Irina was the only one not sleeping. She had been awake all night listening to her chest, which had started hurting the previous evening. She lay there quietly contemplating her pain, not wishing to bother anyone and not getting up early in case the creaking of the bed woke Yasya. She got up as she usually did just after 4 a.m. She boiled the kettle, mixed the Malysh formula milk in a one-litre jar and placed it on the warm lid of the old boiler, which was humming away quietly in the little boiler room. The sweet, warm smell of baby clothes and muslins drifted down from the ceiling, where they had been hung to dry the previous evening.

Before leaving the house Irina kissed her three-month-old daughter, who was sleeping contentedly in the corner of their cosy bedroom, directly beneath the icon of St Nicholas. Then she went in to her mother's room and whispered, 'I'm off now!' Her mother nodded and reached for the lamp on her bedside table.

As she left the front yard Irina looked back at the house she'd grown up in – a neat brick bungalow built by her own father, who had recently died of liver disease. A gentle glow of light came from one of the four front windows. The metal frame creaked as Irina's mother looked under her bed for her well-worn slippers, wheezing and muttering to herself. But Irina didn't see or hear any of this.

At first they had used firewood to heat the house, and as a child she had loved watching the grey smoke drifting up into the evening sky. But when they installed the boiler her father had dismantled the stove. It made more room in the house, but the chimney on the roof had fallen silent. Even now, on this dark winter's morning, the house didn't look quite right without that grey smoke drifting into the sky!

The snow crunched underfoot. Irina hurried towards the road, not wanting to miss the first minibus taxi to Kiev. The minibus passengers all knew one another; they all knew the driver Vasya, and they all knew that his wife had left him. She'd gone off with one of their neighbours, who was a welder and a Baptist and never touched a drop.

A pair of warm, yellow headlights appeared on the road as soon as Irina stopped. The minibus pulled up without Irina even having to flag it down.

It was warm and quiet inside the minibus. Pyotr Sergeevich, who worked as a security guard on a building site in Kiev, was fast asleep with his head resting on his shoulder. The others were dozing. Several of her travelling companions looked up, their eyes full of sleep; Irina greeted them with a nod and took a seat by the door. Her chest was still hurting but she tried to ignore it.

In an hour's time the minibus would deposit them all near the Zhytomyrska metro station, and she would wait for the first train to take her onwards, to where she was expected, where she was paid.

2

Some stories have a beginning but no end. There simply is no possible way for them to end because their beginning gives rise to dozens of separate stories, each with its own continuation. It's like when a pebble strikes a car windscreen, sending cracks spreading out in all directions, and every pothole in the road causes at least one of the cracks to lengthen. This particular story began one winter's night and is still unfolding today. But all we know for now is the beginning. And just when you think you're at the end, you'll realise you're only halfway through. It would take more than a lifetime to follow every story to its conclusion. But we do know when and where this story began: one night in Kiev, on the corner of Striletska Street and Yaroslaviv Val, not far from the Radisson hotel. Someone parks their pink Hummer there every night. More specifically, it all started in the narrow gap between the Hummer, which was parked half on the pavement, and the wall of the café on the corner. The café was called Shkvarochka and hadn't been open that long, maybe a year or so.

It was the middle of the night, and Eduard Ivanovich Zarvazin, pharmacist and inveterate mushroom gatherer, had a strange look about him as he walked along Yaroslaviv Val towards this corner from the direction of the Golden Gates. He was dressed for autumn in a long raincoat and a hat and wore patent-leather boots with

3

pointed toes, which shone in the light from the street lamps. That's right! It was winter, not autumn – the middle of January to be precise. And everything was gleaming in the light from the street lamps, but most of all the snow and the ice. Eduard Ivanovich was walking at a leisurely pace, as though he were simply out for a stroll on a calm winter's night through the deserted, picturesque streets of Kiev's so-called 'quiet centre'.

At the same time a thirty-year-old woman was hurrying nervously along Striletska Street towards the same corner. She was wearing a long but lightweight fox-fur coat, which had been bought for her two years previously in the summer sales by a lover she could barely remember. The soft light gave her blonde hair a distinctive, subtle sheen and her thin, straight little nose was rather red, either because of the light frost or due to a mild cold. But let's assume it was the frost. Beautiful women don't suffer from colds. At least, not when they're out on the street in the middle of the night.

She stopped briefly outside the Norwegian Embassy to read a sign giving details of the opening hours for visa applications. Not that she needed a Norwegian visa . . . She was just one of those individuals prone to daydreaming, who love to read the names of streets, shops, cafés and restaurants but stop for even longer by handwritten notices such as 'Lost Cat'.

When she started walking again a young-looking, athletic man of around forty started to cross Striletska Street from the Radisson hotel side. He was wearing a dark blue jacket, jeans and brown trainers, and his eyes scanned the winter street with the indifference of a webcam. Even the man walking towards him in a raincoat and a hat failed to arouse his interest. But when the blonde-haired woman emerged from behind the pink Hummer that was parked on the pavement at the corner of the street, the man in the long coat and hat stopped, and a knife gleamed in his hands.

Noticing the glint of the knife, the woman stopped two paces from the man and screamed. The man in the dark blue jacket sprang forward – another second and he knew it would be too late to save the terrified lady in the fur coat. She had backed up against the wall of the café and was standing there rooted to the spot, unable to comprehend what had happened. The man in the jacket grabbed her hand and pulled her after him. She glanced over her shoulder and saw a body lying motionless on the snow-covered pavement between the Hummer and the wall of the café on the corner. And a knife, which was no longer gleaming. The man in the jacket ran down Ivana Franko Street, still pulling the woman behind him. He held her hand tightly in his own and kept looking round and hurrying her along with his eyes and his lips, which were mouthing the words, 'Come on!' She was having trouble running in her high-heeled Italian boots. Her open fur coat fluttered like the flag of an obscure winter country, and shock was frozen in her eyes.

3

Boryspil airport, morning

The world has its share of cheerful souls. Take, for example, Dmitry Kovalenko, the sniffer-dog handler: as he inspected the rows of checked baggage with his German shepherd, Shamil, he was humming a raucous pop song by two schoolgirls that seemed altogether inappropriate for the time of day – 'They'll Never Catch Us.' Shamil had been sniffing suitcases and holdalls since 4 a.m. When he'd started his eyes had been shining, sparkling and burning with professional zeal, but after three hours of work this zeal was somewhat diminished. Shamil was looking forward to the end of his shift. As if to spite him, that morning's air passengers were unusually law-abiding. Not the slightest whiff of drugs in their bags. And all Shamil wanted was to please his master, whose eyes had never expressed anything remotely resembling 'zeal'. He just wished his master would stop yawning.

But that morning Dmitry was yawning for real – not because he was bored at work, but because he hadn't had enough sleep the night before. His younger sister Nadya had been celebrating her twenty-fifth birthday, so they'd partied all night and he'd ended up going straight to work. There had been about twenty of them there, all close friends. Eating, drinking, singing karaoke . . . The karaoke was the reason that song about not being able to catch them was stuck in his head. 'Who the hell wants to catch you anyway?!' Dima thought about the two singers, but try as he might he still couldn't get the song out of his head.

Meanwhile Shamil's wet nose carried on extracting smells from the suitcases and bags, until suddenly one completely new and unfamiliar smell caught his attention.

The smell in question was coming from a black plastic suitcase with wheels. The suitcase was new, his nose told him so immediately, but he could also detect a strange, heavy and ominous sense of exhilaration. Shamil didn't start barking noisily and enthusiastically like he usually did in such situations, but turned to his master in confusion. His master had also stopped but was looking beyond the baggage section at the open doors, the motor trolleys loaded with suitcases and, nearby, the baggage handlers Boris and Zhenya. They were standing there in their green overalls, smoking and chatting quietly.

Boris had an impressively luxuriant moustache, which grew down to his chin. He looked over, saw the dog handler and his dog frozen to the spot and fell silent, watching them. The second man, Zhenya, also turned round.

'Hey, looks like he's found something,' said Zhenya.

'Great, that's all we need,' said Boris sadly, with a sigh. 'Just think, one suitcase full of loot through the back door, and we could retire and live happily ever after.'

They threw their cigarette butts to the floor, squashing them with the tips of their heavy black boots, in accordance with the fire-prevention regulations. They went over to Dima.

'Well?' Boris asked the dog handler. 'Are you going to hand the loot over to your arsehole bosses again, so each of them can upgrade his BMW to a Lexus?'

The two of them fixed Dima with serious, questioning looks. They were both heavyset men in their fifties.

'I don't have a lot of choice, do I?' Dima shrugged.

'Well, the dog's not going to go telling tales,' said Boris, quite reasonably. 'We can get it out of this secure zone in one piece.' He nodded at the suitcase.

'And save its owner from a prison sentence,' added Zhenya. 'It's a win–win situation!'

Dima was feeling stressed. He was paying for his sleepless night – his body ached all over, and now his mind had started to ache as well. And that damn song about not being able to catch those girls was still going round and round inside his head.

'Well?' Boris wanted a firm answer.

Deciding to rid himself of all of his problems in one go, Dima resolutely waved his hand.

Boris the baggage handler nodded, then took a piece of chalk out of his overall pocket and drew a tick on the suitcase.

Shamil sensed that something was wrong and looked up at his master.

'What are you staring at? Get a move on!' ordered Dima, annoyed. 'Your job is to use your nose, not your eyes!'

But Shamil didn't understand why his master hadn't pulled the suitcase out. Usually when this happened his master would take a walkie-talkie out of his breast pocket and speak into it, using words that fell outside the category of canine commands and which Shamil therefore didn't understand. But whatever he said must also have been some kind of order, because literally within minutes several people would come running up to them – one would read the luggage tag with a scanner, and the others would quickly pick up the suitcase and take it off somewhere.

'Didn't you hear me?' Dima yelled at Shamil. 'Do as I tell you!'

Shamil heard him all right. He heard that he and his nose had to continue along the row of luggage. He sniffed a couple of bags, a brown suitcase, a trunk shrink-wrapped in polythene. He picked up the scent of a rather tasty dry sausage, tobacco, a piece of lard. He started drooling with hunger, his saliva dripping to the floor. He stopped and looked back at his master.

'What is it this time?' Dima panicked and glanced back too, at the baggage handlers who were walking towards the motor trolley parked near the open gates. 'I've had enough of this . . . Lie down!' Dima ordered the dog.

He took out a cigarette and walked over to the open doors to smoke.

4

Lipovka village, Kiev region
A blizzard had been howling outside the window all night, but by
4 a.m. it had calmed down, leaving a fresh layer on top of the deep
snow that was already there.

Irina ran out towards the road, tying her fluffy grey scarf on the
way. She stopped at the roadside and peered into the darkness,
expecting two egg-yolk headlights to come into view.

She kept her eyes fixed on the road for about five minutes. The
frost was biting, its needles pricking her cheeks and nose.

Irina started to worry. She couldn't be late. Her boss was strict.
'Don't bother coming back!' she would say. And then what? What
would she do for money?

Then, finally, the glare of two orange headlights distracted
her from her troubled thoughts. She stepped forward onto
the road and peered at them. The headlights were different,
unfamiliar.

'Maybe it's a different minibus,' she thought and put her hand
out to flag it down, just to be on the safe side.

A red Mazda pulled up beside her. The driver, a man of around
forty wearing a black leather jacket with the collar turned up, leaned
across and opened the passenger door.

'Where are you off to at this time in the morning?' he asked.

'Are you going to Kiev?'

'Yes, jump in.'

It was warm in the car. Irina removed her scarf.

'That scarf doesn't suit you,' said the man, shaking his head. 'You're more beautiful without it.'

'Beauty is a distraction,' Irina retorted.

The man looked at his passenger in surprise.

'For whom?'

'You, for example, from the road! It's dangerous . . . And me, from—'

The driver burst out laughing.

'You're distracted by your own beauty?'

'Stop laughing at me!' she said indignantly, her voice completely serious. 'Just because I'm from the country you think you can say anything you like to me.'

'I'm from the country too,' the driver shrugged. 'You can say anything you like to me!'

'I've got a three-month-old baby,' said Irina, offended. 'I'm not some kind of –'

'Look, I'm sorry,' said the man, suppressing his smile.

Irina felt stupidly upset, affronted, although she didn't really know why. Then suddenly she was saved: like the light of a torch leading her out of the dark, she recognised her minibus ahead of them by the side of the road. Nearby she saw several of her regular travelling companions and the driver, down on all fours near the front wheel.

'Oh! It's my minibus!' exclaimed Irina. 'I need to get out!'

'But it's broken down!' the driver exclaimed. 'And you need to get to Kiev! You'll catch your death standing by the side of the road while they fix it.'

'Stop the car! It's my minibus!' Irina repeated stubbornly.

The man shrugged and stopped the car.

Without even thanking him Irina ran up to Vasya, the driver.

'Why didn't you pick me up?' she asked in an aggrieved tone.

The driver looked up at her.

'They changed the timetable by five minutes. I set off earlier now.'

'But what if I hadn't caught up with you?'

'Look,' Vasya snorted with irritation. 'They told me to leave five minutes earlier, so I did!' He nodded at the other passengers. 'They all made it! Because they came out and stood by the road fifteen minutes earlier, rather than lying in bed drooling all over the pillow. You like a lie-in, so you missed the bus! Now, get out of my way!'

Irina stared at the driver incredulously, shocked by his callous indifference. She couldn't believe that someone whose personal life she knew about in far more detail than she would have wished could treat her, his regular passenger, in such a way.

Vasya sighed and stood up.

He told them all to get on. Everyone took their seats in silence. Irina took her usual seat by the door. The engine started and normality seemed to be restored. The day was beginning in its usual rhythm, surrounded by the usual sleepy faces.

Irina took the metro to Arsenalna station, where she left the half-empty carriage. She adjusted her scarf and looked over her shoulder, noticing that she was the only one on the long platform. She went up the first escalator, then the next. She was still alone. And there was no one coming down either. It struck her as odd, although it was the same every day – this station was just particularly dead. For some reason it only got busy later on; she was the only one so early.

11

Her chest hurt. It felt constricted. The escalator crawled slowly upwards. It wasn't in a hurry to get anywhere.

Irina thought about the driver who had given her a lift. She sighed at her own stupid behaviour, then smiled. What a funny man! But she had to admit that he'd been right about the scarf. She would have to dye it.

5

Apartment No. 10, Reitarska Street, Kiev

'Where have you been? Where have you been?' The repetitive jangling of his wife's voice assaulted his ears like a miner's pick.

Semyon opened his eyes. His head was full of noise. His feet were aching, as though he'd been for a long walk in shoes that didn't quite fit.

'Have you gone deaf or something?' The tears filling Veronika's eyes had overflowed into her voice.

Semyon raised his head and looked at his wife in her towelling dressing gown.

'I haven't been anywhere.' He waved his hand dismissively. 'What are you going on about?'

'What am I going on about?' she repeated indignantly. 'You went off somewhere at one in the morning, came back at four and then fell asleep right there in that chair, without even getting undressed! "I haven't been anywhere," he says. And what's that on your sleeve?'

Semyon looked down at the sleeves of his denim shirt. There

was some kind of stain on the right one. At his feet lay his dark blue winter jacket, bought for a trip to Alaska that had never taken place. A group of rich adventure-seekers had promised to take him with them as team masseur and all-round nice guy (with an impressive physique and experience of working as a bodyguard). At the time they'd said, 'Make sure you get yourself the right kit, it's going to be minus fifty!' He'd got himself the right kit, but the expedition had been postponed. Indefinitely. He still had the jacket, though . . . And for some reason it was now lying on the floor.

Semyon looked around. He took his trainers off.

'Well? Aren't you going to answer me?' There was that importunate jangling noise again.

'What do you want me to say?' He stared up at his wife.

Seeing the look on her husband's face, she took a step back, afraid that she'd gone too far.

'I must have been out drinking with someone.'

'Who would you have been out drinking with all night? You never go out drinking!'

Semyon shrugged and felt a sudden pain in his left collarbone. He rubbed the sore place with his hand and looked up at his wife again. She was crying. But at least she was doing it quietly.

Brushing her tears away, Veronika went out into the hallway and stopped in front of the heavy iron door. She opened it decisively and slammed it hard behind her. Thunder reverberated down the stairwell.

When the noise had died away, the sound of footsteps could be heard from below. Veronika adjusted her towelling dressing gown and looked down. Her neighbour Igor was coming upstairs.

'Locked yourself out?' he enquired sympathetically.

'A draught caught it,' she explained. 'Semyon will let me in,' she said, and pressed the doorbell.

As if to spite Veronika, her neighbour stood and waited at the door with her, apparently hoping his services might be required. When Veronika pressed the bell a second time, Igor followed it up by rapping on the door with the back of his hand. Again, thunder filled the landing and stairs.

'It's OK,' Veronika said to her neighbour. 'He's probably just in the bathroom . . .'

Igor nodded and walked over to his own door, which was directly opposite. He stopped and looked back.

'A pharmacist was murdered tonight, just outside,' he said. 'He was a good man. A mushroom-gatherer, too. Used to cure friends with his own medicines. Better than that Kashpirovsky and all his psychic healing!'

Veronika heard the jingling of a key behind her and felt the rush of air displaced by her neighbour's door as it opened and closed.

A moment later her own door opened.

'Make your mind up, will you – are you going out or coming in?' Semyon's expression was one of genuine bewilderment. He looked exhausted and still half asleep.

'Let me in!' Veronika pushed him aside and ran into the hallway.

She stopped in front of the mirror and bitterly examined the new haircut she'd had the day before, which her husband hadn't even noticed.

'A bit shorter and it would be what they call a "gamine crop",' thought Veronika. 'No, it's fine as it is . . . I don't need to start relying on shorter haircuts to make me look younger just yet.'

6

'Fluffy! Fluffy!' Dima heard the voice of his wife, Valya. He had been trying to sleep. 'Fluffy! Where are you?'

Just then he heard from outside the familiar unpleasant snarling of the neighbour's bull terrier, which went by the name of King. Dog and owner were equally objectionable. Instead of taking the dog for a walk its owner would sometimes just let it out in his front yard, whereupon it would make a beeline for Dima and Valya's front yard to do its business – and chase their cat Fluffy if he should happen to be nearby – before retreating to its own territory.

Dima wrenched his head from the cushion and looked wearily round the room. The curtains at both windows were tightly drawn, which made for limited visibility.

'I wish Fluffy and that bloody dog would both just *sod off*!' Dima whispered to himself. He peered at the television stand, with its three shelves for all the video accessories and other gadgets that they didn't yet possess. That was where their grey cat loved to sit, on the top shelf just under the television. Valya called him Fluffy, and Dima called him Scruffy. The cat, who weighed at least ten kilos, answered to both names and ate anything that was put in his bowl.

'Scruffy . . . Hey, Scruffs. Here, puss puss!' whispered Dima, when he saw the cat occupying its favourite spot.

The cat ran over to his master and lowered his head, expecting to be scratched behind the ears.

'Valya!' called Dima. 'He's in here!'

The door opened and Valya came in, wearing fluffy slippers and an apron over her lilac flannel dressing gown. The smell of freshly prepared fish wafted in with her. The cat shot straight through into the kitchen like a creature possessed, and the door closed behind him. Dima resumed his attempts to sleep, but the fish smell was too strong and the noise of traffic kept intruding from outside – their building was near the main road that was used to transport sizeable ferroconcrete structures out of a nearby factory.

'Maybe a double shot of sleeping draught would help,' Dima thought and looked over at the sideboard, where an ordinary half-litre bottle of vodka stood behind a glass door, in case of unexpected guests. On the bottom shelf of the same sideboard stood several bottles of home-brew infused with young nettle leaves. These were for expected guests. Dima loved infusing vodka with herbs and berries – it tasted nicer and was supposedly better for you.

He got up from the sofa, poured himself a shot of home-brew and downed it in one. Suddenly the smell of fish was quite welcome: he didn't have any snacks to hand so chased the vodka with a few deep breaths.

He lay down again and went straight to sleep, as though the double shot were all that his weary body had needed.

After eating his fill of fish guts the cat tried to push his way back into the room where his master was sleeping, where it was warm and cosy. But he was thwarted by the closed door. He had no choice but to stay in the kitchen and watch his mistress from under the ribbed cast-iron radiator. Once she'd put the fish in the oven, she turned her attention to a couple of pigs' trotters. A huge pot stood

16

on the gas ring. 'Ah, we'll be having jellied meat!' thought the grey cat.

Just then there was a knock at the door and his mistress put the sharp knife back into the knife block and went out into the hallway.

'We're from the airport,' explained one of the men standing on the doorstep. 'We need a word with Dima.'

'Well, he's asleep. He's just back from his shift.' Valya felt the need to protect her husband.

'It's really important,' the second man insisted. 'It'll only take five minutes. We've just got to discuss one thing with him, that's all.'

Valya wouldn't let them into the house. She left them standing on the doorstep while she went back inside to wake her husband.

'There are some people from work here to see you, from the airport. They're waiting on the doorstep. Are you coming out?'

Dima gave a deep sigh and swung his feet off the sofa. 'Do you know who they are?' he asked his wife, although he knew perfectly well that she wouldn't have recognised a single person he worked with. Firstly because he didn't socialise with anyone from work, and secondly because Valya herself had never been to Boryspil airport. Or to any other airport, for that matter.

Coming to the door, Dima fixed his sleepy gaze on his visitors and recognised them immediately – it was the baggage handlers Boris and Zhenya. The ones who had talked him into 'not noticing' the black plastic suitcase that had aroused Shamil's interest.

'We've got it!' Boris nodded in the direction of a brown Volkswagen Passat standing on the other side of the fence.

'You should have opened it up yourselves,' said Dima, with a weary sigh.

'No.' Boris shook his head. 'Not without you. It's got to be fair.

17

We'll open it up together, split the contents between us and then forget it ever happened. OK?'

Dima nodded.

'Let's do it in your garage,' suggested Zhenya.

Dima yawned and went back into the hallway to get the garage key.

He went into the garage first and made his way to the space between the back wall and his old BMW. 'Bring it over here, I've got an inspection lamp.'

He switched the lamp on, and the baggage handlers carefully put the suitcase down on the concrete floor. The luggage tag was still hanging from the handle of the suitcase, bearing the code of the destination airport: Vienna.

'Have you got anything to smash the lock with?' Boris asked Dima.

'Let's have a look.' Dima went over to his wooden toolbox in the corner of the garage and took out a hammer and chisel. 'Seems a shame to break it,' he sighed, crouching down.

'Don't worry about it. You wouldn't be able to take it on a plane again anyway – you'd never get rid of the smell, and any dog would start barking as soon as it got anywhere near it.'

Dima placed the blade of the chisel against the combination lock. He struck it with the hammer and the lock split in two.

Boris and Zhenya grinned in anticipation of discovering the secrets within.

As soon as Dima opened the suitcase, he was hit by a sweetish smell that seemed vaguely familiar.

There was cardboard on top, then a layer of corrugated packing paper, then rows and rows of identical little boxes packed in tightly, each about the size of a cigarette packet. One of the boxes was damp. Dima opened it and carefully extracted a broken glass ampoule. He dropped this one on the floor and took out another ampoule, which was intact and full of an opaque liquid. He held it out to Boris.

Boris held the ampoule up to the inspection lamp and looked at it in the light.

'There's nothing written on it,' he remarked, passing it to his friend.

Zhenya also rolled the ampoule around in his fingers, then shrugged and handed it back to Boris.

'Buggered if I know what it is,' Boris said pensively. He looked from the ampoule to Dima. 'Do you know any doctors?'

Dima thought about it. He knew one doctor's assistant and a vet. The latter had cured their cat of constipation the previous year.

'Not a normal one, no.'

Boris carefully snapped the end off the ampoule and held it up to his nose. He sniffed it.

'Smells like valerian,' he said.

'Well, we can soon find out.' Dima left the garage and came back carrying Fluffy. He put him on the floor with a plate in front of him, which had a hardened lump of lard on it. Dima flicked the lard into the corner of the garage and tipped the contents of the ampoule onto the plate.

Boris opened another ampoule, and the quantity of cloudy liquid on the plate doubled. The three men watched the cat.

Fluffy had a little look around then bent over the plate, lapped up the liquid and sat down abruptly on his hindquarters. He froze in this strange, un-catlike pose, like a trained dog obeying the command to sit. A minute later his front paws folded under him as well. He lay down and closed his eyes.

19

'So is that all it is then, just valerian?' Boris sounded disappointed.

Suddenly Fluffy got up, looked around drunkenly and wandered over to the half-open garage doors.

'No, it's not valerian,' said Zhenya. 'Valerian's like catnip, it makes them go nuts.'

He was about to say something else, but just at that moment they heard a shout in the street, followed by a mechanical noise and a feline screech.

Dima ran out into the street, the baggage handlers close behind him.

A bicycle lay on the ground just in front of the garage. About two metres away from it, near Boris's Passat, a man in a tracksuit with a skiing hat on his bloodstained head lay face down in the snow. He wasn't moving. Meanwhile, dragging his hind legs in a strange way, Fluffy was trying to crawl into the garden through a narrow gap between the fence and the ground.

'Get him into the garage!' ordered Boris.

They dragged the cyclist inside. Then his bicycle.

'Is he alive?' asked Dima, looking at Boris, who was leaning over the victim.

'Christ knows!' Boris was searching the cyclist's clothing. He pulled his wallet from the pocket of his tracksuit bottoms. Besides a few notes, the wallet contained a court summons. The moustachioed baggage handler scrutinised the document, and a cunning smile spread over his face. He put the wallet back into the tracksuit pocket but held on to the summons. Then he opened another ampoule and tipped the opaque liquid directly into the cyclist's mouth. The cyclist wheezed and half opened his eyes.

'There we go, he's breathing! Well, we know where he lives.'

Boris showed Dima the summons. 'I'll drop in on him tomorrow, tell him I found it in the street . . . and at the same time I can see how he is after today's dose of medication.'

'Good thinking. He's clearly smarter than he looks,' thought Dima, impressed with the baggage handler's ingenious plan.

A little while later Boris and Zhenya took the cyclist out into the street and sat him on the ground, propping him up with his back against the neighbour's fence. They threw his bike down next to him. Then they left, promising to return the following evening.

Dima shut the garage. He felt worried and depressed. He went to see how Fluffy was. The cat's motionless body lay on the snow under the fence.

Dima lifted Fluffy up and saw that the cat was dead. He laid him back down on the snow. The enormity of the situation suddenly hit him. His wife didn't expect too much from him emotionally – she talked to Fluffy more frequently and in greater depth than she did to him, her husband! What would happen when she found out that Fluffy was dead?

Dima panicked. He found an old potato sack in the garage and stuffed the body of the dead cat into it. Then he walked quickly and nervously down the street, racking his brains as he went, trying to work out where he could hide the body so that no one would find it. Fifteen minutes later he stopped in front of the charred remains of an old building that had caught fire a couple of years previously. Kids came and played here occasionally, but the abandoned front yard was of no interest to adults. Apart from the drunks who would use it to vomit or relieve themselves in on their way home. There was even a well for that very purpose.

Dima glanced furtively around and then, satisfied that he was alone on the street, slipped into the yard of the burnt-out building.

He went straight over to the well and looked down it. He couldn't see any water – the well was full of rubbish – but it must have been at least three metres to the bottom.

'Farewell, Scruffy!' said Dima, as he threw the sack containing the dead cat down the well.

'Have you seen Fluffy?' Valya asked him the minute he got home.

Dima shook his head. 'No, can't say I have.'

7

Lipovka village, Kiev region

Snow was falling heavily. Every now and then a sudden gust of wind would gather it and throw it back up into the air, sending it flying over the roof of the single-storey house so that it fell on the other side, outside the little room where Irina and her three-month-old daughter were sleeping. The baby's name was Yaroslava, shortened affectionately to Yasya or Yasenka by her grandmother, who looked after her every day and gently tried to encourage her to drink more of the Malysh formula milk, so that she would grow up quickly, say her first word and take her first steps.

'Come on, my little Yasenka! Just a little bit more!' Irina's mother – known to her nearest and dearest as Baba Shura – pleaded with the baby in her broad country accent, bringing the bottle of formula milk to the child's tiny mouth. But Yasya stubbornly pushed the bottle away without taking her beady little eyes off the television, which was showing the latest episode of *Gangs of St Petersburg*.

'Now, what am I going to tell your mother?' The old lady shook her head. 'She's off earning money for you in town, and what are you up to while her back's turned?'

The doorbell rang while the main characters of the television show were gunning each other down, but Baba Shura didn't hear it until the crossfire ceased. Then she jumped up, laid Yasya on the sofa and hurried to the door.

'Oh, you're back!' she cried, delighted to see her daughter.

Irina put her heavy shopping bag down on the floor and took off her headscarf.

'Go on into the kitchen, sit yourself down, there's some chicken for you on the stove,' her mother said to her in a comforting, domestic way before returning to her own room, without noticing the tears in her daughter's eyes.

In the kitchen Irina unpacked the shopping. She put the sausage and the herring in the fridge and the cans in the cupboard next to the sink. Then she sat down at the table, buried her face in her hands and started crying, quietly, barely sobbing. The strange emptiness she felt inside scared her. Or maybe it was just tiredness. Either way it was not something that could be solved by a quick nap or any amount of chicken and mashed potato.

Every day she rushed off to Kiev, her breasts taut with milk, to sit in a little room while an impassive woman in a white robe expressed her milk with a little pump before sending her off to the kitchen, where the nurse, a kind old woman, would give her a bowl of porridge and make sure that Irina ate every last mouthful. Sometimes there would be one or two other new mothers like her in the kitchen, and then the nurse would keep an equally strict eye on all of them. After the porridge she would spend a couple of hours walking around Mariinsky Park, which was just across the road from the 'offices' of this private enterprise – in actual fact an

23

ordinary apartment, if a little larger than usual. It resembled a milk kitchen, though in reality it was the exact opposite, because they took milk from new mothers rather than giving it out. And in return they paid these young mothers from the villages only about enough to cover the cost of formula milk for their own babies and the bus fare to Kiev and back.

Irina already knew several other single mothers.

'It's for female deputies from the Supreme Council,' Nastya-from-just-outside-Byshev told her once. 'They take some kind of special tablets straight after giving birth to stop their milk coming in, so their breasts don't sag, and then they raise their babies on our milk.'

Irina could believe it. She didn't think badly of such mothers. She'd never been able to think badly of others, even those who deserved it, although she did wish that she could see with her own eyes the baby being raised on her milk.

But on the way home today she'd had to stand in the minibus taxi for more than an hour. The combination of exhaustion and physical discomfort was probably why she spent the entire journey feeling sorry for both herself and her daughter Yasya, who was stuck at home with her grandmother all day even though her own mother was alive and well.

Irina felt better once she'd had a little cry. She ate some supper. She touched her breasts. Although they'd been emptied only three hours ago, they seemed to be filling with milk again. Irina went into her mother's room, picked Yasya up and brought her to her breast. The little girl latched on immediately and started moving her lips greedily. Irina felt a tickling sensation and a smile appeared on her face.

'Mind you don't spoil her,' called her mother. 'Or tomorrow

they'll say you haven't got enough milk, and they'll tell you not to bother coming back!'

'I'll have something else to eat before I go to bed,' Irina replied calmly, unfazed by her mother's words.

Before she went to bed, after eating some bread and lard and another plate of mashed potato, Irina dissolved the dark green fabric dye she'd bought in Kiev in a bowl and put her fluffy grey scarf in it to soak. She added a bit more water to the bowl, so that the scarf wouldn't come out too dark.

8

Apartment No. 10, Reitarska Street, Kiev, midday

Veronika had a slim-fitting lycra tracksuit that she liked to wear in the mornings. It made her look so fit and healthy that the thought of actually doing a fitness workout at home or walking to the gym brought an ironic smile to her pretty face. Today she had permitted herself the luxury of staying in bed until 10.30 a.m. And now that she was finally up, she had the sudden urge to do some housework.

As she put a load of whites into the washing machine, Veronika suddenly remembered Semyon's shirt. She bent down again, opened the round plastic door and pulled her husband's shirt out by the sleeve. The sleeve she pulled out first was relatively clean, but the other one was a different matter. She took the shirt over to the window to examine the brown stain more closely. She sniffed it and rubbed at it with her fingertips. The more she looked at it the more convinced she became that the sleeve was stained with blood. She started running through all the possible explanations, and her thoughts sent a shiver down her spine. She would have preferred to discover that her husband was having some kind of affair than to discover after twelve years together that he was a murderer!

She stuffed the shirt back into the washing machine, pressed the start button and went into the kitchen, anxious and absorbed in her thoughts.

The apartment was quiet. Semyon had taken a phone call early in the morning from his regular client, Gennady Ilyich, and had left straight away on business. He hadn't been out anywhere the previous evening. Although it had been uncomfortable, she'd kept her arm around his shoulder all night.

Veronika sat at the kitchen table next to the window, beyond which a light snow was falling. She remembered Igor telling her about the murdered pharmacist. 'Maybe I should ask him about it,' she thought. 'He might have more details. He reads the papers and watches all the news channels. They might have already found the murderer . . .'

A cup of tea with honey helped her to relax and eased her anxiety. She could have carried on sitting there for another half an hour, or even an hour. But questions, even unspoken ones, need answers. Otherwise they keep itching like mosquito bites, driving you mad. So Veronika went out onto the landing and rang her neighbour's doorbell. She waited for a couple of minutes before returning to her apartment.

'Oh well, I guess it wasn't meant to be,' she decided. And with that her thoughts turned to fate. What about it? It would have been a sin for her to lament her fate. The only child of a military pilot and a geography teacher . . . At home there were always plenty of sweets and chocolates, expensive fish for dinner and a large globe on the sideboard, which her mother would dust every now and then. An ill-advised first marriage at eighteen. Divorce six months later. Her second marriage, already in its thirteenth year, was a different matter entirely. During this time Semyon had gone from selling video cassettes at the Petrivka market to owning a small but successful firm organising security for various high-level meetings and corporate social events. Strictly speaking it wasn't even a firm, just two old friends – Semyon and Volodka – plus three or four 'robust' acquaintances who worked for him on a freelance basis as required. After four years in the security business Semyon had earned enough for a nice little apartment on Striletska Street, right in the centre. He didn't need an office. All his business was conducted over the phone. His main client, Gennady Ilyich, was a parliamentary deputy, which meant that his life both day and night was a continuous round of business meetings and other undertakings requiring secrecy and security. He and Semyon had known each other for a long time, since Petrivka days. Back then Gennady Ilyich had been responsible for the daily collection of money from the traders and he'd been nicknamed Crocodile Gena, after a popular children's character. 'We are the people, we're all children of the workers . . .' Gennady Ilyich would sometimes sing, and whenever Semyon was within earshot it always took him straight back to pitch No. 47 in the third row of the market. Then the song would attach itself to Semyon's brain like a burr and stay with him for the rest of the day. Sometimes he would still be singing it when he got home from work. Veronika had come to think of it as part of their domestic soundtrack, and whenever she heard it she smiled.

Over the years she had learned a lot from Semyon about the ups and downs of market life. During Semyon's trading years he'd been arrested more than once by the militia, and during his arrests he'd managed to make a number of useful contacts. Former sergeants had become majors and colonels, and now they occupied important positions they treated Semyon like a childhood friend and witness to their professional and career growth. Was this fate too? Of course it was!

Suddenly Veronika gave a shudder. She was gripped by an icy chill, plunged into an abyss. She had just had a flashback of something that had happened seven years previously, something that her psychotherapist had promised she would never remember again as long as she lived.

She looked out of the window in despair, at the fluffy snowflakes falling smoothly from the sky. Her right hand swept across the little table, colliding with her unfinished cup of tea and sending it crashing to the floor. The sound of breaking china brought Veronika to her senses. She looked down at the floor, at the white fragments of the cup. She felt a little better. But now this sudden chill in her soul became physical, and she started shivering. She went into the bedroom, took a thick Norwegian jumper out of her wardrobe and pulled it on over her Adidas sports top. Then she went into the bathroom and wrapped herself up in her emerald-coloured towelling dressing gown – a gift from Semyon the previous Valentine's Day. She did the belt up tight. Focusing her attention on warming her body – and thereby her soul – helped to bring her back to reality.

She picked up the larger fragments of the cup with her fingers and brushed the rest into the dustpan. She washed the floor and then decided to go out for a walk in the snow. The bright, white light always calmed her down. It made her feel like a little girl, curious and defenceless. She could remember being afraid of everything when she was about four or five years old. Afraid of being alone in a snowy field when she went with her parents to visit their friends in a village outside Kiev. Afraid to go too close to the road and the enormous, noisy lorries rushing past. But, strangely enough, she had actually relished this feeling of fear, in the same way that many children like scary fairy tales at bedtime even though they know that afterwards they won't be able to sleep without checking under their bed, or leaving the light on to keep monsters and bogeymen at bay.

Veronika wrapped a pashmina around her neck and swapped her towelling dressing gown for her long, brown sheepskin coat. She was planning to walk along by the tall and imposing rear wall of the St Sophia Cathedral as far as Stritenska Street, then to Rylsky Street and back again, three or four times. It was her tried and tested route for times like this, when she needed to regain her composure. Walking beside the high, white cathedral wall in the falling snow would make everything right with the world. With her inner world, at least. She had no control over the rest of it.

9

9 May Street, Boryspil

Following Fluffy's 'disappearance', life in Dima's house descended into an atmosphere of funereal gloom. Day after day Valya would wander round the town, questioning the ubiquitous old ladies about her missing grey cat. She also sent Dima out about five times a day to different areas of Boryspil where there had been reported sightings of a large grey cat matching Fluffy's description. Flyers featuring his photograph and the plaintive offer of a reward for his safe return had already been plastered up all over Boryspil. Valya had refused even to countenance her husband's suggestion to qualify the reward as 'modest'. Dima wished he'd kept his mouth shut and stayed out of it – the search for their errant pet was a mission doomed to fail from the outset, because Fluffy was somewhere he'd never be found. Well, theoretically it would be possible for someone to find his remains, but Valya would be unlikely to rejoice at such an outcome.

So Dima just waited patiently for his wife to calm down. He kept on going to work, supervising the routine olfactory inspection of airline baggage and paying close attention to Shamil's mood. But when he came home it was to an atmosphere of unremitting sorrow. Anticipating his wife's request, he would take it upon himself to announce, 'Right, I'm off to look for Fluffy!' And he would go out to the garage, where he had made himself a comfortable little corner between the back wall and his old BMW. He'd even rigged up an electric heater, to warm it up a bit.

That was where Boris and Zhenya found him. Of course they went to the house first, but Valya told them that Dima had gone out looking for Fluffy. They put two and two together and headed straight for the garage.

'You'll never guess what,' Boris began excitedly, once they'd installed themselves near the heater at the back of the garage. 'He was missing for three whole days!'

'Who?' asked Dima, whose thoughts were primarily occupied by the 'missing' Fluffy.

'That cyclist!' said Boris. 'His wife was going to pieces. I went round there with that summons three days running and ended up having to try and calm her down. I told her he'd probably gone into hiding so they couldn't hand him the summons in person. Then he comes home this morning, as thin as a rake.'

'He was skinny enough to start with,' recalled Dima.

'Well he's even skinnier now. He looks like he's escaped from a concentration camp – his cheekbones are sticking out and everything. And do you know what he said? Told her that he'd cycled over to Chernigov to visit his nephew!'

'Why?' asked Dima.

'That's what I said – why? But he just shrugged.'

'No,' Zhenya said slowly. It was his first contribution to the conversation. 'He said something about not feeling remotely tired . . . Said he had more energy than he knew what to do with, so he'd just decided to go a bit further afield . . .'

'Anyone fancy a drink?' asked Dima.

Boris shook his head, but Zhenya nodded enthusiastically.

Using the stool as a table, Dima put some salted cucumbers on a plate and filled two shot glasses. But before raising his glass he had a little moan about his wife's obsession with their missing cat.

'She'll get over it,' Boris assured him.

'But when? I can't take it any more. The way she's carrying on, anybody'd think we had a dead body in there!'

'Why don't you just find a cat that looks the same?' grinned Boris. 'Then you can pass it off as Fluffy. He was just an ordinary grey cat, wasn't he? There are hundreds of them running around the streets.'

'She'll know in her heart that it's not him,' said Dima, after a moment's hesitation.

'In her heart? Bollocks! Women come out with that sort of nonsense just to make themselves seem more sensitive. But they –' Zhenya didn't finish his sentence. He grabbed his glass and downed his shot nervously, then took a bite out of one of the cucumbers.

'Anyway, that's enough about cats.' Boris decided to change the subject. He looked at Dima. 'Have you managed to find a doctor?'

'When have I had the time to find a doctor? I've been looking for that bloody cat.'

'Forget about the cat. Find a doctor. Or a pharmacist. Pharmacists are more likely to know about ampoules.'

'Here's what you should do.' said Zhenya, holding up his forefinger to attract their attention. 'Take one of the ampoules into a pharmacy. Tell them you found it and don't know what it is.'

'Why don't you do it?' retorted Dima. 'Why should I have to go traipsing round the local pharmacies?'

'Indeed,' said Boris, smoothing his moustache and looking closely at Zhenya. 'Do it yourself.'

'All right, I will,' he agreed, after an awkward pause. 'Give me three ampoules and I'll . . . Well, I'll just go and get on with it, I suppose.'

Dima took three ampoules out of the plastic suitcase, which had been pushed against the wall. Zhenya stuffed them into his jacket pocket, nodded goodbye and left.

Boris and Dima looked at one another.

'What's up with him?' asked Dima.

Boris waved his hand but didn't reply.

'Go on, I'll have a drink now,' he said.

Dima poured.

'You should have drunk with us,' he said.

'I don't drink in groups of three any more,' Boris said

mournfully. 'Drinking in threes is the second sign that you're an alcoholic.'

'What's the first sign, then?'

'The first sign? Drinking alone.'

Boris downed his shot. 'You know what, I don't actually care what's in those ampoules, whether it's illegal drugs or a cure for cancer. All I want to do is sell them for a good price. Then I can send my daughter to university, pay for her to go privately. And as for your cat, you really should find one that looks the same, roll it around in the mud and bring it home. Tell her that he's been off chasing lady cats and is a little the worse for wear – that'll do the trick. It's not a cat she needs, anyway, it's a baby.'

'That's none of your business!' Dima leapt to his wife's defence.

'You're right,' agreed Boris, rising from the improvised wooden bench. 'But the suitcase is. And the sooner we sort it out, the better.'

10

Lipovka village, Kiev region

The following morning started fifteen minutes earlier than usual for Irina. She carried the bowl containing her fluffy scarf and the dye into the boiler room and hung the scarf on the washing line with the bowl directly underneath it, to catch the dye as it dripped off.

She was in a good mood as she got ready to leave the house. She had a cup of tea and ate a cold cottage cheese fritter, then made up the Malysh formula milk for Yasya. She had a brief moment of panic when she put her coat on: what should she wear on her head? Then her eyes fell on the woollen scarf that her mother had bought from some gypsies at the market in Fastov. It was black, with a pattern of pink roses. Her mother had bought three of them at the time, so there must be another two somewhere. Irina tied it round her head, picked up her bag and left.

The snow on the doorstep crunched underfoot.

The minibus taxi pulled up right on time. Once she had taken her usual place, Irina started to relax and fell into a doze. But instead of dreams her head filled with an unfamiliar blue darkness, and she heard a voice. It said, 'Trust me, he'll come back. He'll definitely come back.'

'Who will?' she asked in her sleep.

And the voice answered, 'He will.'

'But who is "he"?' she asked again. What if 'he' was Yasya's father? That particular 'he' was the last person she wanted to see again. But she wouldn't mind a different 'he', someone who could be a loving father to her daughter and a good husband to her . . . But a 'he' like that wouldn't just turn up. And in any case the voice had said he'd 'come back', not that he'd 'turn up'. People can only come back if they're there to begin with.

Irina drifted in and out of sleep as the minibus continued its journey along the dark road. Kiev was waiting for her, to collect the milk from her swollen breasts and to ask for more. Then it would empty them again, down to the very last drop, before sending her home with just enough money in her pocket to keep Irina repeating this daily routine until her milk ran dry.

'Hey, we're here!' the voice of Vasya the driver rang out over her head. 'Hurry up, or you'll be late.'

The nurse opened the door to her, wearing a white robe and

looking like she'd just woken up. She must have spent the night there.

Irina stripped to the waist and sat at the table. She immediately got goosebumps on her shoulders and arms. The old nurse noticed that Irina was cold and closed the top window, and then she positioned the plastic suction cup over Irina's left breast. She turned the pump on and it started humming, like a battery-operated child's toy. Milk started to run along the tube between the suction cup and the bottle.

'Lilya Petrovna has just upped and left,' grumbled the nurse. 'So now I'm left to deal with all the technical stuff.' She nodded at the pump.

In an attempt to take her mind off things, Irina thought back to the voice she'd heard in the minibus. She tried out the 'he' it had mentioned on all the men she knew. It turned out that she didn't know that many. Leaving aside her elderly neighbours in the village, she could count her male acquaintances on the fingers of one hand; if any one of these five were to return it would be no cause for celebration.

The suction cup migrated to her right breast. The humming of the little pump felt as familiar as Yasya's cries.

After a filling breakfast of porridge, Irina left her bag on the coat stand in the corridor and went for a walk in Mariinsky Park.

It was getting on for 8 a.m. Hordes of smartly dressed commuters, wrapped up warmly, were spilling out of the buses and minibus taxis that were pulling up at the stop. None of them were going to the park. They were all crossing the road and disappearing.

That was fine by Irina. It made her feel as though she almost owned it, this park adjoining Parliament and the pale turquoise building of the Mariinsky Palace. Maybe it was the porridge making her feel so warm and cosy despite the frost . . . Or maybe it was the fact that everyone else was on their way to work whereas her first shift was already over and she had a long break ahead of her, which was a luxury not enjoyed by regular employees, even secretaries!

Irina's face lit up with a smile. She adjusted her mother's gypsy scarf on her head and strolled along the path.

'That scarf doesn't suit you either,' called a voice that sounded familiar.

She turned round and recognised the man with mischievous sparks in his almond-shaped eyes. He was the one who had given her a lift in his red car when the minibus taxi had left without her.

'It's not mine, it's my mother's,' answered Irina.

'Yes,' he nodded. 'That's a grandmother's scarf if ever I saw one.'

'Well, my mother is a grandmother, she's got a granddaughter . . .'

The man was wearing a long, black leather coat with a high fur collar. But he wasn't wearing a fur hat. He wasn't wearing any kind of hat.

'Aren't you cold?' asked Irina, unable to take her eyes off his closely cropped head, as though she were inspecting it for signs of hair loss resulting from his failure to wear a hat in sub-zero temperatures.

'No,' he answered calmly. 'My name's Egor, by the way. What's yours?'

'Irina.'

'Come on, I'll buy you a dodgy cup of coffee,' said Egor.

Irina looked at him suspiciously.

'You can only get good coffee round here after nine o'clock. Unfortunately, at this time of the morning there's no choice.'

She nodded her assent and walked with him towards the bus stop on the main road, where buses and minibus taxis were still 'docking'. They went into the underground pedestrian crossing, taking the exit that brought them out on the intersecting road, and five minutes later they turned right and went into a little food shop with a café inside.

'Two three-in-ones,' Egor said to the assistant.

They drank the sweet coffee from disposable plastic cups, looking out of the shop window.

'Tastes OK to me,' shrugged Irina.

'It all depends what you're comparing it to,' smiled Egor. 'Do you work near here?'

'Yes,' said Irina. 'What about you?'

'Me too. Not far from where we met.'

'In the palace?' asked Irina.

'You could say that,' he answered, after a short pause.

A sudden mechanical voice nearby, practically between them, made Irina jump. She looked around to see where it was coming from, but Egor touched her hand gently to attract her attention and indicated that everything was fine.

'I'm on my way,' he said.

Irina noticed a black wire emerging from the high fur collar of his coat and ending in a small black earpiece, about the size of a fly, right next to his ear. She'd seen them on the television, usually on the President's security personnel.

Irina realised he was going to leave and she suddenly felt like crying. Not because he was leaving, without even finishing his plastic cup of 'dodgy' coffee, but because he seemed to be someone who had managed to turn his dreams into reality. He was relaxed, good-natured, self-confident . . .

'You're always walking in the park,' smiled Egor.

She nodded and smiled too.

'I'll come and find you. Maybe later today. I'll buy you a good coffee next time.'

'This one's not bad,' she said quietly.

Egor grinned and left the shop.

Irina was surprised to notice that he was almost a head taller than her.

'Hey, spare us a hryvna,' rasped a bearded tramp who had stopped before her, wearing a shabby, grey woollen coat and boots without laces. 'I'm freezing!'

Irina put her hand into her pocket. She found some change, counted out a hryvna and emptied it into the tramp's outstretched hand.

'Good,' he said, instead of thanking her. Then, looking over his shoulder, he headed straight for a woman in an expensive sheepskin coat who had just entered the shop.

Irina started to feel cold too. She finished her coffee and decided to return to the warmth of her milk kitchen.

The front door was open and Irina went straight in. She had to make way for two men in identical dark blue jackets, who were carrying a large metal milk churn into the building. They carried it down the corridor then opened the double doors at the end and disappeared into another corridor, which was considerably more luxurious, with a red carpet runner and paintings on the walls. Before Irina could make out the subject of the paintings, the double doors swung shut.

'Irochka, there's still some porridge left on the stove,' said Vera the nurse gently. 'Take your coat off and come on in.'

Irina nodded, without taking her eyes off the double doors.

'What's through there, behind those doors?' she asked, once she was in the kitchen.

'That's where clients come from the main entrance. The consultant sees them in his office. We used to have a Chinese consultant, but the one they've got at the moment is from Moscow, apparently,' whispered the elderly nurse. 'But you and me, we belong here in the kitchen. We're not allowed through there.'

Irina nodded again. She understood. As soon as she started eating her porridge the feeling of warm contentment returned, and all her questions – those that had already been answered and those that hadn't yet been asked – just seemed to disappear. Even her hearing seemed to have been inverted, like a wine glass. It was directed inward. She heard herself chewing her porridge, her breasts filling with milk and the loud, steady beating of her heart.

11

Apartment No. 10, Reitarska Street, Kiev
The winter continued to be mild and unobtrusive. Falling intermittently, the snow would melt in the mysterious warm breathing of the wind and then freeze again, turning to black ice. And then people would navigate the uneven pavements with care, waiting for fresh snow to dust their slippery path.

Semyon left before daybreak, promising to be back by 5 p.m. Veronika went out early to do the food shopping. When she got back she spent about an hour on the phone to her friend Tanya. She heard all about her new husband, her third already, who was apparently three years younger than Tanya but had exceptional life experience. Veronika felt that the details of this 'exceptional life experience' would be best explored when the two women met face-to-face.

Time passed slowly that day. Even the snow kept stopping and starting. With nothing else to occupy her, Veronika's thoughts turned to the health benefits of fresh air, and she decided to go for a walk. As she was in a good mood she didn't head for the back wall of the St Sophia Cathedral but for the corner of the three cafés, where Striletska Street met Yaroslaviv Val.

There she witnessed a scene that could not be described as either tragic or comic.

An elegantly dressed woman of around fifty, wearing an ankle-length polar-fox-fur coat and smart boots, stood outside one of the cafés with a hammer in one hand and a small funeral wreath in the other. The wreath was made of pine branches and decorated with artificial roses. Between the woman and the wall of the café on the corner stood a young man wearing jeans and a dark-coloured jacket. He looked about eighteen. And extremely nervous. He was saying something to the woman and gesticulating awkwardly.

The woman's face, attractive in the severity of its features, expressed incomprehension and anger. Regardless of what they were arguing about, Veronika suddenly felt it imperative that she stand alongside the woman and support her.

As she approached them the subject of the argument became clear. The woman in the polar-fox-fur coat turned to Veronika and vented her outrage. 'He was killed right here, and this jumped-up little jobsworth won't let me hang a wreath on the wall! Can you believe it? A car was blown up over there on Reitarska Street, near the Doors café, and there's been a wreath hanging there for the last five years, not bothering anyone!'

'That building's private property,' muttered the youth, looking from the woman holding the hammer and the wreath to Veronika and back again.

'What if it was your father who'd been killed here?' Veronika suggested, nailing the youth to the wall with a cold glare.

'My father's got nothing to do with it!' exclaimed the youth, faltering slightly. 'This is a café, not a cemetery. People come here to drink beer.'

'And my husband used to come here too!' said the woman in the fur coat, pursing her lips and thus expressing her contempt for this unremarkable young man.

'Look, go and talk to the manager about it, it's nothing to do with me. I was just told to take the wreath down. I'm only the security guard –'

'My husband has forty security guards working for him,' Veronika interrupted angrily. 'I'll tell him –'

The woman in the fur coat turned to Veronika. 'It's all right,' she said calmly. 'Where's your manager?' she asked the youth.

'In there,' he replied, with a glance at the café.

'Hold this,' said the woman, passing the hammer and the wreath over to Veronika. 'Let's go!' she commanded the youth.

The two of them went into the café. Veronika stayed on the pavement, which was covered with a light dusting of snow. She noticed a nail sticking out of the wall of the building. She hung the wreath on it and stood the hammer underneath, with its handle leaning on the wall. Now she felt more comfortable standing there.

The woman in the fur coat came out five minutes later. The first thing she did was to straighten the slightly lopsided wreath. She picked the hammer up from the pavement.

41

'It's all sorted. I'll take it down at weekends, and they'll leave it up there during the week,' she said.

'Why don't you come back to my place for a coffee?' Veronika suggested. 'I live just round the corner.'

12

Boryspil airport

Dima's shift finished at 9 a.m. It had been a quiet night. All the passengers on this particular shift had been law-abiding citizens, so despite his best efforts Shamil's eyes did not once light up with joy. And Boris and Zhenya the baggage handlers weren't at the airport that night – their shift obviously didn't coincide with Dima's.

'Just as well,' thought Dima, glancing at his watch and remembering the black plastic suitcase lying in his garage. 'I can do without any more hassle.'

There was one more flight to go, then his shift would be over and the shuttle bus would deliver the weary night-shift workers to their homes.

'Kovalenko!' barked the walkie-talkie in his pocket. 'Report to the customs manager!'

'I'm on my way,' Dima replied into the machine, looking at Shamil in bewilderment.

His boss greeted him coldly, with a cursory nod. He was sitting behind his desk, turning his tinted glasses over and over in his hands. His computer screen and keyboard had been pushed to the right-hand side of the desk, and several files of paper lay to the left.

'Were you on duty the morning of the twelfth?'

'Yes,' answered Dima.

'Was any luggage delayed in our department?'

'I don't think so . . .' Dima was immediately on guard but tried to maintain a neutral expression, to avoid accidentally raising his boss's suspicions. 'If anything happened, it would have been documented,' he said, nodding at the computer.

His boss took a sheet of paper with writing on it from under a file, put his glasses on and began to read. 'One suitcase, black, plastic. Smart Case brand.' He took his glasses off again and fixed the sniffer-dog handler with a steady stare. 'It was checked in for the morning flight to Vienna but never reached its destination. Does that ring any bells?'

Dima shook his head. 'There was definitely no luggage removed on that shift,' he answered, with greater conviction.

'I see. The baggage handlers must know something, then. All right, you can go.' His boss sighed.

Dima felt in this dismissal the threat of a shot in the back.

By the time he got back to the baggage section the luggage from Amsterdam had arrived. Dima and Shamil made their rounds, but everything was clean.

When he got off the shuttle bus Dima stopped at a café and contemplated popping in for half an hour. He didn't feel like going home. Valya had put a photo of Fluffy in a frame on the windowsill, and she'd even stuck a black strip across the bottom corner. This full-scale mourning for Fluffy had started to get on Dima's nerves.

He went in cautiously, but Valya wasn't there. Under an upturned

43

enamel bowl on a small plate on the kitchen table he found two cottage cheese fritters, which were still warm. The kettle on the hob was also warm.

Dima turned the photo frame on the windowsill round so that it faced the window and ate his breakfast in peace.

He thought about the conversation with his boss, all those questions about the black plastic suitcase. Dima suddenly imagined them carrying out an impromptu search of his house and garage. Fear paralysed his thought processes.

He called Boris the baggage handler.

'I need to see you. As soon as possible,' he said nervously.

'Have you found a doctor?' asked Boris.

'No, it's worse than that.'

'I can come over this evening.'

'Can't you come any earlier?'

'No, I'm at work.'

Their conversation did nothing to calm Dima's nerves. He took two shopping bags from the little cupboard in the hall and took them into the garage. He put the boxes of ampoules into them and started hacking at the empty suitcase with a hatchet. He thought he'd be able to break it up into smaller pieces, which he could put into a bag and throw into a rubbish skip, but the plastic Smart Case turned out to be a worthy opponent. The hatchet made a few small holes and a couple of dents but was not capable of inflicting any greater injury on it. Dima abandoned the enterprise and went home.

He sat down in the kitchen again and wrote his wife a note: 'Valya, gone to look for Fluffy.' Then he took the photograph of Fluffy out of the frame and put it in his inside jacket pocket.

The cold air outside invigorated Dima a little, although the feeling of tiredness from working the night shift still lay like a dead weight across his shoulders.

But Dima had come to a decision and had no intention of backing out. Today he would go to the Bird Market in Kiev and buy a Fluffy lookalike. He was sure he'd be able to find a grey cat for less than twenty hryvnas. Then he'd bring it home and see whether Valya could spot the difference. Grey cats all look the same. And all cats love eating, so it was bound to like lying under the warm radiator in the kitchen just like Fluffy, watching lovingly as his mistress prepared his tea.

It was warm in the minibus taxi to Kiev, and there was a dreadful song playing on Radio Chanson about Aunt Shura from Tobolsk. Dima dozed off in his comfortable seat in the back row.

13

Mariinsky Park, Hrushevsky Street, Kiev

The following day the whole of Mariinsky Park was covered with powdery snow. It lay on the naked branches of the trees and the paths making everything look beautiful, like something out of a fairy-tale wedding.

Irina had already been in the park for half an hour, admiring the whiteness of the snow and the turquoise of the palace building, which was just visible through the trees. The soft colour of the palace matched her new fluffy scarf perfectly. Of course it wasn't new, exactly, but freshly dyed. It was such a lightweight scarf. Yet so soft and warm. Warmth flowed down her light brown hair, right to her shoulders. Maybe this was because she had tied her scarf exactly the same way her mother used to tie her school scarf around her head before sending her off in the mornings. That scarf had been grey too, a mousy colour. But why 'too'? That one had been a mousy colour, this one was now pale emerald! Her breasts felt soft and empty, and she was able to forget about them for a while. Irina continued to take pleasure in her fluffy scarf – changing its colour really did seem to have made it warmer.

There was no one else in the park. For some reason Egor wasn't there either. Irina had expected to see him coming from the direction of the palace, but then she wasn't really thinking straight that morning. Yasya had been awake during the night, crying, so Irina had given her some of her own milk. Just a little. Yasya had gone straight back to sleep again, still on the breast, and Irina had had to carefully prise her daughter's mouth open with her little finger to free her nipple. She hadn't been able to catch up on any sleep in the minibus taxi either because Vasya the driver had been sharing his good mood with the security guard from the Kiev building site, who was sitting directly behind the driver's seat as usual. Vasya was over the moon: his wife had come home. First he'd slapped her face, but then he'd smothered her with kisses and promised to forgive her. He spoke about it with pride but Irina wasn't stupid, she knew that he hadn't said what he really wanted to say to the security guard, which was: 'See, I'm better than that teetotal welder . . . she chose me over him, didn't she?'

Irina had shut her eyes, but there had been no way for her to block her ears. So everything she heard had mingled with her thoughts and her memories of the voice from her dream, and now when Irina tried to recall the voice all she could hear was Vasya the driver. And 'he'll come back' in Vasya's voice sounded neither serious nor convincing. It didn't sound right at all.

'Maybe he's having a coffee in that little shop,' thought Irina.

She looked all around once more. Still nobody.

She found the little food shop easily and went over to the high counter, which was all but concealing a young blonde girl in a red jacket.

'A three-in-one, please,' said Irina.

'MacCoffee or Jacob's?'

'MacCoffee.'

She took the hot plastic cup over to the window and started watching the people walking past the food shop. Suddenly she saw her boss, the one who paid her wages in the milk kitchen. She took a step back in alarm, spilling her coffee. It burned her fingers.

'I don't belong here – I'm scared of the slightest thing!' thought Irina. 'No one really needs me here either. There's just some baby who drinks my milk . . . I wonder whether I'll ever get to see it.'

Irina had no feelings for this unknown baby one way or another, neither affection nor anger. She was simply curious. She wanted to know whether it was a boy or a girl and what its name was, so that she could say to her daughter, if only in her head, 'I'm sorry, Yasenka, but Tanechka (or Mishenka) needs it more than you do.'

'Ah, there you are!' A familiar, pleasant baritone rang out behind her.

She turned round and saw Egor.

He looked at his watch.

'Drink up! Another five minutes and we'll be able to get a good coffee!'

With barely concealed joy Irina finished her MacCoffee in one

47

gulp and looked up at Egor like a diligent Young Pioneer loyally devoted to her Pioneer Leader.

It turned out that there was a café serving good coffee just down the road.

The café was warm and cosy. The only inconvenience for Irina was that she had to take her coat and scarf off. She hesitated between the little table and the coat hooks, on which Egor had already hung his own long leather coat.

'Keep it on if you like, if you're more comfortable that way,' he said, noticing her consternation.

She looked at him gratefully. She unbuttoned her coat and loosened her scarf, then moved it back so that it lay across her shoulders like a pale emerald shawl.

'Where did you get such a beautiful scarf?' asked Egor.

Irina smiled. She didn't feel like explaining that it was possible to dye any item of clothing and wear it like new. Particularly not to him, sitting there in his expensive dark suit, white shirt and claret-coloured tie.

A waitress in a white pinafore came to their table.

'Two Americanos and . . .' Egor turned to Irina. 'Shall we have a brandy with it?'

'I can't.'

'Something sweet, then.' Egor turned back to the young waitress. 'What do you recommend?'

'Everything's good. Try the tiramisu.'

'OK. We'll have two of those.'

The girl went off.

'So, don't you drink at all?'

Irina was a little offended by the surprise in Egor's voice. She looked into his hazel eyes and shook her head.

'My daughter's only three months old,' she said. 'I'm still breastfeeding.'

'A three-month-old baby and you go to work every day? Who looks after her, your husband?'

'My mother.' Irina felt her happiness dissipate. The last thing she wanted to talk to this handsome man about was herself. Talking about yourself basically meant enumerating your problems, and nobody likes listening to other people's problems – Irina knew that from her own experience. As soon as someone she barely knew started sharing their problems with her, she immediately wanted to stick her fingers in her ears and walk away. He would probably switch off immediately; his eyes would glaze over, and . . . No, she wouldn't burden him like that.

'I'm not married,' added Irina, more cheerfully. 'I sent him packing. And he wasn't my husband anyway.'

'And you live out there, in Lipovka?' asked Egor.

She nodded.

'So how come you have such a city accent?' Egor seemed genuinely curious. 'I was born in that area too, just outside Kodra. But I grew up here in Kiev.'

'I studied in Kiev. And I like watching television!' Irina admitted with a smile. 'Mama used to say when I was little, if you repeat everything that you hear on television, you'll speak beautifully. You know how strong the accent is out there. The television hasn't helped Mama much, though.'

'Where do you work?' Egor's questions kept on coming.

Irina's eyes suddenly fell on his black earpiece and followed the wire into the collar of his jacket. She burst out laughing.

The waitress brought their coffee and tiramisus.

'What, is it top secret or something?' smiled Egor.

'You're the one with the top-secret job.' Irina relaxed, relieved that the conversation had taken a turn away from her problems. 'I'm a wet nurse.'

Egor had just raised the little porcelain jug of hot milk over his cup. He froze for a second.

'I see,' he said, somewhat surprised. 'That's quite an unusual profession!'

'I'll find another job when my milk runs out,' said Irina casually.

'Would you like some?' Egor lifted the little jug to her cup.

Irina nodded.

The tiramisu was delicious. Egor drank his coffee and scooped up the rich dessert with a little spoon. He looked thoughtfully at Irina.

'You shouldn't wear your heart on your sleeve, you know,' he said suddenly, sounding concerned. 'You talk about yourself so easily.'

Irina shrugged. She was hot in her coat but couldn't very well take it off now. Especially as underneath it she was wearing a nondescript lime-green top over her pink blouse and a long wool skirt that she'd had for five years. A packet of dye might have given her scarf a new lease of life, but the skirt was a lost cause.

'Number Five, where are you?' crackled a mechanical voice from the region of the earpiece.

'Near the Officers' Club,' answered Egor.

'Got a pregnant woman in a black coat wandering around here, near the viewing area. Could be the one who tried to top herself the day before yesterday.'

'Right,' said Egor. 'Keep an eye on her, I'm on my way.'

'Do you have to go?' asked Irina.

'No. Do you want another coffee?'

She didn't.

'You know, Irina,' began Egor. Then he leaned across the table and switched to a light-hearted, conspiratorial whisper. 'My job really is top secret. I can't tell anyone my own secrets, of course, but I can find out other people's. I could find out about yours too, if I wanted to.'

'What kind of secrets?' asked Irina.

'You know, who, what, where . . . Do you read those celebrity gossip magazines?'

'Yes,' Irina admitted. 'Can you really find out anything?'

'Anything. Apart from state secrets.'

Irina grew thoughtful. She looked searchingly into Egor's hazel eyes. They were more serious than his lips, which were fixed in a joking smile.

'Well, there is one thing I'd quite like to know . . .'

Egor leaned closer to Irina, almost knocking his cup over with his elbow.

'The thing is, I don't know what happens to my milk after they express it. I guess they must give it to the baby's mother, or the nanny. They're really strict about hygiene, you know. I have to have a medical check-up every two weeks, all kinds of tests . . . even really intimate ones. Sorry, you don't need to know that. I'd just like to know a bit about the baby, really. The one that's being raised on my milk . . .'

Egor gave a broad smile.

'I'll see what I can do,' he said. 'Come on, let's go. You can show me this milk kitchen of yours.'

They left the warmth of the café and came out into the cold. Irina took Egor to show him the doors of the building where they relieved her of her milk. As she walked, she buttoned her coat up and straightened her pale emerald scarf.

The winter sun was shining brightly over the Pechersk district. The powdery snow that had fallen that morning melted in its rays then refroze, adhering to the previous day's snow, which had already hardened into a brittle crust.

14

Apartment No. 10, Reitarska Street, Kiev

Darya Ivanovna felt comfortable in Veronika's apartment and began to relax. She shed a few tears for her late husband, the pharmacist. She lamented her fate. She praised Veronika's coffee. She questioned her hostess about her own family situation.

Veronika was inclined to be open, but not about her personal life. What little she said about Semyon was wholly complimentary. This made the pharmacist's widow frown sceptically but only briefly, and then she carried on talking about herself and her own husband.

'Mine was wonderful too,' she said, her eyes full of sincere warmth. 'Sometimes he would call and say, "I'm on my way, darling! Put the coffee on!" And the coffee would turn out just like yours.' She gave her hostess a significant look. 'I could only make coffee like this for him. Whenever I made it for myself or a girlfriend it was never quite as good. It's rather warm in here, isn't it? But at least it doesn't smell of cigarettes! You don't smoke, do you?' Darya Ivanovna ran her gaze over the two white Italian radiators. 'When we had our place done up, we left the old cast-iron ones in. We just painted them. It's not so warm in our place. Cold helps to keep you young, you know!'

Veronika's guest fell silent for a moment, apparently contemplating her youth.

'Don't you have any children?' she asked.

Luckily, just at that moment the front door creaked open. Veronika leapt up and looked into the hall. She saw her husband.

'Senya, we've got a visitor,' she said.

Darya Ivanovna got up to leave. She went into the hallway and put on her fur coat. She looked Veronika's husband up and down appraisingly.

'I've left my card on the table. Give me a call,' she said on her way out. 'You must come to mine for a coffee next time. What's your number, by the way?'

Veronika quickly scribbled down both her home and mobile numbers. She received another farewell smile from her guest. Then she followed Semyon into the kitchen.

'You look a bit down. What's the matter?' she asked.

Semyon was more tired than anything else. He'd already poured himself a shot of brandy.

'Why don't you get changed?' suggested Veronika, looking at his jumper and ripped jeans. 'I'll wash those.'

'Who was that?' asked Semyon.

'The wife of that pharmacist, the one who was murdered. Remember, when you stayed out all night –' She stopped suddenly without finishing her sentence.

Semyon flinched, as though startled. He drank his brandy and poured another.

'I'll have one too,' said his wife.

Semyon was surprised. His eyes glowed with affection and compassion. He fetched another shot glass, filled it and handed it to Veronika.

'I met her in the street,' she told Semyon, sipping her brandy. 'When I got to the corner there was a woman arguing with a young lad. She was holding a funeral wreath and a hammer. Turned out she'd hammered a nail into the wall, right where he was killed, but the café's security guard wouldn't let her hang the wreath on it. He said it would scare their customers off . . .'

'So what happened?'

'She went in and saw the manager, and they agreed that the wreath could hang there Monday to Friday and she would take it down at the weekend.'

'Hmm,' Semyon exhaled. 'Well, we had an emergency situation. We were providing security cover for one of Gennady Ilyich's business picnics and there was this bunch of dickheads hunting nearby, probably some other deputies. I sent my lads to move them further away from the picnic, and they responded by deliberately shooting one of them in the leg. We took him to the local hospital, but they stupidly went and called the militia so now they're going to start hassling me . . . I'll have to get Gennady Ilyich involved to get them off my case.'

The conversation created an unexpected closeness between husband and wife. Semyon even allowed Veronika to calm him down. He changed into a clean set of clothes, although he wasn't planning on leaving the house again that night. Outside, the early evening was filling with a lead-coloured frost. Patterns glittered at the edges of the windowpane.

Veronika decided that she wanted another brandy and, separately, a breath of fresh air. She opened the little top window and waited until she felt the cold touch her cheek, then downed her brandy in one.

15

Bird Market, Kurenivka, Kiev

After wandering round the Bird Market for nearly an hour, Dima was just about at the end of his tether. Feline merchandise seemed to be represented exclusively by kittens, and mainly pedigree ones at that. One old woman was selling two adult Siamese females, but she had evidently been trying to get rid of them since they were kittens too: her face and hands were covered with scratch marks.

Dima was more drawn to a couple of plump parrots in a large red cage. He stood there admiring the intelligent birds for five minutes, before reluctantly returning to the task in hand. He walked up and down the tramline outside the market. The woman with the Siamese cats had told him that there were always tramps there, selling grey strays for three hryvnas. The words 'grey' and 'stray' made Dima think of Fluffy. But that day it just so happened that there were no tramps selling cheap cats by the market fence. Eventually, a thoroughly frozen Dima found himself back in the market, standing in front of a woman wearing a warm, village-style sheepskin jacket and peasant boots. At her feet stood a woven basket full of grey kittens nestling under a scrap of blanket, which she was selling for twelve hryvnas apiece.

'I need a big grey one,' said Dima with a sigh.

'How big?' asked the well-insulated woman.

Dima held his hands up, indicating Fluffy's approximate size. Then he explained the situation. He told her all about his wife's grief, about the photograph of the cat in the frame with the black mourning strip.

'Oh, I know what she's going through – I had a stroke when my dear Napkin got run over!' The woman clasped her hands together. 'Your wife is lucky to have a husband like you. Mine called me a fool every day for three weeks straight!'

Dima lapped up this praise with pleasure. He was about to start criticising the woman's husband, for the sake of prolonging the conversation, but stopped himself just in time. He had seen the spark of an idea in the woman's eyes.

'Come to think of it, there is one grey cat . . . It doesn't belong to anyone, as far as I know. I live on the ground floor, so I've taken to putting food out for it,' she said with a friendly smile. 'What was yours called?'

'He had two names. My wife called him Fluffy, and I called him Scruffy . . . But it needs to answer to Fluffy.'

'They'll answer to anything for a bit of fish or sausage! Come back in a week's time. I'll get him house-trained and teach him his new name.'

'How much will it cost?' asked Dima cautiously.

'Whatever you can afford, plus the price of a bit of sausage and his other food . . . Let's call it fifty hryvnas.'

Dima nodded and took the woman's phone number, as he couldn't remember what shifts he was on the following week. With a spring in his step, he headed for the little watering hole he'd noticed on the way into the market. Now he could legitimately order a shot of vodka, not only to warm himself up but also to toast the impending return of the 'prodigal Fluffy'.

16

Lipovka village, Kiev region

Yasya started crying at about 2 a.m. It was quiet outside. Irina lowered her feet from her bed to the wooden floor, rubbed her face with the palms of her warm hands and opened her eyes. She picked Yasya up and brought her little mouth to her left breast, and once again silence reigned in the house. She no longer felt like sleeping. The touch of the cold wooden floor on the soles of her feet was invigorating.

Irina started thinking about Egor. What a gentleman! Strong, tall, well mannered . . . And he had good taste in clothes. The way he'd commented on her scarf like that in the car! Most men wouldn't have said anything. Most men couldn't care less what a woman is wearing, particularly one they've only just met. But he had made a point of saying something, and it wasn't because he'd taken a liking to her at that point. How could anyone have liked the look of such a scarecrow, wrapped up in that grey scarf? She had made a conscious decision to dress like a scarecrow, so that she could walk home in peace after the minibus taxi dropped her off. She would have done anything to avoid attracting the attention of the local men, with their permanent smell of alcohol and their rough hands. Once upon a time she thought that if she made an effort with her appearance, her life would improve. So she made an effort, started wearing make-up, and what happened? Mikhail Yakovich, her old primary school teacher, dragged her back to his peasant's hut. He said he had some old photographs to show her. It all ended with wine, chocolates and the sofa, which was overlooked by a tapestry of a goggle-eyed green mermaid that hung on the wall. So much for happily ever after.

Yasya fell asleep again, her mouth clamped around Irina's nipple. Irina used her little finger to prise her daughter's lips apart and free her nipple, but she didn't take her back to bed. She just held her closer.

She thought about her old teacher again. A fat lot he'd taught her. He'd just left her a 'homework assignment' for many years to come – Yasya. But Irina had no regrets.

She remembered the day she had told Mikhail Yakovich she was pregnant. He'd turned pale as a sheet and clutched at his chest. Then about a week later she'd heard the news that he had sold his hut and moved out of the village.

Irina had been puzzled by Yasya's father running away like that. She just couldn't believe that a man from the village, even a teacher, could organise himself so quickly, sell his hut and just disappear into thin air. A gypsy family moved into the hut as soon as it was vacated by its former occupant: husband, wife and three children. Shortly afterwards the husband was imprisoned for drug dealing. A month later the militia caught the gypsy mother with drugs too, but they let her off. The village youths started calling round in the evenings – the gypsy children would bring out bags of grass and sell them for ten hryvnas. That went on for three or four weeks, then early one morning the hut somehow caught fire. It burned completely to the ground. The gypsy woman managed to escape with her children, although her hair was singed. Suffering from morning sickness and with her bump already starting to show,

Irina went to have a look at the site of the fire. She could just make out the charred remains of the sofa where Yasya had been created, but she looked in vain for the tapestry of the goggle-eyed mermaid – cloth always burns faster than wood. She hadn't thought any more about her old teacher, until that night. But why had she started thinking about him now? Irina shrugged, unable to come up with an answer. She liked this internal, nocturnal conversation with herself. She liked the silence inside and outside. It was a little chilly but Yasya, wrapped up in a blanket, shared her warmth with her mother.

Her thoughts turned again to Egor. She thought about the café with the coat hooks and remembered how uncomfortable she had been sitting there at the table in her coat. She really ought to buy herself something more fashionable. But with what? She was paid sixty hryvnas a day for her milk. Less twenty-one hryvnas for transport, that left thirty-nine. After food and other bits and pieces for Yasya, that left the grand total of . . . nothing.

That evening the news came on after the soap operas. The Donbass miners were on strike over unpaid wages, the air stewardesses in England were demanding a pay rise . . . Everything in the world revolved around money and how much everyone was paid. Maybe she should ask for a pay rise too? After all, the cost of living had gone up recently: buckwheat had gone up by fify kopeks a kilo and Malysh formula milk by forty. How much should she ask for? Seventy hryvnas a day, at least. Seventy-five would be even better.

Somehow in Irina's mind her fantasies became reality. Recalculating her budget according to this new purchase price on her milk, she worked out that in exactly three weeks she would be able to hang her coat on one of the hooks in that café without any qualms.

It really was quite chilly in her room. She got under the heavy quilt, laid Yasya down beside her and fell asleep immediately.

17

Apartment No. 10, Reitarska Street, Kiev

A strange force made Semyon get out of bed at 1 a.m. It dressed him and put his shoes on, and it brought him outside onto a street that was crunchy underfoot with snow. He reached the corner of the three cafés and stopped in front of the funeral wreath that was hanging from a nail hammered into the wall. He stood there for a little while, looking at the wreath with a kind of nervous curiosity. Then he crossed Yaroslaviv Val, walked to the top of Ivana Franko Street and began heading downhill. He went slowly and took small steps, trying not to slip. Nevertheless, after a few dozen paces he lost his footing and crashed to the ground, banging his hip on a step covered with black ice. He sat for a minute, rubbing the injured place through his jeans. Then he got up and continued walking down the street, holding on to the metal railings.

In the morning, when Semyon woke up and started walking around the room in his underwear, Veronika noticed the enormous bruise on his hip.

'Where did you get that?' she asked, looking pointedly at the injury.

Semyon stopped. He looked at his bruise in surprise.

'I don't know,' he said. 'Maybe I caught it on the kitchen table?'

Their conversation was interrupted by the telephone ringing. Veronika picked up the receiver.

'Nikochka,' rang out Darya's voice. 'I need to ask you a favour. I've got to go to the hairdresser's, but I forgot to take the wreath down yesterday. You live nearby, don't you? I don't suppose you could take it down for me, could you?'

'OK. But what shall I do with it?' asked Veronika.

'Hang on to it for me, and I'll pick it up on Monday morning.'

Veronika went out. Alone in the apartment, Semyon spent a long time inspecting the mark on his hip. His whole body felt battered, bruised and worn out. He wanted to go back to sleep, but there would be a car coming to pick him up in an hour's time. A few of the deputies had decided to go on a Saturday skiing trip with a picnic afterwards. Semyon could picture the scene: a campfire, shashlik, ski poles stuck in the snow . . . he'd seen it all before, on more than one occasion. The main thing was to wear plenty of warm clothing. But first, coffee, strong coffee! Otherwise he'd never be ready to face the day.

18

9 May Street, Boryspil

'Someone's seen him!' Dima gave his wife the good news as he stood in the hall, brushing off the snow that had stuck to his heavy work boots. 'On the outskirts of the city, near the Baptist church.'

He took the photograph out of his jacket pocket and held it out to his wife.

'Put it back in. Soon you'll be able to take the black strip off, too!'

Dima thought he saw a fleeting smile cross Valya's face. He smiled too, but for a different reason. He couldn't believe how easy it was to lie to women. It was almost as though they expected it.

At around 7 p.m., when it had started snowing again outside and the weather forecast was on ICTV, there was a knock at the door. It was Boris. Dima had no choice but to put his coat and boots back on.

They went into the garage. Dima switched the lamp on and plugged in the heater. They sat down and Dima told the baggage handler about the little chat he'd had with his boss.

'Yes,' Boris exhaled. 'They must know what's inside it . . . But they can't be that bothered about it, or they'd be making more of an effort to track it down.'

Dima nodded. The little chat with his boss no longer seemed like such a big deal. Sure, he'd asked about the suitcase, but then he'd said, 'All right, you can go.' Hardly a thorough search operation.

'OK, here's an idea.' Boris looked up at Dima. 'Why don't I take the suitcase and dump it over the airport fence, near the VIP terminal?'

Dima thought the idea seemed perfectly sensible, and he got out two shot glasses and a bottle of nettle home-brew. After they'd downed their shots Dima suggested to his partner in crime that they just split the goods three ways, so that each of them could deal with his own share as he saw fit.

The baggage handler was silent for three whole minutes.

'I've already made a fool of myself once,' he said eventually. 'I went into Kiev, took one of the ampoules into the pharmacy on

Vladimirska and asked a man in a white coat to check what it was for. Told him I'd bought it at the market and that it was supposed to be a cure for cancer.'

'What did he say?' asked Dima.

'What do you think he said?' Boris snapped. 'Nothing! He broke the top off, had a good old sniff, tipped a few drops out onto a bit of glass, held it up to the light and then just shrugged. Said it looked more like a "hyaloid body" than a cure for cancer.'

Dima cleared his throat.

'So, shall we split it then?' he repeated.

Boris waved his hand. 'What the hell,' he said. 'We might as well.'

Dima found two bags, spread a copy of *Democratic Ukraine* on the floor and divided the boxes of ampoules into three equal piles. There was one box left over, but Dima gave it to Boris.

'I'll get the bag back to you,' said Boris.

He left the garage carrying a bag containing two shares of the ampoules – his own and Zhenya's – and the battered suitcase. Dima shut the garage door behind Boris, but he himself stayed inside. The little heater, with its red-hot spiral wound round a piece of asbestos-covered pipe, was doing a good job of warming up his cosy corner. Dima thought it would be a shame to let such warmth go to waste. He poured himself another shot of home-brew and drank it. Then he looked down at the floor, where his share of the boxes containing the ampoules lay on the newspaper. 'What am I going to do with them now?' he wondered. But his brain didn't want to answer this question. Dima suddenly remembered that he was on duty the following day, which meant he needed to get to bed. He knew he'd have no trouble sleeping well that night, because he'd managed to get rid of the black plastic suitcase and two-thirds of the ampoules, so Zhenya and Boris the baggage handlers would no longer be bothering him. And as for what to do with his share of the ampoules – well, he'd think of something!

He went back into the house, got into bed and started to doze off. He would have fallen asleep straight away if Valya hadn't taken it upon herself to indulge her husband in recognition of her gratitude for his efforts in finding Fluffy. Dima reluctantly accepted Valya's caresses, falling asleep immediately afterwards. Valya fell asleep too, without taking the slightest offence at her husband's sudden tiredness. He was always like that. And she was the same. That was just the way they were.

19

Hrushevsky Street, Kiev

The motion of the minibus taxi lulled Irina straight to sleep. She was vaguely aware of the hum of the engine, but it didn't disturb her in the slightest. Vasya drove his GAZelle in silence. The winter road appeared to be covered in more snow than usual. Even in her sleep Irina felt the minibus swerve a couple of times.

Irina began to emerge from her somnolent cocoon at precisely the moment the GAZelle should have been pulling up outside the metro station. But today the minibus was still crawling up the final hill beyond which lay the city, as if in the palm of a giant hand. The city brought Irina fully out of her sleep. At first there's nothing but pitch darkness on the road ahead and out of the windows all around, but then suddenly the glow of city lights rises up before you, and although it's still some way off, at least ten kilometres, your heart responds by beating faster, in time with the state of your soul.

It was all a trick, of course, this illumination. Merely an advert for city life. The lights were on, but the city was still sleeping. It was just pretending to be awake. The village might have been poorer but at least it was honest – if the village was sleeping, all the lights were out.

As she approached the main entrance to the grey Stalinist block, which was marked by a sign indicating apartments numbers 25–37, Irina recalled her nocturnal train of thought. She adjusted her fluffy scarf, took a deep breath of cold air and went inside.

Nurse Vera greeted her cheerfully. She made Irina drink a cup of tea in the kitchen before taking her through to the office, where the air itself, warmed by a quartz heating lamp, seemed to invite her to undress.

Once her breasts had been emptied of their milk, Irina ate two bowls of sweetened porridge and had another cup of tea. Then it was time to go outside and start building up the milk for her 'second shift'. She put her coat on then stopped in the doorway and looked back at Nurse Vera.

'What time does the boss get here?' she asked.

'Nelly Igorievna? The car brings her at about ten. Come back a bit earlier if you get cold, I've got some raspberry jam.'

Paths had already been trampled in the morning snow, and one of them led directly from the main entrance to the pedestrian crossing.

Irina walked through the park to the viewing area. She stopped by the railings. She wanted to look across the river at the city on the opposite side but there was a blizzard approaching. Well, not a blizzard as such, just a wall of snow, moving towards her. Whiteness erased the buildings on the other side and half of the Metro Bridge. Then the Dnieper itself disappeared, followed by the remainder of the bridge. Another five minutes and the white snow was falling on her too, on her scarf, her coat. She raised one hand up to the sky and watched as a whole flock of snowflakes landed on it.

She looked around. She couldn't see the Mariinsky Palace or the trees. It was like something out of a fairy tale. If only Yasya were a little older – she would have marvelled at such beauty.

The cold wind grew stronger and started biting her cheeks. Irina decided to go back to the milk kitchen. She had remembered the raspberry jam.

'Everything all right?' A man in a long black coat appeared out of the blizzard, startling her. He peered solicitously into Irina's face. An earpiece was sticking out of his right ear, just like Egor's.

'I'm fine,' Irina answered with a smile.

He stepped back behind the solid white wall of falling snow and disappeared again.

'Oh, you're covered in it!' exclaimed Nurse Vera as she let Irina into the corridor. 'Hurry up and get your things off, and come into the kitchen.'

Irina shook the snow from her scarf. She hung it up carefully on the wooden coat stand, assigning her coat to a different hook. She looked at the double doors at the end of the wide corridor then started walking towards them, conscious of the noise made by the chunky heels of her boots. She went back to the coat stand. She took a pair of slippers out of her bag and changed into them, then returned to the double doors. She opened them slightly, just a crack, and peeped through. She could see a middle-aged woman holding a pug dog and an elderly man in a suit. He was wearing a deputy's badge on his lapel.

The entrance door slammed behind her. She looked round. Two men in green overalls had come in carrying a large milk churn. They stood it next to the wall and went out again, presumably to fetch the next one. They usually brought the churns three at a time.

Tea with raspberry jam lifted Irina's spirits and warmed her up. Nurse Vera's mobile phone rang in her pocket. She made a big fuss of taking it out, then pressed a button and brought it to her ear.

'Yes, Nelly Igorievna, they're already here. My goodness, how did that happen? OK, fine. Irinka's here too, we'll manage.'

Nurse Vera put her phone away and cast a worried glance back at the open door, through which the three milk churns could be seen standing in the corridor.

'Nelly Igorievna's bodyguards have been attacked,' the old woman informed her. 'They're both in hospital. Now there's no one to carry those churns into the treatment room. Will you give me a hand?'

'Of course,' Irina answered readily.

'Here, put this on.' The nurse gave Irina a clean white gown. 'You're not allowed through there without it.'

Irina looked at herself in the little mirror hanging in the kitchen above the sink. The white gown made her look like a nurse.

They both took hold of the handles on the side of the first churn. They raised it slightly and Irina's legs almost gave way. It was the heaviest thing she'd ever had to lift in her life.

'Let's do it bit by bit,' said the nurse seeing the look of panic on Irina's face.

They lifted the first churn up and set it down again about twenty times before they managed to move it to the double doors. Vera was clearly worn out but didn't complain. Irina's arms and shoulders ached.

'Nelly Igorievna asked for our help – I couldn't very well refuse,' said the old nurse dejectedly. She opened one half of the double doors. They took hold of the handles again, picked the churn up and put it down on the other side of the doors. Then they made their way slowly to the third door on the left and carried the churn through, into a room that was completely covered with delft blue tiles. Against one of the walls stood a special medical bath with a control panel on the outside of it. Buttons, handles, little lights . . . Irina had never seen a bath like it. There were clean white towelling robes hanging on a coat stand in the corner and several pairs of identical slippers on the floor nearby.

'Nearly there, Irochka,' said the old woman with a weary sigh. 'We just have to tip the milk in there, into the bath.'

'No way!' Irina cried in alarm. Even her stomach had started to hurt.

'What do you mean, "no way"? Look at me, I'm sixty-seven years old and I'm not complaining.'

Vera folded back the lid of the milk churn. She grasped one of the handles with both hands and Irina took hold of the other.

'We can do it,' the old woman assured her. 'The main thing is to keep it straight and make sure we don't spill it . . .'

They managed to tip the milk into the bath on their third attempt. Although the empty milk churn was still fairly heavy, it felt as light as a feather to Irina when they carried it back to their half of the corridor.

'What's all that milk in the bath for?' asked Irina.

'It's goat's milk,' said Nurse Vera, casually. 'For treatments.'

They needed extra help emptying the other two milk churns into the bath. Luckily a doctor from the office next door responded to Nurse Vera's request for assistance. He looked at his watch once they'd emptied the last churn into the bath and shook his head in dissatisfaction. 'It's a good job Gennady Ilyich is always late,' he said.

Irina's cup of tea shook in her hand as though it were alive. She ached all over after the milk churns. Her shoulders, her arms, her stomach, even her knees. She'd only felt like this once before – after giving birth. But that time, despite the pain and exhaustion, she'd been deliriously happy.

It was time for the second expressing. The cold suction cup stung her breast unpleasantly. This time she found the whole mechanical pumping process extremely irritating and disagreeable.

'It'll pass, don't worry,' Nurse Vera told Irina, supporting the cup with a shaking hand. 'I don't feel too good myself after those milk churns.'

Then there was only the humming of the pump as it expressed her milk. The nurse was silent, her face full of self-pity.

Without a word, she held a damp flannel out to Irina so that she could wipe her breasts before getting dressed.

'Where's the boss's office?' asked Irina, once she'd done up all the buttons on her red woollen cardigan.

'Through there, opposite the treatment room – the one with the bath in.'

As Irina walked along the corridor she felt every movement of her body. She opened one of the double doors carefully, feeling a pain in her wrist. She stopped outside the room with the bath in. From behind the closed door came a deep male voice, singing a familiar old song. She stood there for a minute, just listening. Over the sound of the milk splashing in the bath the man was singing quietly, *'We are the people!'*

Irina knocked on the door opposite.

'Come in,' called a pleasant voice.

'What do you want?' Her boss's voice changed abruptly as soon as Irina appeared in the doorway. 'You shouldn't be here uninvited!'

Her boss was sitting behind an attractive dark brown desk. On the wide windowsill behind her flourished an entire winter garden – there were at least a dozen flowerpots containing young palms, cacti and decorative ferns.

'Nelly Igorievna . . .' Irina gathered all her resolve and attempted to articulate it. 'I wanted to ask you something . . .'

'Yes, what is it?' Nelly Igorievna looked at the young woman with obvious disdain. 'What do you want?'

'I was just wondering whether you might, by any chance, consider increasing my wages. Maybe . . . to seventy . . .'

Nelly Igorievna's eyes filled with anger. Her face grew flushed. She undid the top button of her maroon jacket, as though she needed more air.

'You already get nearly four hundred dollars as it is! Isn't that enough for you?'

'Yes, but getting here costs . . .' Irina didn't finish her sentence. A tear rolled down her cheek.

'What about the cost of the food you eat here? You should be more grateful! My people could find someone within the hour who would be prepared to come here and work for less than we pay you. Do you understand me?'

By now tears were streaming down Irina's cheeks. She nodded and went out into the corridor. She stopped by the coat stand, where she slowly changed her shoes and took her fluffy emerald scarf from its hook. She heard the telephone jangling in the kitchen.

Behind her the old nurse went through to the other half of the corridor and came straight back, carrying a box of chocolates.

'These are for you,' she said to Irina, who already had her coat on. 'From the boss.'

Irina took the box of chocolates in one hand and her bag in the other. Then she left, without saying goodbye to Vera.

She felt like having a good cry. Not alone, though. She needed a shoulder to cry on. Even if that wasn't a very attractive thing to do.

It was still snowing outside, and it was already getting dark. The early twilight accentuated the fairy-tale magic of the street lights, cocooned as they were by the falling snow.

'Maybe I'll go for a little walk in the park,' thought Irina as she approached the zebra crossing.

She peered at the traffic lights, which were partially obscured by the falling snow that was sticking to them. It occurred to her that Egor might be there too, in the park.

She started to cross the road, feeling a nagging pain in her knees. She heard a car sound its horn at someone nearby, and suddenly she was knocked off her feet and thrown into the air. Her eyes were wide open and she felt as though she were flying with her back to the ground and her face to the sky. She flew through the snowflakes, leaving a trail of them behind her, and then she hit the ground. The snow-white sky grew dark. All she could feel was the pain in her knees. The world around her grew smaller – it seemed to float away, recede, roll back; it was packed away into little boxes, like props from a puppet show.

20

There was an invigorating nip in the air on Saturday, which was somewhat at odds with the way Semyon was feeling. Fortunately he never had any trouble switching into 'classified mode' (which was how he referred to the process of ensuring someone else's safety) – he was used to it. There's a soldier inside every man, although he tends to spend most of his time asleep and it takes a certain internal command for him to spring into action. If you can learn how to master this soldier within there is no end to what you can achieve, particularly when it comes to your career. Most men today are civilian through and through: their main aim in life is to take it easy, physically and mentally. Semyon was one of a dying breed, but when called upon his inner soldier would be alert and on duty for several days at a time. So naturally vim and vigour were a distinct advantage, though not essential.

Semyon's old friend Volodka was at the wheel of the Niva. He was wearing camouflage overalls. They were already on the Old Obukhiv Highway, about ten kilometres from where the skiing party were to meet.

'I wanted to ask you a favour,' Semyon said to his friend. 'It's sort of personal. A bit of nocturnal surveillance . . .'

'Male? Female?' asked the driver.

'Male.'

'No problem. When do you want me to start?'

'Tomorrow, about midnight.'

'Have you got a photo?'

'You won't need one. It's someone you know.'

'One of ours?' Volodka turned his head and cast a worried glance at Semyon.

'Yep,' confirmed Semyon, with a deep sigh.

Volodka assumed there was a traitor in their midst and wondered who it might be. He mentally ran through the close-knit team that Semyon had gathered around himself. They all seemed like fairly normal guys . . . but appearances could be deceptive.

'Who is it?' asked Volodka.

'This is just between you and me,' said Semyon, even though he knew that he ran the risk of offending his old friend with this unnecessary proviso. 'The thing is,' he began, then stopped short and fell silent.

'Go on,' Volodka prompted him without taking his eyes off the road, which had been well cleared of snow.

'It's been going on for some time now,' Semyon continued, with greater conviction. 'Something's not quite right . . . I wanted to ask if you would follow me.'

Volodka pulled over onto the snowy verge and stopped the car directly underneath some pine trees, which made up the forest that grew on both sides of the highway. He turned and looked at Semyon.

'I don't get it.' Volodka looked closely into his friend's eyes. 'Is everything all right?'

'I wouldn't be asking you to follow me if everything was all right!' Semyon looked at his watch. 'We're going to be late,' he said calmly, in an impassive and businesslike voice. 'So, will you do it?'

Volodka nodded.

'There's a little window on the second floor of the block opposite mine, in the stairwell. It'll be warmer in there than outside. Make sure you're there from about midnight. If I come out and start behaving strangely, stop me – using force if you have to.'

Volodka pulled back onto the highway. A little while later they stopped at a fork at the beginning of the road that led through the forest. It was already well marked with the wide tracks of jeep tyres. They stopped near a Lada, which was occupied by three more strapping young men. Now the whole team was there. The 'skiers' would be arriving in half an hour. A car containing two lads who worked for the skiers had arrived ahead of them and already disappeared into the forest. They had gone to get the picnic site ready, set up the barbecue, the folding chairs, the table . . .

It wasn't long before Semyon was convinced of their professionalism. When two jeeps bearing Ukrainian flags and three-digit government number plates appeared, Semyon and Volodka waited until they'd passed then took their place at the rear of the convoy. They came out into a large clearing, which looked more like a permanent holiday camp. Semyon was impressed. Wood was already burning in the barbecue, and a large square area of snow had been trampled down to make a cosy picnic area, where four wooden chairs stood around a little table covered with oilcloth. The presence of a red electric cool box gave this country idyll a high-tech feel.

As soon as the jeeps stopped, the two lads ran up to the cars and unfastened four identical pairs of skis from the roof racks.

Semyon knew two of the skiers well: Gennady Ilyich and another deputy from the opposition, who was rather fond of giving television interviews. He didn't recognise the other two, but it didn't matter who they were anyway.

The men were all wearing professional ski suits, despite their evident lack of sporting physique. Semyon went over to them and greeted his client, then rejoined his team.

They sent the Niva about two hundred metres away in the direction of the Old Obukhiv Highway. The Lada stayed nearer the picnic. They switched their walkie-talkies on and spread out around the perimeter. The main rule was to remain as inconspicuous as possible. The clients were there to relax, and visual intrusions were not welcome.

For Semyon and his team the winter air in the forest was as invigorating as a glass of fresh juice. The forest was still young and the pine trunks were thin, which naturally facilitated surveillance. Their job would be fairly straightforward. The skiers would inevitably curb their sporting enthusiasm towards nightfall and take their places at the table, where they would drink vodka, eat shashlik and discuss the state of the national economy and their personal finances, regularly confusing the two. There was more danger once twilight fell, of course, but these deputies were all used to living with fear. And they had good reason to be afraid: each of them knew what he'd done to deserve punishment, although not one of them would recognise the emissary sent to deliver it.

The 'skiers' spent no more than half an hour actually skiing. Once they'd finished one of their employees strapped all the skis back onto the roof rack and assumed the role of waiter.

Semyon stood under a pine tree about forty metres from the clearing. He listened to the sonorous twittering of the winter birds and thought about Veronika. He decided that he ought to treat her better, be a bit more affectionate towards her. Maybe even bring her flowers every now and then. He liked just standing there in the light frost, thinking his thoughts.

He could smell shashlik. Twilight had started to fall. The table talk grew louder and sometimes whole sentences reached Semyon's ears. He realised to his astonishment that the skiers were arguing about religion and which church was the best.

The campfire was rekindled, but this time clearly more for atmosphere than for shashlik. The fire was giving off a resinous pine-wood smell, and you don't cook shashlik over pine wood. Every schoolboy knows that.

Eventually the conversation died down, and Semyon took this as a sign that the picnic was coming to an end. He approached the clearing and waited for the skiers to leave the table. Two of them walked over to the barbecue where the campfire was glowing, spitting sparks. The other two stayed at the table.

Before getting into his car Gennady Ilyich beckoned Semyon over.

'We're going to my place,' he said, his voice pleasant but tired. 'I want to show my friends something. Your lads can have a cup of tea.' He nodded in the direction of the security team, who were standing a little distance away.

The Niva and the Lada followed the three jeeps. When they got to the main road they turned right, towards Obukhiv. After about ten kilometres they turned left onto a paved road that twisted and turned as it ran alongside a succession of high fences. Tall young pines grew on the other side of the fences, like the ones in the forest.

Eventually the jeeps slowed down and drove through some open gates. The Niva and the Lada stopped outside the gates. Semyon and Volodka got out and continued on foot. Semyon gave his lads strict instructions not to get out of the other car unless it was absolutely necessary.

A straight driveway, illuminated by low-level lighting, led directly from the gates to a massive three-storey country house.

'Oi, Senya, get a move on!' This exhortation came from the vicinity of the jeeps, which were already standing by the steps to the house.

Semyon quickened his pace. Striding decisively, Gennady Ilyich led the group along a cleared path behind the house.

There was no light on this side of the house. The snow looked grey in the twilight, and the trunks of the pine trees were like watercolour brushstrokes on canvas.

'Are we all here?' the owner of the country estate enquired imperiously.

Without waiting for an answer he shone a pocket torch at a metal box attached to the trunk of the nearest tree, the front of which bore a red zigzag warning sign. He opened the box, grabbed the handle of the knife switch inside and pulled it sharply upwards. A spark flew out but was lost in the sudden glare from the powerful floodlights that were fixed to a number of pine trees, about ten or twelve metres from the ground. The floodlights illuminated three sides of a red-brick church with three gilded cupolas. It was a tall and imposing structure, architecturally far more impressive than their host's three-storey country house.

'Well, what do you think?' asked Gennady Ilyich, relishing the look of surprise on the faces of his guests. 'Come and see inside!'

Motioning them to follow, he headed for the forged gates of the church.

Semyon thought it seemed colder inside than out. There were several weak lamps on the walls. Piles of dismantled scaffolding lay on the stone floor.

'Petya, where's the brandy?' their host asked his assistant, and Petya shot out of the church like a bullet. The resonant echo of his quick shuffling steps had barely died away before he returned with a bottle of Hennessy and some disposable plastic cups.

77

'You're all invited to the first service!' promised their host. 'But for now, let's drink to God! May He never forsake us!'

Volodka and Semyon moved away and stood to one side. Their host didn't offer them any cognac. They weren't expecting to get the tea they'd been promised, either.

Semyon couldn't help smiling as he took in the scene: four burly men in ski outfits standing in a church, drinking expensive cognac and raising their disposable plastic cups to God. Volodka kept looking up, trying in vain to make out the interior cupola of the church. The weak lighting was deceptive and created the illusion of a low ceiling, which was confusing him.

Back in the city both cars stopped by the embankment. Semyon gave the lads $100 each from the amount he had received from his client. He kept $200 himself, being the boss.

The Lada continued its journey towards the Podil district.

'So, tomorrow at midnight, then?' asked Volodka, when he dropped Semyon off at home. Semyon nodded.

As he got to his front door, Semyon looked at his watch: 12.30 a.m.

'I bet Veronika's already asleep,' he thought as he opened the door.

He put the light on in the hall and immediately noticed the wreath, which was standing on the floor under the coat rack. It scared the life out of him. He froze for a second, mentally running through all of his close relatives.

'Wait a minute, I've seen that somewhere before!' Semyon suddenly realised. As he thought about it he remembered the corner of Striletska Street and the café wall. He remembered his wife telling him about the pharmacist's widow.

He swore under his breath and went to bed.

21

Bird Market, Kurenivka, Kiev

By coincidence, Dima's second visit to the cat woman at the Bird Market was also straight after a night shift. It had been a particularly successful shift that night. Shamil had found 200g of opium in a suitcase arriving from Damascus; Dima had called the shift supervisor, as was standard practice. A report had been drawn up and the passenger had been stopped right there in baggage reclaim and taken off somewhere, although Dima hadn't witnessed that part of the operation. It was no longer his and Shamil's concern. Still, his boss had commended him and this praise had assuaged Dima.

He took the work shuttle bus home, had a shower then called the cat woman.

'You can come and collect your Fluffy,' she said. 'What time is it now, nine o'clock? Let's meet in the same place as before, at eleven. The price has gone up a little bit, by the way. It'll be seventy-five.'

Dima grimaced silently at the increase in the price of a grey alley cat to the price of a bottle of good cognac, but the cat woman was oblivious to his reaction.

The bright sky over Kiev was turning a deep blue. The pavements were covered with trampled-down snow. Trolleybus No. 18 didn't seem to be in any particular hurry . . . It was virtually empty. Dima sat in the back row. His warm Turkish coat with its polyester wadding was doing a good job of keeping him warm, as the seller in the bazaar had promised it would. He was wearing woollen long johns under his old work trousers, too, so he knew he wouldn't freeze. On his knees was an empty shopping bag for the cat – the one he'd been storing his ampoules in. He'd had to take them out and put them back on the newspaper in the garage.

'Is this the stop for the Bird Market?' he asked an old man who got on with two jute bags full of empty beer bottles.

'Next one,' answered the old man.

Stopping at the little watering hole he'd discovered on his last visit, Dima looked at his watch. Ten minutes to go. He went in and ordered a double vodka. Knocking it back, he felt his good spirits multiply.

He recognised the cat woman from afar. She was wearing the same clothes and standing in the same place. She had the same basket at her feet as well, and next to the basket stood a grey army rucksack.

He approached her, took his money out of his pocket and counted out seventy-five hryvnas. She nodded at the rucksack.

'He's all yours!'

'Can I let the cat out of the bag?' Dima cleared his throat and then, realising what he'd said, burst out laughing. That was the last thing he wanted to do.

She unfastened the rucksack and held it open, and Dima saw an enormously fat grey cat, which was clearly considerably larger than the deceased Fluffy.

'But he's . . .' Dima spread his hands wide, disappointment in his voice. 'He's huge!'

'I know. He likes his food, this one! That's why I had to put the price up.'

'But he doesn't look anything like the one he's supposed to be replacing.'

'Fluffy, Fluffy!' the woman called in demonstration, and the cat turned his fat face towards her and miaowed. 'See? I spent all week training him.'

'Scruffy,' said Dima, half whispering, as he looked the fat grey cat up and down.

The cat looked back at Dima with interest.

'He's yours, take him. You won't find another one like him!' The woman launched into a flurry of sales patter, clearly wanting to get rid of her buyer as quickly as possible.

'What about the bag?' Dima asked despondently.

'I'll throw it in for free.'

Dima squatted down, transferred the cat to his shopping bag and put the empty rucksack in too. Then, without saying goodbye, he headed for the exit. He was no longer in a good mood. The cat clearly weighed more than ten kilos. He couldn't imagine anyone feeling sympathy for a cat like this. Especially not Valya.

Reaching his street, Dima carried the bag containing the cat into the garage. He left it there and went into the house.

'What are you doing?' Valya met him at the door.

'I'm just –'

'Have you been to the church?'

'Not today.'

'Well, you should,' she retorted. 'Maybe today's the day you'll find Fluffy.'

All Dima really wanted to do was to eat his dinner and forget about the Baptist church. But he wasn't about to start arguing with his wife. He had enough in his wallet for a portion of *pelmeni*, and eating dinner alone wasn't such a bad prospect. Particularly when he had to decide what to do with this fat cat that answered to Fluffy, and Scruffy, and probably any number of other names.

In the nearest trailer café, over a plate of hot *pelmeni*, Dima did indeed come to a decision. He decided to leave the cat in the garage without any food for a few days, until it lost some weight, and then he could take it into the house.

As he left the trailer café, Dima saw an advert glued to a lamp post.

FOR SALE
imported cancer medication
$20 per ampoule
call Zhenya on 8 063 4320985

'Ha!' Dima smiled to himself and nodded. 'I see Zhenya's got his scam up and running.'

And he went home to report back to his wife that someone had spotted Fluffy near the church that morning, but that he hadn't managed to find him. He would have to go out looking for him a couple more times.

22

Hrushevsky Street, Kiev
The light from three spotlights fixed to the surprisingly low ceiling made everything in the room look yellow.

'Don't worry, you haven't broken anything. It's just a few

bumps and bruises.' Egor leaned over Irina and smiled at her reassuringly.

'We can't be too sure,' cautioned another, unfamiliar male voice. 'She's probably got concussion.'

Irina looked at the doctor in his white coat. He was a young man with a thin moustache and a thin nose. His head was shaven and he wore a tiny silver earring in one ear.

She looked around and realised that she was lying on a stretcher in an ambulance. The square window was dark. Inside herself she felt somehow empty and echoing.

'Where are you taking me?' she asked.

'Nowhere,' the doctor answered. 'You just need to lie down for a bit. Try to wiggle your fingers and toes.'

Irina wiggled them. She immediately felt her body and it seemed a little less empty and echoing. In fact, her toes wiggled a little too easily. She raised her head, then propped herself up on her elbow so that she could see her feet. Ah, of course! They'd taken her boots off, that's why her toes felt so free.

'Irina, I'm taking you home. Don't worry, you're not going to hospital.'

'Yeah, you don't want to go there,' nodded the doctor. 'You might catch something.'

'That's not funny,' Egor admonished him. 'Can't you be a bit more positive?'

'You try living on my salary and maintaining a positive frame of mind.'

Irina lay on the stretcher listening to the conversation between the two men. She started thinking about money too, wondering whether or not she earned more than the doctor.

'OK, time to get up!' Egor distracted her from her thoughts.

'Let's sort your feet out first. We need to get these boots back on . . .'

He carefully put her boots on and did up the zips.

'Now try to stand up . . .'

Irina stood up and saw that they'd taken her coat off too, and she was suddenly ashamed of the way she was dressed.

Egor helped her out of the ambulance. Cars were driving past them, making sighing and sobbing noises as they drove over snow that had already been kneaded by countless tyres. She recognised the bus stop and the park, which was completely dark.

'Oh my God! It's late already!' Irina panicked.

'Come on,' whispered Egor. 'I've left my car in the courtyard of your milk kitchen.'

Irina looked up at her workplace as they walked. All the windows of the first-floor apartment were filled with bright yellow light.

Egor sat Irina in the passenger seat. He shut the door and she felt as though she were in a snow-covered hut. It was cold and dark. She could hear the rustle of the little broom that he was using to brush the snow off the windscreen.

They drove slowly through the city. The flow of traffic only started moving more quickly once they got to Victory Avenue.

To take her mind off her aching body and to stop herself trying to work out which bits were hurting because of the milk churns and which from being hit by a car, she told Egor about the talk she'd had with her boss and about the milk churns that she and the old nurse had carried.

Her story didn't take long to tell, and when she finished a conversational lull ensued. She wanted to hear Egor's voice: confident, decisive and preferably full of concern. But Egor didn't say anything. He remained silent for about five minutes. Then he said, 'Her name's not Nelly Igorievna. She changed it to make herself sound more distinguished. And don't worry, you had every right to ask for a pay rise.'

'Did you manage to find anything out about the baby?' Irina asked, with hope in her voice.

'Not yet, but I've got people looking into it. We help one another out. I put them in touch with certain people, and they do the odd bit of digging for me. They've already checked out your Nelly Igorievna. Turns out her real name is Galina Timofeevna Slepchenko. Only three years ago she was removing the evil eye from people for twenty hryvnas, and look where she is now . . .'

'You don't think she had me run over because I asked her for a pay rise, do you?' Irina was aghast.

'Irochka! You shouldn't think like that!'

'Oh, my bag!' Irina remembered. 'My bag and the box of chocolates! I bet someone's taken them.'

'I'll have a look and see if I can find them,' Egor promised.

Half an hour later Egor's red Mazda turned into Makariv, then Kodra. He drove right to her house and helped her out of the car.

'Here.' He held out a few large-denomination notes. 'Consider it a bonus, and paid leave. Stay at home for a week and look after Yasya. Forget about Kiev. I'll come and check on you soon.'

Irina nodded and stayed by the wicket gate until the red car dissolved into the strange, purple darkness of that winter evening.

23

Apartment No. 10, Reitarska Street, Kiev

Semyon didn't wake up even when Veronika brought a cup of coffee into the bedroom and sat on the edge of the bed.

'Senya,' she said, leaning over her sleeping husband.

He muttered something in response from under the blanket.

'Senya, wake up! It's eleven o'clock!'

'Eleven o'clock?' her husband repeated sleepily.

Semyon ran his hand over his injured hip. He assumed he'd been tossing and turning all night because of it. He raised himself up on his elbow.

'How did you sleep?' he asked Veronika. 'Was I fidgeting last night?'

'No. You slept like a log!'

Semyon got out of bed and went into the bathroom. He took a cold shower and listened to his body. He glanced at the bruise on his hip again. It had turned a dark, pearly shade of purple. He dried himself off with a towel.

As he went past the coat rack in the corridor, he looked down at the wreath.

'Nika! Put that thing somewhere else, will you? I nearly broke my neck tripping over it yesterday.'

'You mean the wreath? Darya Ivanovna's coming to pick it up today. She promised to be here by twelve.'

Semyon stuffed the wreath into a carrier bag and hung it on the coat rack.

He put on his tracksuit and was immediately reminded of the 'skiers' from the day before. He was as bad as they were. Wearing an Adidas tracksuit was about the extent of his sporting activity. He really ought to make more effort to stay in shape.

He had a banana and a cup of green tea for breakfast and thought about suggesting to Veronika that they go out somewhere. It was Sunday, after all.

He had just gone into the living room when the telephone rang. Veronika picked up the receiver and Semyon could tell straight away by his wife's expression that the conversation would last at least a quarter of an hour. He went back into the kitchen and heard his mobile ringing in his jacket pocket, where it had been since the previous night. It was Volodka.

'Hey, Senya, can you meet me for half an hour?' he asked. 'I'm in McSnack, not far from yours.'

The café was nearly empty. The only other customer was a girl sitting at a table with her laptop.

'Well, that was quite a night you gave me!' said Volodka, as Semyon sat down opposite him. Volodka did look genuinely tired. Semyon stared at him, confused.

'You asked me to follow you,' Volodka reminded his boss.

'Yes,' Semyon nodded. 'I know I did. But I thought we said tonight . . .'

'What's the difference? I couldn't sleep last night anyway, so –'

'Hang on a minute. Are you saying I went out last night?'

Volodka nodded.

Semyon recalled the morning. He remembered feeling as though he'd had a decent night's sleep. Veronika hadn't raised any grievances with him, and he'd only seen the wreath in the hall twice – when he got home at 11.30 p.m., and this morning after his shower.

'Where did I go?' asked Semyon, perplexed.

'You left the house at twenty past two. You walked to the corner of Striletska Street and Yaroslaviv Val, wandered past the Radisson, then turned round and walked to the top of Ivana Franko Street then down to Khmelnytskogo. I can draw you a map if you like. That's not the most interesting bit, though.'

'Go on,' said Semyon, warily.

'There was someone waiting for you, on the corner of Chekhov Street and Olesya Gonchara Street. A tall blonde in a full-length fur coat.'

'You're kidding!' Semyon exclaimed in disbelief. 'Then what happened?'

'You kissed her. You barely spoke. You escorted her up Chekhov Street, stood by her front door together for about five minutes, and that was it. She went home, and so did you. You went up Olesya Gonchara Street.'

Semyon felt strange. He looked around.

'Where does this blonde woman live?'

Volodka smirked. He handed Semyon a piece of paper with an address written on it.

'And what's her name?' asked Semyon, his voice barely audible.

'No idea, I didn't talk to her. You were the one doing the talking. Or rather, the kissing . . .'

There was a pause.

'You should go and see a doctor,' whispered Volodka, leaning over the table. 'Seriously. You need to see a psychiatrist, or a psychologist.'

'I'm not crazy!' Semyon shook his head. 'There's nothing wrong with me.'

'You're sleepwalking,' said Volodka, still whispering. 'And I'll tell you another thing – there was someone else following you, but when he noticed me he disappeared.'

Semyon's head started aching. He felt a sudden, unpleasant heaviness in his body.

'You should go and get some sleep,' he said to Volodka.

'Shall I follow you again?' suggested his friend.

Semyon nodded. 'That's probably not a bad idea,' he said.

24

9 May Street, Boryspil

Valya's happiness seemed to know no bounds. Dima stood at the kitchen door with a lopsided grin on his face, watching his wife pirouetting around in her lilac dressing gown with the grey cat in her arms.

'You'd be struggling to do that if he hadn't spent a week in the garage on a diet,' thought Dima.

Now it had lost a bit of weight and been rolled around in some dirt and dust, the cat bore an uncanny resemblance to the late Fluffy.

Valya was dumbstruck when her husband brought him 'home'. She stood rooted to the ground for about five minutes. Then she wiped the tears from her eyes, went up to her husband, took the cat from him as if it were a baby and carried it into the bathroom.

The cat's enforced starvation had sapped its resistance as well as its energy. It was like a limp scrap of cloth, a collar ripped from an old coat. Dima had swept up a pile of rubbish and tipped it out in the corner of the garage. Then he had put the cat in the rubbish and spent some time making sure that it was completely covered in it. The cat hadn't even reacted. It had just looked at Dima every now and then with a vacant expression in its eyes, like a drunken tramp.

However, now that Valya had washed and brushed the cat it had acquired the look of a pampered pet, albeit a rather skinny one. Its eyes were no longer dull but cunning. And right now they were fixed on the painted wooden floor, clearly anticipating the appearance of a bowl of cat food.

It didn't have long to wait.

'There, Fluffy, you get yourself nice and cosy in your favourite spot,' said Valya, putting him down near the radiator underneath the window. 'Now, let's get you something to eat, shall we?'

Dima soon tired of watching his wife and her fraudulent feline co-star acting out this comedy. At the same time he couldn't help feeling a certain modest pride, like the director of a successful stage show.

Half an hour later, after gazing admiringly at 'Fluffy' as he gobbled down his food, Valya suggested to her husband that they go to a café.

'We can celebrate Fluffy's return,' she said softly.

As they left the house they heard a familiar unpleasant growling. King, their neighbour's bull terrier, stood on their side of the fence, his sharp, gleaming teeth bared maliciously.

Their neighbour's door was open, and the dog's owner stood on the doorstep holding a cigarette. He was about fifty years old, with a receding hairline and a beer belly. Rumour had it that he used to work as a butcher at the market.

'Hey, get your dog out of here!' shouted Dima.

'Here, King! Come here, boy!' their neighbour ordered the dog in a hoarse voice.

The bull terrier returned lazily to its own territory through a hole in the fence. Dima looked at this hole in the fence and was filled with rage. He had already boarded it up at least five times. The dog couldn't possibly have taken the boards down by itself; its owner must have been doing it each time so that his bull terrier could continue fouling the neighbouring yard.

'I ought to put some poison down, that would serve him right,' thought Dima.

By the time he and Valya reached the nearest trailer café, Dima's rage had abated. They ordered a plate of *pelmeni* each and 100ml of vodka to share. They looked at each other as they ate. Neither of them felt the need to talk. The television set mounted up near the ceiling of the trailer was quietly babbling away to itself. The actors' voices were indistinct. Sometimes there was a burst of music. This sound, the sound of life going on around them, seemed to suit the mood of their meal perfectly.

Valya filled the shot glasses with vodka herself. She also proposed the toast: 'To Fluffy's return!'

They drank. Then they realised that they'd already finished their *pelmeni*, so they ordered another portion each.

'The portions definitely used to be bigger,' said Valya, sounding wistful. 'You used to get fourteen *pelmeni* in a portion, or seven *varenyky*.' She gave a deep sigh, as though she had just crossed some kind of threshold, leaving her youth behind.

'It's no big deal.' Dima waved his hand dismissively, suddenly filled with the desire to placate his wife. 'There's nothing to stop us cooking *pelmeni* ourselves at home. As many as you like.'

'Fluffy likes *pelmeni* too,' recalled Valya. 'I'm going to take a couple back for him.'

They walked home slowly, arm in arm. A light snow was falling obliquely. They passed other people but they were all walking alone, as though Dima and Valya were the only couple in the whole of Boryspil to be strolling along the street.

As Dima opened their front door he saw a note: '*Call me on my mobile when you get back, Borya.*'

The new Fluffy met them in the hall. He immediately started rubbing himself around his mistress's legs.

'He's missed me!' She was delighted. 'Well, I've brought *pelmeni* for you.'

His wife went into the kitchen with the cat, and Dima headed for the living room to call Boris. He felt apprehensive.

'I'm coming over,' said Boris, sounding completely calm. 'I need a word with you about something.'

He arrived twenty minutes later and asked Dima to step outside.

'Listen, I need to buy your ampoules off you,' he said. 'I'll give you ten hryvnas each for them.'

'Did you manage to find out what's inside them?' asked Dima.

'No, but people are buying them and that's all that matters! Come on, I thought you wanted to get rid of them.'

Dima recalled the sign advertising imported cancer medication and a slight smile crossed his lips.

'Ten? That's a bit low . . .' he said.

'All right, twenty then.' Boris readily doubled his offer.

'Thirty,' declared Dima.

Boris was clearly in a hurry. It occurred to Dima that he might actually have a customer waiting for the ampoules. Just around the corner, looking nervously at his watch.

'Fine,' sighed Boris.

'Wait by the gate,' Dima told him. He went back inside, fetched the cat woman's rucksack and went into the garage.

He put nearly all the remaining ampoules into the rucksack, keeping a dozen boxes back for himself, just in case. What if it did turn out to be a cure for cancer after all?

The transaction was concluded by the dim light inside the car. Boris settled up with large-denomination notes. Dima counted the money three times and got muddled each time, because a voice in his head kept saying: 'You should have asked for more!'

At last the deal was done. Boris left, and Dima smiled as he watched him drive off. He could feel the whole unpleasant business of the black suitcase disappearing into the distance with him.

25

Lipovka village, Kiev region, morning

'She was using her powers to get back at you,' Irina's mother assured her that morning, after hearing what had happened to her daughter the previous evening. 'Go to Kiev! Tell her you're sorry. Tell her you made a silly mistake!'

Irina looked at her electric alarm clock. Beneath it lay the money that Egor had given her the day before.

'And don't go getting your hopes up!' Her mother followed her look. 'He's not going to keep giving you money. He just felt sorry for you, that's all.'

Irina kept looking at the hundred-hryvna notes, trying not to listen to her mother. Just then Yasya woke up and started crying, and Irina realised that it was already gone 9 a.m. That she had slept long and deeply, and her minibus taxi had already been to Kiev and back. So she wouldn't be going anywhere that day. She touched each of her swollen breasts, then picked up her daughter and lifted the woollen blouse she was wearing against her bare skin. She brought Yasya's mouth to her nipple and immediately felt her daughter's strong, warm lips.

Outside the sun was shining, and its rays danced on the pattern frozen onto the windowpane.

'I'm going to take her out for a bit,' said Irina, looking down at her child.

'Well, I don't know how you think we're going to manage on my pension,' remarked her mother. She left Irina's room and went into her own. She switched the television on, turned the sound up and went into the kitchen.

In a funny way the indistinct voice of the presenter restored harmony to their little household. Irina took the baby off her left breast, turned her round and brought her to her right breast. About five minutes later Yasya released the nipple.

'Fast asleep!' whispered Irina.

She put her daughter down on the bed and covered her with the blanket.

Then Irina put on her coat and went out into the yard in her slippers. The chilly air stung her exposed ankles. She went behind the house to the shed. The chickens were making a racket in the adjacent outbuilding and Irina looked in on them as well, just out of curiosity. Her life had been on a crazy schedule for the past three months, and now that the first minibus to Kiev had left without her and she had woken late as the winter sun was already rising she was bursting with an unfamiliar childlike curiosity. It was as though everyone else had been playing a fun game in her absence, and now she wanted to see what she'd missed out on.

At some point Irina forgot why she'd gone to the shed in the first place. Motherhood might have sharpened her instincts, but it had numbed her brain! She'd heard that phrase a few times now but couldn't remember who'd said it.

'Ah, yes! My old sledge!' she remembered.

The door to the shed opened with a terrifying creak. Her father never oiled the hinges. He maintained that any potential burglars would get the fright of their lives if they tried to open the door. Maybe that really was the reason they'd never been burgled, whereas the other villagers seemed to be reporting break-ins almost every day.

Fighting her way past the piles of firewood stacked up against the left-hand wall, Irina made her way towards a couple of bicycles with flat tyres that were propped up in the far corner. Hanging on a nail in the wall above them was a sledge with metal runners and a wooden seat.

Half an hour later she was pulling Yasya on the sledge – still asleep and wrapped up in her blanket – along the frozen path leading to the outskirts of the village, towards the pine forest and the small hill she and her friends used to sledge down when they were children, not so very long ago. Of course Yasya was still too young to enjoy sledging down hills, and Irina's swollen breasts were aching . . . But this wasn't going to stop them, the two of them together, flying down the hill of her childhood.

At the top of the hill Irina picked up her sleeping daughter, sat on the sledge with Yasya on her knee and leaned forward a little, nudging the sledge downhill with the weight of her body.

A rush of cold air on her face, eyes screwed up tight. A spontaneous smile, undeterred by the icy wind or the snow that was falling on them, both from the sky and from the tops of the pine trees.

She got home an hour later, happy as a child, thinking of nothing but Yasya. She left the sledge on the doorstep.

'You had a visitor,' her mother told her, nodding at the door that led to Irina's room. 'Probably the one who gave you that money.'

On the bed next to an empty carrier bag lay a box of sweets, a carton of apple juice, a few oranges and a bar of chocolate.

'As if you were laid up in hospital!' Her mother shook her head, following Irina's gaze into the room.

'Did he set it all out like that?' Irina asked in surprise. Yasya had woken up, and Irina laid her down next to the gifts.

'No, I did. I wanted to see what he'd brought,' her mother confessed readily. 'You're not allowed citrus fruits, they'll make your milk bitter,' she added.

'Are you hungry, my little Yasenka?' Irina began to disentangle her baby daughter from her blanket cocoon. 'Come on, have a little bit of Mama's milk – my breasts are about to explode!'

Irina's mother looked at her daughter and gave a heavy sigh.

'She's never going to drink all your milk. It's too much for her anyway. Look how full they are! You'll need to express some. You should go to Kiev – at least they'll pay you for it.'

Irina moved the gifts from Egor to the edge of the bed and lay on her side, with her back to her mother and Yasya at her breast.

26

Apartment No. 17, Vorovsky Street, Kiev

While Darya Ivanovna was making another pot of tea in the kitchen, Veronika looked around the room and noticed that her hostess didn't have a single photograph of her late husband on display. What she did appear to have, though, was pretty good taste as far as furniture and decor were concerned. Good taste in clothes too, although Veronika couldn't help thinking she was a bit overdressed. Veronika herself wouldn't dream of wearing a business suit around the house, but Darya Ivanovna evidently thought nothing of it. Actually, her matching dark red pencil skirt and fitted jacket seemed perfectly in keeping with her surroundings. There were two leather armchairs and a leather sofa, all light brown, and a coffee table in the centre of the room. There was a vase of red roses on the table, along with two china cups and saucers. The cups had red roses on them too. There was an enormous clock, which must have been at least fifty years old, ticking away on top of a little chest of drawers. The windowsill was full of pot plants, and near the radiator in the corner of the room stood a lemon tree in a wooden tub. There was a portrait of Darya Ivanovna on the little chest of drawers: oil on canvas, a gilt frame.

It was odd, but it suddenly occurred to Veronika that there wasn't a single trace of her husband in this room. It was almost as though he'd never existed.

Darya Ivanovna came back into the room carrying a china teapot, which she set down on the little table.

'I really appreciate your help – I've got so many things to do, so much to think about, without having to remember to take that wreath down at the weekend . . . Are you going straight home when you leave here?'

Veronika nodded.

'It gets dark early these days,' continued Darya Ivanovna. 'I don't think anyone'll notice if you hang it back up on your way home.'

A moment later the cups were refilled with aromatic tea.

Veronika kept looking at the ruby signet ring that graced the third finger of her hostess's right hand. Darya Ivanovna noticed the direction of her gaze.

'It won't come off,' she said, sipping her tea. 'I need to try and get it off with some soap and a piece of thread, so I can take it to the jeweller's to get it stretched. Edik gave it to me for our thirtieth anniversary. Maybe,' she began but then suddenly fell silent, glancing pensively at the clock. 'Well, I don't know how you'd feel about it, but . . .'

'How I'd feel about what?' asked Veronika.

'You've got guts.' Darya Ivanovna looked into her guest's eyes. 'And you stood up for me the other day . . . Are you free right now?'

'Yes, of course.'

'Good.' Darya Ivanovna suddenly grew serious. 'Finish your tea, then we can go. It's not far from here.'

It had grown cold outside. The twilight had deepened into night. Darya Ivanovna had given the carrier bag containing the funeral wreath back to Veronika, and now the frost was nipping at the back of Veronika's hand and her fingers. She stuck her free hand into the pocket of her coat, which was smart and stylish but not particularly warm.

'It's just round the corner,' said Darya Ivanovna, leading the way.

They walked along Yaroslaviv Val then down Ivana Franko Street. They turned onto Chapaev Street, stopping before they reached the headquarters of the Ministry of Emergency Situations – an unprepossessing building with crumbling plaster walls. They stood in front of an archway that led to a series of courtyards. At one time this archway had been open to pedestrians, but now it was blocked with a pair of metal gates. Darya Ivanovna pressed the button on the intercom.

'Can I help you?' enquired a rasping male voice.

'Number thirty-two slash one,' she answered softly.

The male voice asked her to wait a minute, but one of the metal gates swung open after only a few seconds. A man in padded green overalls – a typical contemporary security guard – nodded at the women and closed the gates behind them.

The women followed the security guard through another arch, stopping behind him when they reached the main entrance to a modern two-storey building. The man started jingling his keys in front of the heavy steel door.

Veronika was intrigued by Chapaev Street. It was short and curved like a boomerang. Often it was completely deserted; other times the only pedestrian might be someone really famous, or perhaps a minor television celebrity. Maybe they lived here. If people like that ever walked anywhere else they usually had bodyguards with them, but here they were always alone. As Veronika listened to the jingling of the keys she thought about everyone she'd seen walking along this street: ministers, politicians . . . But she couldn't for the life of her remember their names. They all had faces that were easy to recognise and names that were easy to forget.

'Are you going to be long?' asked the security guard, as he let the visitors in.

'Fifteen, twenty minutes, maybe,' answered Darya Ivanovna, her voice tinged with sorrow.

'I'll make you some tea, then,' he promised. 'Or you'll freeze!'

A spacious service lift took them down a couple of floors.

The security guard turned the light on, and they saw another enormous steel door.

The room on the other side of this door looked like a cross between a luxurious left-luggage facility and a café in a funeral parlour. Three of the walls were covered from floor to ceiling with black and red tiles. Three large tables stood on the black marble floor, each with four chairs around it. The fourth wall, about three metres high and ten or twelve metres long, appeared to consist of rows of lockers for oversized luggage. But there were no coin slots or operating instructions. Instead, each of the matt metal doors featured a three-digit number engraved on a little plaque, which was attached to the right of each door handle.

'Thirty-two slash one, you said?' asked the security guard, wheeling a chrome trolley over to the locker doors.

He stopped in front of one of the doors and pulled the handle towards him. A long metal box slid slowly out from the wall and hung suspended over the marble floor. Inside was the body of a man, dressed in a suit. The security guard made a few simple adjustments and lowered the box containing the body onto the trolley. Then he turned round and looked at Darya Ivanovna.

'Shall I take him to the meeting room? Or will you be staying here?'

'We've got the place to ourselves.' The chemist's wife spread her hands. 'We might as well sit here for a little while.' She indicated the end table on the right.

The security guard nodded. He wheeled the trolley over to the table that Darya Ivanonva had indicated and left the room.

'Sit down, Nikochka.' Darya Ivanovna nodded at a chair. She herself went and stood off to one side, dabbing at her eyes with her scarf. She unbuttoned her coat but didn't take it off.

Veronika sat down. She looked at the body in the box. She knew exactly who it was. It was the first time in her life that she'd been this close to death, to the cold aura of mortality. A peculiar clammy, metallic chill emanating from the box touched Veronika's hands, her neck, her cheeks. She moved her chair a little further away. She didn't hear Darya Ivanovna coming up behind her. Darya Ivanovna softly placed her hands on Veronika's shoulders, and Veronika jumped out of her skin.

'Hey, what's the matter?' chided Darya Ivanovna. 'There's nothing to be scared of. Let me introduce you. This is my Edik.'

She looked affectionately at her husband's white face.

'I thought you'd already buried him,' Veronika said quietly.

'I can't bring myself to do it,' confessed the widow. 'It doesn't seem right, just sticking him in a hole in the ground. You know what they say: out of sight, out of mind . . . I'd feel like I'd lost him for good, I would start to forget him . . . Burying him would be so final. And I'm not ready to move on. Do you remember the poem "Never Leave the Ones You Love!"?'

Darya Ivanovna took a flat metal flask from one of her coat pockets and a couple of silver shot glasses from the other.

'A drop of whisky to warm us up.' She nodded at the flask. 'It's chilly in here!'

Veronika tried to work out whether it was cold in there or not. It was strange, but she didn't actually feel physically cold. There had been a definite chill in the air a moment earlier but it didn't seem to be there any longer, because Darya Ivanovna was now sitting between Veronika and the source of this cold.

'What kind is it?' Veronika suddenly asked, just to change the subject.

'What kind?' repeated Darya Ivanovna. 'No idea. Edik used to love whisky. We've still got about ten bottles of the stuff in our drinks cabinet, all different kinds. They were gifts from famous people, politicians. He cured them all . . .'

'What do you mean?' Veronika was surprised. 'I thought he was a pharmacist, not a doctor.'

'He used to make up individual medicines to order, sometimes using prohibited old recipes. Even the Prime Minister came to see him, our own Yulechka! He made her a powerful cure for tiredness. He warned her that it had strong side effects, and she said to him, "Side effects don't bother me!" She ordered other medicines from him, too, but she didn't come and pick them up herself. She sent her assistant, a bald chap – you've probably seen him on TV. Oh, I don't know what we're talking about them for! Anyway, to cut a long story short our drinks cupboard is still full of foreign whisky.'

She filled the silver shot glasses.

'So as I was saying,' she said, returning to the thread of their conversation, 'I'm against the idea of burying him. Burying him, digging him up . . . Let's drink a toast to his memory! I think he's going to be missed by a lot of people. No one else would dare to do what he did.'

Veronika took a sip of her whisky. She felt a bitter warmth running over her larynx and down her oesophagus as she swallowed. It was like an anatomy lesson on the oral ingestion of liquids.

'He could stay here for a few years, although it is rather expensive,' continued Darya Ivanovna, finishing her whisky. 'It's a private cryogenic storage facility. Mainly for foreigners who are waiting to be transported home, back to their own countries, to be buried. You know, until all the documents are in order and their relatives come to collect them, and so on and so forth. Apparently my Edik is the only one in here originally from Kiev . . . But I've decided he won't be here for much longer, I'll be taking him home soon!'

Veronika looked up at the widow in alarm.

Darya Ivanovna met her glance with a smile.

'There's a workshop not far from here.' Her voice dropped to a whisper. 'They used to stuff people's dead cats and dogs as mementos, but recently they bought a licence in Germany for the plastination of human bodies.'

'What's plastination?' asked Veronika, feeling the cold on her cheeks and neck again.

'It's like embalming, only cheaper, quicker and more permanent,' explained Darya Ivanovna. 'Plus you can tell them if you want the body in a particular pose, and they can always change it again for an additional payment. He would have been all for it – Edik loved science. Before he died he was working on a special medicine for one of his regular clients. To cure fear. He called it Anti-Wimp!' The metal flask of whisky shone in the widow's hands. A thin stream of the noble spirit was poured into Veronika's shot glass, releasing a sharp aroma. Darya Ivanovna looked at her companion. She continued in a whisper. 'Maybe that medicine was the death of him. The woman who ordered it has so many enemies . . . There's no humanity in Ukrainian politics. Everyone's watching, listening, spying on one another. And dear Yulia, she didn't order it for herself. She's not scared of anything! No, it was obviously for her more faint-hearted colleagues. He'd already managed to make the first trial batch but was really worried about the side effects. He said they were of a "psychological nature".' She made a circular motion with her forefinger near her temple and gave a sad smile.

When the widow made this teenage gesture Veronika thought her face looked younger, just for a second. Her wrinkles disappeared and her nose grew a little thinner. 'No, it must be a trick of the light!' she told herself firmly, drinking her second shot of whisky in one gulp.

'What do you mean, a "psychological nature"?' she asked carefully. 'Like when people go crazy?'

'No. Like when suddenly, out of the blue, they start behaving with honesty and integrity . . . Bear in mind I'm talking about politicians here, not normal people. Normal people buy their medicine over the counter. I never really questioned Edik about it in detail, but I can remember the bits he told me himself. He had an office in his pharmacy, but he would make up the trial batches at night somewhere in the Darnytsya area. He had a friend in a pharmacological manufacturing plant there. I'm going to sell the pharmacy. We could go there now, if you like? I could show you Edik's office.'

Veronika had no desire to visit the late pharmacist's office, but she had even less desire to continue sitting at this table with Darya Ivanovna, who was only partially concealing from view the metal box containing the frozen Edik. Who had been killed, incidentally, a stone's throw from her own apartment. The same night that Semyon had come home in the early hours of the morning in a strange mood and with a brown stain on the sleeve of his shirt.

She was overwhelmed by the conviction that her own husband

had been Edik's cold-blooded murderer. But no! Despite his line of work her husband was a kind, gentle man, incapable of cruelty. It was just an absurd coincidence, that was all.

Veronika started to feel cold and she looked at Darya Ivanovna, silently imploring her to refill her glass.

27

9 May Street, Boryspil

After Fluffy 'returned', life in Dima and Valya's home went back to normal. Valya decided to get a job and soon found a position as a cashier in a small amusement arcade near the bus station. She worked from 8 a.m. until 5 p.m., so now Dima had to heat his own breakfast up when he got home after a night shift. The first thing he did was to lift the lid of the frying pan standing on the hob. Partly out of curiosity, partly in order to stimulate his appetite. He was happy whatever there was for breakfast: leftover *pelmeni*, which went all crusty and delicious when they were reheated in the frying pan, buckwheat with rissoles, or even a fried egg with crispy bacon bits, prepared earlier and left to cool.

This morning was no different. When Dima returned from his night shift tired and hungry, he looked under the lid of the frying pan before lighting the gas. Today's breakfast would be a fried chicken leg with noodles.

A circle of little blue flames simultaneously surrounded the gas ring on the hob and started licking the base of the heavy cast-iron frying pan. Dima lit the adjacent ring too and put the kettle on to boil.

The new Fluffy watched his master from under the radiator, then came closer and rubbed up against Dima's leg.

Dima looked down at the grey cat, which had started putting on weight again. Catching his master's eye, the cat went straight over to his empty bowl and stopped before it expectantly.

'Get out of it, you chancer!' Dima muttered and turned back to the cooker.

After his breakfast Dima shut the curtains in the bedroom and got into bed. It was warm and cosy under the heavy quilt. He pulled it up over his head, moving the pillow to one side out of his way, and fell into a deep sleep.

Suddenly there was a noise, the slamming of doors, the sound of footsteps moving quickly across the wooden floor.

Valya ran into the bedroom without taking her coat or shoes off. She looked as though she'd seen a ghost. She ran over to her sleeping husband and pulled the quilt from his head.

'Dima, Dima! Get up! You're not going to believe this!'

The first thing Dima did was to look at the alarm clock. It was 12.30 p.m.

'What is it?' he grumbled.

Dima got dressed, put some slippers on his bare feet and followed his wife into the hall. He couldn't see anything out of the ordinary, but Valya kept pulling him towards the front door. She opened it wide and stopped still. On the doorstep lay a dirty, emaciated grey cat. There was dried blood on its ears. It wasn't moving, but its eyes were fixed on Dima in an expressionless stare. The cat gave a hoarse, feeble miaow, as though it were its last.

Valya turned to her husband.

'Look!' she said.

She knelt down beside the cat.

'Is it you, Fluffy?' she asked quietly.

The cat gave another hoarse miaow and tried to stand up.

'It's all my fault,' whispered Valya, sobbing.

She picked up the frail grey cat and carried it into the hallway.

Dima moved out of the way to let his wife pass.

She put the cat down on the hall floor and turned back to her husband.

Dima couldn't take his eyes off the emaciated cat. It did look a lot like the real Fluffy, the one he'd thrown into the well in the abandoned yard with his own bare hands. But he'd been dead. Hadn't he?

Valya took her coat and shoes off. She stood for a moment, looking down at the cat. Then, apparently having come to some decision, she took the mat that was lying on the doorstep and turned it over to the side that had not yet been used for wiping dirty feet. She laid it under the coat rack and transferred the new arrival onto it.

'Oh my God!' She clasped her hands together. 'He's barely alive. Wait, I'll be right back!'

She went into the kitchen. Seizing the moment, Dima squatted down and looked into the cat's face.

'Scruffy, is it really you?' he asked, as though he were expecting at least a nod in response. But the cat didn't react at all. It just kept staring at Dima with a forlorn, devoted expression.

Dima shuddered. He wondered what Valya had meant about it being all her fault.

Valya came back into the hallway from the kitchen carrying a bowl of milk, which she set down before the cat. It lowered its face right into the bowl and drank greedily, its entire emaciated body shuddering with every gulp.

The new Fluffy emerged from the kitchen. He went straight up to his suffering kinsman and started hissing. Valya grabbed him.

'What do you think you're doing?' she scolded, stroking him behind the ears. 'You were scrawny and half dead at first, too. And now look how gorgeous you are!'

From the lofty vantage point of Valya's chest the new Fluffy looked with open hostility at the dirty grey cat, which had already drunk all the milk from the bowl and lowered its face back down onto the mat.

'Come on, I'll get you some milk too,' Valya said gently, carrying the fat grey cat back into the kitchen.

'Why did you say it was all your fault?' asked Dima, when Valya had finally calmed down and come back into the living room, shutting the kitchen door carefully to keep the fat Fluffy away from the skinny one in the hallway.

Valya sighed and sat down in the armchair.

'I need a drink!' she exclaimed.

Dima fetched a bottle of home-made nettle vodka and poured a shot for his wife. She drank it in one gulp.

'I went to the church, to pray for Fluffy to come home, and when that didn't work I went to see a psychic. She told me that Fluffy was alive but was stuck in a deep hole and wouldn't be able to get out until something else was thrown in. She also said that I would hear Savaofa's voice in my dreams, saying, "He'll come back!" I had to count the number of times I heard it. She said that as soon as I heard it thirteen times Fluffy would come back. But I only heard it seven times, and then you found him yourself . . . Psychics work for the Devil, don't they? So basically I ended up asking for help from God and the Devil at the same time. God sent us one Fluffy, and the Devil sent us the other . . .'

Dima tried to make sense of what his wife was saying but couldn't. He was obviously too tired after his sleepless night.

'I mean it's the same cat, he's just come back to us two different ways,' she added.

'Have you joined some sort of cult?' Dima asked in alarm. He'd never heard his wife talk like this before.

'I went twice,' Valya admitted. 'I thought it would help bring Fluffy back.'

Dima stared at Valya. 'Has she gone mad?' he wondered.

'I'm going to the garage, I need to be by myself,' he said and went into the hall.

Dima's cosy corner of the garage was a little chilly. He switched on the electric heater, sat down on the little wooden bench and poured himself a shot of vodka, to warm himself up and help him think straight. He thought about the day the baggage handlers had brought the suitcase. He remembered everything. Including the way Fluffy had lapped up the contents of the ampoule and then run out of the garage, right under the wheels of that cyclist.

'Well, there's only one way to find out if it's really him,' he decided.

He went back into the house, picked up the emaciated cat and the mat it was lying on and carried the bundle into the garage. He downed another shot and then took an ampoule out of one of the boxes, broke the top off and poured the contents onto a plate that had the remains of an uneaten sprat stuck to it. He put the plate down in front of the grey cat. The cat raised his head. Its eyes lit up. It moved spasmodically towards the plate and lapped it all up, every last drop.

Dima cleared his throat. He knew he was being silly – any cat would have lapped up that stuff!

'Maybe I should go and have a look in the well. What if this one's an impostor too?' he thought, but then he shook his head. He no longer felt like going anywhere.

28

Lipovka village, Kiev region

Irina had a languid, unhurried start to the day, as though she were a child again. She lay in bed with Yasya until nearly 9 a.m.

She'd been aware of the front door creaking several times, opening and closing, as her mother went out to feed the chickens.

She didn't feel like getting up. She did feel like some chocolate, though. She picked up the Alyonushka bar that Egor had brought for her the previous day and unwrapped it, listening to the sweet crinkling of the foil.

For some reason – maybe it was the silver foil against the dark brown of the chocolate, maybe the bitter-sweet taste, or maybe for no reason at all – she suddenly thought of Mariinsky Park and the low turquoise palace behind the thin, black tree trunks. She remembered the crunch of the snow under her feet. Although she was warmer and cosier under the blanket than she'd ever been before, thinking about the park made her feel uncomfortable. Her breasts were aching too. Yasya didn't drink half as much milk as her mother was producing.

A car pulled up outside.

'It's Egor!' Irina thought happily.

She got up, quickly but carefully, so as not to wake Yasya, and looked out of the window.

No, it wasn't Egor's car on the other side of the fence. Egor's was red, but this one was dark blue.

Someone knocked at the door.

'Are you expecting anyone?' asked her mother, looking into the room. 'I'll go and see who it is.'

'Is Irina Anatolievna in?' came a deep, unfamiliar male voice from the front of the house.

'She is indeed,' answered her mother.

'Tell her to hurry up and get ready.'

Her mother came bursting into her room, looking terrified.

'There are two of them out there with their heads all shaven, like something out of *Gangs of St Petersburg*! They're wearing black coats,' garbled her mother, her voice low and urgent. 'You must have upset someone important. Maybe you left one of the ministers' babies without any milk.'

Irina got dressed as quickly as she could. Her mother's fear had communicated itself to her too – her hands shook and her feet refused to go into the warm brown tights. It took her about ten minutes to get ready. Then she went out into the hall.

She saw two tall men in leather coats standing stock-still by the front door, as though they were guarding it. Their eyes were cold and indifferent.

'What time will I be home?' asked Irina, following them out into the front yard and looking back at her mother.

'Same as usual.'

One of the men got into the driver's seat. The other bundled Irina into the back of the car before getting into the front passenger seat.

The engine started. Fine icy crumbs flew up from under the front wheels, and the dark blue car lurched forward so abruptly that it

111

swerved to the right on the icy dirt track and almost flattened their wooden fence.

The driver was in a hurry. Looking out of the windscreen, Irina was horrified to see the same image repeating over and over again: he would drive at top speed right up to the rear lights of the car in front and sound the horn, which made an unusual noise like an air-raid siren from an old war film, and the car in front would immediately swerve out of the way.

'They could at least put the radio on,' thought Irina with a sigh.

They may well have put the radio on if Irina had asked them to, but she remained silent. She was surprised to find herself feeling a sense of mute resignation rather than fear. Her breasts, full of milk and unpleasantly heavy, were sore and tender. Her back was aching too, and her right shin felt numb.

The car raced along the Zhytomyr Highway towards Kiev. A traffic police officer directed his radar at the blue Lexus, purely out of curiosity, and whistled in awe.

'A hundred and ninety-three!' he said to his colleague, nodding at the car as it flashed by.

His colleague shook his head, disapproving of his delight.

'As long as it crashes into a tree, and not a bus,' he muttered.

About a quarter of an hour later the car stopped outside the familiar building, in which Irina had left gallons of her milk. The car's passenger escorted her inside and upstairs to the milk kitchen. She pressed the buzzer herself, and the door was opened by Nurse Vera. The man in the leather coat pushed Irina inside and slammed the door behind her, remaining outside on the landing.

'What did you have to go and do that for?' Nurse Vera asked, reproachfully.

Irina felt ashamed of herself. She took her scarf from her shoulders and hung her coat up on the coat stand.

'She's expecting you,' the old woman said guardedly.

The room opposite her boss's office was open, and Irina saw out of the corner of her eye that the bath was full of milk again. A young woman in a white robe was testing the temperature of the milk with a thermometer.

'Close the door!' barked a familiar, bad-tempered voice. Irina realised that she was already in the office, although she hadn't been aware that she'd crossed the threshold.

'So you think you can just inconvenience me like that and get away with it, do you?' asked her boss. 'You think you deserve a pay rise, do you? I've a good mind to throw you out on the street naked and barefoot!'

Irina looked at Nelly Igorievna more in surprise than in fear. Surely she hadn't gone to the trouble of sending a car to fetch her back to Kiev just so that she could throw her out on the street naked and barefoot?

Irina's boss fell silent for a while, her words having evidently failed to produce the desired effect on the young woman.

'How much more will it take to stop you going AWOL again?' she asked coldly.

Irina hadn't been expecting this question so just looked at Nelly Igorievna in even greater confusion.

'Well, say something!'

Irina shrugged. She felt a sharp pain in her shoulder.

'Oh, go and get on with your work! Come back after lunch and we'll talk again.'

When both her breasts were soft, emptied with the help of the little pump, Irina felt some relief. She was ready to go for her usual walk in Mariinsky Park, but as soon as she got to the coat stand she no longer felt like going out. Maybe Egor would be there, in the park . . . He'd told her to stay at home for a whole week. Well, he hadn't exactly 'told her to', he'd just suggested it, but it was the same thing really.

She ate the porridge that the nurse had made for her. She went over to the window and tried to picture herself outside, fashionably dressed and beautiful and walking arm in arm with Egor along one of the snow-covered paths in the park. She went to the bathroom and looked at herself in the mirror. She decided that she didn't like her hair. It was neither long nor short. Should she dye it? Which colour did men prefer these days?

After her second shift, Irina remembered her boss and went to see her. She was expecting her to shout and be rude to her again, but this time her boss looked at her with complete and utter indifference. She held an envelope out to her.

'Your salary will increase by three hundred hryvnas a month. And this is a bonus. Just don't think for one minute that it's got anything to do with me.'

29

Apartment No. 10, Reitarska Street, Kiev

Waking up in the armchair where he'd fallen asleep that afternoon, Semyon looked at his watch: 5.30 p.m. It was already dark outside. The apartment was quiet.

He pressed his nose up against the window. It turned out to be a good conductor of cold.

'I wonder where Nika's got to?' he thought.

Thinking about his absent wife somehow led to other thoughts, about the blonde woman Volodka claimed he'd kissed the night before. 'I bet it's just some kind of stupid joke,' he concluded.

He found the piece of paper with the address on it, put on his favourite warm jacket and went out.

He stopped for a moment on the corner of Striletska Street and Yaroslaviv Val and looked at the familiar funeral wreath. Then he strolled on inconspicuously until he reached the building on Chekhov Street indicated in Volodka's note.

At the main entrance he was intercepted by an elderly concierge in a dark blue jumper.

'Which apartment?'

'Number eleven.'

The old man nodded.

He stopped in front of the door on the third floor. He pressed the bell. There was the sound of footsteps on the other side of the door.

A woman opened the door just a crack. 'Who are you looking for?' she asked, peering at Semyon. She was definitely blonde. A short, slim blonde, about thirty-five years old. Wearing jeans and a black polo-neck jumper.

'Don't you recognise me?' asked Semyon, cautiously.

'No,' said the woman.

Semyon's heels began to itch – he wanted to leave immediately. The situation had started to seem absurd.

'Is your name Vera?' asked Semyon, attempting to win back the situation with an 'I've got the wrong address' ploy and hoping that the blonde's name was anything but Vera.

'No, Alisa,' said the blonde. 'You must have the wrong address.'

'Looks like it . . .' Semyon gave an idiotic smile. 'Sorry!'

Turning round, he hurried down the stairs.

'I'll get him for this!' Semyon thought about his friend Volodka. 'It was just a wind-up!'

As he reached home, Semyon heard his phone ringing.

'I've got some news for you,' said Volodka.

'Same here. Where are you?'

'Let's meet in La Quinta in half an hour,' suggested Volodka.

30

9 May Street, Boryspil

After three days Dima knew without a shadow of a doubt that the emaciated grey cat that had crawled up to their doorstep was indeed the original Fluffy. He didn't say anything to Valya. Her superstitious nonsense about the two cats being one and the same no longer freaked Dima out. On the contrary, it actually suited him perfectly because it meant that he didn't have to explain anything to her or confess what he'd done. In every other respect Valya was as sensible as before.

The two cats managed to divide the house up between them without ever coming face to face. The new Fluffy simply stayed in the kitchen, the door to which now remained closed, and the real Fluffy/Scruffy assumed territorial control over the other rooms, the hall and all nooks and crannies. The only inconvenience in this new arrangement was the second litter tray that stood under the kitchen table.

It soon became apparent to Dima that the grey impostor he had ordered and paid for at the Bird Market had been adopted by Valya, which meant that protecting the interests of the real Fluffy/Scruffy was now down to him. Although, to be honest, his interests didn't really need protecting. Valya fed both cats generously. Kitchen Fluffy did spend more time courting favour with his mistress and rubbing himself against her legs than the real one, but on the other hand the real Fluffy had started paying more attention to his master.

'What's up, Scruffs?' asked Dima, getting out of bed.

Scruffy ran up to him and looked into his eyes. Not in an ingratiating, grovelling way like Kitchen Fluffy but amicably and with a certain air of entitlement.

Dima knew what the cat liked. So on Scruffy's fourth day back, when he had begun to move about his territory with more confidence, Dima lured him into the garage, where the animal lapped up the contents of yet another ampoule from the plate. For some reason Dima had begun to suspect that this medicine would help the cat recover his lost energy.

After lunch Dima blocked up the hole in the fence – yet again – to prevent next door's bull terrier coming into their yard. He barricaded it with two planks of wood, hammering at least a dozen nails into each one.

Then he went back into the house and turned the television on. The local cable channel was showing an interview with some cyclist, whose face looked familiar to Dima. Peering more closely at the television, he recognised the man who had fallen off his bike in front of his garage doors the same day that Boris and Zhenya brought the suitcase full of ampoules.

Dima turned the sound up and learned that a postman by the name of Vasyl Ledenets had set a new speed record two days previously during a competition for amateur cyclists in the local stadium.

'No wonder,' thought Dima with a grin. 'If I was a postman and had to spend my days cycling away from one mangy cur after another, I'd probably be breaking records too.'

31

Lipovka village, Kiev region
Irina felt warm and comfortable in the minibus taxi home that evening. Vasya the driver even greeted her with a smile and asked where she'd been, and a couple of the other regular passengers acknowledged her with a nod. Everything was the same as it always was. She managed to get a good seat too, over the left rear wheel. Irina had long forgotten the laws of physics she'd learned in school, but she knew for a fact that the seat over the left rear wheel was the warmest on the whole minibus. Irina sat among the other homeward-bound suburban commuters and waited for the minibus to set off before taking the 'bonus' envelope from her boss out of her bag. She opened it and took out two new 500-hryvna notes, bearing the portrait of Hryhorii Skovoroda. A thousand hryvnas!

Irina's spirits lifted. She smiled. She hid the envelope back in her bag and thought about how she was feeling – physically rather than mentally. Right now she was more concerned with the state of her body than the state of her mind. She could feel the warmth from her seat through the fabric and lining of her coat and through her other clothes. It was so subtle, so relaxing, that Irina fell into a light sleep. She kept a tight hold on her bag, though. This defensive instinct was perfectly natural: she was used to being vigilant, even in her sleep.

Her mother opened the door with a strange smile on her face. Irina didn't pay any attention to it at first, but once she'd taken her coat and shoes off she went into the kitchen and realised they'd had a visitor.

There were two empty cups on the table, and a half-eaten cake.

'You had a gentleman caller.'

'Egor?' asked Irina.

'Yes. A proper gentleman he was too. He gave Yasya a cuddle and played with her for a bit. He's from round here, you know, just outside Kodra. His mother's paralysed and can't leave their hut, and he pays one of their neighbours to look after her, feed her and so on. I said to him, I said, you should sell that hut and buy one near us, there's three empty huts on our lane . . . Then I could look after his mother . . .'

Irina looked at her mother in surprise. Only now did she notice that her mother was dressed differently too, more formally. Although the dark blue woollen blouse she had on was old, it was the smartest thing she owned. She was even wearing a brooch on it.

'What about Yasya?' Irina asked suddenly. 'If you start looking after a paralysed old lady, who's going to look after Yasya when I'm at work?'

'Well . . .' Her mother hesitated and then just waved her hand instead of answering. 'I'm just saying! Selling a hut, buying a new one, it doesn't happen overnight. Anyway, he brought you another present. Said he'd come tomorrow morning, before ten.'

'Before ten?' I'll already be in Kiev by then.'

'Maybe you could go in a bit later? He's such a good-looking lad . . .'

Irina sighed and shook her head.

She lay awake that night, thinking about Egor and about the way her mother had taken such a sudden liking to him. Thinking about Mariinsky Park and the never-ending winter. Why never-ending, though? In another month or two the thaw would begin, and spring would soon follow.

Irina imagined how she would look in the spring, her hair dyed and restyled after a trip to the hairdresser's in Kiev. She pictured herself looking elegant and sophisticated.

She woke up early, as usual. She got dressed. She went into the kitchen and boiled some water. She mixed up the Malysh formula milk for her daughter. Then a vague feeling of guilt forced her to return to her room and put her sleeping daughter on the breast. Without waking up, Yasya began to move her lips automatically. The feeling was almost the same as the pump that they used to collect Irina's milk in Kiev's Pechersk district. Only the pump in Kiev was always cold, whereas her daughter's lips were warm.

The early-morning silence intensified the creak of the wicket gate as it opened and closed, then all was quiet once more. Irina walked to her stop. The road was still and silent. The sky was full of stars. In about five hours' time Egor would call at her house again, but she wouldn't be there – she would be walking in Mariinsky Park, already halfway through her working day.

Two yellow automobile eyes emerged from the distance. Irina recognised the headlights and the sound of her minibus taxi's engine. She thought about Egor again and wondered whether he'd be cross with her.

Thinking about Egor, Irina gradually stepped away from the road. When the minibus taxi pulled up at her stop she squatted down behind the old oak tree at the top of her road. The minibus taxi stood there for a few minutes before setting off again. Peeping out of her hiding place, Irina watched it leave. Then she emerged from behind the oak tree and started walking home.

32

La Quinta café, Great Zhytomyr Street, Kiev

Volodka left, and Semyon ordered another coffee. He didn't feel like leaving this cosy cellar café now. He felt as though he were in some kind of fortress, immune to confusion and safe from harm. Protected from what in any other situation he would dismiss as drunken ramblings.

While he waited for his coffee, he recalled the details of his conversation with Volodka. Volodka appeared to have treated Semyon's request like an order from a commanding officer and acted on it accordingly. He might even have risked his life to carry out this order, but fortunately that hadn't been necessary. It turned out that the other man following Semyon was Igor, his neighbour from the apartment opposite, and apparently he was doing it because Veronika had asked him to.

Eager to placate his friend and boss, Volodka had assured him that he'd intercepted Igor before Semyon met the blonde woman.

'It doesn't even bear thinking about,' thought Semyon. He was already convinced that Volodka was telling the truth and had no wish to imagine his neighbour Igor reporting back to Veronika that her husband was having an affair.

'So what do I do now?' thought Semyon. 'None of it makes any sense. That Alisa didn't even recognise me.'

Suddenly he remembered the murdered pharmacist. And the puzzled and hesitant look on his wife's face when she'd told him about the murder and noticed the stain on his shirt. Now she was having coffee with the pharmacist's widow and asking their neighbour to follow her own husband! What does she think I've done? Cheated on her or murdered the husband of her new best friend?

Semyon sighed. 'They can all take a running jump,' he murmured, attempting to give his brain at least a temporary respite from the blizzard of thoughts and doubts.

33

Amusement arcade, Boryspil

When the shuttle bus dropped Dima off at work mid-morning, there was a surprise waiting for him.

'They've taken your Shamil away,' said Vanya, a junior sniffer dog handler.

'Where to?' asked Dima, surprised.

Vanya shrugged. He stood before Dima in his green padded trousers and jacket, holding an empty dog bowl.

'It was last night, when he was on another shift,' he continued, his gold tooth flashing. 'They said he wasn't well or something . . .'

Dima went to see the kennel manager.

'I don't know anything about it,' he said, spreading his hands. He didn't bother getting up from his desk. In front of him, as always, lay an album containing photos of all the working dogs and a sheet of paper divided up into 'duty squares'. The names of dogs were written in the squares in pen. Circular marks left by the bottoms of glasses and teacups indicated that this reference document also served as the kennel manager's tablecloth. 'The boss said you can have a couple of days off.'

'Days off?' repeated Dima, surprised. Something wasn't right.

He took the bus back to Boryspil, feeling disheartened. He'd made the effort to go to work and had been sent home again, without any explanation.

He got out near the station and decided to call in and see Valya at work.

It was quiet in the amusement arcade. The only noise came from the slot machines themselves, which periodically jingled their coins and made gurgling, electronic noises. Looking around, Dima noticed the little cashier's window in the corner. He took out a one-hryvna note and held it through the little window. His wife's hand took the note and exchanged it for two fifty-kopek coins.

'Right,' he decided. 'I'll try my luck, and then I'll stick my head in at the window so she can see who it is!'

He dropped a coin into one of the machines and pressed the big start button. Bananas and apples flashed before his eyes. The machine made a jingling sound. The images stopped several times, but he didn't win anything. He put the second coin in and pressed the button again, and this time three identical little bottles of cola stopped in a row! A waterfall of coins jangled into the metal 'trough' at the front of the machine. Dima took a step back. He watched, fascinated, as the bronze fifty-kopek coins poured out. His mouth fell open. Because of the noise the coins were making he didn't hear his wife's footsteps as she came up behind him.

'What are you doing here?' She was surprised to see him.

'Shamil's not well. They sent me home. So I thought I'd come and see you,' said Dima, turning round. Then he looked back at his winnings.

'Is that all yours?' asked Valya, staring at the machine's trough. Dima nodded.

'Wait there,' Valya instructed him.

She went over to the till and came back with a green cloth money bag. She started grabbing handfuls of coins and putting them into the bag.

'Maybe I should have another go?' Dima suggested cautiously. Valya shook her head.

'You're not supposed to. Relatives of employees aren't allowed to play.'

The two of them emptied the trough. Valya hung a sign on the outside of the entrance doors informing patrons that the arcade was closed due to 'technical reasons', then they both went into the tiny cashier's booth. Inside the booth there was a strange machine with a handle standing on top of a little cabinet. It looked like a meat grinder.

'You tip them in, and I'll turn the handle,' ordered Valya.

The black metal machine also had a kind of trough for coins, only it wasn't as big as the one on the slot machine. It was more like a funnel. Dima tipped the coins in, Valya turned the handle and the coins disappeared into the machine.

'What does it do?' asked Dima.

'Counts it,' answered his wife.

'Can we get it out again?'

'Of course!'

After swallowing Dima's winnings, the machine informed them that the bag contained a total of forty-eight hryvnas.

Valya tipped all the coins back into the money bag. Then she put the money bag into a large shopping bag.

'Are you going straight home now?' she asked semi-rhetorically, as she gave the heavy bag to her husband.

He nodded.

As Dima entered their front yard, he noticed another hole in the fence. He went over and squatted down beside it. The splinters remaining from the two high-quality planks of wood bore jagged marks made by an axe.

'Right!' he breathed threateningly.

Leaving the shopping bag containing the money bag in the hallway, he went back outside, grabbed the garden shears from the garage and made straight for the abandoned courtyard. Tearing wire from the demolished fence and thinking regretfully about the pliers he'd left in the garage, which would have come in very handy, Dima glanced at the well. The one he'd thrown Scruffy's body into. He went over to it and looked inside. Now there was even more rubbish in it, including a broken chair and a smashed chandelier.

'How on earth did he manage to get out of there?' wondered Dima.

After half an hour's work Dima had managed to pull loose and cut off about twenty pieces of rusty barbed wire, which he put into a cardboard box he'd found in the yard. Then he went home and got straight to work. He put on some protective gloves, picked up the pliers and with care and determination used his barbed thread to sew up the ill-fated hole in the fence.

34

Maryanivka village and Lipovka village, Kiev region
Egor had never even thought about Saratov before. He knew a town by that name existed, but that was all. As far as he was concerned Saratov was as remote as Santiago – they were both equally foreign, the only difference being that they spoke Russian in Saratov.

It was getting light outside the hut. His paralysed mother was still asleep in her iron bed with its chrome-plated rails. As soon as she woke up she would start coughing, and then he would put the kettle on and prepare an infusion of dried raspberry and blackcurrant leaves, to ease her breathing. Their neighbour usually did this and she would be coming soon, but she knew that Egor had spent the night at his mother's place so she wouldn't be in any particular hurry.

The hut was small, and every time Egor spent the night there or even just called in for a brief visit he was embarrassed by it. He wasn't embarrassed that he'd been born there – being born is no cause for embarrassment, of course – but he was embarrassed by the fact that his mother still lived there. He was embarrassed by the fact that even though the country's name had changed, life in this village, and in this particular hut, had not changed in the slightest. His father had been planning to build a brick house but back then, before independence, the village council had refused permission. Now there was no point building a new house – his father was dead, and his mother didn't have long left either. If he was going to build one for himself he would build it nearer to Kiev, and that would require a different budget altogether. Money that Egor didn't have. And now there was this application form that he and his colleagues had been given 'to think about' by the deputy director of security. He'd asked them not to show it to anyone else. It was an application form for those interested in highly paid work and free accommodation in the Russian city of Saratov. Anyone willing to move there would be guaranteed a 'family-sized' apartment and reimbursement of the cost of moving furniture and personal items.

Egor threw some firewood into the masonry stove, opened the valve of the gas canister beneath the cooker and lit the gas ring. He put the kettle on and went outside just as he was – wearing dark blue tracksuit bottoms, a black T-shirt and slippers. He liked the way the frost stung his elbows and ankles.

The yard was quite small. There was an outdoor cooking area opposite the porch; to the left of it stood a large walnut tree and a fence, with a mature orchard beyond. Everything was old, but alive and fertile – even the old grapevine, its trunk a gnarled and dormant fist all winter, would assert its vitality every summer by weaving a green canopy over the little yard.

His father had welded a metal framework for this canopy so that in the summer he could sit in the shade at a table brought out into the yard, listening to the sound of the birds singing and drinking tea, or sometimes even vodka.

There are no eternal idylls, and this idyll too had run its course. Egor's mother was coming to the end of her life; the hut was on its last legs . . . Even the gas in the canister was about to run out.

While he was in the yard, their neighbour Baba Sonya arrived to start work. She came through the gate, nodded at him and went straight into the hut.

'You ought to park your car in the yard,' she said, when Egor went back into the warmth. 'There are a lot of drunks around at night. It's only a matter of time before someone slashes your tyres. They don't like rich people round here.'

'I'm not rich – that car's all I've got! I haven't got a house, or an apartment, or . . .'

Half an hour later the red Mazda's engine rumbled to life. Egor's first stop was Irina's house.

'Oh, come in, come in!' Seeing her guest, Baba Shura broke into a smile. 'Irinka's just taken Yasya out sledging, they're over there,' she said, indicating the direction with her hand.

Egor had no trouble finding the little hill by the frozen lake. At first he watched from a distance as Irina sledged down, holding Yasya wrapped in her blanket. Just like a little girl herself. Then he approached them.

'I've got to be at work by twelve,' he said. 'Are you in any pain, after what happened?'

'No,' answered Irina. 'I was late for the minibus taxi today –'

'You promised me you'd take a week off!'

'There's something I need to tell you,' she said guiltily. 'I don't have a choice. I have to keep going there, to Kiev . . .'

As they drove back to the house she told Egor about them sending a car for her the previous day. And about her conversation with her boss.

Egor's mood darkened.

'You don't have to keep going there,' he said after a short pause.

Irina didn't say anything. For a little while they drove in silence. But when they reached the village they exchanged quizzical looks, because they both felt that this silence wasn't right.

'Do you know anything about Saratov?' asked Egor, glancing at Irina.

'No. I got a C in Geography.'

Egor smiled sadly.

35

Lukyanivka, Kiev

In the morning, Semyon called Sergei, an old friend from Petrivka days, a former sergeant and now a colonel in the militia. He asked him to find out the latest on the pharmacist's murder case.

Sergei called back half an hour later.

'The case doesn't exist,' he said. 'Maybe it did, but it doesn't any more. Nobody knows anything about it.'

Perplexed by this news, Semyon stayed sitting for some time in the armchair by the telephone. Then he stood up, got dressed and went outside. He walked to the pharmacy that Veronika had told him belonged to the deceased. He went in. An elderly woman in a white coat was sitting next to the counter, reading a newspaper.

'Excuse me,' Semyon said, interrupting her reading. 'Was the bloke who owned this place murdered?'

'Have you come in for a chat, or for some medicine?' the woman asked sternly.

'I'll have some of those.' He pointed at a packet of condoms lying under the glass of the counter.

'Eight hryvnas,' she said drily.

Once he'd paid and stuffed the condoms into his jacket pocket, Semyon looked searchingly at the woman.

'So, was he murdered?'

'This place is owned by a woman, not a "bloke",' she muttered and took her seat again.

He could tell by the look on her face that he wasn't going to get any more information out of her.

Semyon went outside and looked around. He saw an old woman with a little dog sitting on a bench outside the next entrance along. He approached her and asked about the murdered pharmacist.

'Of course! Murdered, he was! Stabbed to death! They say he was concocting a youth drug for some deputies, and that's why,' said the old woman, looking up at the sky, 'his dispensing days are over!'

Semyon was keen to continue his conversation with this well-informed old woman, but just then his mobile phone rang.

'Senya.' It was Gennady Ilyich. 'I've got a job for you. I'm in Parliament – we're trying to stop those bastards from the opposition taking the floor – but I'll be out of here in half an hour. Go to the National hotel and wait for me there, in the café. OK?'

It would take Semyon exactly half an hour to get to the National. He reluctantly took his leave of the old woman. On the way, he recalled one of Gennady Ilyich's recent picnics, at which he'd been drinking and doing business deals with one of 'those bastards from the opposition'. They're all bastards when they're shouting at one another in Parliament, thought Semyon, but as soon as they're out of there, off to the woods for shashlik, they're as thick as thieves.

He got to the hotel café first. He ordered himself a cup of coffee, sat down at a table and looked around. The clientele all looked like they'd just wandered in off the street – they were all somewhat bedraggled. But when Gennady Ilyich came in, you could tell immediately that he wasn't just anyone. You could tell by his coat, and by his boots.

'Right!' exhaled the deputy, sitting down at Semyon's table. 'Listen, I've just fired my assistant and I want to offer you his job. It's basically the same as what you do now, only you'll get paid by Parliament rather than by me personally. You just need to hand in your work record book, and you'll get your assistant's ID. For you it's a promotion, a decent pension plan and more respect, and for me . . . well, I'll be happy. It'll be good for both of us!'

'OK,' agreed Semyon.

On hearing this positive response, Gennady Ilyich smiled and ordered them both a double brandy.

'Gennady Ilyich, have you heard anything about a "rejuvenating" medicine from Germany?' Semyon asked quietly.

The deputy burst out laughing. He looked at Semyon, his eyes twinkling.

'Medicine? Are you kidding? It's full of chemicals! Medicine will kill you, not make you younger. I'll tell you what you need if you want to knock a few years off.'

'What?' asked Semyon.

'Dairy products,' said Gennady Ilyich with a smile. Lowering his voice to a whisper, he added, 'And best of all a young mother's breast milk. You don't get milk kitchens for kids any more. Now they're for grown-ups. "Hormone cafés" for women. Just don't ask me what's on the menu, it makes me want to puke. My wife goes. She's getting on for forty-five, but her bottom is as soft as a baby's.

No need for drugs or surgery . . . What do you need it for anyway? Are you planning on getting into politics?'

'What's it got to do with politics?' asked Semyon, confused.

'Well, it's important for a politician to look the very picture of health. Like a piglet, in the natural, most positive sense. You get more votes.'

Semyon looked at Gennady Ilyich and assumed he was talking about himself. He didn't have a single wrinkle, his lips were plump and he always had a healthy glow about him. Like most of the other deputies, in fact. They were all smooth, shiny and full of the joys of life.

'So why did you want to know, then?' the deputy suddenly asked.

'Apparently a pharmacist was murdered recently near our building. And they're saying that he was dealing in some kind of youth drug.'

'Rubbish! Pharmacists deal in hardcore pain relief and shit like that. Take my word for it. Right, I'd better be off.' He looked at his watch. 'This session is doing my head in! Anyway, they'll call you and tell you where to bring your work record book. OK? I'll see you soon.'

Left alone, Semyon lingered over his brandy. As he drank it he thought about the pharmacist who'd either been murdered, or had never existed at all. He thought about his wife, who'd become friendly with the pharmacist's widow. He thought about the breast milk that politicians had to drink in order to get elected. Eventually Semyon stopped thinking altogether, because each of these thoughts individually – let alone in combination – could qualify as the ravings of a madman. And Semyon didn't consider himself to be a madman.

36

Apartment No. 10, Reitarska Street, Kiev

That evening, Semyon told Veronika that he was going to be a parliamentary deputy's assistant. He told her in a cold, indifferent voice. Then that night he went missing again. Veronika woke up, noticed he wasn't there and started crying. She cried until 3 a.m. then fell back to sleep.

The next morning, Semyon got dressed and went out as though nothing had happened. Half an hour later, washed, dressed and made up, Veronika telephoned her neighbour.

Igor invited her over immediately. He put on his noisy coffee machine and opened a packet of biscuits. Despite the early hour he was already dressed in a grey suit, shirt, tie and thick red socks. He was clearly on his way out but managed to give the impression that he wasn't in any kind of hurry.

'Did you find anything out?' asked Veronika, sitting down at the kitchen table.

'I did, but not much,' he said, looking at her ingratiatingly. 'And I won't be able to find out anything else. I've been warned off.'

'What do you mean?' Veronika was genuinely surprised.

'I followed him the other night, like I promised, but it turned out that someone else was already following him. A short, tough-looking chap in civilian clothing. He held me up against a wall and made it pretty clear that I was getting in the way. So it looks like your suspicions were correct.'

Veronika turned pale. She hadn't even touched her coffee. She fixed her neighbour with a cold stare. Now he was scared for himself as well as for Semyon.

'Who are they, whoever it is who's following him?' she asked, after a short silence.

'Not the militia,' he said pensively. 'Probably the Security Service.'

'I'd better go,' said Veronika, getting up. Unable to hold back any longer, she let out a sob.

'But what about your coffee? Stay a bit longer!' said her neighbour. 'At least wait until you feel better.'

Veronika left anyway. She went home, but even there she couldn't manage to compose herself.

She called Darya Ivanovna and invited herself round, although it was hardly an imposition – any conversation they had these days ended in them arranging to meet. But they didn't stay long in Darya Ivanovna's apartment. No sooner had the lady of the house put a bottle of brandy on the coffee table than the telephone rang. Darya Ivanovna barely said a word but listened to the unseen caller for about three minutes, then said into the receiver, 'I'm bringing a friend.'

'You know what,' she said, turning to Veronika once she'd hung up. 'Let's take the brandy with us. A good friend of mine needs some support. It's not far from here, on Vorovsky Street.'

On the way, Darya Ivanovna and Veronika stopped for a while by the wreath. The widow straightened it up, and they continued on their way.

'Just to warn you, she's a bit odd,' said the pharmacist's widow as they walked. 'She's also had some bad luck recently. Just before me. Her husband wanted to leave her for a younger woman, but he didn't get round to it. Died of a heart attack. He was a good-looking chap, not even that old. Liked playing chess. They brought him home this morning. That was her on the phone just now, in tears. But you have to get used to it. It's even worse being on your own.'

'Did they bring him home for the funeral?' asked Veronika.

'No, he's already been "done". You'll see. They're going to do the same with my Edik. He's scheduled for the day after tomorrow.'

'To be plastinated?' Veronika had already added this word to her vocabulary.

'Yes,' nodded Darya Ivanovna.

The owner of the apartment, a brunette of around forty, greeted them with a warm smile on her tear-stained face.

'I'm Anna,' she introduced herself to Veronika.

There was a round table in the middle of the living room with three glasses on it. Darya Ivanovna took out the bottle of Ararat brandy. She looked about the room, then her quizzical gaze came to rest on their hostess.

'Where's Vasya?' she asked.

'In the bedroom.' Anna nodded towards the closed door.

They sat down and started drinking the brandy. Veronika found the silence in the apartment unsettling, and her feeling of unease was strengthened further by the weight of her own thoughts and doubts.

'Oh, girls,' she sighed bitterly.

Darya Ivanovna and Anna looked at her.

'Something terrible has happened,' Veronika continued. 'My Senya's being followed! It's either the militia, or someone else.'

'Why, what's he done?' whispered Anna.

'I don't know. He might even have killed someone . . .'

Veronika was so alarmed by her own revelation that she poured herself another brandy and took a sip.

'What are you *doing*, you idiot? Are you going to tell Darya Ivanovna that Semyon might have been the one who stabbed her husband?' Veronika's inner voice echoed resonantly in her head.

'What makes you think he might have killed someone?' asked Anna, carefully. 'Just because someone's following him?'

The two women were so calm, so composed, that Veronika suddenly felt exposed and vulnerable before them. She felt like crying and tears spilled from her eyes of their own accord, washing away her inner tension.

'Don't cry,' Darya Ivanovna begged her. 'You shouldn't think such things of your husband! Maybe it's someone else's husband following him, not the militia.'

'Someone else's husband?' Veronika repeated through her tears. She looked from Darya Ivanovna to Anna. Anna nodded.

'Maybe you're right,' Veronika said weakly. 'But what would someone else's husband want with my Senya?'

'Nikochka.' Darya Ivanovna reached out and stroked Veronika's shoulder. 'You need to reconcile yourself to the life of a woman. There's a widow inside every one of us. The fact is, we live longer than they do. Anna and I are already widows but your husband's still alive. You ought to think better of him, because sooner or later you'll have to live without him. Do you think my Edik was perfect? Hardly! But I only ever praised and flattered him, and now I stick to the old rule, "If you don't have anything good to say about the deceased, don't say anything at all." Do you see what I'm saying? Now, Annushka,' Darya Ivanovna turned to their host, 'can we see Vasya?'

Anna got up from the table and opened the door to the bedroom slightly. Darya Ivanovna went over to it first and peeped through the gap. Veronika followed suit.

A man in a smart denim jacket and velvet trousers lay on the bed with his eyes closed. He was lying on his back. The colour of his face made it look as though he were alive and simply sleeping. Veronika even thought she could see his chest rising and falling, as though he were breathing.

'I can't decide where to put him,' sighed their hostess, slightly bewildered. 'They said it would be best to put him in an armchair near the window.'

'Yes, the armchair would be good,' agreed Darya Ivanovna. 'You just need to check the feng shui.'

Veronika thought the room had a 'medicinal' smell. She was finding it hard to breathe. And Darya Ivanovna's comment about all women being widows had made her think about her own future widowhood, which only increased her need to get out into the fresh air.

She said she had a headache, and Anna and Darya Ivanovna let her go home.

Veronika walked along Vorovsky Street to Lviv Square, thinking about Semyon. She felt so bad for jumping to conclusions that she was almost in tears. She knew that she loved her husband. She knew that nothing bad had happened to him yet.

In the food shop on the corner of Olesya Gonchara Street and Yaroslaviv Val she bought some smoked sausage, which Semyon loved, a fresh loaf of black bread and a bottle of dark beer. All for him.

'I'll give him a big kiss as soon as he gets home today, right there in the hallway,' she decided.

37

9 May Street, Boryspil

Dima was vaguely aware of his wife getting ready to go to work. Although still technically asleep, he was already looking forward to having the house to himself. He didn't have long to wait. A 'clean' morning silence soon descended upon him, like freshly washed bedlinen. A winter bird was singing outside. Shafts of sunlight forced their way through the gaps in the dark curtains, revealing tiny motes of dust suspended in the air. Noticing these airborne particles, Dima got out of bed with his mouth closed and started breathing through his nose, imagining that its natural hair filter would prevent such pollution entering his body.

Dima pulled on a tracksuit, washed, shaved and generally made himself look presentable. Then he went out onto the doorstep, where he noticed to his delight that the barbed wire he'd used to fix the hole in the fence was still in place. He went back into the kitchen.

He'd just lit the gas under the frying pan containing his breakfast when the doorbell rang.

On the doorstep stood a woman of around forty, wearing an expensive sheepskin jacket, and a young militiaman.

'We're looking for Boris Khansky,' said the militiaman. 'Has he been here in the last two days?'

'Khansky?' asked Dima, puzzled. 'Who is he?'

'He works at the airport with you. In the baggage section,' said the woman in the sheepskin coat. 'He told me all about you.'

'Ah, Borya!' Dima nodded and took a step back into the hallway, inviting the woman and the militiaman inside. 'No, I haven't seen him. Why, what's happened?'

'He's been dealing in medicinal drugs recently,' said the woman, who was obviously his wife. 'One of his customers called two days ago. Ordered a thousand hryvnas' worth. Borya went to meet him and never came back.'

Dima felt a sudden chill. His fleeting look of panic aroused the militiaman's suspicion.

'I don't suppose he told you where he was getting this medicine from, did he?' asked the militiaman.

Dima shook his head but his face had turned pale, and now even the woman was looking at him suspiciously.

'He's got this friend, Zhenya,' said Dima, trying to deflect their attention away from himself and onto somebody else. 'Maybe they were in on it together.'

'Zhenya was buried four days ago,' Boris's wife said dismissively.

'What happened?' asked Dima, with a rising feeling of dread.

'He was poisoned. Counterfeit vodka.'

Dima sighed with relief.

'Can I ask you something, in private?' The militiaman nodded at the kitchen door. 'Don't worry, he's known for going off on drinking binges,' whispered the militiaman once they were in the kitchen. 'He's been missing for two days before, even three. His wife's just a bit worried, it's always the way. But the thing is, I need to buy some of that medicine he was selling. My elder brother's ill, you see. I bought a few ampoules off Borya, and it helped him straight away – I saw it with my own eyes! He went outside for a walk and jumped in front of a car to stop the neighbour's kid being run over, and then managed to jump out of the way himself. And only the day before he hadn't even been able to get out of bed! Did Boris tell you where he was getting the medicine from? I'm willing to pay whatever it costs.'

'No, he didn't,' whispered Dima. 'But I can try and find out.'

The militiaman took a notepad and pen from the pocket of his uniform jacket and wrote down his phone number.

'I'll make it worth your while,' he promised, looking imploringly into Dima's eyes as though asking a favour of a close friend.

Dima's visitors left him feeling slightly concerned about what the future held in store for Boris, and for himself. The militiaman was young, which made Dima inclined to believe that he really did need the medicine and that it wasn't a trap, although that thought had crossed his mind.

He drank a shot of nettle vodka to pull himself together then lay down for a nap. He slept for quite a long time, and when he got up again it was already turning to dusk.

He went out onto the doorstep in the hope that the frosty air would raise his spirits.

He stood there for a while then walked over to the fence separating his front yard from his neighbour's. The barbed wire was still intact.

He went back to his doorstep and lit a cigarette. The neighbour's door creaked open and King the bull terrier came flying out as though he'd been kicked. He dashed straight over to the blocked-up hole in the fence but stopped right in front of it. He stood there for a moment, looking completely confused. Then he went over to the young apple tree in his own yard, raised his hind leg and went about his business.

'Yeah, you'd better get used to it,' Dima whispered gloatingly. 'Keep your mess in your own yard!'

38

Hrushevsky Street, Kiev

'How come you're so late?' asked Nurse Vera by way of a greeting, as she let Irina into the hallway. 'It's a good job we've got two new recruits today, otherwise there might not have been enough milk.'

'Are they young?' asked Irina, taking off her coat.

'Yes, both about twenty,' the old woman answered in her usual friendly voice. 'Anyway, go on in and sit down, get yourself ready.'

Irina unbuttoned her red woollen cardigan and lifted her bra, freeing her left breast.

A few minutes later the familiar buzzing sound came from the pump and a stream of Irina's milk began to flow into the glass receptacle.

Her left breast grew lighter. It would soon be empty: time to swap breasts.

'Those new girls are a fair size, both of them,' sighed Nurse Vera. 'They ate all the porridge between them! I'm afraid there's none left for you. Why don't you go and see Nelly Igorievna, to apologise for being late?'

Irina's eyes immediately filled with tears. The old woman noticed this.

'Ah, don't worry about it.' She waved her hand. 'I'll tell her you apologised next time I see her. Are you coming back again today?'

Irina nodded. She put her coat on and went out.

She stopped in the courtyard and listened to her body. She was used to eating after giving milk, and now she could feel her hunger growing. She headed towards the road, looking down the paths of Mariinsky Park in the hope of seeing Egor, but there was nobody there. She walked past the Officers' Club to the little food shop, where she bought herself some boiled sausage, a bread roll and a cup of 'dodgy coffee', which as far as she was concerned tasted no different to 'good coffee'.

Once she'd finished her snack she headed back to Mariinsky Park to wander along the paths. Her thoughts mingled with her dreams, and she walked until she came out onto the viewing area. The frozen Dnieper and the whole of the left bank lay out before her. Irina looked down at the city and felt completely alone, with only the forest, the hills and silence behind her. Everyone else was down there, completely oblivious to her existence. Their lives were different somehow. They had different jobs, which didn't involve milk. Maybe they raised their children with more love than she did, but so what? Maybe she would also learn how to lead a better and more fulfilling life. Maybe someone would show her the way. Maybe this someone would be Egor, who was his own master and relied on no one but himself to change his life for the better.

Irina remained standing there, motionless. About a hundred metres behind her, near the metal barrier that closed off one of the paths leading onto the square in front of Parliament, stood Egor. He was wearing a long black leather coat with the collar turned up, and he was watching Irina. Nearby, right up against the barrier, two Communist veterans were holding a banner protesting against NATO. They didn't bother him – all their enemies were inside Parliament, and anyway Egor's responsibilities did not include parliamentary security. Parliament and Mariinsky Park had their own separate security teams. The members of these teams recognised each other by sight and would sometimes greet one another with a nod, but they were not friends. They weren't enemies either. They just had their own specific responsibilities, like working dogs. One shift on, two shifts off.

Time seems to speed up in winter, and the air loses its transparency more quickly than in autumn. It took Irina a while to notice the lights on the other side of the Dnieper coming on, and when she did she looked at her watch. She listened to her body again and realised that she was cold, that her body wanted to be somewhere warm. There was only one place in Kiev where this warmth was on offer, although the warmth there was not freely available like it was at home – she had to pay for it with her milk.

'Oh well,' thought Irina with a sigh, 'I'll sit in the kitchen for a couple of hours to warm up. Then after my second milk shift I can go home.'

The red light on the pedestrian crossing turned green. Irina ran across the road and stopped on the other side to catch her breath. As she approached the main entrance, she bumped into two men unloading empty milk churns from a Niva. She followed them into the building.

'So, did you get something to eat?' asked Nurse Vera.

Irina nodded. She took her coat off and hung it on the wooden coat stand next to two sheepskin coats, one short and one long.

She could hear the familiar buzzing noise coming from the expressing room and glanced in out of curiosity.

A young woman with short hair and enormous breasts was sitting at the table. There was already a lot of milk in the pump's receptacle, and a vigorous, exuberant stream of it was running along the transparent tube. The girl was nodding her head in a strange way. Looking more closely, Irina noticed that she was wearing headphones.

'Come on in,' called Nurse Vera.

There was another young woman that she didn't know sitting at the kitchen table. She immediately held out her hand to Irina.

'I'm Zhanna,' she said. 'What's your name?'

'Irinka,' the old nurse answered for her. 'She's our star performer!'

Irina looked at Nurse Vera in surprise. 'What are you talking about?' she asked.

'You've got no idea, have you?' The nurse brushed her aside. 'Do you honestly think Nelly Igorievna would keep you here otherwise? No!'

After a pause, the nurse looked significantly at the puzzled Zhanna and went on. 'Her milk,' she nodded at Irina, 'is worth its weight in gold. Her milk gets chauffeur driven in a black Mercedes!'

On hearing this, Irina grew embarrassed. She glanced out of the window at the dark blue winter sky beyond.

She felt the frost on her cheeks again as she left the building that evening, pausing briefly at the main entrance to adjust her scarf before heading towards the metro station.

39

Apartment No. 10, Reitarska Street, Kiev

'What's the matter with her?' wondered Semyon. The sudden increase in Veronika's affections towards him had not escaped his notice. She was either throwing herself at him in the hallway the minute he got in from work, or bringing him coffee when he hadn't even asked for it.

Of course, women are unpredictable creatures with their own eccentricities. Semyon had never doubted it. But now he was increasingly doubtful about his friend Volodka's version of events. The night before, in La Quinta, Volodka had maintained that Semyon was still visiting the blonde woman at night.

'He's talking nonsense,' thought Semyon, looking into the bathroom mirror as he had a wash. 'Making out that I'm perfectly normal during the day but out of control at night . . . He and I need to have a serious chat.'

The day ahead was already fully booked. He wouldn't be free until late that night and he wouldn't be going anywhere then – he would be accepting the kisses and caresses that he deserved from his wife. He needed to make the most of it, because it wouldn't last for ever . . .

Smartening himself up a bit, Semyon looked out of the window. Volodka's Niva was already parked at the main entrance next to the black Bentley belonging to one of his neighbours, a district judge.

Before leaving, he ran into the kitchen and kissed Veronika on the lips.

'What time do you want to eat tonight?' asked his wife.

'Nine o'clock.'

An hour later he and Volodka drove up to the grounds of Gennady Ilyich's estate. A security guard opened the gates to let them through and told them that Gennady Ilyich was busy in the church, so they'd have to wait in the car.

They sat in the car for at least half an hour, listening to the radio. Semyon was on the point of broaching the subject with Volodka several times but kept stopping himself, because he knew they could be called at any moment and then he would have to start the conversation all over again.

When Gennady Ilyich came out of the house he was not alone. He was accompanied by a bearded priest, who wore a long black sheepskin coat over an even longer black cassock and strode confidently down the path, which had been cleared of snow.

'This is Father Onophrios,' Gennady Ilyich told Semyon. 'He'll be coming with you. Is the boot empty?'

Volodka nodded.

'You'll be picking up three churns of goat's milk from a building opposite Parliament, then taking them to an orphanage. Father Onophrios knows the address. It's not far, just the other side of Vyshhorod.'

Radio Chanson played quietly in the background. For the first ten minutes of the journey the priest sat on the back seat in silence, then he began talking in a pleasant baritone.

'God commanded us to share our worldly goods with those less fortunate than ourselves, did He not?' he asked, out of the blue.

Volodka turned the radio off straight away. He looked at their passenger in the rear-view mirror.

'What I'm saying is that we have to share with the poor,' repeated the priest, although it was no longer in the form of a question. 'Because there are always more of them, and power is with the majority.'

'Do you worry a lot about the poor?' Semyon asked politely.

'Oh, you know, I'm just trying to get myself in the benevolent mood,' yawned Father Onophrios.

His yawn perfumed the car with expensive cognac.

146

'So what do you make of Gennady Ilyich's church?' asked Semyon, smelling the brandy.

'It's a nice church, well built. It lacks one thing, though. A congregation! Nobody goes to any of the services there apart from Gennady Ilyich.'

'Does he actually go, then?' Semyon was surprised.

'He does,' replied the priest, nodding emphatically. 'He's only rung once to let me know he wouldn't be attending the service, so I didn't have a wasted journey!'

Semyon could just picture it: Gennady Ilyich standing alone in the enormous church with Father Onophrios before him, reading a sermon.

'There are quite a number of churches like his these days, without congregations,' added the priest. 'Deputies build them at their dachas, and bureaucrats. It's no bad thing, though. A deputy is mortal, he'll die one day, and what will his children want with a church? They'll give it to the people, in memory of their father . . . Here, this is the address we're going to.'

They had no trouble finding the building indicated on the piece of paper. Semyon and the priest went up to the first floor. They rang the bell, and the door was opened straight away. Two men in green overalls carried three large metal milk churns down and placed them carefully in the Niva. Then a woman of around forty-five, wearing a fur coat thrown over her white robe, came down to the car.

'Now you're going straight to the orphanage, aren't you?' she asked the priest anxiously.

'Yes, yes, we're going straight there!' he assured her.

'If the milk curdles, they can make curd cheese out of it,' she said. 'Just don't let them tip it away, whatever they do.'

'I'll pass that on,' promised Father Onophrios.

Volodka was about to hit the accelerator like he usually did, but he caught sight of the milk churns in his rear-view mirror and thought better of it. The Niva carefully moved off the pavement onto the road.

They got caught up in three traffic jams before Shevchenko Square, but from then on the road was fairly clear. It didn't take them long to find the orphanage.

The two-storey building was nice and clean, and the portraits of five deputies hung on the wall of the corridor in expensive frames, beneath the inscription 'Our Sponsors'. The central position was occupied by a portrait of Gennady Ilyich.

The older boys collected the milk from the back of the Niva. Then Semyon, Volodka and the priest went over to speak to the director.

When they got to his office, the first thing the director did was to thank his guests for the milk they had brought. Then he fixed his gaze on Father Onophrios, correctly presuming him to be the most senior delegate present, and asked him to pass on a request to Gennady Ilyich: to buy the orphanage equipment for a small cheese-making enterprise. He knew what he was talking about too, because he handed the priest a printout from the Internet with a description and photographs of various models.

'The thing is, not all the children like goat's milk, although they do know it's good for them. But in a different form I think they will all like it.'

'If it be God's will, you will get your cheese-making equipment,' said Father Onophrios in his baritone, taking the printout from the director.

40

Apartment No. 10, Reitarska Street, Kiev

Veronika was happy to have the morning to herself.

The sun was shining. The city and its inhabitants were getting ready for spring, and Veronika was in a good mood. Tomorrow was Saturday, and if Senya wasn't busy they could go somewhere. It was ages since the two of them had been anywhere together.

Veronika tried to decide which would be better: the theatre or a café. Or maybe they could go to the cinema? Darya Ivanovna spoke very highly of the cinema that had opened inside the Ukraine department store.

'No, the theatre would be better,' thought Veronika, screwing up her eyes in the bright sunlight coming through the window.

She sighed pensively, imagining how she would dress Semyon for the theatre. He didn't show the slightest interest in what he wore. All his shirts were white. He had two suits – one grey, one black. Today she would go and buy him a brightly coloured shirt, maybe orange, or a nice dark red. Buying shirts was easy. You just needed to know the collar size.

The doorbell interrupted her thoughts. Veronika tightened the belt on her emerald-coloured towelling dressing gown and went into the hall.

'Can I come in for a minute?' Her neighbour Igor stood on the doorstep. He was wearing a suit and tie again.

Veronika nodded. Igor went straight into the kitchen and sat down at the little table.

'Would you like some tea?' asked Veronika.

'Yes, that would be nice,' nodded Igor. 'I'm sorry to disturb you . . .'

Veronika glanced at the kettle, which was still warm. It would take about three minutes to boil, plus ten or fifteen minutes to drink tea and have a chat, and then she could politely say goodbye. She turned to her guest.

'I hope you don't think I'm a coward,' said her neighbour, looking searchingly into Veronika's eyes. 'I can't deny that they gave me a scare, but I'll carry on if you want me to. Do you want me to?'

'No, don't worry about it,' said Veronika with a dismissive wave.

'Why not?' asked her neighbour, surprised. 'I could find out whether they're still following him.'

Veronika liked this idea.

'OK,' she agreed.

'So shall I follow him?'

'Just once more,' said Veronika.

At that moment the doorbell rang again. Puzzled, Veronika looked at Igor. He suddenly looked uneasy, as though he were frightened that Semyon would find him there.

Veronika went out into the hall.

Darya Ivanovna stood on the doorstep, holding the wreath from the café wall. She seemed upset.

'I'm going to leave it here for the time being.' She put the wreath on the floor, then removed her fur coat and headed straight for the kitchen.

She went in and stared silently at Igor.

'This is Igor, my neighbour,' said Veronika.

Darya Ivanovna looked so disdainfully at Igor that he immediately jumped to his feet.

'It's time I was off,' he said, making for the door. And then he was gone.

'What an unattractive neighbour you have,' said Darya Ivanovna.

'Well, you can't choose your neighbours!' Veronika laughed it off.

'You know, someone got into the pharmacy last night,' said the widow, her voice shaking. 'They turned the place upside down. I need to sell that pharmacy as soon as possible. I don't know what to do now . . . Should I call the militia or not?'

'Of course you should call them!'

'But what if they didn't find whatever it was they were looking for, and then the militia come and find it?'

Veronika stared at Darya Ivanovna.

'I found something myself, just after he died. And I hid it. But what should I do now?'

'Maybe it would be better not to call them, then? I can come with you, if you like. We can tidy it up a bit . . .'

Veronika was suddenly alarmed by her own suggestion, but Darya Ivanovna perked up immediately.

'Would you really come with me? It won't be so bad with two of us there. When the old woman who works for me got to the pharmacy yesterday morning she was so frightened she just ran off. I suppose I should be glad she called me first, and not the militia.'

41

9 May Street, Boryspil

The idea that Boris the baggage handler had simply gone off on a bender gradually returned Dima to a state of calm. This 'state of calm' was relative, though. He'd already called work twice to ask when he could resume his professional duties, but they'd told him evasively that Shamil was still in the veterinary hospital so he would have to wait a bit longer.

Enforced inactivity in winter is a burden. It's like loneliness – you need to share it with someone to stop you turning to drink.

During the day Dima had only Scruffy with whom to share his loneliness. Valya left first thing in the morning to attend to the slot machines, abandoning her husband without a twinge of conscience to the mercy of the two cats: the kitchen cat, who continued to put on weight due to his limited confines, and the house cat, who only ever rubbed up against his master's legs, even though his mistress was the one who fed him. Sometimes Dima was irritated by this and sometimes he rather liked it, but a cat was better company than none at all, so for the time being Scruffy was in his good books.

Dima thought about the young militiaman's request and tried to recall how many ampoules he had left.

A light, powdery snow was falling. Dima looked at this white 'manna from heaven' and wondered whether or not to go to the garage. Boris the baggage handler could return to hung-over reality at any moment, which would scupper his chances of making any money from the ampoules, but as things stood he could even put the price up a bit. Militiamen were no angels – their 'services' didn't come for free. They knew how it worked, so they shouldn't have a problem paying the market price.

In the absence of competition Dima imagined the current market price of the ampoules and their questionable contents to be as high as $40 or even $50, but he knew it was important not to push his luck. So when he suddenly found himself holding the piece of paper with the militiaman's mobile phone number on it, a random yet plausible price popped into his head: $43.55. Dima didn't know where this particular figure came from but it already felt somehow official, as though it had been announced on television.

The militiaman responded positively to Dima's call. He placed an order for ten ampoules from Dima's fictional seller. They agreed to meet at Dima's place at 7 p.m.

After breakfast Dima went to the garage with Scruffy. He counted out the ten ampoules that had been ordered and one extra, which he gave to the cat, breaking the top off and tipping the contents onto the unwashed plate.

They went back into the front yard together. King the bull terrier was sitting on the neighbour's doorstep. Seeing the cat, he snarled and dashed towards the blocked-up hole in the fence. Scruffy darted over to the fence as well and hissed, baring his sharp little teeth.

'Oi, pack it in!' Dima shouted at him. 'Get inside, quickly, or he'll rip you to shreds!'

The cat seemed to understand and obey him. In any case

the two of them went into the house, while King carried on growling.

It stopped snowing at about 5 p.m. Valya came home from work. She took off her fake-fur coat and her Romanian boots, then put her slippers on and went into the kitchen.

The militiaman arrived late. Dima made him a cup of tea and poured him a shot of his home-made nettle vodka, which the militiaman really liked. Then, getting down to business, Dima laid the ten ampoules on the table.

'There's your order. I'm afraid the price has gone up, though. Don't forget that I'm not the one selling them, it's one of your colleagues.'

'He's in the militia?' his guest asked in surprise.

Dima nodded.

'In the Boryspil force?'

'Uh-huh,' answered Dima.

'So, how much do I owe you?' The militiaman took a leather wallet out of the pocket of his uniform.

'Four hundred and . . . fifty,' declared Dima.

The militiaman handed over the cash. He shook his host's hand and then left.

Dima poured two shots of home-made vodka to celebrate. He drank one himself and took the other into the kitchen, where Valya was leafing through a brightly coloured magazine. She smiled gratefully and thought what a considerate husband she had after all. She drank the vodka then turned her attention back to the article she was reading about the unfortunate Britney Spears.

42

Maryanivka village, Kiev region

The red Mazda flew along the deserted Zhytomyr Highway like a rocket. It shot past the traffic police checkpoint, which still had its lights on. The arrow on the speedometer reached 180kph. But Egor wasn't thinking about the road; he could still hear the screeching voice of Irina's boss: 'That girlfriend of yours can go and jump off a bloody cliff, for all I care!' And what had he said to provoke such a reaction? He had merely gone in, sat down opposite her and asked her, firmly, to leave Irina alone. How could he have known that she would react so hysterically?

'Anyway,' thought Egor, peering ahead at the patch of road illuminated by his headlights, 'now I just need to find her another job. Somewhere normal, and not necessarily in Kiev.'

Egor remembered that there was a roadside café in Kalinovka belonging to an old friend of his, the son of a former divisional inspector from Makariv. Maybe there would be a job there for Irina? It was a nice, clean café, with bar stools and a television.

Egor imagined himself calling in to this café on the way to work and being served coffee by Irina, and then calling in on the way back to take her home.

Just then the road sign for Kalinovka flashed past. Perfect timing. Egor braked and pulled up next to the café he'd had in mind. He looked at his watch: 1.30 a.m. The café lights were still on.

He looked inside. There was a film showing on the television, and a group of drunken men sat around one of the tables, with two bottles of vodka and several bottles of beer on the go. They looked up simultaneously at the new arrival. A woman of around forty looked at Egor from behind the counter. Her hair was dyed bright orange, and she wore a quilted jacket over her dark blue woollen cardigan.

'Have you got any coffee?' asked Egor, going over to the counter.

'Machine's broken,' answered the woman. 'They're coming to fix it tomorrow.'

As he turned the car into Makariv, Egor started driving more carefully. The road here was narrow and slippery.

He came to a stop once he got to Lipovka. He took a pen and a piece of paper out of the glove compartment and wrote a note, then walked down the ice-covered track to Irina's house and stuck the folded note in between the door and the frame. Then he got back into his car and drove home.

It was chilly in the hut. Their neighbour obviously hadn't put enough wood on the fire.

His mother was asleep, with two quilts over her.

Egor stoked the fire in the masonry stove, threw in some pine logs and firmly closed the cast-iron door. The smell of smoke filled the room.

Egor went out into the yard to have a look at the pipe on the roof. A column of smoke drifted straight up into the sky. There was no wind.

He made up a bed for himself on the old sofa and lay down, covering himself with a blanket. He heard his mother muttering something in her sleep in the next room. A mouse scrabbled somewhere behind the fridge.

Egor lay there looking at the ceiling and listening to the silence. He didn't feel like sleeping.

43

Apartment No. 10, Reitarska Street, Kiev

Semyon woke up with a headache. Even the cup of coffee that Veronika brought him in bed failed to improve matters. The previous day had ended badly: he and Volodka had gone to a bar in the evening, and Volodka had suddenly flown off the handle when Semyon had mentioned that he thought Volodka's reports about the blonde woman were some kind of joke. Of course Semyon had been drinking brandy, whereas Volodka had been as sober as a judge; maybe his sobriety was the reason he'd lost his temper so quickly. He'd even jumped up from the table. 'I've not slept for days because of you!' he'd declared in an injured tone. Then he'd told Semyon that he had a surprise for him but he probably wasn't going to like it.

'You're looking a bit pale today,' said his wife, sitting on the end of the bed. She sounded worried.

'Have you ever tried goat's milk?' Semyon asked suddenly.

Veronika thought about it.

'No, I don't think so,' she answered after a pause.

'What about goat's cheese?'

She shook her head.

'I have to get up,' said Semyon, trying to look at Veronika with affection and gratitude.

After taking a cold shower he felt a little better. He'd virtually forgotten about his argument with Volodka, but he couldn't stop thinking about goat's milk and goat's cheese.

'I'm going out for a walk,' he told Veronika.

As he put his jacket on Semyon caught sight of the familiar funeral wreath, which was standing on the floor in the hall.

'Is it Sunday today?' he asked.

'No, Saturday,' said Veronika, glancing into the hallway. 'Oh, Darya Ivanovna forgot the wreath! The pharmacy was broken into yesterday evening. I went there with her –'

'Did they take anything?' asked Semyon, putting his shoes on.

'I don't know,' his wife shrugged. 'All the medicines seemed to be in place.'

'He was probably dealing drugs on the side –'

'Don't be silly!' Veronika exclaimed, jumping to the defence of the deceased. 'He was developing new medicines.'

'To make people younger?'

'All sorts! Darya Ivanovna and I found his secret hiding place yesterday. That was probably what the burglars were looking for.'

'And what was in it?'

'Notes, chemical formulas, jars, ampoules . . . And a book of erotic sketches! Darya Ivanovna gave it to me. Do you want to see it?'

'Not really.' Semyon waved his hand dismissively. 'By the way, are you sure he was murdered?'

'Yes! I saw his body with my own eyes.'

Semyon gave a strange shrug and left the apartment.

Once she had the place to herself, Veronika took the pharmacist's notebook from her bedside table. It was full of pencil drawings of nude female figures, which were actually rather good. As she turned the pages she found notes written in fountain pen at the beginning and end of the book. She tried to decipher them, but the handwriting was so appalling she gave up.

Semyon came back an hour later with a fresh baguette and a packet of French goat's cheese.

Veronika put the kettle on and spread the cheese on slices of the bread. They sat down at the table.

Semyon ate one of the slices and cleared his throat, disappointed.

'Well, I like it!' said Veronika. Then, out of the blue, she said, 'Why don't we go to the theatre today?'

Semyon's eyes widened. 'Which theatre?' he asked, surprised.

'Nothing too heavy . . . I was thinking about the operetta? At least we won't have to concentrate too hard! We haven't been out anywhere together for ages.'

'OK,' agreed Semyon. 'Only I have to pop out for an hour this afternoon. I need to sort things out with Volodka.'

They met in the café nearest the apartment. Volodka wore the same injured expression as the day before.

Semyon put a piece of goat's cheese on the table, wrapped in foil.

'Do you know what that is?' he asked, pushing it towards Volodka.

'Looks like cheese to me.'

'It's goat's cheese, the kind they were talking about making yesterday in the orphanage. Try it.'

'I'll try the cheese, while you look at these.' Volodka took an envelope out of his inside jacket pocket and handed it to Semyon.

The envelope was full of photographs of Semyon and the blonde woman from Chekhov Street. In the first three photos they were standing and talking, but in the last two they had their arms round each other and were kissing.

'So, do you still think I'm making it up?' whispered Volodka. He put a piece of goat's cheese in his mouth. 'And shall I tell you something else?'

Semyon, whose mood had sunk lower than the skirting board, gave a barely perceptible nod.

'Two days ago you spent *three hours* in her apartment. At night! Any idea what the two of you got up to in there?'

Semyon didn't answer.

'A double brandy,' Volodka said to the waiter. Then he pointed at Semyon and added, 'For him.'

44

Amusement arcade, Boryspil

That morning Valya asked her husband to walk her to work. They set out along the freshly fallen snow. Of course they could have got there in ten minutes in a minibus taxi, but the weather itself seemed to suggest that they walk. Valya really wanted to breathe in the cold, crisp air. Overloaded GAZelle trucks rushed past them on their way to Kiev. They walked the length of the street in silence, each of them thinking their own thoughts.

'Dima,' Valya began suddenly, turning towards him as they were walking. 'What's going on with your job?'

Dima snapped out of his reverie. 'I told you, Shamil's not well. I might have to start working with a different dog.'

'Or maybe you could get a different job?' Valya's gaze grew serious, more focused.

'Doing what?'

'You could help me.'

The sheer unexpectedness of this stopped Dima in his tracks.

'Help you with what?' he asked.

'We're going to have a baby,' Valya whispered, with a slightly silly, self-satisfied smile.

'Oh!' exclaimed Dima. 'When?'

'In about seven months. You could work in the arcade for me while I'm on maternity leave, and then we could take it in turns. It's nice and cosy in there, near all the money, and the pay's good . . .'

'We'll see,' said Dima. But as he looked ahead towards the bus station something in his attitude had changed – he felt different, more decisive.

They continued on their way in silence, each thinking their own thoughts. It's impossible for any two people to think the same thoughts at the same time, unless they're thinking out loud.

Valya started her shift at the amusement arcade. She waited until her colleague Sonya had left, and then she gave Dima twenty hryvnas in fifty-kopek pieces.

'Here, see how you get on. Today might be your lucky day!'

He walked along the rows of slot machines and stopped in front of one that seemed to freeze as Dima approached, as though it were afraid of him. Its buttons even stopped flashing.

Dima put a coin into the machine's slot. He pressed the start button, and the machine's three reels began to spin. Bananas, lemons and oranges flashed before his eyes.

About five minutes later coins started jingling into the winning trough. Dima turned round and exchanged glances with his wife, who was looking through the little window of the cashier's booth. She came over to her husband holding a grey money bag.

'For the baby!' said Dima, nodding at his winnings.

He felt a surge of pride, although he wasn't quite sure whether this was down to his forthcoming fatherhood or his success on the slot machine.

45

Lipovka village, Kiev region

Irina read the note in the hall, on her way back from the doorstep.

'Irina, you've been fired. You don't have to go to Kiev any more. Will come and explain everything tomorrow, around 11 a.m. Egor.'

Irina took off her coat, scarf and boots and went into the kitchen holding the note. She remembered not wanting to get out of bed this morning – she must have known this was going to happen.

'Oh well,' she thought, 'so I've been fired. It's not the end of the world.'

Irina went back into her room. Her daughter was awake, so she picked her up and put her on the breast. When Yasya had drunk her fill of her mother's milk she dropped off again, and Irina lay down in bed beside her. She fell asleep straight away, like a child.

She woke again when light suddenly flooded in through the window, accompanied by the sound of doors slamming and foot-steps on the wooden floor. Opening her eyes, she saw her mother standing over her.

'I thought you'd left already,' her mother said in surprise.

'I got the sack,' Irina said quietly, so as not to wake Yasya.

'Lord help us! What did you do?' Her mother clasped her hands together.

'Nothing,' Irina answered sadly. 'Egor's coming at eleven. He said he'd explain everything then.'

'At eleven?' cried her mother. 'Look at the state of me!'

She disappeared and the door closed behind her. Moving carefully away from Yasya, Irina got out of bed. She glanced at the clock: 9.30 a.m. She had plenty of time.

In the kitchen her mother was heating up a big pan of water, to wash her hair. Once it was hot she carried it into the bathroom.

Irina had a cup of tea. She decided she probably ought to wash her hair too, but there was no way she'd have time to dry it. Or would she?

Both Irina and her mother managed to wash and comb out their hair by 11 a.m. Irina's hair was thicker, which meant it took a little longer to dry.

Irina left Yasya with her mother and went into the little boiler room to try and dry her hair more quickly. It was always warm in there, warm enough to dry freshly washed nappies in under an hour. She took a dark blue towel and started rubbing the ends of her hair. She was still in the boiler room when the knock came at the front door.

It wasn't Egor, though. It was Nurse Vera, wearing a heavy grey overcoat and holding a black shopping bag. She was flanked by two unattractive, cold-eyed, shaven-headed men in long black leather coats.

'They sent us here to find you,' said the old nurse.

One of the men shoved Vera aside and barged into the hall.

'Where's the kitchen?' he barked at Irina's mother.

She looked over at the closed kitchen door.

'Get on with it,' he said to the old nurse, pointing at the door and motioning to Irina to follow.

Nurse Vera sat down wearily at the table in her coat. She looked sadly at Irina, then reached into her bag and took out the breast pump and all its attachments.

'I'm sorry,' she whispered. 'It's not even Nelly Igorievna. She doesn't care any more. One of the clients kicked up a fuss and promised to fire the lot of us if we couldn't get hold of your milk for him. He's used to it. Apparently it has a particular taste . . .'

'One of the clients?' repeated Irina, flabbergasted. She couldn't understand what the old woman was saying.

'Yes,' Vera nodded, holding the transparent plastic suction cup out towards Irina's exposed left breast. 'Here, put it on,' she said.

Irina automatically positioned the suction cup over her breast and felt the table start to vibrate under her elbow. She watched the machine extract her milk, drop by drop, until a thin white stream of it was running along the transparent tube into the storage bottle.

'What client?' Irina asked quietly.

'Gennady Ilyich,' she said. 'He's someone really important. Always comes with two or three bodyguards, like those two out there – they made me come here with them. I've got no idea how they're going to deal with it longer term . . .'

After about twenty minutes, when the pump had extracted every last drop from Irina's breasts, Nurse Vera gathered her things together. She sealed the bottle of milk with a rubber lid and left without another word, trying to avoid catching Irina's eye.

Egor found Irina in tears and her mother unusually pale and frightened.

Irina clutched his shoulders, buried her wet face into his chest and started sobbing. With tears in her voice, her mother told him what had happened.

Egor stood there for a while just holding Irina and then sat her down on her bed and left in silence, without even saying goodbye.

46

Bekhterevsky Street, Kiev

Alone and still looking at the photographs that Volodka had given him, Semyon finished his brandy and dialled the number for directory enquiries on his mobile. He asked for the address of a private psychiatrist working in the city centre. It turned out that there were quite a few of them; the closest was at number 8 Bekhterevsky Street, near the Pokrovsky Monastery.

Semyon decided to go straight there. He walked down Reitarska Street to Lviv Square and continued along Artema Street. On the way he watched the minibus taxis and trolleybuses as they drove past and compared the US dollar exchange rate offered by different currency exchange booths. He reached the Berlin bar and was surprised to find that it was now called Courchevel. 'Typical,' thought Semyon. 'Only the names change quickly in this country.'

He found the psychiatrist's office easily enough. It was in a basement and had a nice wooden door. There was a nameplate: Dr P. Naitov.

As soon as Semyon pressed the bell, the door opened and a young girl in a white robe – like an angel from an old-fashioned

Christmas card – smiled at him and said, 'Come in.' Closing the front door behind him, she asked, 'Do you have an appointment?'

'No,' replied Semyon. He was instantly on guard.

'First-timers are always just dropping in without appointments!' She smiled again. 'Well, you're in luck – Pyotr Isaevich is free right now.'

There was no hallway. Instead the front door opened directly into a kind of lobby, the walls of which were covered in photo wallpaper depicting a series of tropical scenes: islands, palm trees, sandy beaches and emerald water. A brown leather sofa stood beneath the palm trees. To the left of an internal door was a small desk with an exercise book on it. The angelic girl sat down at the desk, picked up a pen and looked at Semyon, her face open and innocent.

'Could I have your name and address, please?' she asked.

Semyon gave her his details.

The doctor's office was startlingly white. The desk and chairs were painted white, there was a couch covered in white imitation leather and the doctor himself, of course, was wearing a white coat. A white sheet of A4 paper lay on the white desk. Only the doctor's close-cropped ginger hair violated the sterile colour spectrum of the room.

'Take a seat.' The doctor's voice was soft, almost velvety. 'Talk to me!'

Semyon sat down opposite the doctor. He moved his tongue around his mouth as he thought about what to say, and it brought back the taste of the brandy he'd drunk.

'I've got a few problems,' began Semyon, but then he stopped.

'Don't worry, your problems will become mine.'

Pyotr Isaevich's penetrating gaze came to rest on Semyon.

'The relationship between a doctor and his patient must always begin with trust. Otherwise we'll never get anywhere,' he said. 'OK?'

Semyon nodded. He hadn't expected the psychiatrist's voice to be so easy to listen to. It slipped into his brain and seemed to stay there, deep inside him. It was like being hypnotised.

The angelic girl in white came into the office without knocking and placed two cups of tea, a sugar bowl and spoons on the doctor's desk. Semyon waited until the girl left and put two spoonfuls of sugar into his cup, and then to his own surprise he began to talk. He told the psychiatrist that he had suspected himself of sleep-walking so had asked a friend to spy on him, and that he'd learned from this friend that he was going out at night to meet up with a woman. He thought about showing the doctor the photographic evidence but decided against it. He merely added that the woman he was meeting at night hadn't recognised him when he went to see her during the day.

'Very interesting! So she is your colleague in misfortune,' said the doctor in a light, friendly voice. 'Or fortune. It all depends on how you look at it. But I'd leave your friend out of it from now on, if I were you. From his point of view, clearly, somnambulism is a terrible disease.'

The doctor got up and gestured to Semyon to lie down on the couch. He asked him to focus on the pencil he was holding while he moved it from side to side, and then he checked Semyon's reflexes.

He turned away and put the pencil on the desk. 'Stand up,' he said. 'Physically, there's nothing wrong with you. I can't detect any obvious mental pathologies either, but as far as your sleepwalking is concerned . . . Do you remember the first time it happened? I don't mean in childhood but from the age of, say, twenty?'

Semyon thought about it.

'No, I can't remember. It used to happen when I was little, though. My mother used to say that I wandered around the apartment at night with my eyes open.'

'Nearly all children walk in their sleep. It's perfectly normal. But what about later?'

Semyon shook his head.

'Have you ever been involved with drugs?'

'I tried smoking grass, but that was a long time ago. Nothing else.'

'All right,' sighed Pyotr Isaevich. 'This is how I see it. Are you married?'

'Yes.' Semyon sat down opposite the doctor again.

'If your sleepwalking is bothering you, you could ask your wife to lock the front door at night so that you can't get out. If you suffer only mildly from somnambulism, then the worst that can happen is that you'll get up every now and then and wander around your apartment at night, like you did when you were little. Eventually, it might even stop of its own accord. But if it's more severe . . . Which floor do you live on?'

'The third floor.'

'That could be dangerous. I assume you don't want to fit bars onto your windows?'

'No,' said Semyon.

'You need to understand that there is no cure for somnambulism, as such,' said the doctor. 'It is possible to suppress it temporarily . . . but if something is suppressed it will invariably find a way to reappear elsewhere, or at another time. If you are managing to

168

exercise even the slightest control over your nocturnal behaviour, you're doing well. If you want to stop yourself getting up in the night, I suggest you have a few drinks before you go to bed, and I'm talking something stronger than wine or champagne.'

'So I'm not going mad?' Semyon asked carefully.

'When the patient is unaware of their condition they are able to live a calm and fulfilling double life, in two dimensions. However, I'm afraid that now you're aware of your sleepwalking the chances of you succumbing to mental illness have undoubtedly increased.'

'This woman, the one I meet at night, you said she's also a sleepwalker?' asked Semyon.

'Of course. And I would advise you not to try and contact her during the day again. The female psyche is considerably more fragile than the male.'

On his way out, Semyon paid the girl in the white robe a hundred hryvnas and was given a business card in return.

Outside, on the street, he felt an incredible lightness in both his body and his soul. It was as though the spring he was so sick of waiting for had finally begun inside him.

In reality it was cloudy and still cold. There was no frost, but it was unpleasantly damp. The little square patches of earth around the trees were hidden beneath heaps of filthy snow, and all the cars driving past were dirty. The external world just didn't correspond to the way Semyon was feeling inside. He carried this feeling home with him, guarding it protectively from loss or damage.

That evening he went to the operetta with Veronika. Even though their seats were in the fifth row of the stalls, Semyon asked in the cloakroom for a pair of opera glasses and then proceeded to spend the entire performance peering through the glasses at the boxes of the second and third tiers.

'You're supposed to be admiring the actresses!' whispered Veronika, surprised at her husband's behaviour. 'Do you want me to think you're looking for someone?'

Veronika had heard that all the actresses in the operetta theatre were old, and that they had to spend two hours before the show being made up to look like twenty-year-olds.

But Semyon, who wasn't actually that interested in the performance, started to wonder what he'd been doing. When he thought about it he realised that he'd been hoping to see Alisa, in close-up.

47

9 May Street, Boryspil

The news of Shamil's death took Dima by surprise. It had been several days since he'd thought about his canine colleague, and for genuinely good reason: Dima had been contemplating his future fatherhood and the changes that the birth of a child would bring to his life. He'd felt in need of a change for some time now. He wouldn't mind changing his job, or moving house. He sometimes even thought of finding a new wife. It was simple enough and not uncommon, but it would be fairly unpleasant.

Now it was as though Valya herself had sensed that it was time for them to make some changes in their lives. Initially the news about the baby had come as a huge shock to Dima, but he'd soon come to view the pressures and responsibilities of parenthood in a more positive light. He wasn't nervous at all, because he knew that the burdens of parenthood were borne first and foremost by the mother of the child. Before the telephone call from the airport he'd been imagining Valya with a child in her arms. But now this news!

He was upset about Shamil, of course. In a manly way. After all, it had been seven long years that they'd worked together, seven years that they'd spent looking into each other's eyes, seven years that Shamil had given Dima his paw before the start of every shift. But men are notoriously frugal with their emotions, regardless of the circumstances.

Having promised his boss that he would call in for a chat at 6 p.m. the next day, Dima started to wonder what sort of a chat it would be. What would they talk about?

Scruffy rubbed against his legs, as though he'd picked up on his master's mood. Dima glanced at him. Scruffy had come back from the dead, hadn't he? Maybe Shamil would too.

It occurred to him that he needed to drink to the memory of his friend. Shamil had been his friend, after all, not just a dog.

Dima sighed and put his coat on, then went out to the garage. He placed a bottle and a shot glass on the stool and poured himself a drink. He called to mind an image of the German shepherd and silently downed the shot, with a nod to his own obedient imagination. A thin, hot stream of home-made nettle vodka flowed directly into his soul. He poured another shot and downed it. He remembered the two of them walking along the endless rows of suitcases and bags, the way Shamil would stop and sniff . . . The way he'd stopped and sniffed that black plastic suitcase, the one that the two baggage handlers had subsequently brought to this very garage. Dima didn't feel like remembering any more.

At some point he began to feel cold, so he got into the car. He switched on the engine and turned the heater up. He was soon feeling warm and cosy and started drifting off. He was no longer thinking about Shamil. Suddenly there was a sound like someone banging their fist on the locked garage doors for all they were worth. Dima woke up and opened the car door, noticing how weak his arm seemed to be. He could smell mustard. He gulped in mouthfuls of air but it didn't seem to be enough, he couldn't inhale deeply enough – there seemed to be something wrong with the air in the car. Then it hit him: he was dying! Dying a banal death in his garage, from carbon monoxide poisoning. Using his last reserves of energy he clambered out of the car and took several unsteady steps towards the garage doors. He flung the left-hand door wide open and, as the cold air hit him in the face, fell forwards onto the snow. Something warm brushed against his face. It was only ten minutes later, once Dima had regained consciousness and got his breath back, that he reached out his hand and his fingers made contact with a warm, soft ball of feline fur. It was Scruffy. The cat was using his body to warm the right-hand side of his pale, terrified master's face.

Several of his neighbours went by on the street, but not one of them stopped to ask what had happened. They just looked at him warily and went on their way. Dima could still hear the sound of their footsteps.

'You idiot! You absolute idiot!' Dima muttered to himself, as he ventilated the garage half an hour later. All four car doors were wide open, as were the garage doors. Scruffy kept wandering off then coming back to rub up against his legs.

Dima had lost all sense of time. It was already dark outside. There were lights on in the windows of the building opposite. There were lights on in his house too, although he never left the lights on when he went out.

When he and Scruffy returned home, only the kitchen light was still on. Valya was already asleep, and the clock said 10.30 p.m. Dima had a cup of tea then undressed and lay down under the warm blanket next to his wife.

'You smell funny,' said Valya. Dozy with sleep, she turned away from her husband.

'Shamil's dead,' whispered Dima, by way of explanation.

But Valya didn't hear him. She'd already dived back into her dreams.

48

Lipovka village, Kiev region

Egor's pursuit of the dark blue car with three sixes on its personalised number plate was not crowned with success.

At the speed he was going it only took Egor about quarter of an hour to reach the traffic police checkpoint at the entrance to Kiev. He pulled onto the verge and turned the engine off. His eyes fell on the low rampart of dirty, black snow that separated the forest from the highway and he tried to concentrate, to imagine what would have happened if he had managed to catch up with the car. Seriously, what would he have done?

This sudden confusion might simply have been down to exhaustion. A fifteen-minute car chase, the stress, his anger . . . That was all it was. As soon as he turned off the Mazda's engine, his own engine stopped as well.

Egor got out of the car. He kicked the dirty crust off the pile of snow with the toe of his boot, then bent down and used the fingers of both hands to prise two chunks of snow from the frozen, solid mass. He rubbed them over his face, his cheeks and his forehead.

Like a cold shower, the icy feeling of the snow made Egor feel a little more alert. He wiped his wet hands on his trousers and got back behind the wheel.

His agitation gradually dissipated.

'What would I have done?' he wondered, already thinking about it more rationally. 'Would I have punched someone?' But who? The two men that Irina's mother had told him about were the same as Egor himself, just someone's security guards. They were given orders, and they carried them out. So who had given this particular order? Egor thought about it and remembered his last conversation with Irina's boss, though it hadn't exactly been a 'conversation' – more an exchange of unpleasantries. Could it really have been her? Maybe he should borrow an air rifle from his friend and shoot out the windows of that milk kitchen one night, like a final warning. But if that didn't do the trick, then what? Maybe he should hide Irina and Yasya, take them to his place. Only where was 'his place'?

The red Mazda pulled back onto the road then turned round and began heading away from the city. Egor needed caffeine. He wanted to sit alone at a table in a cosy little roadside café, and he knew just the place – another fifteen kilometres or so and a squat green building would come into view just after the petrol station.

He stopped at the café and went inside to think it through again over a coffee. He knew he had to do something. He just needed to decide what.

There was a sudden sleet shower as he turned off the Zhytomyr Highway into Makariv. He could still taste the bitter coffee he'd drunk at the roadside café.

Then he was in Lipovka. Just before the village cemetery Egor took the turning into Irina's road. His car rolled down the frozen track, over the wet snow, towards her house.

Light poured from all four front windows – a soft, comforting evening light.

Irina opened the door. The house was warm and quiet.

'Would you like a cup of tea?' she asked, almost whispering, and then she grew flustered, realising that it was the first time she had addressed Egor using the familiar form of 'you'.

'That would be nice,' he answered, his voice equally low.

They went into the kitchen and Irina half closed the door.

'Mama fell asleep with Yasya. Today's all been too much for her . . .'

'I'm going to buy you a mobile phone tomorrow,' said Egor. The determination in his voice somehow communicated itself to Irina. 'So you can call me if anything happens. If that lot come back, don't open the door – just call me straight away!'

49

Apartment No. 10, Reitarska Street, Kiev

The night tormented Semyon with insomnia. He tossed and turned, one minute putting his arms around his sleeping wife, the next getting as far away from her as he could. The noise in his head kept dying down then growing louder again. His injured hip was hurting, and absurd thoughts flashed through his headache as he drifted in and out of sleep. These thoughts were suddenly followed by an image of Alisa; her name also flashed through his mind several times. Eventually Semyon had had enough of this. He got up, went into the kitchen and sat down at the table without turning on the light. He placed his elbows firmly on the plastic tablecloth.

After sitting there for a few minutes he felt calmer. The noise in his head had died away, but an unbelievable heaviness remained. He felt it pressing down on his shoulders and throughout his body.

'There's something wrong with me,' Semyon whispered to himself.

He thought about Pyotr Isaevich, the ginger-haired psychiatrist he'd visited. He'd said something about there being no cure for sleepwalking. But sleepwalking is not the same as insomnia. The insomnia made him ache all over – he could feel a dull tremor drumming away at him, inside and out, whereas the sleepwalking had no adverse effects on his body. It just surprised him.

'You idiot!' exclaimed Semyon, suddenly remembering that Veronika had some sleeping tablets somewhere. She'd suffered from insomnia in the past, although she seemed to be over it now. So it obviously wasn't worth getting depressed about.

Semyon switched the light on. He got the first-aid box out, found the packet of barbiturates, took two tablets and went back to bed.

He woke up to the intense smell of coffee. He opened his eyes and saw a cup of espresso on the bedside table, and Veronika sitting on the edge of the bed in her pale green nightdress.

'Did you have a bad night?' she asked sympathetically.

'I had a headache,' admitted Semyon.

'Is it still hurting?'

'No, it's fine now.' Semyon reached his hand out to the bedside table.

He picked up the cup, but a few drops of coffee spilled into the saucer so he put it back down. He sat up in bed next to his wife and reached for the coffee again. After a few mouthfuls the caffeine buzz would begin to tighten his body's inner strings, tuning them up. And then everything would be fine, absolutely fine.

Veronika went to have a shower. He went into the kitchen. There was a small window between the bathroom and the kitchen, up near the ceiling, and the sound of the running water soothed him. It was snowing again outside, but in here it was warm and cosy.

Semyon closed the first-aid box that he had left out on the table the night before and put it back in the cabinet.

Over breakfast he kept glancing at Veronika. That emerald-coloured towelling dressing gown really suited her, particularly this morning.

'I promised Darya Ivanovna I'd be at hers by eleven. She wants me to give her a hand,' said Veronika. 'They're bringing her husband home today . . .'

'Haven't they buried him yet?' asked Semyon, surprised.

'No. Are you at home today?' asked Veronika.

'Until lunchtime, but after that I don't know. Gennady Ilyich was going to call.'

Veronika left at 10.30 a.m. Semyon called Volodka and asked him how things were going. Things were going fine, although Semyon thought Volodka sounded tired.

'Let me know in advance next time you're going to have a good night's sleep, OK? So I can get some sleep too,' said his friend.

'I was awake half the night,' complained Semyon.

'Well, you should have come out then, we could've had a chat! I had something to show you.'

'You mean there's more?' asked Semyon, irritably.

'Why don't you wait and see what it is first, before you get upset about it? Have we got any work on today?'

'It looks like it, but not until later. You can show me whatever it is then.'

Semyon changed into a tracksuit, feeling a growing sense of unease. He went over to the door that led to the balcony and looked out at all the snow that had accumulated on it. He thought about what Volodka had said. He had certainly piqued his curiosity. What was it that he had to show him?

Semyon turned round and glanced at the telephone. Should he call him back? Or wait until that afternoon?

In the end, his nervous curiosity got the better of him and he called his friend back.

'I don't suppose you're planning on coming into town any earlier, are you?' he asked.

'I'll be there in an hour,' answered Volodka. It was obvious from his tone of voice that he had been expecting Semyon to call back.

50

Apartment No. 17, Vorovsky Street, Kiev

They brought Eduard Ivanovich home naked. Not completely naked, of course, but in nothing more than a white robe. Veronika had already been at Darya Ivanovna's apartment for about an hour by the time he arrived but they were still waiting for Anna, who had promised to be there first thing in the morning. Two hospital orderlies in white robes brought the plastinated corpse into the hallway on a stretcher and asked Darya Ivanovna where she wanted him.

She told them to put him on the bed.

'But he was wearing a suit!' Darya Ivanovna looked at her husband's naked feet. 'And socks and shoes . . .'

'They'll bring all that later,' promised one of the orderlies.

Alone again, Darya Ivanovna and Veronika exchanged glances.

'Anna's a bit late,' said the pharmacist's widow.

The doorbell rang.

'Talk of the devil!' Darya Ivanovna smiled and went out into the hall.

'Sorry!' Veronika heard Anna's voice in the hall. 'I got held up at the Baykov Cemetery, but at least I managed to sort it all out. They're going to reserve us two adjacent graves, under an old pine tree. It's a perfect spot.'

They assembled in the living room.

'So.' Darya Ivanovna looked at her friends. 'Let's get him dressed first! I thought they'd be bringing him in his suit . . .'

In the bedroom she opened the wardrobe and ran her hand along her husband's jackets, shirts and suits.

'Something casual,' she said to herself, selecting and rejecting one jacket after another. 'This dark blue one will do.'

It took the pharmacist's widow another fifteen minutes or so to select a shirt and trousers. Then she took out underwear and socks.

At first Veronika found it rather unnerving. To make matters worse she had trouble getting his left sock on.

'Here, let me help,' offered Anna.

Veronika lifted the pharmacist's feet while Anna skilfully pulled the socks on. Working together, they managed to get it done quickly.

'It's weird, he doesn't feel cold at all,' said Veronika, surprised.

'Mine's room temperature too,' nodded Anna.

For a second Veronika remembered the warm body of her

husband, tossing and turning all night. He'd kept hugging her, then pushing her away. A warm smile appeared on her face.

'They've already come up with the idea of installing an electric heater, set to body temperature,' added Anna. 'I don't fancy that, though. It would be a bit strange, having to plug your husband in!'

The process of putting on his shirt, trousers and jacket took place under the strict supervision of Darya Ivanovna.

'What about his shoes?' asked Anna.

'Slippers,' the widow corrected her. 'He's going to be sitting in the armchair.'

They placed the armchair according to the rules of feng shui, so that it faced the window and the right-hand corner of the room, where a large vase of dried roses stood on a narrow chest of drawers.

Once they'd finished dressing the pharmacist and positioned him in the armchair, the women stopped to catch their breath. They all felt a certain relief.

It wasn't long before Darya Ivanovna proposed a toast. 'We should drink to his homecoming,' she said, placing an opened bottle of Martell on the table. 'Annushka, there are some slices of lemon in the kitchen. Bring them in, would you?'

Once she'd taken her seat at the table, Veronika yielded to a slight internal panic. If she looked straight ahead, her eyes fell on the nape of the pharmacist's neck.

She jumped up, moved her chair round to the other side of the table and sat down again with her back to the dead man.

Darya Ivanovna and Anna exchanged smiles.

'You'd better get used to it, Nikochka – yours won't be alive for ever!' said Darya Ivanovna.

'Why do you need two graves at Baykov?' asked Veronika, glancing first at Anna and then at Darya Ivanovna.

'What do you mean?' Darya Ivanovna seemed surprised by the question. 'For our husbands, of course.'

'But they're at home! If you're going to . . . why did you . . .' Veronika faltered, unable to hide her confusion.

'Practicalities, my dear,' said the pharmacist's widow, without a hint of criticism. 'Both Edik and Vasya are officially dead, and dead people are supposed to have graves. What if Edik receives a posthumous award for medicine? Where will the President bring the wreaths? He won't have anywhere to put them if there's no grave and no gravestone. Think of it as a residency permit. Everyone has to have one, but you can live wherever you like. So Edik's officially resident at the cemetery, but lives at home.'

Veronika nodded, deep in thought. She looked at the bottle of Martell, at the saucer of pale yellow lemon slices, at the glasses. 'I'm going to get Semyon to drink brandy with me tonight,' she thought smugly, realising how much better and more complete her life was than either Anna's or Darya Ivanovna's.

'Come on then, girls,' said Darya Ivanovna, picking up the bottle of Martell. 'Let's get stuck in!'

51

9 May Street, Boryspil
When Valya got up and started dressing the next morning, Dima screwed up his eyes. He had a bit of a headache. He clearly didn't look too good either.

'Did you overdo it a bit last night?' asked his wife.

'Shamil's dead,' he said mournfully.

'Dead? What did he die of?'

'They said he got sick. Some kind of infection, apparently, but I think . . .' Dima stopped and shook his head.

'It's a sign,' said Valya, looking pointedly at the ceiling. 'You need to leave that place.'

'What about my pension?'

'Have a drink,' Valya suggested unexpectedly. 'It'll help you put things in perspective.'

Dima looked at his wife with surprise and respect. He decided that pregnancy had changed her for the better – she'd suddenly grown wiser, or something.

As soon as Valya was dressed, she left for work.

'I overslept this morning,' she said on her way out. 'So you'll have to get your own breakfast.'

When the door had shut behind Valya, Dima got up and went into the kitchen. He poured himself a shot of vodka. He fished a pickled tomato out of a litre jar, then cut a slice of Ukrainian bread and rubbed it all over with a clove of garlic.

After he'd downed his morning shot and chased it with his snack his eyes fell on Kitchen Fluffy, who was lying lazily under the radiator, staring at Dima with a stupid and satiated look in his eyes.

Dima suddenly felt like throwing something heavy at the cat. He looked around the kitchen and spotted the old copper mortar standing on the windowsill, but he couldn't be bothered to stand up and get it. Or maybe the desire wasn't strong enough . . . He knew deep down that he didn't really want to hurt the animal. He was just tormented by a vague feeling of injustice: good, loyal dogs die mysterious deaths, while this fat good-for-nothing cat lay under the radiator without showing the slightest respect for Dima, his master.

Pulling on a tracksuit, Dima called his boss. He apologised for not making it in for their 'chat'. Then he asked where they'd buried Shamil.

'Are you out of your mind?' his boss roared at him. 'Why the hell would we have buried him? He was a dog, not a person!'

'But there's a pet cemetery. I read about it in the paper,' said Dima.

'He wasn't a pet, he was just a dog. One that belonged to the state. And when state-owned animals die they get thrown in a hole, or somewhere similar. All right? Now, stop going on about it!' And with that his boss hung up.

'They'll probably throw me in a hole as well. I'm just a state-owned employee,' Dima thought sadly. He remembered what his wife had said that morning. 'She's right. It's a sign. I have to get out of there. I belong at home, not to the state.'

Dima imagined himself sharing Valya's shifts at the amusement arcade. He imagined the two of them sitting there, or even the three of them – the baby waking up or going to sleep to the sound of coins jingling into the winning troughs. 'That's how it should be,' thought Dima. 'A calm life, a steady job and a happy family.'

That evening Dima called in to pick up his wife. They walked home in companionable silence, each feeling that they were needed by the other. They ate fried fish and mashed potato for dinner, and afterwards Valya had indigestion. 'It must be the pregnancy,' thought Dima and sent her to bed. He stayed in the kitchen and started leafing through a pile of free newspapers, looking for new ideas. The section that interested him most was 'Cars for Sale'. He studied the make, model and age of the vehicles listed and compared this information with their price, trying to understand the logic behind it. He found at least a dozen 'twins' of his own car, all of which were priced fairly consistently – between $3,000 and $5,000. Not a lot, but not exactly peanuts either.

Before going to bed, Dima opened the little top window in the kitchen. A rush of cool evening air darted inside, carrying with it some strange metallic noises.

Dima stood on a stool and looked outside. To the left, just over the fence, he noticed a man squatting down. And then there was a short, suspicious 'clink'!

Dima's eyes gradually grew accustomed to the dark.

'He's sitting by that hole in the fence,' he thought, recognising his neighbour, the owner of the bull terrier.

There was another 'clink' and Dima realised that his neighbour was cutting the pieces of barbed wire that he'd used to seal the hole in the fence.

Dima's fury wasn't strong enough to propel him out into the cold night air, into open conflict with his neighbour. In any case it would have been difficult to predict the outcome of such a conflict – there was every chance that the neighbour's bull terrier might 'step forward' in his defence.

'Whatever,' thought Dima, climbing down from the stool. 'There's plenty more wire out there. I'll fix it again tomorrow.'

52

Lipovka village, Kiev region
Irina soon got the hang of using her first ever mobile phone. After listening attentively to Egor's instructions, she was able to key in

her own PIN code and save Egor's number into the phone's address book. She needed Egor's help to select a ringtone, though. Irina didn't like any of the pre-programmed ones and she asked Egor to find a simple lullaby, so that it wouldn't frighten Yasya if the phone happened to ring while she was holding her. Strangely enough, when he searched through the phone's memory he found a lullaby he hadn't noticed before. Once the phone was set up, they drank tea in the kitchen and then Egor went off to work in the city.

Irina glanced at the clock: 8.30 a.m. She had got up later than usual that morning, but she felt a lot fresher for it.

Yasya drank a little of her milk but then pushed her mother's breast away with her hand and started crying.

'Give her some of that Malysh formula,' suggested Baba Shura. 'She normally drinks it straight away when I give it to her.'

Irina's mother was right, as it turned out. Yasya quickly emptied a 300ml bottle of formula and promptly fell asleep.

Irina's swollen breasts ached, making it impossible for her to think about anything else, so she decided to manually express a little into a jar. Just then a car pulled up outside, and Irina felt the hairs on the back of her neck stand on end. She looked out of the window and saw two men coming through the wicket gate and behind them Nurse Vera, carrying the familiar bag.

When the doorbell rang Irina was still sitting at the kitchen table, completely numb with fear.

It rang again. And again. Then there was a long, continuous ring. Irina worried that Yasya would wake up and start crying. She got up to check on her and bumped into her frightened mother, who was on her way to open the door.

'Don't,' Irina begged her.

Her mother stopped in the hallway and looked at her

daughter. She spread her hands and said, 'We've got no choice.'

The bell stopped ringing, but then a fist began banging on the door.

'Open up!' demanded a deep, gruff male voice.

'Hang on! Hang on!' cried Irina's mother and rushed to the door.

The two men burst into the hallway. One of them turned to Nurse Vera who'd come in behind him and nodded towards the kitchen, and she went in silently. Irina had already run into the kitchen when her mother opened the door.

Nurse Vera's hands were shaking as she took the breast pump out of her bag and laid it on the table. She was trying not to look at Irina, who was crying silently. Irina couldn't even feel the tears – they seemed to be spilling from her eyes of their own accord. Drop after drop ran down her cheeks, either stopping or gathering strength from the next tear, and they fell onto her bare knees or the edge of her short dressing gown.

Once she'd emptied Irina's breasts, Nurse Vera sealed the jar of milk with a rubber lid, placed it in her bag and left. One of the men who had come with her looked into the kitchen.

'You're making things complicated,' he said quietly, with a hint of menace in his voice. 'If you're not at work by seven tomorrow morning, you'll be creating big problems for yourself. You can't hide from us!'

He slammed the kitchen door shut.

When the car left, Irina picked up Egor's present in her shaking hands. She called his number, and all she said was, 'They came back!'

Egor put his phone back into his coat pocket. Irina didn't see the colour drain from his face, the way he looked around him, the cold hatred he wasted on the innocent winter trees of Mariinsky Park and the ordinary passers-by.

Egor had a bad feeling. He tried to shake it off, to literally stamp it out of his system along the paths of the park, but the rage he felt would not leave him. He walked over to the other side of the park. The area behind the Mariinsky Palace was kept under the watchful eye of his colleage and friend Seryoga. He was from Brovary, just outside Kiev, and he and Egor were almost the same age. Egor knew that Seryoga liked hunting.

Seryoga was exactly where Egor had expected to find him – about twenty metres away from the military tents that were set up opposite the Cabinet of Ministers. In 2004, this 'tent city' had been occupied by the drummers of the Orange Revolution; now the flags on either side of the camp were white and pale blue, signalling the shift in political power. There were only four or five 'political tourists' in residence.

Egor and Seryoga greeted each other warmly, like old friends. Egor started a conversation about hunting, and Seryoga recounted a hare-hunting expedition he'd been on just recently. Egor listened to the story very attentively, then asked if he had a gun with a good aim that he could borrow for a day or two. He said that he fancied taking some time off to go hunting too.

53

La Quinta café, Great Zhytomyr Street, Kiev
By midday the winter sky had grown lighter and the sun had come out.

Semyon had already ordered himself an espresso and had a good look round before Volodka came down the steep steps into La Quinta, wearing a black leather jacket and a skiing hat.

'Sorry for hassling you on the phone today,' said Semyon, pulling a guilty face.

'Don't worry about it.' Volodka waved his hand dismissively. Then he looked over at the bar. 'Believe me, if you were the only one hassling me everything would be hunky-dory. At least you're paying me. The others aren't, and they're giving me more hassle than you are.'

'A cappuccino and a double Hennessy,' Semyon said to the barman. And then recalling his last meeting with Volodka he added, with the accompanying gesture, 'For him!'

Volodka grinned.

'So, what did you want to show me?' Semyon asked casually.

'All in good time,' said Volodka, unbuttoning his jacket. He took an envelope out of the inside pocket.

He pulled some photographs out of the envelope and gave one to Semyon. It was a photograph of Alisa looking preoccupied, her gaze directed off to one side.

'I think she's waiting for you,' whispered Volodka.

'When was it taken?'

'Last night. About one in the morning.'

'And what are those?' Semyon nodded at the other photographs his friend was holding.

Unlike the first photo the others had been taken during the day, in normal light. Alisa looked considerably more attractive in these photos. There was one of her standing on the edge of the road with her hand up, flagging down a cab. One of her going into a building. One of her coming out of the building.

'Where was this one taken?' Semyon looked up at Volodka.

Volodka took a sip of his brandy and cast a sidelong glance at the photo Semyon was holding.

'The Ministry of Health,' he answered. 'Your Alisa works there.'

'She's not "my" Alisa,' hissed Semyon.

'Whatever. Do you want me to find out more about her?' asked Volodka, with a sly smile on his face. 'Or not?'

There was a pause, during which Semyon looked at the photographs again. He spent a particularly long time studying the last photo, a close-up of her face. She looked preoccupied, her thin lips tense. There was a barely noticeable scattering of freckles on both sides of her fine, elegant nose.

'So do you want me to or not?' Volodka asked again.

'Do I want you to or not?' Semyon echoed mechanically. 'I guess not. I'm not planning on marrying her. At least not during the day, and the registry offices aren't open at night. What's that you've got there?' Semyon had noticed his friend holding an official form.

'You'll laugh,' said Volodka, with no trace of humour in his voice.

'I won't,' Semyon assured him.

'It's from her personal file at the civil registry office,' said Volodka. 'She lives alone, and she's registered as single. Born in 1973 . . . Here, have a look through it at home. Just make sure you hide it from your wife!'

Semyon said goodbye to Volodka and started walking in the direction of the Lukyanivka district. He wasn't consciously heading for Bekhterevsky Street, but that was where his feet took him.

The Pokrovsky Monastery was at the far end of the alley. A couple of gypsy women were standing to the right of the monastery gates, which were light blue and freshly painted.

Semyon wasn't sure whether or not he wanted to see the doctor again. But his feet had brought him here!

The same angelic girl opened the door.

'Oh, why didn't you call? Come in, come in! Pyotr Isaevich is with a patient at the moment. Would you like some tea?'

Semyon nodded and sat down on the sofa. He closed his eyes.

About fifteen minutes later an attractive young brunette came out of the psychiatrist's office. She was wearing tight jeans and a short fox-fur coat. She squinted at Semyon and stopped by the secretary's desk.

'Innochka, book me in for three o'clock on Friday,' she sang, with another sideways glance at Semyon.

Angelic Inna made a note of the appointment in her exercise book, and the young woman sashayed out.

'What's wrong with her?' Semyon asked Inna.

'Nothing!' replied Inna. 'There's nothing wrong with the people who come here. They just have certain issues. You can go through, the doctor's ready for you.'

'Ah, it's you!' Pyotr Isaevich greeted him with a benevolent smile. 'Take a seat. So, what's on your mind? Tell me all about it.'

'What do you mean?' asked Semyon, surprised.

'Well, try and remember what it was you wanted to talk about when you decided to come and see me. We can start from there.'

Semyon thought about it. There had to be a reason he'd ended up here, in this basement with photographic ocean scenes and palm trees on the walls.

'Right,' said Semyon. He took a deep breath. 'I wanted to ask you . . . Remember I told you about the woman I sometimes meet at night?'

'Yes, of course.'

'Well, I can't stop thinking about her. I want to find her, to see her . . .'

'You know where she lives, don't you?'

'Yes, but you said I should try to avoid seeing her during the day.'

'So I did,' nodded the doctor. 'By the way, how does your wife react to your sleepwalking? Is she even aware of it?'

'She's noticed it a few times and had a go at me about it. But everything's fine between us now.'

'And so it should be. It appears that you have one woman during the day and a different one at night. I would advise you to start making a clearer distinction between your diurnal and nocturnal activities . . . There's really no need for you to meet your nocturnal acquaintances during the day.'

'There's something else I wanted to ask.' Semyon looked earnestly at the doctor, like a diligent pupil. 'Is it possible to find out how long I've known this woman?'

'Sleepwalkers don't keep diaries.' Pyotr Isaevich spread his hands. 'You might have known her for as long as a year, or maybe only a month.'

Semyon frowned.

'Is there no way for me to control myself at night?'

The doctor gave Semyon a strange look. 'I hold a night clinic on Wednesdays,' he said. 'If you come and see me while you're actually sleepwalking, then I can help you a lot more. But don't worry. I can write you a certificate in the meantime to put your mind at rest, attesting to the fact that you genuinely suffer from somnabulism and cannot be held responsible for any actions you may take at night!'

'Is that true?'

'Officially, yes. From a legal point of view you are ill at night and perfectly healthy during the day. It might be a good idea to keep this document with you at all times, in your wallet or your passport. You never know when you might need it. What if you get arrested one night? You can attach my business card to it too. Anything could happen!'

Semyon agreed. The psychiatrist took a form out of his desk drawer, filled it in and formalised it with a bold, violet stamp.

The sun was shining, and Semyon could feel its warmth on the skin of his cheek. He stopped on the corner of Observatorna Street and read the document he'd been given carefully one more time, then folded it and put it in his wallet. Then he took the photograph of Alisa and slipped it inside the folded document.

'I can no longer be held responsible for my actions,' whispered Semyon, and a thoughtful smile began to play across his lips.

54

9 May Street, Boryspil

Scruffy was walking round the house in a state of some excitement. He could obviously sense the coming spring. He rubbed himself against his master's legs, but then ran his fluffy tail across his mistress's legs too.

'Wait a minute,' Valya told him. 'I'm just going to get myself ready, and then I'll give you something.'

Soon afterwards, Valya left for work. Dima opened the little top window and watched a droplet of water fall from the tip of an icicle, catching the sun.

'The thaw has begun,' he thought happily.

Just then he heard the unpleasant snarling of a dog in the front yard. Pressing his cheek to the cold glass, he saw King, the neighbour's bull terrier. The dog had obviously only just done his business and was now pacing around the young apple tree, which was still wrapped in the cloths that had been used to protect the lower part of its trunk the previous autumn, in case of severe frost.

'You little bastard!' exclaimed Dima.

He remembered the clinking of the wire-cutters the night before. He quickly pulled on his tracksuit bottoms and jacket and ran into the hall. He stuck his bare feet into his boots and hurriedly did the buckles up, then grabbed a wooden mop from the boiler room and charged out of the front door.

'Go on, bugger off!' he shouted as he ran towards the bull terrier. 'Get back to your own yard!'

The bull terrier didn't scare easily. He crouched down and sprang at Dima. The first blow with the mop hit the dog square in the chest, but King turned out to be heavier and more dangerous than Dima had realised and the blow from the mop just knocked him sideways onto the snow, where he crouched down ready to spring again.

Then a strange thing happened. Something hit the window ledge with a thud. Dima spun round and saw Scruffy running across the snow towards him. King froze for a second. He looked from Dima to the cat, as though trying to decide which of them he hated more. Then he looked back at Dima and headed towards him, his jaws open wide. Scruffy responded with a loud hiss. Dima could scarcely believe what happened next: Scruffy launched himself at the dog, sank his teeth and claws into the scruff of his neck and hung there like a furry collar.

King shook his head, fell onto his side and started squirming.

He was snapping his jaws, trying to bite Scruffy's paw or his tail, but the cat managed to stay out of reach without loosening his grip until the bull terrier rolled onto his back. Then Scruffy jumped off. King leapt at him, but instead of running away and jumping up a tree, Scruffy threw himself at the dog again. He swiped at King in mid-air like a boxer, with the claws of his right paw drawn, and Dima saw three bloody stripes appear on the bull terrier's short-haired pelt. King started growling more ferociously, but Scruffy had managed to jump to the side and now stood about two metres away from his canine adversary.

The bull terrier's small, round eyes filled with blood. Dima was panicking. He tightened his grip on the handle of the mop in case King jumped at him, but the dog lunged at the cat again.

Scruffy launched himself high into the air and landed on King's back, sinking his sharp teeth into the dog's fat neck. King turned round and round in circles, trying to shake the cat off. He fell onto his side and rolled on his back in the snow, but the cat opened his little jaws briefly only to clamp them shut again, this time on the dog's throat. The bull terrier rolled over onto his stomach, pressing the cat's head into the snow with his chest, but still Scruffy did not release his grip. The snow around the cat's head turned red and Dima stared at it, trying to work out which animal the blood was coming from.

Dima knew that Scruffy's number was up. He would not be coming back to life again this time. As this realisation sank in, Dima brought the wooden mop down on King's head so hard that the force of the blow caused the lower part of the mop to fly off to one side. King immediately went limp, dropping his bloody jaw onto the snow. Scruffy's head, also covered in blood, was just visible beneath it.

Dima used the mop handle to push King's lifeless body off Scruffy, rolling him onto his side on the blood-covered snow; Scruffy was still wrapped round his neck, gripping tightly with his sharp little teeth. His grey fur was covered in blood. Dima tried to separate the animals with his hands and eventually managed it on the third attempt, although Scruffy came away with a piece of the dog's flesh hanging from his teeth.

'He can't be dead,' whispered Dima.

He was suddenly filled with remorse for the cat, who had already died once before. And this time he hadn't just died – he had lost his life heroically, defending his master. Dima's eyes filled with tears. He wished he had a glass of vodka to raise in silent, mournful homage.

Just then Scruffy's paw twitched.

'He's alive!' exclaimed Dima, joyfully.

He picked Scruffy up and carried him into the house. The cat weighed next to nothing, and his fur was wet and sticky from the snow and the blood. Dima took him into the bathroom and placed him in an enamel basin.

Dima washed the blood and snow off his hands, and then used a wet towel to wash Scruffy. He applied some antiseptic to the cat's wounds and scratches, wrapped him in a dry towel and placed him on the floor. Then he went into the kitchen and looked out of the window. King was exactly where he'd left him, lying on his side in the red snow.

'What if he's still alive too?' Dima panicked. He knew that such dogs bear grudges and attack their enemies in silence.

He went out into the yard, squatted down and tilted the dog's head to one side. He looked, and he listened. The bull terrier was definitely dead. Dima sighed with relief. He glanced at his neighbour's house – he obviously wasn't in, or he would have come running out into the yard when he heard the fight.

Dima looked again at the dead dog.

He fetched a shovel from the shed, stuck it into the red snow and spent a few moments formulating his plan of action: he would stuff the dead King in an empty potato sack and drag him to the abandoned yard, where he would throw him in the well – the same one he'd thrown Scruffy in. Then he would remove the snow from the site of the scuffle to avoid arousing the suspicions of his neighbour, who would soon notice that his dog was missing.

It took Dima a couple of minutes to stuff the bull terrier into the sack, which smelled of damp and potatoes. Then he dragged the sack to the wicket gate. At the gate he turned round and saw that the sack had carved a bloody, red trail in the snow.

Tutting, Dima hoisted the sack onto his shoulders and carried it over to the garage. He looked all around. The street was deserted. Dima hid the sack in the boot of his car. He had already realised that the sack was too heavy to carry on his shoulders to the abandoned courtyard. In any case, someone carrying a heavy sack down the street was bound to arouse curiosity, even if the sack wasn't dripping blood.

When Dima got back to his front yard he tried to cover up the blood with fresh snow, but it was no use – the blood showed through immediately. Dima thought about it for a little while then cleared the snow from that part of the yard. The black rectangle of earth looked strange, of course, but it was nobody else's business – it was his front yard, and he could do what he liked in it.

Standing there contemplating the stark-looking patch of bare earth, Dima came to the conclusion that the neighbour was bound to notice it.

He picked up the shovel again and cleared the rest of the yard.

He went back into the house and looked in the bathroom. The cat was lying exactly where he'd left him in the enamel basin on the floor, covered in green antiseptic ointment and wrapped up in the fluffy towel like a baby.

When twilight fell, Dima drove the sack containing the dog's body to the abandoned yard and pushed it into the well.

When he got home he carried Scruffy into the garage, where he switched on the heater and set up a bed of old jumpers for him nearby.

Remembering how the cat had lapped up the contents of the ampoules, he got one out and tipped the liquid onto the dirty plate. Then he left the garage, closing the doors carefully behind him so that they didn't make a noise.

55

Lipovka village, Kiev region

When Irina got out of bed in the morning, the only sound was the creaking of the bed frame beneath the mattress. She went barefoot into the kitchen, put the kettle on the hob and looked out of the window. It was still dark out there, but probably not quite as cold any more. The winter was nearly over. It was getting light earlier these days – not long until spring, and then Yasya would be able to bask in the warm sun in her pushchair! And if she brought some sand back from the river and sifted it, to get rid of the fragments of broken beer bottles, then she could even make a little sandpit for her. Right here on the doorstep. Irina let her mind wander, lost in her daydreams.

Just then the door to the kitchen opened and her mother looked in.

'Are you off to Kiev?' she asked.

Irina shook her head.

'They'll only come for you again,' warned her mother. 'They'll take your milk, and they won't pay you for it. They didn't pay you for it yesterday.'

Irina considered this. It was true, they hadn't paid her, but she hadn't even thought about it. She'd been too frightened.

'Your Egor won't be able to stop them, you'll see,' her mother said sadly.

'Yes, he will,' said Irina, stubbornly.

Her mother shrugged and quietly closed the kitchen door behind her.

Egor called her mobile at about 8 a.m.

'Call me as soon as the car turns up,' he said.

Irina knew they would come, and she no longer felt afraid. She washed in cold water, brushed her hair and put on warm tights and a dress that she could undo easily at the top. Then she sat down to wait.

The car pulled up at around 9.30 a.m. Irina called Egor immediately. 'Right,' he said. 'Call me again as soon as they leave.'

Irina opened the door herself, and the same two men as before came in silently. Their faces looked cold, either due to the temperature outside or because they had no soul. Nurse Vera took her bag straight into the kitchen and Irina followed, closing the door behind her.

Everything was the same as before, only this time Irina had more milk.

Irina stood by the door sadly, watching the car leave. She called Egor straight away and then went back to Yasya. Her breasts were empty. Yasya was already awake, her beady little eyes roaming over the white ceiling.

Meanwhile Egor hid behind the dirty snow-covered embankment at the edge of the highway, holding an automatic rifle. His eye had already grown accustomed to the rangefinder. He had been practising, focusing on the drivers and passengers of other cars.

He had chosen a comfortable spot with a wide field of vision. All the Kiev-bound cars came down a long, gently sloping stretch of road so it would be possible to pick out the one he was waiting for from some way off. Besides, there wasn't much traffic at that time of the morning.

Egor looked at his watch. He worked out again how long it should take them to get this far. According to his calculations it was already time for him to be on the alert. He positioned himself slightly to the left, so that he had a clear view of the slope of the highway, then began to watch the cars through the rangefinder, scrutinising the unknown faces of their passengers. He wouldn't recognise any of the people in the car he was waiting for either, but he would definitely recognise the car itself, not least because it had a personalised number plate. Number plates like that cost a small fortune. Well, they'd certainly be paying for it now!

After about seven minutes he spotted the dark blue BMW with three sixes on its number plate. It was tearing along at top speed, but the minibus taxi from Zhytomyr in the left-hand lane was apparently oblivious to the agitated flashing of headlights coming up behind it.

Egor put his finger on the trigger. He looked through the range-finder at the driver, then at his passenger. He noticed the old woman, too, on the back seat. Irina had told him about her. Something was stopping him pulling the trigger. Who were these people? They'd been sent to do a job, and they'd just carried out their orders. It didn't mean they weren't guilty . . . but how could he single out just one of them? Egor hesitated, and immediately grew annoyed with himself for being so indecisive. Suddenly he noticed the minibus taxi from Zhytomyr pulling over into the right-hand lane to make way for the BMW. Worried that he'd miss them altogether, Egor quickly aimed at the car, located the front right-hand wheel in the rangefinder and fired. Still looking through the rangefinder, he saw the wheel explode. Then he put the rifle down and watched what happened next: the car veered to the right, hit the minibus taxi and spun off the highway onto the side of the road. It rolled over several times before colliding with one of the metal posts of an enormous advertising board and coming to a standstill, wrapped around the metal post like a horseshoe. Smoke was coming from the bonnet, which had been crumpled and forced open by the impact.

Egor lay on the snow without moving, looking at the wreck of the car. He was going to call the emergency services just to be on the safe side, but he noticed a lorry stop nearby, followed by a Zhiguli. The drivers of both vehicles ran to the scene of the accident.

One tugged at the doors on the driver's side, but they were jammed shut. The doors on the passenger side wouldn't open either. The voluntary rescuer eventually managed to open one of the back doors, and the old woman fell out onto the snow. Her face was covered in blood but she was still alive – you could see her breath in the cold air. She was clutching a torn shopping bag, which was leaking milk onto the snow. Blood dripped after it.

Egor didn't see any of this. He was already walking back through the woods to the country road where he'd left his Mazda.

56

Apartment No. 10, Reitarska Street, Kiev

If the phone hadn't rung, waking her up, Veronika would have slept until lunchtime. When she went into the kitchen she found a note from Semyon on the table: '*Back later, GI called – urgent, love S x*'.

There was nothing unusual about this, but on the way to the kitchen she'd noticed her husband's winter boots next to the front door – they were covered in mud, and his tracksuit bottoms were in a large bowl underneath the bathroom sink, soaking wet and also covered in mud. If Darya Ivanovna hadn't called Veronika would have given more thought to what she had seen, but after a five-minute conversation with her friend she was thinking about something else entirely: the pharmacist's widow had asked her to go shopping. This suggestion was very timely – the sun was getting warmer and warmer every day and you could hear the dripping of the icicles as they melted, heralding the impending arrival of spring. Veronika hardly had any tights left without holes in, and her wardrobe was in dire need of a general overhaul. After all, spring was like a new start and it was only right to greet it in a new outfit!

Striding confidently along Striletska Street, Veronika suddenly remembered her husband's dirty boots and clothes. Where on earth had he managed to find so much mud in the middle of winter?

Veronika recalled that they had gone to bed at the same time. She recalled not particularly wanting to respond to his amorous advances, but knowing what Semyon was like she had given in straight away to avoid provoking him. Everything had then followed the same old and oft-repeated formula: he had started kissing her face and roughly caressing her breasts, trying to act like a considerate lover, although he was ultimately incapable of focusing on anything but his own satisfaction. His hundred-metre sprint, as Veronika called it. It hadn't taken him long to reach the finishing line, and then he had buried his nose in the pillow and fallen asleep, his right arm still around her shoulders.

Then what? Veronika had fallen asleep too, after removing her husband's heavy arm. She couldn't remember anything beyond that.

'Maybe he went out, fell over somewhere, came back, got changed and fell asleep again?' she thought.

'Nikochka!' called her friend. 'I thought you'd be late! Come on, they've got a sale on in Vidivan!'

'But that's a men's shop!' exclaimed Veronika. Darya Ivanovna's outfit was less stylish than last time, but suitably warm: dark blue trousers, boots and a long dark blue cashmere coat.

'I know. Let's get the easy stuff out of the way first. I need three pairs of socks and a couple of shirts for Edik. You can buy something for your husband too . . . if he deserves it, that is!'

They took a half-empty minibus down to Independence Square.

It was fairly quiet in Vidivan, despite the eye-catching signs in the windows advertising the sale.

Darya Ivanovna headed straight for the shirts.

'Can I help you at all?' enquired an impeccably dressed young man wearing eye make-up. Veronika thought he might be wearing lipstick too.

'If you like,' answered the pharmacist's widow. 'I need a couple of shirts, large, for a man with neither taste nor pretensions.'

'Are you looking to spend a little more or a little less?' asked the well-groomed sales assistant.

'Why would anyone spend a little more on a man like that? Mind you, it is his birthday soon . . . I think I'll go for one more expensive one and two less so.'

The young man ushered Darya Ivanovna over to a display unit stacked full of shirts in clear cellophane packaging. Veronika stayed by the other display, which was obviously where the less expensive shirts were to be found.

'Maybe I should get one for Senya,' she thought.

She remembered how he'd refused to let her iron his new shirt before they went to the operetta. He'd just taken it out of its packaging and put it straight on.

A green long-sleeved shirt caught Veronika's eye, so she picked it up and looked at the price. It was ninety-nine hryvnas, which struck her as being rather a lot.

'Do you need any help?' asked a sugary-sweet voice behind her.

She turned round. A young man in a suit stood leaning slightly towards her, like an obliging waiter.

'Could you tell me where the sale shirts are?' asked Veronika.

'On the first floor,' the young man replied.

Veronika glanced at Darya Ivanovna and the sales assistant obligingly showing her shirts and knew that she had at least twenty minutes. She went up to the first floor and chose three shirts for Senya all by herself: a bright red one, a dark green one and a smart black one. All three together came to ninety-nine hryvnas.

She went back downstairs carrying her purchases in a Vidivan bag. Darya Ivanovna was at the till, counting out banknotes.

'I got two gorgeous shirts,' she boasted. 'And you should see the socks I bought – a hundred per cent cotton!'

'Why are you buying clothes for him?' Veronika asked her friend, once they were back outside on Khreshchatyk Street.

'What do you mean?' Darya Ivanovna asked in surprise. 'His shirt collars still get grubby, and his armpits smell. It's probably just the dust or something . . . I have to wash his socks too. It's the same as when he was alive! The human body is animal, not mineral – alive or dead, it still has to breathe! It reacts to the weather, the atmospheric pressure and so on. What did you buy for your husband?'

'Why don't we go and sit in a café somewhere? Then I can show you,' suggested Veronika.

'If we go to a café we won't have time to get anything for ourselves! Let's go to TsUM first, then we can go to a café.'

Veronika agreed and they walked along Khreshchatyk Street, past the town hall, towards Kiev's main department store. It seemed like only yesterday that the shop windows had been full of glittering Christmas decorations.

57

City centre, Kiev

Gennady Ilyich had been in a wonderful mood all morning, which was probably why he noticed the miserable look on Semyon's face when they met near the monument in Mariinsky Park.

'What's up with you?' the deputy asked his assistant.

'A few problems at home,' Semyon lied, trying to adopt a more nonchalant expression.

'Money troubles?' Gennady Ilyich enquired sympathetically. 'Why don't you let me help you out?'

Semyon shrugged. It would be stupid to refuse the offer of money under any circumstances. Moaning about not having enough money was a bit embarrassing, but it was better than trying to explain to his boss that he'd come home the previous night soaking wet and covered in mud, even though the temperature was still below zero at night and there wasn't a single puddle or patch of mud to be found anywhere in the city.

'Well, I had to spend the night in a hotel.' Gennady Ilyich waved his hand in the direction of the Kiev hotel. 'We were in Parliament until three in the morning, thrashing out a new law that even future deputies will thank us for! From now on, when deputies are issued with their ID they'll also get a special gold crucifix on a chain, to wear under their clothes. Quite a big one, too. Now Ukraine will be closer to God . . .'

Semyon listened attentively, nodding. Hearing that Gennady Ilyich had spent half the night in Parliament somehow put his own problems into perspective.

'Where's your car?' asked Gennady Ilyich, switching to a more businesslike tone.

Semyon looked at his watch. 'It'll be here in fifteen minutes,' he said.

'Good. You'll be escorting a delivery lorry today, to that orphanage outside Vyshhorod. A crane truck will be there by twelve to unload. I want you to make sure that they unload and install everything carefully.'

'What's in the lorry?' asked Semyon.

'A second-hand cheese-making machine, for the production of goat's cheese,' said the deputy. 'Just be sure to tell the director of that orphanage that it's not a gift, it's an investment: they'll be giving half of their output to me! Oh, and you'll need to call in and pick up the milk churns from Hrushevsky Street first. The same place as last time.'

Semyon nodded.

'The lorry with the cheese-making machine will be waiting on Shevchenko Square, near the bus station. It's a Kamaz with a dark blue canopy.' The deputy glanced at his watch. 'Right, then. Time for me to go and serve the people!'

He nodded goodbye and set off towards Parliament. Halfway to the door he turned round and called out, 'And tell them not to use the cheese-making machine until the priest has sanctified it!'

Semyon came out of the park onto the road and saw Volodka's Niva straight away. It was standing in front of the main entrance to the building where they had to pick up the milk churns.

'I don't suppose you were watching me last night, were you?' asked Semyon, as they shook hands.

'Nope.'

'Shame,' sighed Semyon. 'Because I came home covered in mud, and I've got no idea where . . . Ah, never mind, let's go!' he said, with a nod at the front door.

Three heavy milk churns migrated from the corridor of the milk kitchen into the boot of the Niva. A sour smell immediately filled the car.

'We're a couple of jolly milkmen, you and me!' said Volodka, as he started the engine.

'Speak for yourself. I'm not feeling too "jolly" at the moment,' said Semyon.

The Niva drove carefully onto the main road and turned left, heading towards European Square.

Semyon saw the Kamaz with the dark blue canopy straight away. They pulled up in front of it and sounded the horn, and then both vehicles started driving along the Vyshhorod Highway towards the Kiev Sea.

It was already dark when Semyon got home, tired and still unhappy, though now for a different reason. He, Volodka and the driver of the Kamaz had waited for over two hours for the crane truck to show up, and they hadn't finished unloading the cheese-making machine until nearly 5 p.m. One of the workshops had been prepared in advance for the new arrival: the workbenches and tools had been removed and stood outside on the snow. The crane lifted the cheese-making machine, the base of which was clad in a sturdy wooden crate, and a crowd of excited teenagers applied themselves enthusiastically to the task of installing it in its new home . . . but their efforts were in vain. Even with the double doors open as far as they would go the crate simply would not fit through the doorway. They disassembled part of the wooden crate and eventually manoeuvred the machine in through the doorway of the workshop, where it got stuck. Semyon, Volodka and the driver of the Kamaz had no choice but to help the boys from the orphanage finish the job. Once the cheese-making machine was finally inside and was being moved into position, Semyon paused for breath and passed Gennady Ilyich's message on to the director of the orphanage.

'Investment?' he cried. 'What kind of bullshit is that? I suppose he wants me to send him detailed accounts of our cheese production too!'

'You'd better discuss that with him,' said Semyon. 'I'm just the messenger. You need to take the milk out of the Niva too.'

The director didn't even acknowledge their departure. He just went into the orphanage and slammed the door behind him, although he did send some of the older boys out to collect the milk churns. It took four boys to carry each of the full churns, two on either side. They brought the empty churns straight back.

'Do you want anything to eat?' Veronika came into the bathroom just as Semyon was splashing his face with cold water, trying to wake himself up.

'I suppose so,' he answered gloomily and followed her into the kitchen.

'What's the matter?' Veronika asked tenderly, as she put a plate of buckwheat and meatballs in tomato sauce on the table in front of Semyon. Then she sat down opposite her husband, without taking her eyes off him.

'You don't want to know! Where's that from?' Semyon was looking at her new pale pink cardigan.

Veronika didn't answer. She just smiled.

'I washed your tracksuit bottoms, and your boots. They're drying on the radiator,' she said.

Semyon tensed up. The piece of meatball on his fork almost missed his mouth entirely.

'Thank you,' he said warily.

'Did you fall over somewhere?' Veronika asked solicitously.

Her husband nodded. He had been expecting this interrogation, but he hadn't imagined that it would take place in such an amicable atmosphere.

'I went down into the basement,' he lied, coming up with a relatively plausible explanation. 'When I went out this morning I noticed steam coming from the basement, so I went down to have a look. I thought a pipe might have burst or something. But I slipped over, so I had to get changed.'

'And was there a burst pipe?'

'No, it was just damp. The pipe was dripping, there was mud everywhere . . .'

'I went shopping with Darya Ivanovna today. I bought you some new shirts,' Veronika began but suddenly stopped, worried that she might say too much. She considered any mention of the deceased pharmacist's presence in his widow's apartment 'too much'. 'I've already ironed them.'

'Oh, right. Did you take the pins out of them too? Last time one of them pricked me when we were in the theatre!'

'Well, that was your fault for just taking it out of the packet and putting it straight on! I don't know anybody else who does that. Do you fancy going somewhere tomorrow?'

'Tomorrow?' Semyon thought about it. 'OK, why not. I just have to go and pick up my wages in the morning.'

After dinner Veronika went into the living room to watch television, and Semyon stayed in the kitchen. During his supper he'd felt happy with himself for the first time that day. Or rather, he'd been happy with his fabricated account of his morning foray into the basement. But as soon as his wife left the kitchen Semyon felt a vague sense of unease, because he'd suddenly realised that as far as he knew his 'fabricated' story might well have been absolutely true.

'I've got to go down there,' he decided.

It was dark outside. It would be dark in the basement too, as always, and he didn't have a torch. Going down there without a torch would be a complete waste of time.

He stuck his head around the living-room door.

'I'm just popping out for a bit. I won't be long,' he said to Veronika.

He went out onto the landing and rang the doorbell opposite.

His neighbour Igor opened the door just a fraction, as though he were worried it might be a burglar, or uninvited guests.

'Good evening,' Semyon greeted him very politely. 'Do you have a torch I could borrow, by any chance?'

'Yes,' said Igor, slightly puzzled. 'Have you had a power cut?'

'No, I just need it for something. I'll bring it back tomorrow.'

Igor gave Semyon a large torch and closed the door straight away, without even saying goodbye.

Semyon put on his old boots and an anorak over his jumper and went downstairs. Access to the basement was through a little door inside the next entrance along. It wasn't locked. Semyon switched on the torch and stepped into the dank world of underground utilities. He took three steps then squatted down and shone the torch around: pipes, valves, rubbish . . . The torchlight flashed over the floor just in front of him and Semyon noticed a set of heavy footprints. They looked familiar. He peered at them more closely and realised that that they had, in fact, been made by his own winter boots. This discovery made Semyon feel neither happy nor relieved. He stood up and followed his own footsteps further into the basement, using the torch to light his way. He walked through puddles and patches of mud, round the concrete partitions that divided the basement into sections, and finally came to a dead end. The footsteps led him to another corner, where he stopped in front of a tangle of pipes that were giving off heat. He squatted down, stuck his hand in underneath the pipes and shone the torchlight around. He inspected every crack and crevice picked out by the artificial yellow light. Nothing out of the ordinary. He shifted to the right and shone the torch under the pipe again. This time there was a rustling sound and his hand brushed against something made of paper, or maybe plastic. He put his left hand under the pipe and pulled out a parcel. The rustling sounded too loud in the damp, dark silence. He froze for a moment, listening tensely to the sounds coming from the surrounding darkness. He could hear water dripping and a kind of hissing noise but none of it seemed out of place – these were standard basement noises.

The light from the torch slipped inside the parcel and Semyon's hand slipped in after it. He pulled out a little booklet with a cardboard cover, about the size of a passport. There was an inscription embossed in silver on the front cover: Church of the Embassy of the Moon. Semyon opened it. There was a photograph of him on the right-hand page, with his own signature beneath it. He looked at the left-hand page.

'Brother Seramion, baptised into the Church of the Embassy of the Moon on the 23rd day of November 2006, commits himself to all secrets of the Church and vows to keep them from all who know him. Anyone breaking this vow of silence will be condemned to death by drowning, as a sign of their expulsion from the Church of the Embassy of the Moon.'

Semyon closed the little booklet and noticed that it was shaking in his hand. Then he opened it again and shone the torch on his photograph. He was wearing a black jumper and looking away from the camera, his lips involuntarily parted.

Semyon put his hand inside the parcel again and pulled out a rosary with green stone beads. He was shocked by how familiar and comfortable this rosary felt in his hand, by the way his thumb and index finger instantly took hold of one of the beads. He released the rosary immediately and it fell back into the parcel. He put the membership document back in as well and replaced the parcel under the pipe where he had found it.

He retraced his steps out of the basement.

Outside on the narrow pavement the cars were parked up close to one another for the night. A single star shone above Striletska Street.

Semyon took his mobile out of his trouser pocket and called Volodka.

'Hey, milkman,' he said.

'You sound weird. What's up?' asked his friend. 'Have you got a cold?'

Semyon told him that he hadn't, but he could hear by his own voice why his friend had asked. 'Are you free tonight?' he continued. 'I've got a bad feeling . . .'

'All right. Just try to stay up till at least midnight, or I might miss you!'

Semyon looked at his watch. 'OK,' he promised his friend. 'See you later.'

'Have a good night,' replied Volodka, tongue firmly in cheek.

58

9 May Street, Boryspil

Dima couldn't sleep that night. He was warm and comfortable with Valya lying beside him, but some inner anxiety kept turning him from side to side and wouldn't let him close his eyes. Valya had already woken up a couple of times and sleepily asked what the matter was.

Eventually Dima got up, trying not to make any noise. He put his tracksuit and slippers on in the dark and went out onto the doorstep.

A half-moon shone brightly in the sky, and the stars twinkled with a cold, distant light. An aeroplane rumbled overhead. The area where the snow had been cleared three days earlier was still a stark black rectangle. It was bordered on one side by the fence with the hole that had not yet been fixed, beyond which his neighbour's front yard was still and quiet. There wasn't a single light on in his house either.

Dima decided that there was no rush to fix the hole. The bull terrier was out of the picture, which meant the hole was no longer in use, and in any case it would have aroused his neighbour's suspicions.

He already suspected something, of course. Earlier that evening, after Dima had thrown King down the well in the abandoned court-yard, his neighbour had asked, 'You haven't seen my dog, have you?'

Dima had been tempted to reply with a few choice words, but he'd managed to bite his tongue. Some dogs were just better than others. His Shamil had been so smart! He'd answered his neighbour with a brief 'No' and then, as though he shared his concern, he'd added, 'He's probably out looking for a mate. It's nearly March – they're all at it! The same thing happened with our cat. We spent weeks looking for him, and then he just turned up out of the blue.'

'Do you think I should put a notice up?' asked his neighbour.

'Maybe, but you should probably include a photo of him. And don't forget to offer a reward!'

'How much do you think I should offer?'

'Whatever you think your dog's worth.'

His neighbour then asked why Dima had cleared and dug over part of his yard.

'I was drunk,' said Dima, making it up as he went along. 'I'd had a row with the wife, so I did it just to get back at her.'

His neighbour shook his head and tutted disapprovingly, but Dima couldn't have cared less.

The bare patch of earth in the yard reminded him of Scruffy, who was currently languishing in his heated sick bay in the garage. Dima took the garage key from the nail in the hall and went to pay him a visit.

It was cold inside the garage and Dima shivered as he entered, but thanks to the glowing spiral heater the air in the far right-hand corner of the garage was pleasantly warm, and there was a comforting, familiar smell of petrol and engine oil.

Scruffy lifted his muzzle as Dima approached and looked at his master, narrowing his eyes.

'Hey, it's OK, lie down,' Dima said gently, squatting down and stroking Scruffy. He was happy to see that he was no longer bleeding. Valya had got hold of some ointments and lotions from an old woman she knew and had used them to treat his wounds again yesterday. She'd said that everything seemed to be healing up surprisingly quickly.

'Now then, do you want some drugs?' smiled Dima.

Dima looked into Scruffy's eyes and felt a kind of bond between them. If the cat were a person he might even have said they were kindred spirits. But he wasn't, so Dima didn't know what to say. He didn't have to say anything, though, he just felt it.

He stroked the cat again, carefully avoiding his wounds. Then he took out an ampoule and flicked the thin top off. He tipped the contents out onto the dirty plate that Scruffy had already licked with enthusiasm several times before.

This time was no different. The cat immediately leaned forwards and licked the plate clean, lapping up the liquid and managing at the same time to remove the dried-out remains of a former meal that were stuck to the china.

Dima calmed down in the garage. He felt his anxiety evaporate.

He went home and got back under the warm blanket.

He was woken by a loud knocking at the window. Opening his eyes he realised that the morning was already almost over and that Valya had left for work long ago.

A militiaman – the one who'd bought the ampoules from him – was waving at him through the window.

As he got dressed, Dima worked out how many ampoules he still had hidden in the garage. He assumed that the militiaman had come for more. But when he let him into the house Dima noticed that he was pale with fright. The militiaman didn't even greet him, he just said, 'I need to talk to you, urgently!'

Dima sat him down at the kitchen table.

'The thing is,' his visitor began nervously, 'I need to speak to your contact, the one in the militia. The one selling the ampoules . . .'

It took Dima a while to realise who the militiaman was talking about.

'You see,' said the militiaman, 'my brother, the one I bought the medicine for . . . well, basically he died.'

'Of cancer,' nodded Dima sympathetically.

The militiaman shook his head.

'No. He jumped on three armed thugs, just like that! They were dragging the wife of a businessman into a jeep, and she was shouting for help. Everyone was just walking by, like people do, but he ran over to help her. And they killed him!'

'So, I guess he won't be needing any more medicine, then,' sighed Dima, disappointed.

'No, he won't,' whispered the militiaman, then he started speaking in a normal voice again. 'But I really need to see your contact!'

'I can't just hand over his details like that, you know.' Dima grew nervous. 'I need to call him first and explain who wants to see him, and why –'

'Well, in that case I hope you don't mind –' the militiaman's voice dropped to a whisper again – 'but I'll have to hand you over to them, and they'll soon shake it out of you.'

'Who are "they"? What are you talking about?' Dima was starting to panic.

'Special investigators, from other agencies,' said his guest. 'They're studying cases of "civilian bravery" all over the country at the moment. They searched my brother after he died and found the ampoules, and apparently they contained exactly what they were looking for. So they came to my house and interrogated my wife, trying to find out where I'd got them from. They said the ampoules were stolen from a secret laboratory and that the scientist who'd developed this medicine had been murdered. They told my wife that it makes people go mad – their sense of justice is sharpened and they're not afraid of anything . . . My brother used to be such a coward. He would never normally have dreamed of trying to rescue somebody! So it must be true.'

'Are they going to arrest the person selling the ampoules?' Dima asked his guest fearfully.

'They just want to talk to him,' said the militiaman, staring intently at his host.

'Have they already spoken to Borya, the baggage handler?'

'Borya's dead. So he's unlikely to be helping them with their inquiries.'

This news came as such a shock to Dima that he started coughing and doubled over, wheezing so badly that the militiaman jumped up from the table and slapped him on the back as hard as he could, assuming that his host was choking on something.

When Dima's coughing fit was over he looked up at the militiaman.

'I'm scared,' he wheezed.

'Me too,' said the militiaman. 'I've got a wife and an eighteen-month-old daughter to worry about! Where did you get the ampoules?'

Dima didn't answer.

'All right, have it your way then.' The militiaman stood up. 'They're coming to my place this evening, and I'll be sending them straight round here.'

For a long time after the militiaman left Dima sat at the kitchen table without moving, like a statue, with his elbows resting on the tabletop and his face buried in his hands.

Then he locked the house and went into the garage. He sat down in the heated sick bay next to Scruffy and immediately started to feel a bit better.

This was his fortress. Every man needs his own secret hideaway, a cellar or a garage, where he can be alone with his problems or hang out with his friends without worrying about getting under his wife's feet. A garage, of course, was better than a cellar. A garage was not only a fortress – it was an explanation, a convincing alibi and exclusively male territory. It also represented the possibility of escape.

Dima looked over at his BMW and thought about getting away from it all. He imagined himself and Valya grabbing their most essential possessions in the middle of the night and driving away from Boryspil. But where would they go? To her relatives in Belarus? To his uncle in Transnistria?

He was so preoccupied with the idea of escaping that he didn't notice Scruffy crawling up to him and rubbing himself against his legs. Dima glanced down at the cat. He was barely able to stand, and Dima gently carried him back to his bedding.

'Some things are even scarier than bull terriers,' he said, looking into the cat's eyes.

Then he took out his glass and the bottle of home-made nettle vodka. He poured himself a shot and looked at Scruffy again.

'I know,' breathed Dima. 'Drinking alone is a bad habit.'

He got out an ampoule, flicked the top off and poured the liquid onto the plate.

'Cheers!' he said to the cat, raising his glass.

After downing his shot he looked around for something to chase it with, even though he knew that there was nothing to eat in the garage.

'I'm scared,' he whispered, looking at Scruffy. 'I'm scared.'

His gaze fell on the empty ampoule. Dima cleared his throat, picked it up and sniffed it. The sweetish smell of valerian hit his nostrils.

Dima looked over at the shelf with all his tools on. He took another ampoule out of the toolbox. He flicked the glass top off and poured the contents into his glass. Then, as though it were a shot of vodka, he exhaled sharply and knocked it back.

59

Mariinsky Park, Kiev

'Number Five! Check the viewing area!' the familiar voice of his colleague crackled in Egor's earpiece. 'That pregnant woman's heading over there again!'

'On my way,' answered Egor.

He looked around. It was nearly 11 a.m. The sun was shining weakly, and the melting snow squelched underfoot. His head was throbbing. He must have caught a cold the day before, when he was lying on the snow with the rifle . . . It was either that or lack of sleep.

He walked past the monument, peering intently down the paths leading to the viewing area. An elderly couple were walking towards him with a pug dog on a lead. The dog was wearing a bright red quilted outfit, which was presumably so that they could see it from a distance and also to stop it freezing to death.

Egor quickened his pace, but when he reached the viewing area he couldn't see anyone there. Just to be sure he leaned over the side and looked down.

'Number Four!' said Egor. 'There's no one in the viewing area.'

'Roger that. But keep an eye out anyway,' answered Seryoga.

On his way back towards Parliament Egor spotted the woman his friend had told him about. A young pregnant woman, wearing a dark-coloured coat and a man's fur hat over her curly hair, was walking over to a bench on the path closest to the road.

'She's going to sit down,' thought Egor. 'Then she'll take her mittens off and start biting her nails.'

She did sit down on the bench, but she didn't take her mittens off. She looked all around and her eyes came to rest on the Parliament building.

'She's not quite right in the head,' thought Egor. Then he realised that his own head didn't feel quite right either. What had been mild discomfort was now a full-blown, splitting headache.

Egor looked over at the anti-NATO picket, and then out of the corner of his eye he saw the pregnant woman get up from the bench and start walking quickly towards the elderly protesters. Egor was initially surprised but soon realised that the woman wasn't actually heading for the anti-NATO pensioners at all – she was hurrying towards a stout gentleman who had just come out of the main entrance to Parliament. He had stopped and was talking to someone on his mobile phone. At first he didn't even notice the woman approaching him from behind, but when he did he immediately took a step backwards and looked around, as though he were hoping to be rescued.

Egor couldn't hear the argument that started up between them, but he had no trouble interpreting their facial expressions and the way they were gesticulating. Their altercation culminated in the man slapping the woman across the face; she burst into tears and ran back into the park, covering her face with her hands.

Egor watched her walk to the nearest bench. By the time she got there the man had already disappeared.

Egor thought about the events of the previous day. His conscience had started to bother him, mainly because of the elderly woman in the car.

He looked at the main entrance to the Stalinist building across the street, at the doors that Irina had gone through several times a day.

'I wonder if there's anything about it in the papers,' he thought.

Egor picked up *Facts* and *Kiev News* at the kiosk and took them back to the bench near the anti-NATO picket. He sat down and went through both newspapers. The car crash on the Zhytomyr Highway didn't even get a mention, although there was an entire page devoted to other road accidents, including photographs.

Despite his splitting headache, Egor somehow made it to the end of his shift. While he was pacing out the hours along the paths of the park, he really felt like a shot or two of vodka. No more than that, though – he didn't drink much or very often, and it was always for a reason.

When his shift was over Egor went to a food shop and bought some sausages, butter, buckwheat groats and a kilo of semolina for his mother, who had lost all her teeth a long time ago.

As he walked out of the alley onto Hrushevsky Street he glanced again at the grey five-storey Stalinist building opposite the park.

After Egor had turned off the Zhytomyr Highway towards Makariv he remembered that he wanted a drink. His head didn't seem to be bothering him so much any more. As his car approached Lipovka he found himself thinking more and more about Irina, and now he couldn't decide whether or not to call in and see her. He would have called in without hesitating but his mother had taken a turn for the worse – she'd been awake for most of the night, feeling sick. He and Baba Sonya had sat by her bedside until she fell asleep just before dawn, and then Egor had left for work. He wondered how she was now.

The Mazda drove into Lipovka, then took the turning to Kodra and continued for about two hundred metres before pulling up outside a café at the side of the road. Egor got out of the car and looked at the green neon sign.

He opened the door and looked inside. He'd never been to this café before. There used to be a kind of metal trailer here, where they sold beer and vodka, then the owners had upgraded it to a brick building with an outside terrace. It was too cold to sit outside in the winter, so customers had taken to leaving their bicycles there.

Inside, one of the tables was occupied by a drunken old man in a quilted jacket and another by three young lads. The television was on, tuned to a pop music channel.

Egor didn't like the atmosphere in there at all. He'd already gone off the idea of having a drink, so he turned round and walked out again. Back outside, the air seemed remarkably clean and fresh. As he opened the car door Egor noticed a horseshoe lying on the road, and he picked it up and put it on the rubber mat under his feet.

He decided to go and see Irina after all, so he could fix the horseshoe above her door for luck. Irina loved the idea. Her mother came out onto the doorstep in her old coat to admire the way the horseshoe looked hanging over the front door.

'Shall I fry you up some potatoes?' she asked Egor.

'No thanks, I need to get back. Mother had a bad night last night.'

He promised to call in again the next morning and hurried to his car. He didn't notice Irina come out and stand by the wicket gate, watching until his red tail lights disappeared into the darkness.

60

Apartment No. 10, Reitarska Street, Kiev

'Oh, what happened to you?' exclaimed Veronika, when she met her neighbour Igor on the landing.

Igor was about to turn away but then changed his mind, obviously realising how silly it would look. He stopped in front of his blonde neighbour and sighed.

Veronika was intrigued by the large bruise under his left eye.

'I got that because of your husband,' said Igor. 'I was just trying to help you out . . . And I got punched in the face!'

'By Semyon?'

'No, by the bloke following him. Short chap, he was, about this high. And he said that if he saw me again, he'd kill me!'

'Gosh, you're so brave,' said Veronika, with a touch of irony. 'Come in, I'll make you a coffee.'

Igor perked up straight away. He even started smiling.

'Where's Semyon?' he asked warily.

'He's working for one of the deputies at the moment, so he won't be home until late. Go on through into the living room, I'll just put the kettle on.'

Igor went into the living room and had a little look around, then went over to the balcony door and looked out onto the street. He couldn't wait for spring to come. Winter only ever seemed to emphasise his loneliness and the lack of stability in his life. Igor lived for the times he had a young female client looking for an apartment – he would arrange several viewings a day and they would end up spending three or four hours together. But his last client had just signed a contract, so his services were no longer required. As the agent Igor stood to make $2,000 from the deal, and yesterday evening this had still seemed like some consolation, but his financial fortunes had been somewhat overshadowed by the black eye he got later that night. He only had himself to blame, though. So thought Igor as he stood in the living room looking out at the old seven-storey building opposite, at the little square with the two benches in the middle of it, at the three tramps – one female, two male – sitting on one of the benches and at the two young students drinking beer on the other.

Veronika came into the living room carrying two cups of coffee on a round nickel tray. 'You ought to get married, you know,' she said.

'Married?' Igor turned round in surprise. 'Why, do you have any young single friends?'

'I do know a couple of widows, actually. One of them is quite young.'

'No, I'm still not ready,' said her neighbour, keen to bring the conversation to an end. 'Marriage should take you by surprise, not be planned in advance according to the availability of potential partners.'

'Marriage happens when it happens,' said Veronika, looking directly into his eyes. 'You know, Igor, it's really not worth you taking any more risks. As far as my husband's concerned, I mean.'

'But he's sneaking off somewhere at night!' Igor spread his hands in agitation. He desperately wanted to insinuate that Veronika's husband might have another woman. Maybe then she would consider popping over to his apartment for more than a cup of coffee . . .

'Don't worry, I'll keep an eye on him,' smiled Veronika.

When her neighbour left, Veronika remembered that today was the late pharmacist's birthday. Right on cue, Darya Ivanovna called.

'Are you coming, Nikochka?' she asked. 'Annushka said she'd be here around three, so why don't you come on over? I've made herring in sour cream.'

Veronika had never been to a dead person's birthday party before. She wasn't sure whether or not to take a gift, and if so, for whom? Or should she just take a bottle of champagne?

In the end, she decided not to think about the pharmacist at all for the time being, and she would buy something for Darya Ivanovna, because she was the one who had invited them – it didn't matter what the occasion was.

On the way to her friend's apartment she bought a fancy cake and a bottle of pink champagne.

The round table in the living room at the pharmacist's widow's apartment was already set for three. As before, the pharmacist himself was sitting in his armchair with his back to the table. Veronika immediately worked out where to sit so that she wouldn't end up staring at the back of his neck.

'I had some culinary inspiration today!' the pharmacist's widow declared happily. 'I made four salads, a pumpkin and parsnip soup and a cake with three kinds of nuts: cashews, hazelnuts and walnuts. Would you like some brandy?'

Veronika nodded.

It wasn't long before Anna joined them. She was carrying a gift bag with a red cord handle.

'Here's a little something for the birthday boy,' she said.

Darya Ivanovna looked inside the bag and nodded thoughtfully.

'I don't know what kind of cologne he used . . . But even if all they're doing is sitting around men should still smell nice, don't you think? It's Hugo Boss,' said Anna.

'Annushka, will you have a brandy?' Darya Ivanovna asked her guest.

'Of course!'

After they'd all drunk their brandy, they sat down at the table. Darya Ivanovna ladled the soup into deep bowls, and Anna picked up the champagne and looked at it carefully.

'I'll do it,' offered Veronika, and she started untwisting the wire that was holding the plastic cork in place.

The loud noise the cork made as it flew out startled Darya Ivanovna, Anna and Veronika herself. Fortunately the champagne didn't come gushing out, so Darya Ivanovna was spared any extra cleaning up.

'To the birthday boy!' Anna raised her glass.

Veronika really enjoyed the soup. She felt relaxed and happy, in the mood for a girlie chat, but then she turned round and her gaze fell on the back of the pharmacist's neck, or more precisely on his left ear, and the feeling dissipated. She had no wish to discuss her personal life in the presence of a man, however impassive he might be. They continued their meal for some time in silence, until Darya Ivanovna turned on the cassette player and their conversation resumed against a background of quiet and unobtrusive jazz.

'I bought the same cologne for mine too,' admitted Anna. 'The chemists in town have got it on special offer at the moment – buy one get one free!'

'Really? Is that just on colognes, or on everything?' asked Darya

Ivanovna. 'I need some washing powder. It's time to start spring-cleaning!'

Anna didn't know whether or not the special offer applied to washing powder as well.

'My neighbour got a black eye last night, while he was out following Semyon,' Veronika announced cheerfully.

'Why's he following him?' asked Anna.

'Because I asked him to. Senya sometimes goes out in the middle of the night . . . But that's the kind of job he has. He's in security. My imagination just started running away with me.' Veronika noticed Darya Ivanovna's gaze fixed upon her, and she abruptly fell silent. It wasn't the first time this had happened.

'Was it your husband who gave him the black eye?' asked Anna.

'No, someone else, another man who's following my husband,' answered Veronika. 'It might have been his bodyguard.'

'My, what an interesting life you lead!' Anna clasped her hands together. 'Mind you, when my husband was alive, I also had a tale or two to tell.'

There was a sudden sadness in Anna's voice. She looked at the half-eaten herring on her plate and put her fork down on the tablecloth.

'I should probably go,' she said.

Darya Ivanovna nodded. Her face had fallen.

'Let's move into the kitchen,' she suggested, after Anna had left.

They carried their plates of food to the kitchen table, and Darya Ivanovna refilled their champagne glasses.

'You know something,' she began in a confidential tone of voice, 'my husband was a bit of a bastard as well. He hardly ever spent the night at home. He's much easier to live with now!'

227

'My husband's not a bastard!' Slightly tipsy from the champagne, Veronika shook her head in protest.

'I never used to say it either. I just thought it. But now I can say whatever I like! I followed him a couple of times, and do you know where he used to go? To his pharmacy! There was a woman he used to meet beforehand, and then they'd go to the pharmacy together. But now he's at home all the time, day and night, and I know for a fact that he's not meeting any other women. That's what it takes for men to start behaving themselves!'

Veronika sighed sympathetically and took another sip of her champagne.

'There, you see?' whispered Darya Ivanovna. 'We started feeling better as soon as we moved in here, away from him. I don't mind admitting it either. I only wish he knew!'

As a parting gift Darya Ivanovna gave Veronika the Hugo Boss cologne that Anna had brought.

'Why don't you give it to your husband instead? I don't like the smell of it,' she said. And then she added, in a hushed tone, 'I dab my perfume, Red Moscow, behind his ears.'

61

Vyshhorod district, Kiev region

When Volodka picked his friend up in the Niva the following morning, he immediately confessed that he was in no fit state to continue driving. Volodka's face was pale and puffy from lack of sleep – he really did look unwell, so Semyon took over.

The task that Gennady Ilyich had given them that day was straightforward and familiar. They had to go to Hrushevsky Street again and pick up three milk churns, then pick up Father Onophrios on Shevchenko Square, then go to the orphanage.

They drove to Hrushevsky Street in silence. Two strong lads in green overalls brought the milk churns out to them and loaded them straight into the boot.

Father Onophrios was waiting for them near the bus station. He was holding an old-fashioned brown leather travelling bag, and his black cassock was hanging down below the hem of his coat.

'With God's help, let us proceed,' he said, getting into the back of the car.

'Yes, God's help wouldn't go amiss,' agreed Semyon.

Father Onophrios attempted to strike up a conversation several times during the journey, to no avail. Semyon just nodded in response to his words, and once the priest heard Volodka snoring he didn't say another word until they reached the orphanage.

While Volodka slept in the car, Semyon witnessed the sanctification of the cheese-making machine that they had helped install the other day. The ceremony was attended by the director of the orphanage, several teachers and their young charges, none of whom showed any particular enthusiasm for the proceedings, and conducted by Father Onophrios, who didn't seem to want to be there any more than they did. He walked around the cheese-making machine several times with the censer, droning psalms and prayers to himself, and then he stuck a piece of paper with a cross on it to the base of the machine.

When it was all over, the director of the orphanage ushered Semyon and the priest into his office, where it was surprisingly warm. An elderly woman from the orphanage canteen served each of them a plate of buckwheat and meat rissoles, generously covering each portion with a thick sauce. The director himself filled their shot glasses with vodka.

'Well, that's that,' he said. 'I hope everything was satisfactory. Thank you for your help. If it be God's will, I hope you might share with us again whatever you can spare –'

'Whatever Gennady Ilyich can spare,' Father Onophrios corrected him courteously.

'Well, yes,' nodded the director of the orphanage. 'God does give him more than others. Let's drink to him!'

Father Onophrios drained his shot glass in one, as did the director of the orphanage. Semyon only took a sip.

'The tool setter has already been,' said the director, after knocking back his shot. 'The machine is fairly easy to operate. My eldest boys made notes on everything he said – now they can start learning a new trade. Maybe one of them will go on to become a master cheese-maker!'

Semyon felt a sudden rush of kindness towards the director. The way he spoke about 'his boys' was affectionate, almost paternal.

Volodka woke up as soon as Semyon started the engine.

'It's freezing in here,' he said, with a glance in the rear-view mirror at the priest, who was looking decidedly flushed after several shots of vodka.

'No wonder, it's minus three out there,' said Semyon.

Volodka rubbed his hands together and rotated his shoulders. Sleeping in a sitting position is never a good idea – it's uncomfortable, and it makes your whole body go numb.

'Let me drive,' he said to Semyon.

'We'll swap before we get to the city,' said Semyon. 'But I'll drive until then. I thought it would be difficult after a seven-year break, but it's just like riding a bike!'

'Have you not driven for seven years?' enquired the priest from the back seat.

'He was in a really bad accident seven years ago,' Volodka explained to Father Onophrios. 'His car was a write-off. It's a miracle that he and his wife survived.'

'Miracles are evidence of God's work,' commented the priest, taking the opportunity to encourage their spiritual improvement.

Semyon had absolutely no desire to remember the accident.

They were already driving along the country road. The priest began to doze on the back seat, and Volodka sat in silence. The gloomy winter forest all around them was starting to make Semyon feel quite depressed, so he turned the radio on to try and cheer himself up.

As they approached Shevchenko Square, at the point where the forest ends abruptly and Kiev begins, Semyon suddenly felt like a coffee. They dropped the priest off – he said goodbye and walked off towards the tram stop, holding his travelling bag – and Semyon and Volodka went to a cigarette kiosk, which had a large sign above the serving hatch proclaiming 'Hot Coffee – 1 Hryvna'. They bought a cup each.

'Do you want me to tell you about last night now, or shall we drop the milk churns off first?' asked Volodka.

'Milk churns first,' answered his friend.

Volodka got into the driver's seat and finished his coffee.

As the car pulled away, the empty milk churns clinked against one another in the back.

By the time they reached the centre of the city, twilight had already descended upon Kiev.

62

Boryspil, evening

As evening approached, Dima set off on foot for the bus station. He kept looking from side to side as he walked down the street.

A couple of times he squatted down to do his shoelaces up, to give him further opportunity to look around, but there didn't appear to be any suspicious-looking individuals heading the same way.

Once he got to the amusement arcade, Dima paused to catch his breath and began to calm down. Valya was sitting in her little booth, changing a customer's notes into coins.

Someone somewhere got lucky, and the sound of fifty-kopek coins pouring into the metal trough filled the entire room. Dima froze, like he did whenever he went fishing and felt a serious bite. He walked towards the sound and saw a boy of about fourteen stuffing his winnings into his jacket pocket.

'He's underage! Who let him in?' Dima thought to himself indignantly.

He wanted to take the boy by the ear and escort him out of the arcade, handing his winnings back through the cashier's window. He felt a sense of social responsibility stirring within him, which reminded him of what the militiaman had said that morning, about the medicine in the ampoules sharpening people's sense of justice and making them fearless.

Dima remembered how afraid he had been earlier and looked down at his fingers to see whether they were trembling. No, they weren't trembling, and furthermore he felt calm and composed – not physically, but somewhere deep in his soul.

The sound of coins had stopped but a golden echo rang in Dima's ears, and this ringing calmed him down even more. There were no windows in the amusement arcade, and each machine gave off so much bright light that anyone walking in off the street could be forgiven for thinking they'd entered some kind of parallel universe. Dima suddenly felt protected by a mysterious, mystical force as well. He went over to the cashier's window, looked through it and smiled at his wife.

'What's the matter with you?' she asked, worried.

'What do you mean?' Dima was surprised.

'Why are you smiling like that?'

'Everything's fine . . . I just came to pick you up,' said Dima, now sounding shaky and lost.

'Oh, right,' nodded his wife. 'In that case you might as well go for a stroll or something. Sonya won't be here for at least another half an hour.'

When they were walking home together in the twilight, Dima tried to look around without Valya noticing.

'You know,' he said quietly, 'maybe we should move away somewhere. With the baby – it'll be a new life! We could sell the house and use the money to buy a two-storey cottage somewhere, a bit further out of Kiev. What do you think?'

'What's wrong with Boryspil?' asked Valya. 'We've always lived here! We've got everything we need, right on our doorstep . . . And who would take care of my relatives' graves? Your sister's here too, and the rest of your family are buried here.'

'Not all of them,' sighed Dima, already resigned to defeat. 'No one knows where my brother's buried.'

'He might not even be dead! Is it ten years since he disappeared?'

'Eleven.'

Dima started thinking about his missing brother. He used to travel to Russia for work, and then one time he never came back.

'Are you hungry?' Valya asked suddenly.

'Uh-huh.'

'Let's go and have some *pelmeni*,' she declared. 'We can both have a couple of portions and get a portion each for the cats.'

Dima licked his lips. He was suddenly hungry for a plate of hot *pelmeni* and had no desire whatsoever to go home, but then he felt a stab of indignation. 'A portion each for the cats,' she'd said – that's what had offended him. He wouldn't have thought twice about buying *pelmeni* for Scruffy – a double portion even – but what had Kitchen Fluffy done to deserve *pelmeni*? He had no idea.

'That's not really fair, you know,' he said to his wife.

'What's not fair?'

'Getting both cats a portion each. My Fluffy saved my life! The other one does nothing but lie under the radiator.'

'Well, I don't know,' Valya spread her hands. 'They're both our cats . . . We could always get a double portion for your Fluffy, if you like?'

They returned home at about 10 p.m., sleepy and satiated. Their wicket gate was wide open, and this instantly put Dima on his guard. He looked cautiously at their porch and saw a square of white paper sticking out between the door and the frame. He hurried over to the porch, pulled the note out and stuffed it into his jacket pocket, then unlocked the door and glanced at his wife.

She didn't seem to have noticed anything. She had just followed him in and started taking off her coat and shoes.

63

Lipovka village, Kiev region
It felt like the middle of the night when Irina woke up in agony, her breasts engorged. The clock said 4.20 a.m. It was quiet and dark outside.

Irina pulled on warm tights and a plain grey dress and went into the kitchen. God forbid Egor should see her like this! The dress was at least twenty years old – it had belonged to her mother – but it had buttons down to the waist, so it was quite practical. She sat at the table in the dark, leaning forward and resting her swollen breasts on the tabletop. Then she began to cry, making as little noise as possible so as to avoid disturbing the peace in the house.

What could she do with all this milk? If only Yasya would drink it . . . But Yasya only latched on to her mother's breast when she was sleepy. During the day she would drink a little, push Irina's nipple out of her mouth and then cry until she was given a bottle of formula milk.

'You silly little thing,' thought Irina through her silent tears. 'The city is full of sickly children, all being raised on formula milk, because their mothers choose to put their breasts on display rather than feeding their own children the way nature intended. And I've got all this milk for you – my own milk, warm and full of life!'

After she'd finished crying, Irina switched the light on in the kitchen. She put the kettle on to boil and held a litre jar upside down over the spout. She held it there until it had 'sweated' inside three times, and then she undid the mother-of-pearl buttons on her dress, placed the jar beneath one breast and began to express her milk.

This activity soothed her, distracted her.

After about twenty minutes she felt better. Liberated of their milk, her breasts no longer ached. The jar of milk stood on the boiler, sealed with a plastic lid that had been sterilised in the steam.

Throwing her mother's coat on over her dress, Irina went out onto the doorstep. The first thing she did was to check that the horseshoe was still there, and then she looked up at the stars. They were twinkling with a cold dark blue light, but there was no frost. Or was it just that she no longer felt it?

Irina started thinking about the spring, about the fact that in a month or so it would be time to stock up on seeds. Then she would be so busy helping her mother that she would forget all about Kiev. But how would they manage without her Kiev money? Her mother's pension was a joke, and you couldn't go and stand by the road with a bucket of new potatoes any earlier than the middle of June. Irina could remember selling potatoes and onions by the side of the road. Sometimes an hour would pass, even two, before a car would stop and the driver would lower his window to ask, 'How much for the bucket?' He would buy without haggling and drive off, and then she would go back for more. She would give the money to her mother, whose hands were dark from the soil that had worked its way under the skin. Her mother would hide the money in the sideboard, and Irina would take her empty bucket back down to the cellar.

She stood on the doorstep for a little while longer before going back into the house, thinking about past and future springs.

Something told her that this coming spring would be different. She lay down with her mother's coat still on and fell back to sleep.

At around 9 a.m. Irina heard the sound of a car approaching. She looked out of the window and smiled happily, then quickly changed her dress and hurried to the door. She took Egor through to the kitchen and made him sit in the warmest place, with his back to the hob, then got out the ground coffee and lit the gas under the kettle.

Her mother joined them in the kitchen. She was dressed smartly, with a brooch on her green cardigan. She sat down at the table opposite their guest.

'I'll have a coffee too,' she said to her daughter. She turned to Egor. 'So, how's your mother?'

'Not great, actually,' Egor sighed. 'Our old stove's playing up too. There's virtually no draught up the chimney and I didn't sleep at all last night because I was worried the smoke would come into the hut, so I sat up by the fire, keeping an eye on it.'

'Oh, there's someone three doors down who knows how to fix those old stoves. Grisha, his name is. Shall I fetch him?'

'It's all right, thanks, I've already found someone.'

Irina poured coffee for Egor and her mother. She took the lid off the sugar pot.

'I'm just going to check on Yasya – she might have woken up,' she said and went out.

As soon as the door closed behind her, Aleksandra Vasilievna looked at Egor. Her expression was different now, more serious.

'You should stay over at our place sometimes,' she said. 'We'll find you somewhere to sleep. We could put a mattress down on Irinka's floor.'

Egor nodded silently.

'And you should take me to see your mother,' she continued after a pause. 'I know she can't get out of bed . . . but I ought to meet her.'

Egor sipped his coffee. 'All right,' he said. 'As soon as she's better, I'll take you.'

Irina's mother felt the need to tell him something about her daughter, something personal, a little secret. 'Irinka's always liked ice cream, you know,' she said. 'Ever since she was a little girl. She loves it, she does!'

Just then the door opened. Irina came in and sat down at the table with Yasya in her arms. Yasya looked at Egor with curiosity.

'She likes you!' exclaimed Aleksandra Vasilievna. 'When my Irinka was little, she used to cry whenever she saw someone she didn't know! Oh, I have to feed the hens!' And with that she jumped up and left the kitchen.

Egor finished his coffee and got up to leave for Kiev.

'I'll call in again later,' he promised. 'Do you want me to bring you anything?'

'Mama loves that dark rye bread,' said Irina.

After Egor had left, her mother came back into the house immediately and changed back into her normal clothes.

'Mama,' Irina called out to her, 'can you ask around the neighbours? Maybe someone in the village could use some breast milk. Either for money, or in exchange for something else . . . It's just such a shame to waste it.'

'I'll ask at the village council office,' said her mother. 'Galya the accountant knows everyone's business. You ought to get yourself down there too, you know. There are all kinds of benefits for single mothers. They might give you some sort of allowance.'

'I'm not on my own, though,' Irina replied and turned away, offended.

She fought back the tears. She could remember her shame, her fear of being seen out pregnant. She'd been convinced that everyone knew who the father of her child was . . . and maybe they did all know, but now she couldn't care less. There were dozens of girls like her in the village. It was a big village – seven hundred families!

64

Dali bar, Yaroslaviv Val, Kiev

At around 10 p.m. the barman of the Doors café asked Semyon and Volodka to move to another establishment, because he was closing early.

Semyon didn't feel like standing up. Not because of the amount of whisky he'd drunk, but because he was afraid it might cause his understanding of the events of the previous night, as described in detail by Volodka and in which he himself had played the leading role, to unravel. If it had all been stored away in his memory, he wouldn't have been so worried about it. Memories can be blurred but the details are all there, waiting to be recalled – all it takes is a trigger, a specific reminder of the past, and everything comes flooding back. But that was the trouble: Semyon had absolutely no recollection of the events in which he had allegedly taken part. To all intents and purposes he hadn't even been there. Finding out what you've been doing from somebody else is not normal. Of course people sometimes drink so much that they can't remember anything and have to ask their friends to supply the missing details, but Semyon hadn't been up to any drunken antics. He'd been living a mysterious double life without even knowing it, and if it hadn't been for Volodka he wouldn't have had a clue about this second self, this second life that was so separate from everything else he knew.

'What was she like?' Semyon questioned Volodka.

'Getting on a bit, sixty or so I'd say . . . I couldn't really see, to be honest. You kissed her hand, and she made the sign of the cross over you, only there was something weird about the way she did it. It wasn't the Orthodox way. Oh yeah, and another thing – she seemed to be having a go at you about something. I couldn't really hear, but you were clearly having some sort of disagreement. Your mobile phone rang and you spoke to someone for a couple of minutes, then you passed the phone to her. She spoke for a bit, and when she'd finished she gave you a carrier bag. You looked inside the bag, and she seemed to be explaining something to you.'

'What time was this?' Semyon asked, getting his mobile out.

'About two.'

Semyon checked his incoming calls. He'd had a call at 1.45 a.m. from a 'withheld' number.

'Where did she go next?'

'I don't know. I followed you home. There were two other men watching you, and I was worried they might follow you too.'

'What about the bag?'

'You took it home with you.'

'Right.' Semyon sighed. He looked over at the bar and met the barman's weary gaze. 'OK, OK, we're just going!' he said.

They cut through the courtyard connecting Reitarska Street and Yaroslaviv Val and went down into the Dali bar, which was situated in a snug and spacious basement.

They ordered a couple of tequilas and sat in a corner, drinking them in silence.

'Wasn't Alisa there?' Semyon asked suddenly.

'No, you didn't meet her this time.'

'Christ,' breathed Semyon. 'Where's this all leading?'

'Down the aisle!' Volodka joked ruefully. Then he looked at his friend as though he'd just had a brainwave. 'Hey, why don't you buy yourself one of those little digital voice recorders and sew it under your collar? Then you'll have a record of all these night-time conversations.'

This idea struck Semyon as eminently sensible.

Veronika was already asleep when Semyon got home. He took his shoes off and went into the living room. He tiptoed round the apartment, looking everywhere for the carrier bag that he had been given yesterday by an unknown female in her sixties. Empty-handed and exhausted, he sat down in the armchair. He listened cautiously to his body, as though it were an unfamiliar machine with the capacity to surprise him.

'Am I going anywhere tonight?' he wondered.

He remembered Volodka's advice about sewing a digital voice recorder into his collar. Why not? He could be his own private investigator!

Semyon started feeling anxious again. He got out the first-aid box, found the sleeping tablets and took two, washing them down with tap water.

65

Apartment No. 10, Reitarska Street, Kiev

In the hours before dawn, Veronika pressed her bottom up against her husband's warm thigh and his raw masculinity animated her nocturnal imagination like a jolt of electricity, generating a tender and romantic dream. In the dream she was running through a field of poppies towards a young man. He was leaping as he ran to meet her, and his green T-shirt kept floating up above the red poppies and then down again. He didn't look anything like Semyon. A happy smile shone on his perfect face as he devoured Veronika hungrily with his eyes. He was clearly younger than Semyon – younger than Veronika too. Veronika tried to jump as she ran, to soar above the flowering carpet of poppies.

The man in the T-shirt was getting closer and closer. Veronika realised that neither of them could stop. She knew that his arms were about to seize her in a strong embrace, that the two of them would fall onto the red carpet of poppies . . . Then just at that moment the green T-shirt flashed past, without the man's arms even touching her. She turned round, startled, and watched him run away from her. A little further off, at the edge of the poppy field, she saw a young girl with long hair wearing a pale blue kaftan. She was just standing there, not running. Standing and waiting. And the man just kept leaping towards her.

Veronika sighed and turned to face Semyon. She placed her left hand on his chest, and then she woke up.

It was light in their bedroom. Veronika looked down at Semyon's handsome, masculine face and brushed her lips against his bristly cheek.

She got up quietly and took the Hugo Boss cologne out of her bag. She dabbed some onto her fingers and ran them behind her husband's ears, then she leaned over him again and inhaled deeply. She liked the smell.

At around 9 a.m., after her morning coffee and a hot shower, she called Darya Ivanovna and told her about her dream. Her friend sighed sympathetically on the other end of the line, but she didn't seem to be interested in discussing it any further. Instead she asked Veronika to come to her apartment as soon as possible.

'We'll talk about my dream again when I get there,' Veronika told herself hopefully.

She glanced into the bedroom. Semyon was still fast asleep, only now he lay on his right side, facing the window.

Veronika left a brief note for her husband on the kitchen table and went out onto the landing, pulling the front door softly shut behind her. The latch clicked and the door closed, and at the same time the door opposite opened and her neighbour looked out with a broad smile on his face. 'Are you in a hurry?' he asked.

'Yes I am, actually,' answered Veronika.

She nodded goodbye and started walking down the stairs, the heels of her white Italian boots clacking noisily.

Igor went back into his hallway and stopped in front of the mirror. He admired his new tracksuit, the healthy glow in his carefully shaved and moisturised cheeks and the way his eyes shone from the vitamin drops he'd put in them. What else would it take for his neighbour to actually notice him? Maybe he ought to go to the steam baths.

Meanwhile Veronika walked the familiar route to her friend's apartment. She greeted her with a kiss on the cheek.

'Annushka's got problems,' Darya Ivanovna confided nervously. 'And so have I.'

'Why, what's happened?' asked Veronika, worried.

'Come in, I'll show you.'

Darya Ivanovna took Veronika to her husband, who was sitting in his chair. She knelt down on the carpet and pointed at his slippers. Veronika knelt down beside her and saw that the soles of the pharmacist's slippers were dirty.

'Oh my God!' gasped Veronika. 'I don't understand . . .'

Without a word Darya Ivanovna showed her the footprints made by the dirty slippers. They were barely noticeable on the carpet but quite obvious in the hallway.

'Anyway, let's talk about your dream! I need something to take my mind off all this,' said Darya Ivanovna.

Veronika recounted her dream once more.

'You know, I used to have dreams like that, when Edik was alive.' Darya Ivanovna looked guardedly back at her husband.

Veronika shuddered. She didn't feel comfortable in her friend's apartment.

'Come on, let's go to Anna's for a coffee!' declared Darya Ivanovna.

Outside it already felt like spring. By 11 a.m. the thin layer of frost that clung to the pavement first thing in the morning had already melted and trickled into the road.

Veronika kept looking down at her feet.

'This Italian leather is so soft,' she said as they walked. 'In the shop they said I should treat the boots with special protective cream twice a day. But the "special protective cream" cost forty hryvnas a tube!'

As soon as Anna opened the door Veronika started feeling uncomfortable again. Anna's eyes were red and tear-stained, and her face looked swollen.

She took her friends into the kitchen and put the coffee machine on. Then she turned to Darya Ivanovna, who had already sat down at the table, and said, 'I can't take it any more!'

'Why don't you start from the beginning?' Darya Ivanovna coaxed her gently.

Anna sat down, straightening her white towelling robe so that it covered her bony knees.

'You'd better go and see for yourself.' She nodded at the door into the living room.

Darya Ivanovna stood up and left the kitchen.

It was quiet in the apartment. The only noises were the quiet humming of the fridge and the ticking of the alarm clock, which was the old-fashioned kind with a bell on top.

Veronika watched Anna, waiting for her to look at her so she would be able to find out what had happened, but Anna just stared at the tabletop in front of her.

Darya Ivanovna returned about three minutes later.

'I don't know . . .' She spread her hands. 'He's under guarantee, isn't he?'

'Yes, he is,' said Anna, without looking up.

'Have you called them?'

Anna shook her head.

'Well, I'm going to call them myself, right now!' Darya Ivanovna declared and left the kitchen again.

'They're on their way!' she announced, coming back into the kitchen and sitting down at the table. 'Annushka, why don't you get dressed?'

Anna sighed and left the room.

'What's the matter?' whispered Veronika.

Darya Ivanovna grimaced. It was obviously something that she found distasteful, but she overcame her aversion in order to satisfy her friend's curiosity.

'There's something wrong with Annushka's husband,' she said. 'His eyes have gone a funny yellow colour. I'm going to go and help her get dressed.'

Veronika was left alone. She drank her coffee and looked out of the window, where the sun was spilling its gentle, warm light over the city.

The doorbell rang. 'Where is he then?' asked a male voice.

Veronika hid in the kitchen. She held her breath, trying not to miss a single sound coming from the hallway.

Darya Ivanovna's voice was louder than anyone else's, but Veronika couldn't work out what she was saying. Then the doors slammed and the voices died away.

Darya Ivanovna and Anna came back into the kitchen. They both looked downcast and tired.

'They took him back,' said Darya Ivanovna. 'We can't do anything right in this country, can we? Even with a foreign licence!'

'I'd better be off,' said Veronika, standing up.

'Oh, stay for a bit!' Darya Ivanovna pleaded with her. 'I want to ask your advice on something.'

The pause that followed these words lasted several minutes. Finally Darya Ivanovna stroked Anna's shoulder and looked at her gently.

'You'll probably have to say goodbye to him for good this time . . . You'll get your money back, though. They said so, didn't they?'

Anna nodded.

Darya Ivanovna turned to Veronika.

'We're not going to abandon Annushka in her hour of need, are we?'

'Of course not,' promised Veronika.

66

9 May Street, Boryspil

Dima spent so long pretending to be asleep that he nearly did drop off to the sound of Valya's whispering. She was lying beside him, asking, 'What shall we call it? Valya, maybe? Or Marina?'

'There's no point talking about it yet,' said Dima. He was pre-occupied with the note he'd pulled from the door but hadn't managed to read yet. 'We'll choose a name once it's born.'

Valya eventually fell asleep, her breath warming the back of her husband's neck. Her breathing might have been what finally wore down Dima's resistance and nudged him into a sweet doze. He soon managed to rouse himself, though. He got out of bed quietly and went into the hall. He took the note from the pocket of his jacket, which was hanging on a hook, and went into the kitchen.

Startled by the sudden bright light, Kitchen Fluffy screwed up his little cat eyes in annoyance.

'*Monument to the Unknown Soldier* – 10 p.m. *Be there, or we'll torch your house.*'

Dima's blood ran cold. He caught sight of his frightened reflection in the window and his fear increased. He checked his watch before turning the light off: 10.30 p.m. Someone had been waiting for him half an hour ago by the Unknown Soldier. Maybe they were still there . . .

Dima sat in the dark kitchen and peered outside, into the dark of the night. The stillness of the barely visible front yard had a calming effect on him for a moment, but then another wave of fear rose up. He had to hide somewhere. 'The garage,' he thought. 'I just need to lock myself in the garage. The cure for this fear is in there!'

He went into the hall and put his boots and jacket on, feeling for the garage key in his pocket.

In the garage the first thing he did was to turn on the heater. Then he poured himself a shot of vodka and downed it in one. He took out an ampoule, flicked the top off and shook the liquid into his shot glass. Then he drank it, running his tongue around the inside of the glass to make sure he didn't leave a single drop.

'There,' he sighed with relief. 'Now I'm not afraid of anything!'

He didn't sound very convincing. His voice was shaking.

He had another shot of vodka, then another.

'I'm not afraid,' he whispered, concentrating on the sound of the words.

The warmth from the heater and the vodka gradually made Dima relax.

'I'm not afraid,' he repeated, and suddenly he felt a profound happiness. His fear really had disappeared.

'So what if they torch the house?' he whispered, with a strange, tired smile. 'We'll see who ends up getting burnt! Right, let's go!' he ordered himself and stood up.

Back inside the house, Dima carefully locked the front door. He closed all the top windows and bolted them. Then he got into bed, which was warmed by his sleeping wife.

67

Mariinsky Park, Kiev

At around 11.30 a.m. Egor decided that he needed a coffee. He would only permit himself a short break, ten to fifteen minutes, so rather than going to a café he walked past the Officers' Club to the food shop. He warned Seryoga by walkie-talkie that he was leaving the zone.

While he drank his coffee he remembered the jar of milk that he'd left in his car. Irina's mother had given it to him secretly that morning, without Irina knowing. She had asked him to take it to the milk kitchen and accept whatever they'd pay for it, so that it didn't go to waste. He hadn't managed to say anything in response because Irina had come out just as he was putting the cloth bag containing the jar on the floor in the back of the car. She'd given him a sandwich to eat on the way. He'd eaten the sandwich – slices of hard-boiled egg with mayonnaise – but had left the jar of milk in the car. The last thing Egor wanted to do was take it to the first floor of the Stalinist building. Irina clearly had more milk than she knew what to do with, but he didn't want to see her getting sucked back into the trap he'd just rescued her from!

Egor tore himself away from his thoughts to speak into his walkie-talkie. 'Number Four! Everything OK your end?'

'Affirmative,' answered Seryoga. 'The big guys are here, by the way. They're checking in the bushes. The President must be coming.'

'I'll be right there,' said Egor.

As he was leaving the food shop he bumped into the local tramp, who for some reason smelled strongly of oranges. He looked lucid and serene and was surveying the customers with divine condescension, although he was already mentally sorting them into categories: those who always gave him something, those who never did, and those he'd never seen before in his life.

Back in the park Egor patrolled the paths, keeping his eye out for the young pregnant woman. She came here every day and had already given him and his colleagues cause for concern a couple of times. On one occasion she'd suddenly turned on a pensioner walking a little dog, for no apparent reason. She'd called him every name under the sun, using such foul language that the old man had sat on a nearby bench for half an hour with his hand over his heart. Egor had called an ambulance, but by the time it turned up the old man had recovered and gone home.

Egor had never heard a pregnant woman swear like that. He had subsequently seen the woman arguing with a certain rather thickset deputy a number of times, although she never swore at him. One evening they'd had to forcibly remove her from the railings around the viewing area. She'd been planning to jump off. It had taken three of them to get her down – two of Egor's colleagues and a militiaman from the Parliament security team.

Today, to Egor's relief, she was nowhere to be seen.

'Number Five!' crackled Seryoga's voice. 'Retreat. The big guys have gone. No one's coming.'

'Roger that,' answered Egor.

The pressure was off. He stopped and looked around, already feeling more relaxed. He looked over at his car – it was a good thing that it was red, and therefore visible from a distance. He'd parked it where he usually did, in the alley by the side entrance to the park. The milk was in there too. It wasn't so cold that it would freeze, although it might turn sour.

Egor looked across at the windows of the first floor of the building opposite, and as he watched a Mercedes 500 drove up to the entrance door and three men in black leather jackets got out. They stood there for a couple of minutes, smoking, then marched into the building.

Egor glanced at his car again.

'What on earth am I going to do with that milk?' he wondered.

He looked back at the building. Just at that moment the three men came out, got quickly into their Mercedes and drove off.

'That's odd,' thought Egor. 'Cars like that usually have only one passenger.'

He looked at the windows again and strode decisively to the pedestrian crossing.

The doors to the first floor were partly open. Egor pressed the doorbell anyway, then went inside. Four empty milk churns with their lids off stood by the wall.

There was a white door opposite the milk churns. He pulled the handle and the door opened, but there was no one inside the little room. Egor was surprised. He kept walking.

He reached the second part of the corridor and stepped through onto the carpet runner. On the right was the boss's office, where she had shouted at him. Egor stopped and listened to the silence. There was something strange about it.

The door opposite the boss's office was partially open. He looked inside and saw a large bathtub full of milk. The milk was a creamy, yellow colour.

Egor wrinkled his nose up as he peered at the contents of the bath. Suddenly he noticed a kind of foam floating on the surface of the milk. There was something underneath the foam. Egor looked more closely, and a shudder passed through him. Beneath the foam he could see an ear and a gold earring. Turning his face to one side, he reached into the milk and pulled a woman's body from the bath. He looked at it out of the corner of his eye and recognised the owner of the milk kitchen, the one who had shouted at him. She was dead. Wet hair sticking to her face, eyes open, milk streaming from her nose, her ears, her mouth . . .

Egor released the body and it fell back under the milk.

Just then he heard doors slamming in the corridor and the sound of running feet.

'In here, in here!' a voice shouted outside the door.

Two men wearing green overalls ran into the room, followed by a middle-aged man in a suit. He pointed at the bath and they put their hands in, pulled the woman's body out and laid it on the floor.

'Oh my God! Why have they done this to her?' cried the man in the suit. 'She had nothing to do with it!'

They didn't see Egor hiding behind the open door in the corner of the room.

'What are you just standing there for?' one of the men in overalls shouted at the man in the suit. 'Bring the milk churns in!'

The man hurried into the corridor. The two men in overalls grabbed the boss's body and carried her out of the room. Egor watched from his hiding place as they dragged her into the room opposite, which had been her office.

Egor ran out into the corridor, past the milk churns and the middle-aged man in the suit. He reached the landing and ran down the stairs, taking them two at a time. He didn't stop until he got to the park.

'Number Five! Where are you?' Seryoga's voice came from his walkie-talkie.

'I'm here,' Egor replied breathlessly.

He could feel himself shaking. He looked all around, then back at the grey Stalinist building. He stood there looking at it for about twenty minutes until his breathing returned to normal and he stopped shaking.

'Now they'll all start turning up,' he thought. 'The militia, the Security Service . . .'

But the front entrance remained quiet. Nobody went in, and nobody came out. At around 3 p.m. a Niva drove into the courtyard of the building. The two men in green overalls he'd seen earlier that day brought four milk churns out and loaded them into the back of the Niva, and then the car drove off.

Egor remained in a state of shock for the rest of his shift. Before driving home he gave the jar of milk to an old woman walking past his car. He gave it to her without saying anything, and she didn't seem surprised. She just said, 'Thank you, my dear!' and walked off.

68

Apartment No. 10, Reitarska Street, Kiev

Darya Ivanovna called Veronika on Friday evening.

'Nikochka, I didn't get round to taking the wreath down!

Could you possibly pick it up for me and hang on to it for the weekend?'

'Do you want to come over for a coffee?' asked Veronika.

'Where's your husband?'

'He's going to be at work all night. He just popped home for something to eat but had to go straight back out.'

'OK, then,' said Darya Ivanovna. 'I'll be there in an hour. You might as well go and get the wreath while you're waiting.'

Veronika walked to the corner of Striletska Street and Yaroslaviv Val, took the wreath off the nail and carried it home. The streets were full of slush, so she left her Italian boots standing on a cloth in the hall to dry out.

She felt energised after her brief outing. The wreath stayed in the hall, leaning against the wall next to the Italian boots, and Veronika went into the kitchen and took her new Italian coffee machine out of its box. It was one of those you could stand on the hob like a kettle. There was no point in putting the coffee on, as Darya Ivanovna wasn't a great one for punctuality. She might be there in an hour, like she'd said, or it might be more like an hour and a half.

To pass the time, Veronika got out the notebook that the pharmacist's widow had given her and sat down at the kitchen table. Before opening it, she marvelled again at the nonchalance with which Darya had given it to her. She could understand her readiness to part with it, though – the pages that weren't littered with illegible handwriting were filled with erotic sketches. These were what Veronika had decided to look at. From the very first page she felt a strange feeling of envy towards this unknown woman, who had been sketched by the late pharmacist with such skill and precision. Her gaze rested on the woman's hair, which was gathered into a bun. For some reason she was convinced that this woman was blonde too, like her. Veronika compared the rest of her body with that of the woman in the pictures and came to the objective conclusion that they were identical. They both had the same straight little nose, the same average-sized breasts, the same delicate neck . . .

Veronika became thoroughly absorbed in the sketches. She studied them carefully and then tried once more to decipher the pharmacist's handwriting, in the hope that she might find some notes to accompany the sketches. Screwing her eyes up and squinting along the lines, she managed to detect a certain pattern in the handwriting – in this way she worked out how to distinguish his k's from his h's and his h's from his n's. She looked closely at the text, and her lips moved as she spoke the words aloud.

'Third experiment with Anti-Wimp did not lead to results I was hoping for. Instead of bravery, the patient feels an exaggerated sense of justice. Looks like I'm going to have to focus on *primal* rather than *conscious* bravery. Yulia getting impatient. She gave A some more money and a threatening note to pass on to me. She's worried I'll sell it to the other side if they offer enough.'

At that moment the doorbell forced Veronika to stop abruptly. She hastily hid the notebook in the cutlery drawer.

'Oh, thank you, my dear!' Darya Ivanovna exclaimed delightedly, as she came in and noticed the wreath leaning against the wall.

Veronika lit the gas under her new coffee machine, which she had prepared in advance, and followed her guest into the living room.

'You're so lucky,' Darya Ivanovna sighed, looking around.

'Why?' asked Veronika.

'Because your husband is still alive. Your place smells completely different to mine. Oh, just ignore me, I'm in a bad mood today!

When I woke up this morning, there were more footprints on the floor. And his slippers were dirty again . . . What a nightmare! Or am I imagining it? I just snapped at your neighbour too. As I rang your bell he stuck his head out of his apartment. "Have you come to see Veronika?" he asked, in a horrible, ingratiating voice. I said to him, "Well, I haven't come to see you, that's for sure!"'

Veronika laughed.

'Has he got a crush on you or something?' Darya Ivanonva lowered her voice to an intimate whisper.

Veronika nodded. 'I feel a bit sorry for him,' she said. 'Poor chap, he hasn't got a clue . . .'

'Yes, people like that do deserve to be pitied,' declared Darya Ivanovna, her tone suddenly cold and ruthless. She seemed to be speaking from experience. 'Anyway, I've come to a decision. It's been a while now . . . No one can question my unwavering fidelity. And Annushka feels the same. So we're going to let our husbands go. They've both got places in the cemetery, side by side. We're going to let nature take its course. It'll be interesting to see how my husband manages his nightly strolls from his new home! You know, I haven't had much joy out of him sitting in that chair. Neither fish nor fowl . . .'

'You might be right,' agreed Veronika. 'Men are better when they're alive!'

'Better? That's debatable!' said her guest. 'Some of us are luckier than others, and some of us don't realise how lucky we are. But I suppose none of us appreciate what we have until it's gone.'

There was a loud spluttering sound from the kitchen, which was followed immediately by the smell of fresh coffee forcing its way through the open doors into the living room.

69

Apartment No. 10, Reitarska Street, Kiev

Sleep induced by pills has its own peculiarities. There are no dreams, no brief spells of wakefulness. Semyon fell into bed and slept like a log. His head certainly felt like it was made out of wood the following morning, when he was woken by the distant but persistent musical ringtone of his mobile. The Beatles' 'Yesterday' sounded as though it were coming from outside, or from another room. When it finally stopped Semyon felt sleep retreating, and a headache approaching. It took him another five minutes to actually get out of bed. Semyon was surprised to see that his mobile was right next to him, on the bedside table. 'I need to stop taking sleeping pills,' he said to himself. 'That's three nights in a row now. What if I get hooked on them?'

He reached over for his mobile and checked his missed calls. Two in the night from a 'withheld' number and three from his boss, Gennady Ilyich.

Semyon got into the shower and turned on the cold water. He stood under the shower for about three minutes, letting the water cool him down; then he dried himself with a rough towel, threw his dressing gown on and went back into the bedroom to call Gennady Ilyich.

'Where have you been?' asked his boss.

'I took some sleeping pills,' admitted Semyon.

'They're a waste of time. You're better off drinking brandy if you want a good night's sleep!' advised the deputy, with uncharacteristic warmth in his voice. 'Now, I want you to go and collect the milk from Hrushevsky Street at eleven. Take it to the orphanage, and pick up some of their cheese for me to taste. The director said that the first batch was a success! Call me on my mobile when you're on your way back.'

After this conversation Semyon sighed with relief. He had plenty of time, so there was no rush. He called Volodka, told him their plan of action for the day and then went into the kitchen. He stopped, puzzled. Something wasn't right. He looked around . . . Everything was neat and tidy. It must have been something else, but what? He went back into the bathroom. Nothing in there was out of place either. As he came out into the hallway he caught sight of the funeral wreath leaning against the wall.

'What day is it today?' he wondered.

He knew that they sometimes looked after the wreath at weekends. But today was Monday, wasn't it?

Semyon went back into the bedroom, picked up his mobile phone and checked the day and date. Yes, it was Monday!

He looked at the bed and only now realised that he had woken up alone, without his wife. He panicked for a moment. What could have happened? Where had she been when he'd taken the sleeping pills?

Semyon looked down again at the phone in his hand and called Veronika's number. She took a long time to answer, but Semyon stubbornly held the phone to his ear. And then suddenly – miraculously! – she answered, sounding sleepy and annoyed.

'Nikochka, where are you?' asked her husband.

'What do you mean?'

'I woke up and you weren't here . . . And that wreath is in the hallway, but today's Monday.'

'Monday?' Now Veronika sounded worried.

'Yes, Monday,' confirmed Semyon. 'Where are you?'

'I'm over at Darya lvanovna's place. I stayed here last night . . . I'm sorry, we were drinking brandy. She had a sort of panic attack . . . Can you take the wreath and hang it up on the corner for me, please? Do you know where it goes?'

'Are you really at Darya Ivanovna's?' Semyon couldn't help sounding suspicious.

'Hang on, sweetheart,' said Veronika. And then he heard a different, deeper, more languid and indulgent voice. 'Semyon, it's Darya Ivanovna. I really did feel dreadful yesterday, you know, so Nikochka spent the night here. Why don't the two of you come together next time? In fact, why don't you come over right now? It's not far. And there's still some brandy left!'

'Thanks, but I can't right now. I've got to go to work. But next time, definitely!' he promised, reassured.

Once he'd got dressed, Semyon walked to the corner of Yaroslaviv Val and Striletska Street, found the nail that had been hammered into the wall and hung the wreath on it. While he was straightening it up, he noticed several passers-by giving him funny looks.

When he got back home, he decided to have some breakfast. He made himself some instant coffee and then opened the fridge and took out the butter, the cheese and some smoked sausage. He took the bread out of the breadbin and opened the cutlery drawer. There was the late pharmacist's notebook, lying on top of the cutlery. Semyon had already seen it in passing, but he was surprised to find it in one of the kitchen drawers. He put it on the table, remembering to grab a knife and fork from the drawer. Then he made himself a couple of sandwiches and sat down at the table with his sandwiches to the left of him, by the window, his cup of coffee to the right and the notebook in front of him. He opened it at random, near the beginning. His eyes scanned the illegible handwriting, then he turned a page and froze, staring at the erotic image before him. The woman in the drawing was dancing, gracefully arching her body; she was looking straight ahead of her with her eyes wide open, hair loose, arms flung out to the sides, as though she were spinning around. She looked so familiar. Semyon grew pensive. He drank some coffee, ate one of his sandwiches, picked up the other . . . And then a sudden realisation pierced his heart. He took his wallet out of his jacket pocket, found the photograph of Alisa and put it on the table alongside the notebook. There was no doubt about it: the woman in the pharmacist's sketches was Alisa. Even the birthmark on her left cheek was the same in the drawing and the photograph. Semyon flicked through the notebook, looking at the other images. They were all of her, and they had all been drawn in a way that made her appear more beautiful, more sensual, than she was in real life. But why 'more sensual' than she was in real life? Why did he think that? How would he know what she was like in real life? Semyon leaned back and looked out of the window. The sunlight was no longer wintry – it was more golden, more restless.

He tried to remember everything that he knew about Alisa. He could remember her face, from the time she had opened the door to him. She wasn't unattractive, but there wasn't anything that special about her either. He certainly wouldn't have looked twice at her if he'd seen her in the street – during the daytime, at least. Apparently he saw things differently at night. She was more attractive in Volodka's photographs than she was in real life, too. Semyon picked up the photo of Alisa and looked at her eyes.

'Maybe it's a kind of inner beauty?' he thought, recalling his teenage years and a conversation with his geography teacher, who loved to tell his older students, 'Every single girl is beautiful. If you can't see it, you're just not looking at them properly!'

Semyon began to wonder when he would see her again. When would he next spend a few hours at her apartment? He wanted to find out more about their nocturnal relationship. Suddenly he remembered his recent conversation with Volodka, about getting a digital voice recorder, and this cheered him up immediately. He glanced at his watch, then called Volodka and asked him to go straight to the milk kitchen at 11 a.m., without calling round to pick him up first. He said he would meet him there.

He carefully closed the pharmacist's notebook and hid it on the top shelf of the kitchen cupboard, where they kept the guarantees and instructions for the vacuum cleaner, the iron and other domestic appliances. He didn't want Veronika looking though this book of drawings any more, as though it were just some glossy magazine at the hairdresser's. This book was now connected to his personal life. Conscious or subconscious – it didn't matter.

As he walked past the wreath that he had hung on the wall earlier that morning, it suddenly occurred to Semyon that there might be an inscription about Alisa in the notebook. He had to fight the urge to go back and start looking through it again.

Semyon bought the smallest digital voice recorder he could find – about the size of a matchbox, only considerably thinner – then took the bus to the milk kitchen. Volodka's Niva wasn't outside the grey Stalinist building yet. According to Semyon's watch it was 10.38 a.m. He went into Mariinsky Park.

The paths had been completely cleared of snow. Despite the fact that the temperature was close to zero, two young women in

261

sheepskin jackets sat smoking on the nearest bench. An old man was walking slowly towards him with a little dog on a lead. Semyon noticed that the man had a military bearing – he was probably a retired general, or a colonel.

He walked until he reached the tents that were set up in front of the main entrance to Parliament. He glanced indifferently at the slogans on the banners, which for some reason were facing the park rather than Parliament itself: 'Crimea Belongs to Russia', 'Justice is Worth Fighting For!', 'No to the Orange Plague', 'NATO Go Home!'

He shrugged and turned down the path leading to the viewing area, which looked out over the whole of the left bank of the Dnieper.

He walked past a young pregnant woman sitting on a bench. She was dressed in a long dark blue coat and over her curly hair she wore a man's fur hat, made of either muskrat or deerskin. Her face was red – she'd been crying.

Semyon stood for a little while in the viewing area, then glanced back at the pregnant woman.

When he returned to the Stalinist building, Volodka's Niva was already waiting outside the main entrance. The men in overalls carried the milk churns down and loaded them into the car.

'Have you ever tried goat's milk?' Volodka asked, as they pulled onto the main road.

'No,' said Semyon. 'But I've tried goat's cheese.'

'What's it like?'

'Tastes a bit sour, and smells like damp. I don't know why it's so expensive.'

An hour later they pulled up at the orphanage. The older boys took the milk churns into the cheese-making workshop and decanted the milk. The director came out to see Semyon and Volodka, and he was noticeably friendlier than usual. His mood may have improved in anticipation of the coming spring, because during their short conversation he looked up at the sky and the sun several times and smiled.

'Ah yes, I've got something for Gennady Ilyich,' the director suddenly remembered. 'Hey, Kolya!' he called, and a thin boy with long legs turned round.

'There's a blue parcel on the desk. Could you bring it out?'

The parcel weighed about five kilos. Semyon put it on the back seat of the Niva and returned to the others.

'You know, it's funny,' said the director. 'The boys were writing about the meaning of life, and judging by their essays about five of them have decided that the meaning of life is work.' He nodded at the cheese-making room. 'They never used to think that. I know them all inside out – they have to write essays on the meaning of life twice a year!'

They parted with the director warmly, almost as friends.

On the way back Semyon showed his digital acquisition to his friend.

'So I shouldn't plan on getting an early night tonight, then?' Volodka teased him.

'I'll call you later and let you know.'

After returning the empty milk churns to Hrushevsky Street, the friends said goodbye. Volodka drove off, and Semyon called Gennady Ilyich.

'Where are you?' asked the deputy.

'In town. Not far from the Officers' Club.'

'Excellent. Come to the Kiev hotel, and I'll buy you a coffee.'

Gennady Ilyich entered the hotel foyer deep in his own thoughts. It was only when he reached the staircase leading to the restaurant on the first floor that he stopped and seemed to remember why he was there. He caught Semyon's eye and beckoned him over.

The waiter took Gennady Ilyich's smart coat as though it were a priceless treasure and carried it off with great care. Then, rather more casually, he took Semyon's leather jacket, with his scarf protruding from the pocket.

'Do you just want a coffee, or something to eat?' asked Gennady Ilyich.

'Coffee's fine.'

'Good. I've got two dinners booked in today already. First with our lot, and then at midnight with the opposition.' Just for a moment, Gennady Ilyich's weary smile made his round face seem attractive and kind.

He ordered a bottle of Borzhomi mineral water for himself and a coffee for Semyon.

'Have you heard anything about an organisation called the Embassy of the Moon?' Gennady Ilyich asked suddenly.

'Why?' Semyon looked anxious.

'Oh, the deputies from the opposition are trying to join it. Some kind of new, unifying ideology. And it doesn't cost much to join.'

'It's not worth it,' Semyon replied nervously, remembering his own membership document with the silver inscription on the front. 'It's like that Great White Brotherhood cult, only the opposite.'

'The opposite?' Gennady Ilyich began nodding. 'Yes, the opposite. They meet every night in different nightclubs. Half of Parliament's already joined . . . But I don't think I've got the energy for it. Anyway, that's enough about that!'

For a couple of minutes the deputy was lost in his own thoughts, frowning and concentrating hard. He gave an ambiguous smile and then sighed.

'Let's forget about the Embassy of the Moon!' The deputy put his hand in his jacket pocket. 'Here, this is for you. I wanted you to be the first to have one. They're for you and your wife.'

He held out two plastic boxes to Semyon.

Semyon opened one of the boxes. Inside, on a little tray coated with velvet, lay a thick gold cross with a trident in the centre. There was a gold chain underneath the little tray.

'It's a deputy's chain,' Gennady Ilyich said with pride. 'Who knows, maybe you'll be qualified to wear it one day!'

Semyon looked gratefully at his boss and nodded.

'Do you have any children?' the deputy asked suddenly.

'No.'

Hearing footsteps nearby, Gennady Ilyich turned round. He paused until the waiter had walked past, then turned back to his companion.

'Would you like to?' He looked expectantly into Semyon's eyes.

'I would, yes,' he admitted.

'What about your wife?'

'I think she would too.'

'Then maybe I can help.' Gennady Ilyich momentarily lost his composure. He chewed his fat lips nervously and looked at Semyon again. 'There's a little girl . . . she's going to be a pretty little thing too.'

'How old is she?' asked Semyon.

'How old? She's not even born yet! She's due in the next week or so.'

'Does she need adopting?' Semyon was perplexed.

'You know, people register pedigree puppies in dog clubs a year before they're even conceived!' Gennady Ilyich declared enthusiastically. Then he sighed and lowered his voice to a whisper. 'Her mother won't keep her, I know that much. In such situations it's better to plan ahead.'

'She'll need breast milk,' Semyon thought aloud.

'That's not a problem.' The deputy waved his hand airily. 'This country has more breast milk than Russia has oil!'

Semyon thought about Veronika and didn't say anything.

Gennady Ilyich glanced at his watch.

'So, what do you think?' he asked impatiently.

'I'm all for it,' said Semyon. 'But I'll need to discuss it with my wife.'

'OK. Have a word with her, and give me a call.'

Semyon nodded. Gennady Ilyich paid the waiter and started walking towards the exit. When he reached the double doors he looked back at Semyon and nodded goodbye.

70

9 May Street, Boryspil

When Valya got out of bed the next morning, the rocking motion woke Dima up. He opened his eyes a little and saw his wife standing there in her nightdress, holding a pair of flesh-coloured tights. She checked the tights for holes, then sat down on the edge of the bed and put them on.

Dima suddenly remembered the note. He felt happy. After all, the morning was starting just like any other. After Valya had finished getting dressed, she would make him something to eat and then leave for work. Then he would get up, have a leisurely breakfast and decide what he was going to do that day. He might take a walk to the newspaper kiosk. He might even buy a copy of *Job Search*. Not because he actually wanted to find a job, more for Valya's benefit.

Outside, the morning sun was shining. A shaft of sunlight entered the room, forcing its way through the gap between the curtains and making Dima think about the summer. Summer was always an expensive time of year – it made you feel like going out, celebrating, treating yourself to ice cream and beer. Furthermore, this summer Valya's belly would begin to swell with their growing child and he would have to indulge her, because pregnant women are notoriously prone to mood swings and cravings!

The door slammed and Dima was left alone in the house. He luxuriated for another half an hour in bed before getting up. Then he remembered the previous day's note, only this time he didn't feel afraid. 'It's just empty threats,' he thought. But at that moment his brain conjured up an image of Boris and Zhenya, the baggage handlers – they were waving at him. 'But they're dead!' Dima's breath caught in his throat and he broke into a cold sweat.

Dima looked at the sunlight penetrating the gap in the curtains and suddenly felt the need to hide, or at least to shut the curtains properly so that no outside light could find its way into the room. He went over to the window, peeped through the gap in the curtains and saw an unshaven man in a dirty padded jacket hanging around near his front yard, on the other side of the fence. The man was just standing there, smoking, looking down the road and off into the distance. Dima drew the curtains firmly, and the room grew a little darker.

He got dressed and sat on the bed. He was hungry, but he didn't want to go into the kitchen. The kitchen curtains were more decorative than useful – they didn't fully cover the window, and they were probably open anyway.

Scruffy seemed to sense his master's mood and padded over on his soft paws to rub himself against Dima's legs. Dima stroked him without looking down.

'What are we going to do?' he murmured.

Dima sighed. He looked at the blank television screen and listened to the silence. Silence is a good thing, he thought, but there's more than enough of it at the cemetery. Noise is a sign of life.

He switched the television on but turned the sound right down. They were showing news footage of President Yushchenko and Prime Minister Yanukovich arguing about something. They both looked cross.

'I wish I had your problems,' muttered Dima, looking at the President.

He went into the kitchen and pulled the curtains shut. Only then did he peer under the lid of the frying pan, to see what he was having for breakfast. The fried potatoes were still warm, as was the pink circle of fried sausage.

After his breakfast he drank a shot of home-made nettle vodka and went back to bed, as though sleep were the best refuge from fear.

His sleep was interrupted by a sudden crash, like a wardrobe falling onto a wooden floor. By rights this noise should have instantly banished all vestiges of sleep, but the home-brew haze in Dima's brain delayed both his hearing and his thought processes, so the sudden crash plunged him into a kind of dull incomprehension, rather than fear. There was dull incomprehension in his eyes too, when he opened them and saw at the foot of his bed two puny men with prominent cheekbones, wearing identical black leather jackets. One of the men was holding a gun.

'Get up!' ordered the man not holding the gun.

Dima tried to get up, but he couldn't. His head felt heavier than usual.

The man's face contorted with rage; baring his teeth, he punched Dima in the mouth.

Dima felt the bitter taste of blood on his lips. The drunken haze was still preventing him from thinking clearly. He just felt exhausted, like an animal that no longer has the energy to run away or hide. He looked at these two nondescript individuals, at their smoothly shaven cheeks, and for some reason he thought of *Job Search*, which he hadn't got round to buying that morning.

'Where are the rest of the ampoules?' asked the man with the gun in a quiet, steely voice. 'Who's selling them?'

Another blow caught Dima on the chin. His head hit the pillow. He raised himself up on his elbow and saw blood on the white pillowcase.

'Listen,' said the man not holding the gun. 'Your dog recognised the smell and brought us to this house twice. We know it was you who stole the suitcase full of ampoules from the airport. You've got no idea what you've got yourself involved in. I'll ask you again: where are the rest of the ampoules?'

'Have you got Shamil?' Dima asked suddenly, licking his cut lower lip.

'We did have him, but now he's dead,' said the man not holding the gun. He rubbed his right fist with his left hand. 'Where are the ampoules?'

Dima thought about Shamil. So they were the ones who had taken him. They had probably killed him too.

Another punch, and Dima's head hit the pillow once more.

'We should finish him off,' said the man with the gun nervously. 'We're not going to get anything out of him.'

'No, he's going to give us the ampoules first,' said the other man. Then he looked back at Dima. 'Where have you hidden them, you son of a bitch?'

Dima pointed at the right-hand corner of the room, in the direction of the garage.

Both men looked into the corner, where a long green skirt of Valya's was hanging over the back of a chair.

The man holding the gun squatted down and looked underneath the chair. He looked up at his colleague with irritation and disappointment, then back at Dima. The man not holding the gun raised his fist to hit Dima again, but all of a sudden Scruffy leapt up like a streak of grey lightning and sank his teeth into the man's wrist, clinging to the sleeve of his leather jacket with the claws of all four paws. Blood spurted from the wound and the man started waving his arm about, swearing and trying to shake the cat off. He looked at the man with the gun.

'Shoot him!' he yelled, still frantically trying to get Scruffy off his arm.

His colleague aimed the gun at the cat but was unable to fire. Blood from the man's wrist was spraying all over the bed and onto the gunman's face.

A shot rang out, and Scruffy fell to the floor with a thud. The cat's victim clutched his chest with his hand. Blood trickled through his fingers. He suddenly made a wheezing sound and fell to the floor beside the cat. His eyes searched for his colleague and then froze. He was dead.

Pale with shock, the gunman spread his arms wide in confusion, still holding the gun in his right hand.

'What the fuck?!' Dima heard him whisper. 'What the fuck?!'

The man turned to Dima. He put the cold barrel of the gun to Dima's forehead and pulled the trigger. Dima didn't even have time to be afraid. But the barrel was empty – instead of a bang, it made a dry metallic click.

The gunman pulled the trigger again. Another click. He stuffed the gun nervously into his jacket pocket and hurried out of the room.

The fear of death caught up with Dima. He sat motionless, staring at the dead man and at Scruffy's body, covered in blood. It felt unusually warm and stuffy in the room.

The pool of blood spreading from beneath the corpse on the floor was approaching Dima's bare feet. When it was only a centimetre away from his toes, he got up and went over to the door. He stood there for about ten minutes, then he started feeling faint and nauseous so went out into the hall and noticed that the front door was ajar, its safety bolt smashed. They had obviously used a master key to open the outside lock, resorting to brute force in the absence of an equivalent for the bolt. Dima shut himself in the bathroom and hung his head over the toilet bowl. He stuck the index and middle fingers of his right hand down his throat and spent about five minutes emptying the contents of his stomach, spitting and coughing.

When he staggered out into the cold hallway, the thought occurred to him: what if Scruffy were still alive?

He went back into the bathroom and got a clean white towel. Giving the pool of blood a wide berth, he laid the towel on the bedroom floor and transferred Scruffy's blood-covered body onto it. The white towel immediately turned red. Dima wrapped the cat up in the towel and carried him into the garage, spurred on by the cold that was pricking his exposed ankles, because he'd come out wearing open-backed slippers on his bare feet.

In the garage he placed the towel and Scruffy on the concrete floor next to the heater and switched it on. He remembered nursing Scruffy back to health in this very same place after his run-in with King from next door. 'Maybe he'll survive this too?' thought Dima hopefully.

He took an ampoule from his toolbox. Breaking the glass top off, he turned Scruffy's jaw to the ceiling and shook every last drop into his mouth.

Then he covered Scruffy with a cloth and went outside.

An old man he knew, who lived two doors down, drove by in his Moskvich. He looked at Dima in surprise. Dima touched his fingers to his cheek and felt dried blood. He quickly locked the garage and went back inside the house to wash it off.

71

Lipovka village, Kiev region

The snow was still clinging to the ground and to the fields. It was more tenacious in the forest but had already started to slip from the top of the little hill by the lake, revealing the naked, sandy summit. Holding Yasya on her lap, Irina was now sledging down the lower part of the hill. Yasya was smiling, either because she was enjoying the sledging or because she liked the sun, which was sitting in the sky directly above them, above their little hill, above Lipovka, and shining more bravely and with greater warmth than usual.

The snow was no longer really snow, as such – it was more of a thin crust, which either crackled and crunched beneath the iron runners of the sledge or made a ringing sound, like metal striking metal.

Irina's legs were aching now, so she pulled Yasya on the sledge to the nearest bench by someone's front gate and sat down to rest.

A fat woman in a bright blue Chinese padded jacket and warm, grey woollen trousers cycled past on the ice-covered verge. She looked over at Irina as she passed. After about twenty metres she stopped and got off her bicycle, then leaned it against the fence and walked back to the bench where Irina was sitting. Irina thought she recognised her.

'Are you Baba Shura's daughter?' she asked, in the same broad village accent as Irina's mother.

'Yes.'

'What's your surname?'

'Koval.'

'Why haven't you brought your daughter for her injections?' asked the woman sternly.

'She doesn't play with other children. She hardly leaves the house!' Irina began to defend herself.

'She hasn't even got a medical card. Do you want to get into trouble for neglecting your child, like Olenka Shyp from Fasivochka? They took her daughter away and put her into care – she'd starved her half to death!'

'But I'm feeding mine – look how rosy her cheeks are!' Irina showed the woman Yasya's face.

'That's just the frost.' The woman waved her hand dismissively. 'Come to the clinic tomorrow, between ten and twelve. And bring her birth certificate – you'll need it for her medical card.'

Irina nodded guiltily. The woman maintained her stern expression as she turned and walked back to her bicycle, shaking her head as she went and mumbling criticisms under her breath.

Irina and Yasya returned home for lunch. Irina's breasts were full of milk again, but after feeding for a couple of minutes Yasya pushed the nipple out of her mouth and started to cry. She wouldn't calm down until Irina brought her a bottle of formula milk from the boiler room.

Then Irina made herself a bowl of buckwheat and took a piece of pork fat from the freezer, slicing it so thinly that it would have looked translucent if held up to the light. That was her lunch: buckwheat and pork fat. Yasya fell asleep while she was eating, and a peaceful silence descended over the house.

Irina's mother returned home at about 3 p.m. She was flushed and out of breath. She pulled her felt boots off and bashed them together out of habit, as though she were knocking snow off them, even though this was no longer necessary. She hung her coat up on a hook.

She went into the bedroom and sat on Irina's bed. The metal frame creaked beneath her weight, and Irina woke up.

'I went to the village council about your milk,' her mother whispered with a glance at Yasya, who was asleep on the other side of Irina. 'They said that three families from Kiev have moved to Gavronshchina, and one of them has a baby boy . . . Maybe they need some milk? Gavronshchina's not far from here. You could give them a jar a day. And maybe Egor could drop it off, on his way to Kiev . . .'

'Well, I'm not going to go and ask them,' Irina said and lowered her gaze.

After being shouted at and reprimanded today by the community nurse she was already carrying twice her own body weight in shame and fear. She would be quite happy if she never had to talk to anyone else ever again, apart from her mother and Egor.

'I'll go and ask then,' said her mother. 'I'm not sure how much we should charge, though. What did they used to pay you in Kiev, sixty hryvnas a day?'

Irina nodded.

'Mind you, everything's more expensive in Kiev. If this lot had any money they wouldn't be living in Gavronshchina . . . But anyway, I'll ask for fifty. If they want to haggle, I'll knock ten off . . . The bus to Gavronshchina leaves at five.'

'Take some milk with you. Then at least their little one can try it.'

'All right, I will. There's an empty lemonade bottle in the kitchen. It'll fit nicely into my coat pocket.'

Irina expressed some milk, almost a third of a litre jar. She tried to express more, but there wasn't any. At first she was surprised and upset, then she remembered that she hadn't had very much to eat, either that day or the day before. There was still enough to fill the lemonade bottle right to the brim.

At 4.30 p.m. her mother put on her felt boots and her coat. She put the bottle of milk into her pocket and went out.

72

'Quiet Centre', Kiev

Veronika arrived at Darya Ivanovna's in tears. Without taking off her shoes or her sheepskin jacket, she went into the living room and sat down at the round table. She stared at the armchair, which was positioned so that whoever sat in it would be able to see both the door and the balcony. She suddenly had a strange feeling, which made her stop crying. She didn't even notice Darya Ivanovna anxiously follow her in, clasping her hands together as if in prayer.

'Would you like a brandy?' the pharmacist's widow asked tentatively.

Veronika nodded.

'Here, drink up,' Darya Ivanovna said gently, holding a glass out to her. 'This'll make you feel better.'

'Something terrible happened yesterday,' began Veronika, looking down at the brandy in her glass. 'Senya came home late. I was already asleep. But he woke me up and asked if I wanted a baby, and then he started saying that he knew of a baby girl we could adopt, a pretty little thing . . . I asked him who she was, how we could adopt her, but he just clammed up. I asked him where she was – was she in a maternity unit? Why didn't her parents want her? But Senya still didn't answer. I asked him how he could bring it up so casually, after what happened seven years ago.'

'Why?' asked Darya Ivanovna. 'What did happen seven years ago?'

Veronika downed her brandy and held her glass out to her friend, silently entreating her to refill it.

'We were in a horrific car accident.' Veronika's voice suddenly sounded like it was coming from far away, as though she were somewhere else entirely, and the light in her eyes seemed to go out. She wasn't looking at her friend any more. 'I had a head injury. When I regained consciousness the first thing I did was to ask about our daughter. But the doctor said, "They only brought two of you in."'

Tears spilled from her eyes, which were staring off into space.

'What was her name?' Darya Ivanovna asked quietly.

'I can't remember,' whispered Veronika. 'I forgot everything. Almost everything. After the accident I had to go and see a psychiatrist every day. He and Semyon proved that our daughter hadn't died, that she had in fact never existed . . . That we never had a daughter . . .'

Darya Ivanovna held her breath. Alarm flickered in her eyes. 'Do you have any photographs of her?'

Veronika thought about it. 'No, there aren't any photographs.' She touched the fingers of her right hand to her lips then looked at her hand. 'And there never were any photographs. I don't remember us taking a single one.'

'But people always take photos of new babies!' Darya Ivanovna clearly felt uncomfortable, and her hand reached for the bottle of brandy.

'Maybe the psychiatrist hypnotised me? The two of them, him and Semyon, assured me that I didn't have any children . . . But I remember her!'

The spark suddenly returned to Veronika's eyes. She looked at her friend.

'Senya must have hidden the photos . . . or burned them!'

'Now, calm down!' Darya Ivanovna begged Veronika. 'Just calm down! And ask him again today where he got the idea about adopting a baby, and what baby he was talking about. A man doesn't suddenly decide that he wants to be a father just like that. It's not normal. It could mean anything. Maybe he suddenly found out that he's incurably ill and is worried about leaving you on your own?'

At these words, Veronika's look of anguish was replaced by one of alarm. She stood up.

'I've got to go,' she said.

73

Semyon's conversation with his wife had unnerved him. He hadn't expected her to jump down his throat like that. What had triggered it? He'd just mentioned that there was the possibility of adopting a cute baby girl. They didn't have any children of their own, but it was about time they thought about it – another couple of years and it would be too late. They could adopt their first child – she would awaken Veronika's maternal instinct, and then Veronika would want a baby of her own! Seven years ago, after the accident, her psychiatrist had told Semyon that they needed a stable and active family life, full of domestic worries and day-to-day concerns. It was strange that he hadn't suggested it to her himself, come to think of it – she'd seen him every day for nearly a year. Her appointments were in the morning and she would always come home happy and focused, but by the evening she would start falling apart again, crying and running around the apartment, looking out through the curtains. She was searching for a daughter who had never existed. She used to go into a kind of trance, as though she could neither see nor hear Semyon. Then suddenly she would stop and collapse into the armchair, pale and in tears. He would go over to her, kneel before her, take her hand in his and kiss her fingers, trying to calm her down. But she would just whisper, 'Go and find her! Bring her home!'

So he would get dressed and go out. At first he just used to stand outside the front door, sometimes for an hour, sometimes an hour and a half. Then he would go back inside to find Veronika sitting exactly where he'd left her, as though she hadn't moved. He would tell her that he hadn't found her, and she would remain motionless for about five minutes. Then she would nod and hold her hand out to him. Semyon would help her to stand and then put her to bed. This went on day after day. Eventually Semyon got fed up with standing outside the front door and began to walk the dark streets, exploring the courtyards. He found that he used to walk past the same people, at the same time, and after a while they would greet him. One night, several months later, he realised with alarm that he really was looking for her now, this little girl they'd never known. Once he even asked someone who greeted him, 'You haven't seen a little girl, have you? She's three years old.' The man offered to help him look for her, and the two of them searched all the court-yards in the vicinity. At some point Semyon had come to his senses and thanked the man, saying that his wife must already have found her.

Almost a year passed before the sessions with the psychiatrist started to help Veronika and she forgot about the accident, and the child. Life was good. Until now! Why hadn't it occurred to him that bringing up the idea of adoption was bound to remind Veronika of the accident?

Semyon shook his head in despair. He bit his lip and thought about how he really did want a baby. This world was too cold . . . and not only in winter. Hope is what keeps you going, and the best form of hope is a child.

Semyon went into the kitchen, climbed onto a stool and took the late pharmacist's notebook from the top shelf of the cupboard.

He sat down with it at the kitchen table and began looking through the familiar drawings. They calmed him down. For some reason he was convinced that the Alisa in the drawings would have wanted to be a mother. He could just imagine the figure of a child beside her. It would have been a kind of 'divine' eroticism! But he was sure that the pharmacist didn't have any children either, otherwise his widow would have had more to worry about than hanging up and taking down that wreath.

The last pencil sketch was followed by another page covered with the fine handwriting so typical of the medical profession. Every paragraph began with a date, which was more or less legible. This page began with the date: 28 February 2000.

Semyon worked it out: the accident happened on 12 October 1999, so that was October, November, December, January, February . . . four and a half months after the accident. Semyon peered more closely at the handwritten lines, which seemed to have been written illegibly on purpose, to prevent anyone finding out about the pharmacist's secret life. Were the pencil drawings also part of his secret life? If so, then there was probably some reference to Alisa in the notes too.

Semyon looked out of the window. The sunlight was refracted through raindrops on the windowpane, turning them gold. One corner of the kitchen table was also painted gold with sunlight. Semyon put his left hand into this light and felt its warmth almost immediately. The warmth of the coming spring. Keeping his hand in the sun, he looked back at the open diary.

'"28 February 2000,"' he repeated, and then continued. '"A left at about 10 p.m. last night. She left her gold watch with the chain strap. She doesn't want to be cured. She asked me just to appreciate her for who she is. My head is aching from the sleepless nights. Good job Darya likes to drink. Nearly finished work on the new sedative

– it will stimulate complete indifference, just a few hours initially, and then a long, healthy sleep. I've already tested it on Darya.'"

Semyon looked out of the window again, at the golden raindrops sticking to the glass.

'A must be Alisa,' he thought. 'What did she have that she didn't want to be cured of?'

Semyon's reflections were interrupted by his mobile phone ringing in the pocket of his leather jacket.

'Why haven't you called me back?' asked Gennady Ilyich.

'I was just about to,' answered Semyon, hesitantly.

'Did you get a chance to talk to your wife?'

'Yes,' sighed Semyon. 'She said no.'

'That's a shame,' said the deputy, his voice wilting. 'A real shame.'

Putting his mobile back down on the table, Semyon returned to the notebook.

'"2 March 2000 – I think I met another 'night' person last night. I walked A home at about 1 a.m. and took a short cut back. Said hello to someone as I cut through a courtyard, and he asked me to help him look for his daughter. We looked for her until 2 a.m., then he apologised and left . . ."'

Semyon was distracted by the phone ringing again, but this time it was their landline ringing in the living room.

'It's Darya Ivanovna. Can you come over? But don't mention it to Veronika.'

'I've never been to your place before,' said Semyon, tentatively. 'Where do you live?'

Darya Ivanovna told him the address.

Puzzled, Semyon carefully closed the notebook and put it back on the shelf.

74

9 May Street, Boryspil, evening

Dima's fear was replaced by a feeling of impending doom, as though he were infected with some kind of incurable disease and knew that it was about to erupt inside him, leading to certain death. He walked to the bus station, his sodden boots squelching through the snow that was melting in the warmth of the sun. What would he say to Valya? And when would he say it?

He couldn't think straight. His thoughts kept interrupting one another, and a growing sense of confusion accompanied his ominous feeling of dread.

The wheels of the passing cars sprayed dirty slush over the pavements.

'What am I going to tell her?' thought Dima. 'Should I tell her about the body in the bedroom? About Scruffy? About the ampoules? No, not the ampoules. What's going to happen now? Will they come back? What should I do?'

Dima knew his train of thought was logical. So, making the most of this sudden clarity, he reviewed the situation once more.

By the time he arrived at the amusement arcade, he'd already decided what he was going to say to his wife.

But Valya was so happy that her husband had come to pick her up at work that she gave him ten fifty-kopek coins and sent him off to try his luck.

Dima went straight to his favourite machine, which had already responded so well on two occasions. The machine started blinking, beeping and flashing its multicoloured lights, as though it recognised him and knew what he was after.

He put a coin into the slot and pressed the buttons below the spinning reels. The dim light in the room made him feel calm and confident. He felt sure it was his lucky day. But it wasn't. The machine cheerfully swallowed all of his money.

Dima returned meekly to the little window.

'Ten more minutes,' said Valya. 'Sonya's always late – she lives near the cemetery.'

'You don't have to live near the cemetery to always be late,' thought Dima. Then he thought about the body lying in the bedroom.

'Now, I don't want you to panic, it's not good for you in your condition,' was the first thing he said when they got to the square near the bus station. 'But there's a dead body in the house . . .'

Valya stopped. She turned to look at her husband, horrified.

'Some thugs broke in while I was asleep, two of them. I was barely awake and they started beating me up, trying to find out where we kept our money!' Dima turned his cut and swollen lower lip inside out, thereby proving the veracity of his story. 'My Fluffy jumped on one of them and bit his wrist. He must have hit an artery, or something. So the man shouted at the other one to kill him – Fluffy, I mean – and the other man shot Fluffy but hit the first man in the chest. I took Fluffy into the garage and wrapped him up in a towel. But the dead man's still on the floor.'

'What about the other one?' asked Valya, her voice trembling.

'He got scared and ran off,' answered Dima.

They stood there without moving, in silence, for about three minutes.

'Shall we go then?' he asked softly, almost tenderly.

She nodded but still didn't move.

'Come on!'

'There's a dead person in there,' she whispered.

'We can get rid of him,' Dima started whispering too. 'I would have done it myself, but he's a bit heavy. If we do it together it won't take long . . .'

They continued walking down the street. They were walking slowly, but Valya still kept lagging behind. It took them over an hour to reach their wicket gate.

There was no indication of what had happened either in the front yard or on the doorstep, which was probably the reason Dima was able to persuade his wife to go inside.

He sat her down in the kitchen, still in her coat, and told her to stay out of the bedroom.

'I'll clean up a bit . . . but then I'll need you to give me a hand.'

'Maybe we should call the militia?' Valya suggested hopefully.

Dima shook his head. 'We'd never hear the end of it. They'd be round here every day, asking all sorts of questions . . .'

Dima filled a large bowl with water, threw a floorcloth in and went into the bedroom.

He managed to wash most of the pool of blood off the wooden floor relatively quickly, although he did have to change the water in the bowl three times. But washing off the dried blood around the edges was more of a challenge. He had to really scrub at it, rubbing the blood-soaked cloth into the floor as hard as he could. Dima tried not to look at the body lying nearby, but a couple of times he had to lift up an arm, or a leg, to wipe underneath it.

Finally he decided the floor was clean. At least, it looked that way in the dim light of the bedside lamp – he'd washed the floor without turning the main light on.

Next he dragged an old East German rug out of the wardrobe, a gift from his mother-in-law. He spread it out next to the dead man, and the smell of mothballs suddenly filled the room. Dima had always hated this smell, but now it seemed appropriate.

He squatted down and rolled the body onto the rug. Then he wrapped one end of the rug over so that it covered the body, before rolling over the other end. You could no longer see the dead man's head.

Dima was grateful to the East Germans for having made such useful rugs.

Now everything was ready, and he knew exactly what to do next.

He went out into the garage, started the car and reversed it into the front yard. He then went back into the kitchen, where Valya was still sitting on the stool buttoned up in her warm coat, just as he'd left her.

Dima poured himself a shot of vodka and drank it. Then he looked outside.

A car went past the house. The light from its yellow headlights swam over the fence of their front yard and disappeared.

'Just don't ask me any more questions for now,' Dima said to his wife. 'I'm just going to have one more, and then we'll load it into the car and get rid of it . . . I know a place not far from here. OK?'

Valya nodded.

After his second shot, Dima turned on all the lights in the house and took Valya into the bedroom. She felt for one end of the heavy rug, and Dima took the other. They dragged the rolled-up rug into the hallway, then carried it out to the doorstep and loaded it onto the back seat of the car. Everything would have been fine, except the back door wouldn't close. Dima had to spend about five minutes fiddling about, rearranging the rug so it lay at an oblique angle, before the door finally closed.

Dima told his wife to sit in the front.

He started the engine and, without putting the headlights on, drove in darkness out of the front yard.

When he reached the demolished fence of the burnt-out building, he stopped the car, switched the engine off and listened. Everything was quiet.

He and Valya pulled the corpse out of the car and carried it over to the well.

'What if someone finds him?' asked Valya.

'If they do, hopefully they'll give him a proper burial,' whispered Dima.

They placed the rug-wrapped corpse on the edge of the well and pushed it in.

'There,' breathed Dima. 'Now, let's go home.'

'I don't want to,' said Valya. 'I don't want to go back there . . .'

'Where do you want to go, then?'

Valya was silent for a while.

'Why don't we go for some *pelmeni*?' suggested Dima. He was genuinely hungry.

'OK,' agreed his wife.

75

Lipovka village, Kiev region

A white Volga stopped by Irina's fence the following evening and a man in a sheepskin jacket got out, holding a briefcase. He looked attentively at the house number, which hung to the right of the front door. He glanced at the horseshoe nailed above the door and smiled indulgently. Then he rang the bell.

Baba Shura opened the door to him. She was dressed smartly, in a green cardigan with a brooch on it and a long black skirt that she had ironed specially for the occasion.

'Oh, come in, come in!' she said. 'Come through to the kitchen!'

He made a formal and rather grand entrance. He placed his briefcase on the floor by the wall; then he removed his sheepskin jacket and hung it on a hook. He glanced down at his short boots then back at his hostess. She understood the question in his eyes.

'Don't worry about it, come in as you are,' she said.

Their guest was relieved that he didn't have to take his boots off. He had just remembered that in his haste that morning he had put on a pair of undarned socks. How could you have a serious conversation with anyone about business or financial matters once they noticed that you had a hole in your sock?

Irina heard someone come in but didn't come out into the hall. She was shy. She knew that their visitor must be from Gavronshchina, come to talk about her milk. He could work everything out with her mother first, and then her mother would call her.

'Please, take a seat. Oh, I've forgotten your name! I know that your wife is Kateryna, like the wife of our President –'

'Ilko Petrovich,' said their guest, looking around the kitchen and simultaneously pulling down his brown hand-knitted jumper, which was a bit on the small side and had ridden up above the belt of his trousers to reveal a dark blue shirt that was straining at the seams. He sat down.

'Would you like some coffee?'

He nodded, and looked around the kitchen again.

'What's your name?' he asked. He spoke with the same strong accent as Baba Shura.

'Koval. Aleksandra Vasilievna.'

'A good, solid family name,' remarked their guest. 'One of my colleagues at work studies Ukrainian surnames. He's got a doctorate. Is your husband's name also Koval?'

'It was. He passed away.'

'What did he die of?' asked the guest, with cautious curiosity.

'Liver disease.'

'Did he drink?'

'Only on special occasions.'

'Are there any hereditary diseases in your family?'

'Diseases? Of course not!' Baba Shura looked at Ilko Petrovich in alarm.

'You have to understand—' his voice grew more serious – 'milk is like blood. Nationality is poured into a child through milk, as a way of establishing its identity. If a Polish woman breastfeeds a Ukrainian baby, then the child will be Polish, not Ukrainian. There have already been such cases. The country's done enough damage to itself already with that dreadful formula milk that everyone's using!'

Baba Shura listened to Ilko Petrovich with growing concern. Even when he'd opened the door to her in Gavronshchina he'd provoked various thoughts, none of them pleasant. To start with, he was no dashing young bridegroom – he must have been at least fifty. He had little round piggy eyes, fat lips and a fleshy mole on his right cheek, just like a woman. And his wife, Kateryna, can't have been more than twenty years old. Sitting there on the sofa in her traditional embroidered blouse, all pale and skinny and silent, like his complete opposite . . . He spoke on behalf of his young wife, just as she, Aleksandra Vasilievna, was speaking on behalf of her daughter. But as a parent she had every right to speak on her daughter's behalf. Why didn't he let his wife speak for herself?

'Do you have a family archive, by any chance? Any old photographs?' he asked unexpectedly.

'Yes, there are some photographs,' she said.

Baba Shura got up and poured a cup of freshly brewed coffee, then placed it in front of her guest.

She went through Irina's room to her own and took the old photo album out of her wardrobe. She brought it into the kitchen and gave it to Ilko Petrovich.

He glanced in irritation at the weak light given off by the bulb hanging from the ceiling. Then he opened the album and his face brightened. Thanks to Baba Shura's husband and grandfather there was an extensive photographic record of their family history. There was a photo of her grandfather himself, a tall good-looking man with a moustache. He had been a landowner and was known for being strict with lazy farmhands. And there was his wife, wearing an imperious look and a coral necklace. Even though it was nearly a century old and captured in black and white, this necklace seemed to glow with its true colour.

A gentle smile crept across the face of her guest and it transformed him, making him look more attractive, more agreeable and endearingly vulnerable.

'Everything's going to be fine,' thought Baba Shura, noticing this change.

After leafing slowly through the whole album and drinking his coffee without sugar, which also surprised her, Ilko Petrovich looked pensively at his hostess.

'I picked up the results from the laboratory today. Your daughter's milk is very healthy. Top quality. It's a shame she's a single mother . . .'

Aleksandra Vasilievna's mood darkened. Now she was going to get a lecture on single mothers from this one too! Oh, poor Irinka. She needed a marriage stamp in her passport. Why was that Egor dragging his heels?

'Excuse me, Ilko Petrovich,' said Baba Shura, 'but our country herself is a single mother. Where are all the real men? They're all out for what they can get, but do any of them think of marrying her, of taking some responsibility? Not a bit of it!'

'Our country . . . a single mother?' repeated her guest thoughtfully and without taking the slightest offence. 'What wise words! You're quite right!'

The respect with which he spoke put Baba Shura back in a good mood.

'Ukraine is like a single mother,' he said again, listening to each word as he spoke. 'Everyone wants to sleep with her, but no one will marry her! You are a wise woman, Aleksandra Vasilievna. I will use that in one of my lectures, to demonstrate the wisdom of the people.'

Baba Shura felt a little embarrassed.

'Right, well, we've got a bit sidetracked!' Ilko Petrovich suddenly glanced at his watch. 'What's your price per litre?'

'I told you yesterday, fifty hryvnas.'

'Aleksandra Vasilievna, I might be a professor but I don't earn much. Maybe you could knock a bit off? We're Ukrainians born and bred, just like your family!'

'How much can you offer?'

'Well, what about thirty per litre?'

Baba Shura multiplied thirty hryvnas by thirty days: nine hundred hryvnas a month. She added her own pension to the amount, and that took it over a thousand.

'Fine,' she said. 'Come on, let me introduce you to my daughter.'

'I can meet her another time,' said Ilko Petrovich. 'We've already agreed on everything – there's no need to disturb her! I'll pick up the milk myself . . . And now I must be off. Kateryna's probably expecting me. Since she had the child she's been terribly weak. Although she's from a good family, she seems rather sickly. Oh, I nearly forgot – I brought you a couple of journals with my articles in.'

Before leaving, her guest took two academic journals from his briefcase, Linguistics and Nation & Culture, and presented them reverently to his hostess.

76

'Quiet Centre', Kiev

Darya Ivanovna greeted Semyon cordially. She sat him in the kitchen and brewed some strong coffee, waiting until he relaxed a little before attempting to engage him in conversation.

'Veronika came to see me,' she said, looking into his eyes. 'She was really upset. She started telling me about the accident . . .'

Semyon froze, his coffee cup at his lips. He didn't want to talk about the accident. He never wanted to think about it again.

'I'm sorry.' Darya Ivanovna smiled guiltily. 'I know it's personal. I don't mean to pry . . . I lost my own husband recently . . .'

Semyon nodded.

Darya Ivanovna began talking about her husband, about his foibles. Semyon was fascinated. Not only because Darya Ivanovna knew how to tell a good story, but also because she was talking about the author of the notebook that had riveted Semyon's attention so unexpectedly that morning.

'So he used to invent new medicines?' asked her guest.

'That's probably a bit of an overstatement.' Darya Ivanovna shook her head. 'He just put together new combinations from various medicines that were already in use. A couple of times he even fulfilled orders for private pharmacological mini-factories . . . But most of all he played around with sedatives. He was obsessed with making the world a calmer place. I think he was deeply irritated by the world. He only ever smiled in the evening, when darkness had fallen . . . Even then, he didn't smile very often.'

'What do you mean by mini-factories?' asked Semyon.

'They're like private laboratories. The oligarchs don't have any faith in the products of mass medicine – they want special medicines, medicines that you won't find in ordinary pharmacists. Primarily to cure their exhaustion and to enhance their virility. So chemists, the smartest ones, conduct all kinds of experiments in their pharmacies and promise their clients miracles. And sometimes they even manage to deliver! Edik did.'

Darya Ivanovna was thoroughly absorbed in her own blend of thoughts and memories. The rapt attention of her guest, who was hanging on her every word, encouraged her to reveal more.

'And he liked the night?' Semyon asked tentatively.

'He loved it! He could walk the streets for hours at night.'

Semyon closed his eyes and cast his mind back seven years. He remembered asking a man who had greeted him one night to help him look for his missing child. He couldn't remember what this man looked like, how tall he was or how old. Maybe he hadn't even seen his face in the darkness. But reading about this incident in the pharmacist's notebook had somehow reawoken his memories of the recent past. He found that he could replay several other nocturnal walks from his personal video archive. He could remember how certain windows burned with light late into the night, how there was always someone smoking on the first-floor balcony of a building on Chapaev Street, the little light from their cigarette tracing abrupt, agitated arcs between the edge of the balcony and their mouth.

'Did you hear me?' asked Darya Ivanovna.

'Yes, yes,' he answered distractedly.

She fell silent, and Semyon looked up at her.

'How did it start?' he asked.

'How did what start?'

'You know, his love of darkness, the night . . .'

She thought about it. 'He told me once,' she whispered. 'I can't really remember . . . I think it was when he was a child and couldn't get to sleep – his parents punished him by shutting him out on the balcony in the evening, and he used to look up at the moon and stars. He used to love the moon, more than the sun . . . He loved the shadows cast by trees . . .'

'Did he go to church?'

'To church? No. Various sects tried to get him to join them. A few "brothers" and "sisters" even came knocking on the door. I sent them all packing!'

Semyon suddenly remembered something and glanced at his watch.

'Damn! I need to make a call!' He frowned, taking his mobile phone out of his pocket.

'Go ahead. I'll leave you to it.'

'No, it's fine. I don't have any secrets.'

'Even dead men have secrets.' Darya Ivanovna stood up and left the kitchen with an enigmatic smile.

She went into the living room and sat down at the table with her back to the window. She thought about her husband.

The door to the living room creaked as it opened.

'I'm sorry,' Semyon said, looking in. 'I have to go to work. Thanks for the coffee.'

Darya Ivanovna nodded. 'We didn't finish our little chat. You'll have to come again,' she said quietly.

Outside Semyon stopped for a moment. He glanced up at the

second floor of the old brick building in which the pharmacist's wife lived. He would have been happy to continue their conversation, but he had to meet Volodka in forty minutes at the milk kitchen and go to Vyshhorod again. They were to wait there for Gennady Ilyich, who was supposedly bringing the next instalment of humanitarian aid.

After saying goodbye to her guest, Darya Ivanovna called Veronika and invited her over.

Veronika arrived half an hour later. She seemed preoccupied and had a carrier bag of shopping with her.

'I should have gone home first.' She nodded at the carrier bag in the hallway.

'I won't keep you long,' said Darya Ivanovna, her voice full of secrets. 'I had a little chat with Semyon.'

'On the phone?'

'No, he was here. I made him a coffee. He's very sensitive, isn't he? I never would have thought it.'

'What did you talk about?' Veronika asked warily.

'About my husband, Edik. Semyon asked me about him. I have no idea why I started telling your husband all about mine . . . But that doesn't matter. The point is that your Semyon is very sentimental.'

'So?' Veronika didn't understand.

'Men like that always carry photographs of their children in their wallets, and sometimes their wives too. Do you see what I'm getting at?'

'You mean he might have a photo of our daughter in his wallet?' Veronika's eyes lit up with a mixture of joy and desperation.

Darya Ivanovna was unnerved by the look in her friend's eyes, but she knew from experience not to let her feelings show. So she maintained a neutral expression and merely nodded.

Veronika grew thoughtful. 'But what if there isn't one?' she asked.

Darya Ivanovna shrugged, but Veronika smiled serenely. She went over to the window and lifted her face to the sun.

'Did he go home after he left?' she asked, without turning back to Darya Ivanovna.

'No, to work.'

'I should go too. I need to get his dinner on.'

77

Vyshhorod district, Kiev region

Gennady Ilyich had a big row with Father Onophrios just as the celebrations were about to commence. It started outside, in front of Semyon and Volodka, but Semyon immediately moved away out of courtesy. He focused his attention instead on the pine forest surrounding the orphanage, where white patches of snow still remained, sheltered from the warmth of the sun by the prickly green canopy. Thus he managed to avoid hearing a single word of the verbal skirmish between his boss and the priest.

A cool, light breeze ruffled his short hair. Semyon looked up at the mighty pine trees and thought of Alisa. He was sure he would be able to find out more about her from the pharmacist's notebook. The pharmacist was lucky – he used to meet her in his waking life, during the day. Or maybe he also used to meet her at night? In any case she had talked to him, greeted him, smiled when they met . . . No, of course they must have met during the day – sleepwalkers don't keep notes, the psychiatrist had said so! Semyon wondered whether she really had posed for him, or were all those erotic sketches simply the product of his imagination?

'Hey, boss!' Volodka called to him.

Semyon looked round. The deputy and the priest were nowhere to be seen. They had already gone inside.

The orphanage's modest assembly hall could accommodate around thirty people. Wearing dull brown school uniforms, all nineteen children sat in the first two rows together with the director. In the back row three old women sat chatting among themselves – they were probably the cleaners, or the cooks. Three men, one of them quite elderly, sat in decorous silence at the opposite end of the third row. Semyon and Volodka sat next to them.

The stage was set with three chairs and a coffee table, on which stood a carafe of water and some glasses.

All of a sudden the Ukrainian national anthem began blaring out. The director stood up and looked around expectantly, and there was the clatter of tip-up seats as the assembled group did likewise, albeit rather slowly and reluctantly. By the end of the national anthem they were all on their feet. Then they sat down simultaneously. The director of the orphanage, Father Onophrios and Gennady Ilyich walked onto the stage, the latter holding a folder full of certificates.

'Today is a day that you will remember for the rest of your lives,' began the director. 'Much of what adorned my childhood has been missing from yours. You have not joined the Octobrists or the Young Pioneers, you've never been on Pioneer camps or played the war game Summer Lightning . . . You don't know what it's like to sit around a Pioneer campfire or to eat potatoes baked in the fire. Of course I must take some of the blame for this, but we are bound by official educational policy and specific instructions from the Ministry of Education. On the other hand, my childhood seemed to go on for ever, whereas you have the opportunity of becoming responsible adults far earlier. Most of you are ready for this. Thanks to Gennady Ilyich some of you have already embarked on your first profession – cheese-making. And what is about to happen—' the director looked at the deputy – 'could never have happened to me when I was your age . . .'

The director nodded at Gennady Ilyich, who stood up and straightened his jacket. His eyes swept the room.

'My dear children!' he said, his voice unusually loud. 'Good deeds and acts of kindness do not come easily to many people. To be honest, it is not a very rewarding business – and I say this as a politician, not just as one of the people. Collectively, people don't understand acts of kindness – they don't often benefit from them themselves, nor do they notice them when they benefit others. And I don't blame them for this. Kindness is like love – it's impossible to share it out equally among everyone. Yes, true kindness is like love! And you can only truly love a specific individual. You love her, and she loves you back, as it were. If you try to love the people, they just shrug. Do you understand what I'm saying? Real, tangible kindness is that bestowed upon a specific individual. Our Prime Minister says the same thing – only real kindness can change life in our country for the better. And I'll say it again – everything has to be real, no empty words, no "kindness for all"! Kindness for all is a myth. But first and foremost every specific individual must have real faith in their own future and in the future of our country.' Gennady Ilyich looked at Father Onophrios, who had just stood up and adjusted his cassock. 'And so today you will experience your first rite of passage, as it were. What you are about to receive is essentially a travel pass to your adult life – a real piece of political kindness, as it were. You'll be able to touch it, to hold it in your hands for the very first time. I may be breaking some trivial regulation or other today –' the deputy looked at the priest again – 'but if that is the case, may God forgive me.'

Father Onophrios walked silently over to Gennady Ilyich carrying a large box, which was covered in dark blue flocked paper. Gennady Ilyich took a little gold cross on a chain out of the box and held it up to show the whole hall.

'My dear children, these crosses are marked with your names and today's date. They will accompany and protect you throughout your adult life. Together with the cross, which Father Onophrios will present to you, you will receive a certificate confirming that the cross truly belongs to you. The number on the certificate corresponds to the number of your cross and is effectively your lucky number, as it were. It guarantees you a place at Kiev State University, without having to take any tests or exams, and it will open many other doors for you in the future. I'm telling you all this so that you understand the importance of today. Look after your cross and its accompanying certificate in the same way that young people of my generation looked after their party membership cards!'

Gennady Ilyich took his glasses from the breast pocket of his jacket, put them on and read the name on the first certificate. One of the older students, a long-legged boy, bounded up onstage. He reached out his hand to take his certificate, but Gennady Ilyich indicated that the boy should go to Father Onophrios first. The priest had already placed the open box on the coffee table and was holding one of the crosses, which he put over the boy's head, carefully tucking it beneath his clothes and making sure it lay correctly on his chest. Only then did Gennady Ilyich give the boy his certificate.

The ceremony lasted about fifteen minutes, and when it was over the director invited everyone present to the canteen.

On their way Semyon and Volodka were intercepted by the director, who grabbed Semyon's elbow.

'Please come to my office,' he whispered.

A table had been laid in the office as well, with a bottle of brandy, a plate of pickled cucumbers and sour cream, Russian salad, meat rissoles and boiled potatoes. The meal was an exclusive affair: the only participants were the director, the priest, Gennady Ilyich and Semyon and Volodka. The first thing that Gennady Ilyich did was to give the director a certificate too, and Father Onophrios gave him the corresponding cross. The director bowed to show his deep gratitude and immediately began pouring the brandy.

Semyon started feeling a bit peculiar. He didn't feel like drinking anything. Or eating anything, for that matter, so he apologised and said that he was just popping out to get some fresh air and would be back shortly.

It was almost evening, and the sun had already started to slip from the sky. It wasn't long before Volodka emerged from the orphanage and joined him. They stood side by side in silence.

'I wouldn't mind having one of those travel passes to life myself!' said Volodka, after they'd stood there for a few minutes. 'I'd swap my car for a proper jeep, for a start.'

Semyon glanced back at Volodka's Niva. Next to Gennady Ilyich's Lexus, which was parked nearby, it looked like a mechanical dinosaur. One of the back doors was open, and there were three empty milk churns in the boot. 'I wonder how many milk churns you could fit into the back of a Lexus?' thought Semyon.

The director, the priest and Gennady Ilyich came out onto the doorstep of the orphanage. The deputy was holding a bulging parcel.

'Goat's cheese, I bet,' thought Semyon.

Their parting was un-Slavically brief. Gennady Ilyich was particularly curt with Father Onophrios, after which the priest got straight into the back of the Niva. Gennady Ilyich shook hands with Volodka and then Semyon.

'Once you've unloaded –' he nodded at the Niva – 'drop your colleague off and then call me on my mobile.'

The Lexus pulled away abruptly as soon as its passenger got in. Dirt and slush flew from under the wheels.

On the way to Kiev Father Onophrios took the opportunity to vent his outrage.

'He wanted me to hand out the certificates so he could hang the crosses round the children's necks himself! And as if it weren't enough that each of the crosses has a number stamped on the back of it, they've also put the state trident on it in place of the crucifixion! I said to him straight away, I do God's work, I said. Crosses are a gift from God, whereas these documents with numbers stamped on them are from the Devil! Yes, I know they're from the government, not the Devil, but it's the same difference. Now I bet he'll have me run out of town. He's bound to complain to the archbishop, who'll banish me to some godforsaken parish in the back of beyond!'

Volodka glanced back at the priest. 'No, he won't,' he said attempting to reassure him. 'It's not like that any more.'

'Maybe not for you laymen, but it's different for us men of the cloth.' Father Onophrios sighed heavily and a sudden fury flashed in his eyes. 'Well, if they *do* send me away I'll just go to the press and tell them a thing or two about Gennady Ilyich . . . No Parliament will ever take him again!'

Intrigued, Semyon turned round and stared at the priest. Sensing a sympathetic audience, the priest launched into a tirade.

'I'll tell them how he forced me to baptise his German shepherd puppies in that little church of his. I can't give my friends heathen puppies, he said! Every Ukrainian dog deserves to be baptised, he said! I'll tell them how the two of us once sat in his church playing cards by candlelight, when there was a power cut!'

'Erm, perhaps it would be better not to mention that,' said Volodka.

The priest thought about it. Then he nodded.

'OK, maybe you're right. I've got enough other material anyway!' he said, then sulked in silence for the rest of the journey.

It was raining when they got to Kiev. The priest asked them to drop him off on Shevchenko Square, near the tram stop. It didn't take them long to get from there to Hrushevsky Street, where they carried the empty milk churns up to the first floor and left them in the hallway.

Volodka went home. Semyon stood in the porch, out of the rain, and called Gennady Ilyich.

'Meet me at the restaurant in the Officers' Club in fifteen minutes,' said the deputy.

There were no concert performances that evening, so the Officers' Club was empty.

Gennady Ilyich entered briskly and spotted Semyon sitting at a little table by the window. As he passed a sleepy waiter he ordered two double brandies, some lemon slices and two cups of tea.

Sitting down, the deputy took a small parcel out of his pocket. It contained a numbered cross and a certificate. The certificate had been stamped and there was a bold, important-looking signature in the bottom right-hand corner, but the space for the recipient's name had been left blank.

'This is for you. When you have a child, you can write his or her name in here.' He nodded at the certificate. 'By the way, don't tell anyone else about the baby girl we discussed. Just forget I ever mentioned it. It's a shame, of course, that your wife . . .'

Gennady Ilyich didn't finish his sentence.

The waiter brought their order and laid it out on the table. The deputy looked at his watch. He downed his brandy in one, placed a hundred-hryvna note on the table and left, with a nod goodbye.

Semyon stayed and thought about Veronika.

'Maybe I should try talking to her again? Or ask Darya Ivanovna to talk to her?'

He tipped his brandy into his tea and drank it, remembering how they used to call it 'officers' tea'.

He thought about Alisa and immediately became aware of a strange feeling within himself, a kind of reluctant enthusiasm. Not even reluctant so much as stubborn, challenging the resistance of his own body, which was already tired and wanted to rest.

Semyon realised that the night hadn't lured him out onto the city streets for a while now. Or maybe it had, but he just didn't know about it because he hadn't asked Volodka to follow him. He recalled the last few mornings, but there had been no indications of any nocturnal excursions. Maybe this strange unwelcome enthusiasm was a kind of nocturnal alarm clock.

Semyon left the Officers' Club in a state of some anxiety and called Volodka on his way home.

'I've got a bad feeling about tonight. Are you free later?'

'Don't forget to put your new gadget in your pocket,' Volodka reminded him.

Semyon's feeling of unease grew the closer he got to home. The rain had stopped, but the puddles beneath his feet reflected the headlights of the cars going past. Semyon quickened his pace. He wanted to be standing in front of his own door as soon as possible.

78

All-night *pelmeni* café, Boryspil

'You've got blood on your hands,' the owner said to Dima, when he and Valya entered their usual *pelmeni* café.

Dima looked at his hands. 'I cut myself by accident,' he said.

'There's a washbasin over there,' said the café owner. 'Shall I find you some antiseptic?'

'No, it's all right,' Dima said over his shoulder. At the washbasin he began scrubbing his hands with soap, while Valya waited at the counter.

'Pork or beef?' the café owner asked her.

'Which do you want, Dima?' She looked at her husband.

'A double portion of mixed, with a "surprise"', said Dima.

'We don't do mixed any more,' said the café owner. 'I can do you one portion of pork and one of beef.'

Dima wiped his hands on the towel hanging there. He went back to the counter.

'Two pork and one beef,' he said, with greater conviction. 'In the same bowl.'

'I'll have the same,' said Valya.

'Do you want a "surprise" as well?' the owner asked.

Valya nodded.

'Anything to drink?'

'A carafe of vodka,' said Dima.

'Me too,' said Valya.

'You're not allowed to!' Dima looked at his wife in surprise. 'You're pregnant!'

'What's she having then?' the café owner asked Dima.

'A double brandy.'

They sat down opposite one another at the little wooden table. Dima now sat facing the counter, with his back to the elderly couple drinking beer at the next table. He watched the owner of the *pelmeni* café, whom he'd known for about twenty years. He used to be a fireman, here in Boryspil, until he got the sack for drinking on the job. He stopped drinking and went into business, starting off as a market trader. Then when he turned fifty he bought this trailer, set it up here in a relatively quiet part of town and opened a *pelmeni* café.

It occurred to Dima that he'd never seen him smile. For some reason it made him want to smile himself, but he couldn't. It just made his cut lip sore, causing him to grimace in pain.

Valya reached out and covered Dima's hand with her own. They looked into one another's eyes tenderly. He covered her hand with his other hand and they sat like that, Dima pressing Valya's hand gently between his, until the café owner brought over Dima's vodka and Valya's brandy.

'The *pelmeni* won't be long,' he said as he walked away.

Their hands separated reluctantly.

Dima sipped his drink and immediately felt his cut lip pinch again. He finished the vodka in one go and looked at Valya, sniffing her brandy.

'Is it OK?' he asked.

Valya nodded. She took a sip and put her glass back on the table.

Their triple portions of *pelmeni* looked particularly appetising, piled up high with steam rising from them. Cubes of butter were melting into pale yellow tongues and sliding down the sides.

'Will it be my lucky night?' wondered Dima as he took his first bite.

It was. He pulled the 'surprise' out of his mouth – a three-kopek Soviet coin.

In exchange for the coin the café owner silently placed a five-hryvna note on the counter.

'I'd rather have some more vodka,' said Dima.

He returned to the table with a full glass of Khortytsia vodka.

Valya ate her *pelmeni* slowly and with great determination, washing them down every now and then with a mouthful of brandy.

Dima tried to pace himself too, but his appetite got the better of him. He'd cleared his plate before Valya was even halfway through hers.

Suddenly she stopped eating and started crying quietly, with a kind of childish helplessness.

'What's the matter?' Dima leaned across the table towards her.

She shook her head. 'I'm scared to go home,' whispered his wife.

'There's nobody there any more,' Dima also whispered.

He glanced at his watch. It was nearly 1.30 a.m.

He looked into his wife's eyes and saw a fearful obstinacy.

'OK,' he said. 'Let's go and sit in the garage. I put the heater on in there earlier. We can check on Fluffy!'

Twenty minutes later they drove the car into the garage, shutting the doors behind them. They settled down in the far right-hand corner near the welcoming warmth of the home-made heater.

The first thing Valya did was to unwrap the cat, removing the cloth and folding back the edge of the blood-soaked white towel. She leaned closer, trying to examine him more closely in the dim light of the forty-watt bulb hanging down from the ceiling.

'He's dead,' she whispered.

'Are you sure?'

'Yes. Look at him. Look how much blood he's lost . . .'

They both fell silent.

'Shall we go to bed?' Dima suggested tentatively.

'No, I can't go in there,' she whispered.

So they sat there until the morning, repeatedly drifting into a kind of half-sleep then suddenly waking with a start.

Whenever Valya was dozing Dima poured himself a shot of home-made nettle vodka from his garage supply and downed it in one.

79

Mariinsky Park, Kiev, night-time

Everything seems more imposing and mysterious at night. Everything looks meaningful and larger than life. Not like during the day.

Thus when patrolling the viewing area that night Egor looked out across the Dnieper and marvelled at the beauty of Kiev's left bank, its sea of lights spread out before him; he marvelled also at the stern and ominous bulk of the Parliament building and at the Mariinsky Palace, which looked bigger in the artificial light than it really was.

A brisk wind blew across the park in the direction of Parliament and the palace where it seemed to split in two, as though coming up against an insurmountable barrier. The stronger of the two currents flowed like a powerful invisible river of air to the edge of the hill and downwards, picking up speed as it headed towards the Dnieper. The weaker current flowed into the city streets, rolling down Hrushevsky Street onto Sadovaya Street, and Shelkovichnaya Street, losing its energy as it went. Its barely perceptible remnants drifted down Institutskaya Street to Khreshchatyk Street where they vanished, dissolving in the air of Kiev's main street.

Egor liked the feeling of the wind in his face. It kept him awake and alert, and it elicited a kind of inner resistance. He walked into the depths of the park, into the wind, and his body fought against it. This opposition of man and wind gave Egor a feeling of inner strength, deep in his soul. It wasn't even strength so much as a conviction that everything was going to work out just the way he wanted it to. He would build his life like a fortress around him, and no one else would be allowed in unless he invited them. He was thirty-six years old, physically capable and in good health. His life-fortress would be ready before he was forty, and there would be room inside for gentle happiness and something new, something he'd never experienced before.

Egor stopped in front of the arched entrance at the side of Mariinsky Park. He looked at the dark windows of the food shop on the corner opposite, then at his Mazda parked in the alley. Then he turned round and headed back into the park.

But something felt wrong. The wind was at his back now and

seemed to be exerting a physical pressure on him, urging him on, pushing him so hard that Egor was forced to lengthen his stride. When the wind pushes you around like that it makes you feel very small. You realise how insignificant you truly are in the natural order of things, while everything around you remains majestic and awe-inspiring.

Egor paused near the monument. He looked along the deserted paths of the park, at the street lamps and the benches that were illuminated by their weak, yellowish light.

He decided to go back to the viewing area at the edge of Pechersk Hill and stand there for a while, looking out over the Dnieper.

As soon as he got there Egor felt calmer, happier somehow. He was still being buffeted by the wind but it was no longer pushing him forward. He stood at the railings looking out across the river, with the wind at his back.

Egor's feeling of inner strength returned. He looked back at Parliament and the palace, at the deserted square between Parliament and the park, and he felt as though he too were part of the silent energy of this 'hill of power'. At night it sometimes seemed to Egor that he was owned and controlled by the anonymous and elite group of people who gathered up here to control the whole country, the entire population. The President hovered above them all, keeping a watchful eye over everyone and everything, so feared and obeyed that he never even needed to leave the building. Whenever he did appear in person everything would stop and fall silent; it was a silence that no one would dare to break, not even the President himself.

The lights on the left bank were twinkling in the distance, and the wind continued to blow over the edge of the hill. If you really concentrated you could hear the noise it made, a kind of humming sound. The wind was surprisingly mild, as though winter had finally retreated, chased away by the approaching warmth of spring.

Egor stood there, looking out at the nocturnal expanse of the left bank. He turned up the collar of his leather jacket. The short fur tickled his ears, and the wind receded.

The lights were still twinkling down below, on the other side of the Dnieper. There was something magical about them. Suddenly a distant, high-pitched noise rose up to meet him. It was high and pure, like the sound made by a bow gently caressing a violin string.

This noise surprised Egor. Maybe it was the wind whistling through some wires? He looked around but the noise had disappeared, as though it had decided to play hide-and-seek. All he could hear was the howling of the wind. Egor forgot about the noise. Only a few more hours to go . . . then at 8 a.m. he would hand over his walkie-talkie and go and check on his mother, then drive to Lipovka to see Irinka. If his mother was well enough he could take Aleksandra, Irina's mother, to visit her – she could tell her about herself and her daughter. His mother could still hear and understand everything that was said to her, and sometimes she even said a word or two in response.

Nearly 5 a.m. It was getting harder and harder for Egor to keep his spirits up. He turned his face to the wind, trying to blow the tiredness away. He closed his eyes and stood there for a little while then opened them and walked through the park towards the street, heading into the wind. He stopped in front of the main entrance to Parliament. He could hear a kind of rustling sound. He went over to the metal barrier at the edge of the park, which was covered in bits of cardboard and plywood from the anti-NATO banners. It had been like that for as long as he could remember. There was a one-man tent nearby, on the other side of the metal barrier, but he knew it was empty. In the morning an old lady would turn up with her vacuum flask to set up camp for the day; then the Communist veterans would arrive to voice their stolid opinions. Beyond the tent there were trees and bushes. The trees were young and you could easily see through their thin trunks that there was nobody there.

Egor walked along the path towards the arched entrance at the side of the park. Then he turned round and walked back again. Just at that moment he saw someone run across the square in front of Parliament. He couldn't hear much, though, because the howling of the wind was drowning out everything else.

Quickening his pace, Egor came running onto the square. It was deserted. All he could hear was that high-pitched sound again. He headed for Hrushevsky Street but there was no one about – no people, no cars. It wasn't usually this quiet. There was something eerie about it.

'If they were still running, I'd be able to hear their footsteps,' thought Egor, puzzled. 'They must be hiding somewhere . . .'

'Number Four, Number Four,' he said into his walkie-talkie. 'Someone just ran across the square. I think they were heading your way.'

'Roger that,' answered Number Four. 'I'll check it out.'

Egor went back to the square and heard the high-pitched sound again, only this time it seemed to fluctuate more expressively. He looked everywhere, and then his eyes came to rest on the steps in front of the entrance. There was something strange about them – they seemed uneven, as though someone had put something on one of them.

He walked over to the steps and stopped, flabbergasted. There was a bundle lying on the top step, just in front of the door, and it was crying.

Egor picked up the bundle, pulled back a corner of the blanket and saw a newborn baby's face, all red from crying. Its little mouth was wide open and it was still crying, but rather half-heartedly, as though the baby knew that it was a waste of time because no one would hear.

'Number Four,' said Egor into his walkie-talkie in a dismissive voice. 'Don't bother . . .'

'What?' said Number Four.

'You don't need to check it out. It's just another abandoned baby . . .'

'So, I guess we follow the protocol then?'

Egor paused before answering. He peered at the baby, every wrinkle of its screwed-up little face expressing unhappiness. The remote and clinical word 'protocol' somehow didn't seem appropriate.

'No,' Egor finally said into his walkie-talkie. 'I know what to do with it –'

'Number Five, don't do anything stupid!'

'No, honestly, I'll take care of it.'

'Then you didn't tell me anything, and I don't know anything.'

'Roger that,' said Egor.

He took the baby to his car and placed it on the passenger seat in its raspberry-coloured blanket. He started the engine and turned the heater on. He noticed that the baby had stopped crying.

Egor put his hand to its tiny mouth and felt its warm breath on his skin.

'Have a little sleep,' he whispered. 'I'll come and check on you again in a little while, and then we'll go home.'

He locked the car and then, looking all around, walked yet again down the path towards Parliament.

80

Veronika kept looking at her watch while she waited for her husband to get back from work. She wanted to talk to him, and she was planning to be more conciliatory than last time. He was probably still upset about their recent conversation, which could technically have qualified as an argument. Darya Ivanovna was right about him being in touch with his feelings!

Every now and then she would sit down in the armchair and browse her stack of glossy magazines. She only bought them once in a while but when she did she would buy ten at a time, as though she wanted to revitalise her sophisticated and cosmopolitan life – a life that only really existed in her imagination. She had several cups of tea and coffee. She thought about her friend's advice to look in her husband's wallet. This idea now seemed eminently sensible, so much so that she wondered why she hadn't thought of it herself. And not only to look for a photo of their daughter. After all, a man's wallet and its contents are like an instruction manual for the television or the fridge – a useful point of reference to understand how things work, and essential for troubleshooting. But obviously on some level she didn't really want to understand her Senya, otherwise she would have started going through his wallet a long time ago. Or would she?

Veronika suddenly realised that she didn't consider her husband to be her property – she never had. At least not in the way you can own an inanimate object, like a hairdryer. She couldn't even remember the colour or size of his wallet, as though she'd never seen it before in her life. Maybe she hadn't.

At around 8 p.m. Veronika finally relaxed and changed into her towelling dressing gown. The deep twilight outside also had a calming effect on her. But she really wished that Semyon were there!

Her husband didn't come home until 8.30 p.m. and he was clearly preoccupied. She kissed him and put her arms around him. He hugged her back, but his face was expressionless, and Veronika knew his mind was elsewhere.

'Sorry, I'm just tired,' said Semyon.

Nevertheless she did manage to get him talking a bit, by asking where he fancied going on holiday in the summer. The question seemed appropriate, with spring getting nearer every day.

'Where do *you* want to go?' he asked and looked at her eagerly, clearly ready to fulfil any reasonable desire his wife might have.

Veronika smiled. 'Maybe we could find a little place near Odessa?'

'OK, I'll find out what there is to do down there.'

Then he started looking for something and forgot all about Veronika. He found the digital voice recorder he'd bought recently, set it to automatic so that it would switch itself on at the first sound and tucked it into the small breast pocket of his jacket. Then he kissed Veronika, undressed and went to bed. Contrary to his expectations, he fell asleep immediately.

Veronika suddenly remembered his wallet. She went into the hallway, ran her hand along the lining of his leather jacket and found it straight away. She extracted it from the pocket and went into the kitchen. There were no photographs in the special little see-through windows, so she started emptying the various pockets of the wallet, pulling the contents out onto the tabletop, and then she froze. A photograph had fallen out of a piece of paper folded in half – it was a photograph of a blonde woman in her forties, and Veronika didn't recognise her. She picked up the photo. The woman was not posing for the camera but looking off to the side, as though she didn't know it was being taken. There was nothing written on the back of it.

Veronika opened the piece of paper. The layout of the document and the words 'To Whom It May Concern' at the top made her assume it was some sort of medical certificate, but when she read the rest of it she stood up abruptly, her stool falling back onto the air vent at the bottom of the cooker.

'"Does not bear any responsibility for his actions,"' she read aloud. 'Why not?'

She studied the psychiatrist's bold violet stamp closely. Then she looked at the business card stapled to the top left-hand corner of the certificate.

'"Pyotr Isaevich Naitov, Psychiatric Doctor",' she read. She looked at the address of his office.

Veronika really felt like calling Darya Ivanovna, or better still running round to her apartment with this certificate and the photo of the blonde woman. But it was late, and in any case Veronika felt that she had already burdened her friend too much with her problems. Darya Ivanovna had enough problems of her own!

So Veronika decided to postpone the solution of this unexpected riddle until the morning. She put the wallet, the certificate, the photograph and the other bits of paper and money on the windowsill, so that Semyon would be able to find it and at the same time realise that Veronika knew there was something going on and that she was waiting for an explanation.

81

Apartment No. 10, Reitarska Street, Kiev

Semyon quietly got out of bed in the middle of the night. He glanced at his sleeping wife with cold detachment, and then he got dressed. In the hallway he took his leather jacket from the coat rack and put it on, zipping it up almost to his chin. He tied the laces of his boots in a double bow.

Volodka was dozing in his Niva so he didn't actually see Semyon leave the building, but something – either the sound of the front door slamming or intuition – suddenly made him open his eyes and look through the car window. When he spotted Semyon, Volodka was instantly on the alert. He quickly poured some bitter coffee from his vacuum flask into a plastic cup and drank it. He waited until Semyon reached the corner of Yaroslaviv Val, then he got out of the car and followed him.

Semyon was 'led' towards the Golden Gates. Suddenly he stopped and took his mobile phone out of his jacket pocket. The ringtone grew louder and then stopped. Volodka hid behind a tree near the post office, about twenty metres away from Semyon. He thought it was strange that he couldn't hear a single word, or any other sound, even though he could clearly see that Semyon was talking on his phone. In fact, Volodka couldn't hear anything at all – it was as though someone had put the whole city on mute. Overwhelmed by a sudden surge of frustration, he stamped in a puddle and was relieved to hear it splash. He saw Semyon turn and look in the direction of the noise, with his phone still clamped to his ear. Volodka hid behind the tree again. He slipped his hand into the right-hand pocket of his jacket, feeling for his digital camera.

'Where's he off to next?' he thought.

Putting his phone back in his pocket, Semyon set off again. He crossed Vladimirskaya Street and went down Proreznaya Street to Khreshchatyk Street. Volodka followed him, increasing his pace, but he couldn't seem to get any closer. Wherever he was going, Semyon was clearly in a hurry.

The city was still shrouded in silence, and for some reason all the traffic lights were simultaneously flashing orange.

A taxi stood outside the Dnieper hotel with its headlights on. The driver was asleep inside, his head resting on the steering wheel.

Semyon walked right across the middle of European Square, skirting the flower bed in the centre with its mantle of dirty black snow.

Volodka stayed on the even-numbered side of Khreshchatyk Street, slowing down a little as he reached the corner near the Ukrainian House exhibition centre.

Heading towards Podil, Semyon turned right just after the concert hall that was home to the Kiev Philharmonic and went down some stone steps that led to the Dnieper. Volodka followed him, maintaining a distance of about fifty metres. He saw him turn right again, onto the path that led to the pedestrian bridge and Trukhanov Island.

Puzzled by Semyon's unfamiliar route, Volodka increased his pace again. He turned onto the path but couldn't see Semyon in front of him. He started running. There was the bridge . . . but Semyon was nowhere to be seen. In a panic Volodka ran to the end of the square in front of the bridge, and then he finally saw him – he was walking rapidly along the Dnieper embankment in the direction of the Metro Bridge.

'Should I try and cut him off?' wondered Volodka. 'But there's nowhere to hide on the embankment, there aren't enough trees . . . No, I'll go that way, along the tramline,' he decided. Taking the steps two at a time, he went down to the rails.

Volodka was surprised to see cars still speeding along the Naberezhny Highway. A black Mercedes with a government number plate sprayed him with mud, as though it had crossed into the lane closest to the rails specifically for this purpose.

He looked nervously across at the isolated figure of Semyon, striding along confidently on the other side of the street. Where on earth was he going? It was a complete mystery to Volodka, although Semyon himself probably had some idea. In all his nights of surveillance, this was the first time that his boss had walked so far from home, and this was precisely what was bothering Volodka. Something might happen right here, on the street. Maybe a car would stop and someone would either shoot Semyon or tie him up and throw him in the boot before driving off with him, and then the night would become an ellipsis in Semyon's fate. Date of death: unknown.

Why was he thinking like this? Where were these ominous thoughts and feelings coming from? Volodka tried to analyse the reason for his feeling of unease, this apprehension, but his thoughts ran ahead of him and refused to comply.

They continued walking like this, on opposite sides of the street, until they reached the fish market and the Metro Bridge. Then Semyon turned onto the bridge. Volodka ran across the wide street, with headlights bearing down on him from both sides. Semyon stopped by the railings and looked down at the black water of the Dnieper.

Volodka watched suspiciously. Semyon remained in that position for about ten minutes, and then suddenly he clambered up onto the railings and jumped off.

Volodka gasped. He ran to where his friend had been standing, leaned over the cold metal railings and saw concentric circles spreading out in the water. Without even thinking about it he climbed up onto the railings and jumped off after him. The icy water seared his hands and face, and he was suddenly aware of the unfamiliar heaviness of his own body. The water closed up over his head but he had enough air in his lungs, or at least he thought so. He dived deeper and felt the current seize him. It wasn't fast but it was strong, and he surrendered to it, drifting with the flow. He came to the surface to take a breath, then was dragged under once more. Just as Volodka's strength began to desert him, his hand brushed against something under the water. He reached his hand out again and kicked hard, although his legs were heavy and restricted by his wet trousers and boots. This time he managed to grab Semyon with his fingers, which were already numb with cold.

The concrete bank was about five metres away. Volodka used his left arm to paddle towards it with all his remaining strength. Then he heaved Semyon out of the water onto dry land. His friend wasn't moving. He started trying to resuscitate him by the method that had been drummed into him in childhood, bringing Semyon's arms together up over his chest and apart again, in a kind of repetitive pumping motion. Water gushed from his mouth. Volodka turned Semyon's head to the side and released his unresponsive arms for a moment. He checked to see whether Semyon was breathing. Hearing nothing, he resumed his endeavours.

Semyon coughed, twitched and then was still again.

Volodka stopped and leaned over his friend's face. He was breathing, albeit barely. Volodka was suddenly overcome with a primal exhaustion. And he was freezing. He looked all around, and his eyes came to rest on the stone steps leading from the bank up to the road. He grabbed hold of Semyon's jacket with both hands and dragged him towards the steps. He had to keep stopping to catch his breath. Once he got to the top he squatted down next to his motionless friend and stared at the road. A car hissed past on the wet tarmac.

'How the hell am I going to get him home?' he thought.

His own legs threatened to give way, and this made him panic. He staggered to the edge of the road and saw two pairs of headlights approaching. He raised his hand, but the cars rushed past. Volodka stood there with his arm still up, swaying like a drunk. His cold, wet clothing was sticking unpleasantly to his body, but he couldn't exactly strip off by the side of the road.

More headlights rushed past. Time stood still. Semyon coughed, but Volodka didn't turn round. He was peering intently into the darkness, where the oncoming cars were concealed beyond the invisible horizon.

There were no cars for several minutes, but then a pair of headlights emerged surprisingly slowly from the horizon.

Volodka was suddenly vigilant, roused from his trance. His right arm had begun to droop disobediently, but he used his last remaining energy to haul it back into position. He even tried to wave it. The driver of this vehicle had resisted the temptation to increase his speed just because it was the middle of the night, unlike the others, so Volodka became convinced that he would notice him and stop.

And he did. It turned out to be an old yellow VW minivan, empty but for the driver and one passenger in the front seat.

Volodka reached out for the car door and opened it.

'Guys, I need your help! My friend almost drowned, and we're both soaking wet. I need to get him home.'

'Where does he live?' asked the middle-aged driver.

'In the centre, Reitarska Street.'

'Get in.'

Volodka felt a surge of energy. He turned back to Semyon, grabbed him under the arms and dragged him to the car.

The driver and the passenger got out of the minivan and helped Volodka lay Semyon across the seats in the middle. Volodka himself climbed into one of the seats in the back row.

'Did he have one too many?' asked the driver. They were already driving past the Metro Bridge.

'No, he tried to drown himself,' said Volodka.

The driver shook his head. 'Yes, life's no picnic these days,' he said, after a pause.

They drove the rest of the way in silence.

The driver and the passenger helped Volodka take Semyon up to his floor and waited until Veronika opened the door. Veronika was in her nightdress. Before opening the door she asked several times, 'Who is it? Who is it?' Then when she eventually opened the door and saw Volodka and two other men she didn't know holding her husband up against the railings on the landing, she almost cried out. In fact she did cry out but Volodka put his finger to his lips, silently imploring her to stay calm, and she froze with her mouth open. Only when they had carried Semyon into the hallway of the apartment did she ask, 'What happened?'

'He tried to drown himself,' muttered the driver.

'Rub him with vodka,' said Volodka.

She nodded.

'Do you want me to stay?' Volodka asked hesitantly. He looked down at the wooden floor, where a puddle of Dnieper water was spreading around his feet.

'No, it's all right,' she whispered, barely audibly.

Volodka was relieved. On his way out, he caught up with the men from the yellow minivan.

'Hey, how much do I owe you?' he asked. Then he added, apologetically, 'I'm afraid my money's a bit wet.'

'Don't worry about it,' said the driver. 'If we lived in a world where people only bothered helping one another for money, I'd be trying to drown myself too. Who knows, maybe you'd be the one to rescue me!'

The minivan drove off and Volodka walked to his Niva. He sat behind the wheel, started the engine and turned the heater on full. He felt in desperate need of warmth. It takes a while to generate, in a car as in life, but it's always worth waiting for.

82

9 May Street, Boryspil

Dima was woken early the following morning by a pale and sleep-deprived Valya. He had been asleep sitting up on the floor, his body twisted in such a way that his head was almost touching the red-hot spirals of the heater. Maybe that was why the first thing he felt when he opened his eyes was an unpleasant dryness in his mouth and nostrils.

'Dima,' said Valya, 'bring me some water, would you, so I can have a wash? And something to change into.'

'Why don't we just go home?' Dima straightened his sore back and looked around.

'I can't,' said Valya 'Maybe later . . . But I can't go back in there just yet . . .'

Dima sighed, then got up and left the garage. He noticed that the air outside was milder than it had been recently. It was still fresh, but it no longer had that wintry chill.

An old man cycled past, his wheels spraying up the slush of the melting snow. Dima moved closer to the fence to allow the cyclist to pass.

Back at the house he filled a three-litre jar with warm water and put some of Valya's clothes into a canvas overnight bag. He even found some clean tights in the bottom drawer of the wardrobe. He stood there in the bedroom for a little while, in the exact spot where only yesterday the stranger's body had lain. He could still smell mothballs. The wooden floor looked clean enough, but when Dima squatted down to inspect it he noticed a couple of spots of blood. So he took a cloth from the bathroom, held it under the tap and sprinkled it with washing powder, then carefully washed the floor one more time.

'I don't know what her problem is,' he thought with a shrug. 'That house in the next street along was on the market a while back, after the son hacked his father to death when he was drunk . . . And did they have any trouble selling it? Of course not!'

Valya got changed next to the heater, standing on a classified ads paper taken from the shelf. Droplets of water fell onto the heater as she washed herself and the spiral hissed irritably, turning them to steam.

'Do you want me to get you something to eat?' asked Dima.

'No, I'm fine. I'll get something to eat on the way.'

Once he was alone Dima did a couple of squats and stretched his arms out several times, like the exercises they used to do at school. His legs ached, his neck ached, his back ached . . . everything ached.

He caught sight of the dirty cloth covering Scruffy's body and was overcome with grief and sorrow.

'I'm going to bury you today,' he whispered, looking down at the floor. 'You deserve a proper funeral . . .'

Locking the garage, he went back into the house. He spent a long time under the shower, scrubbing his body vigorously with the loofah as though trying to wash off the top layer of skin. He was thinking about Valya, about how she should be sleeping properly in a bed rather than propped up on the floor in the garage. Anything could happen! It might cause a miscarriage, or some kind of birth defect. He had to convince her that everything was fine and that there wouldn't be any more problems.

'But what if they send someone else?' Dima thought suddenly, and the hand holding the wet loofah froze on his left hip.

Just then there was a ring at the door. Dima turned the water off abruptly and listened intently. The doorbell rang again, but it didn't sound particularly urgent. Naked and wet, he stood on the slippery enamel base of the cast-iron bath for several moments, just listening. Then he turned the water back on and quickly rinsed the soap from his body, then got out of the bath and dried himself off. He crouched down and crept into the kitchen in his underwear. He looked out of the window, but there was nobody either on the street or in the yard in front of the house.

He put the kettle on the hob and sat down at the table. He didn't feel like eating anything, but he was really thirsty. Without waiting for the kettle to boil he ran a glass of cold tap water and drank it in one long gulp.

Then he called the militiaman who had bought the ampoules from him.

'Hello, who is it?' The young voice on the other end of the line sounded tense.

Dima told him.

'What do you want?' asked the militiaman. He didn't sound particularly friendly.

'We need to meet, to talk . . .'

'Are you at home?' The militiaman sounded surprised. He had obviously looked at the display panel on his phone and recognised the number. 'Are you OK?'

'Me? I'm fine. My cat was murdered, though.'

'Your cat?' said the militiaman. 'Who murdered your cat?'

'The men you sent round. Remember, about the ampoules –'

'I don't know anything about any ampoules. And I never sent anyone round to your house . . . You never had anything to do with any ampoules. Do you understand?'

'No,' sighed Dima. He looked at the phone in confusion.

'Fine,' said the militiaman after a short pause. 'I'll come to your place. I'll be there in an hour.'

The militiaman turned up half an hour earlier than he'd said. He came into the hall and looked over Dima's shoulder, as though he were checking to see whether anyone was hiding behind him.

'I've only got a minute,' he said, peering at Dima.

Dima returned his rather bewildered stare.

'Last night –' he began.

The militiaman cut him short with a gesture.

'I don't want to know,' he said. 'Nobody's looking for the ampoules any more. I've been instructed to forget about them, and you should too! The President is about to dissolve Parliament.' The militiaman's voice dropped to a whisper. 'Just don't tell anyone about that yet either. You wouldn't believe what's going on in this country. Our collective-farm minister has gone mad! Right, I've got to go. Oh, and one more thing – you don't know me and have never seen me before in your life. Got it?'

Dima nodded. 'What about my cat?' he asked suddenly.

'Your cat, your problem,' the militiaman replied curtly and left.

Dima closed the door behind him and bolted it.

He started thinking. He thought about Scruffy, wondering where he should bury him.

He plodded slowly into the bedroom and called directory enquiries.

'How can I help you?' trilled a cheerful female voice.

'Yes, I was just wondering, is there a pet cemetery in Boryspil?'

'I'm afraid we can't help with that kind of enquiry,' replied the voice.

'Fine, we'll go to Kiev then,' thought Dima.

He went over to the window, parted the curtains and screwed up his eyes as the sunlight fell on him. He could hear the drip, drip, drip of the ice melting outside. He reached up and opened the little top window, and a gust of fresh air chased the smell of mothballs away.

Two hours later Dima was carrying the canvas overnight bag

down the main path through the Baykov Cemetery. The bag contained Scruffy's lifeless body, wrapped up in a towel. It also contained a folding spade that he'd grabbed from the garage and a separate little bag containing 250ml of birch-bud vodka, a shot glass, a piece of salted lard, a crust of black bread and a peeled onion.

The sun was approaching its zenith. Birds were singing among the dark, shiny gravestones and monuments. Marble busts, bas-reliefs and engraved portraits of the great and the good drifted slowly by, but Dima kept walking into the depths of the cemetery, further and further from the world of the living. After another two hundred metres or so, he reached a fork in the path, stopped and looked around. He was completely alone. One path now went off to the right, another to the left. After looking around again, Dima's gaze came to rest on the bust of a high-ranking military official. He walked over to the grave. Two star medals carved on the breast of the memorial statue indicated that the deceased had twice been awarded the title Hero of the Soviet Union. Dima looked at the next grave along. This one belonged to a general too, although he only had one star.

Dima put the bag down. He craned his neck and looked up at the sky, as if checking to see whether anyone up there was watching.

The clear blue sky was completely empty: no birds, no aeroplanes, no clouds.

'Well, here goes,' Dima said to himself, as he began digging a hole between the two graves. The earth yielded easily to the sharp blade of the spade.

When the hole was about half a metre deep, Dima placed the towel and Scruffy inside. He scattered earth over the little grave and patted it down neatly with the back of the spade. Then he sat on the bench in front of the memorial to the first of the two Heroes of the Soviet Union and spread out his funeral repast. He drank a shot of vodka, then rubbed the crust of bread with the onion and the lard and took a bite. The birdsong suddenly grew louder and cleare. Dima felt an overwhelming sense of inner calm and well-being. He poured himself another shot of vodka and looked around with ponderous serenity and contentment. The world was a good place, he thought to himself – so accommodating, and occasionally even quite miraculous. He contemplated the sudden, spontaneous happiness you sometimes feel, for no particular reason. Even on sad occasions such as this.

He sipped his vodka and chewed the aromatic black bread. He didn't feel like going anywhere. He didn't want to leave the seductive silence of this cemetery and return to the bustling, noisy world, overflowing with other people's lives, other people's voices and other people's problems.

The sun shone down with the warmth of spring, and Dima unzipped his jacket and lifted his face to the sky. At this moment he felt more than ever before like a creature of God, whose only aim was to live and enjoy life, entrusting his fate and protection to the Almighty celestial powers.

83

Lipovka village, Kiev region
The baby woke up and started crying just as Egor was approaching Makariv. It was another six kilometres to Lipovka. The dawn was

turning the edges of the sky silver. There were no other cars on the road, so it was an easy drive – he just had to concentrate on keeping his eyes open.

Dirty snow was piled up along the sides of the road. Spring would begin a little later here than in Kiev. Everybody knew that the best things came to the city first and the villages later . . . if they made it there at all. But spring would come, as it always did. And it would be here soon.

He passed Makariv. The baby was still crying, but he didn't mind – its frail, high-pitched mewling was strangely appropriate and timely. Egor hoped it would cry all the way to Lipovka, because the noise would keep him alert and ensure that he didn't doze off at the wheel. Such lapses in concentration, however brief, could be fatal. After about twenty minutes his drowsiness would gradually recede, only to return in the hope of defeating him later.

Turning into the little lane where Irina lived, Egor saw the windows of her house. The sight of these yellow squares of light made him feel warm inside.

He lingered on the doorstep with the baby in his arms, looking up at the horseshoe he'd recently nailed above the door. The door-bell here was harsh and strident, so he decided not to press it in case Yasya was sleeping. He knocked on the door instead.

Irina's mother opened the door. She was wearing an old black dress, an apron and a red cardigan, and she looked the very image of a gypsy woman. When she saw Egor she immediately stepped back inside to let him in, but then her gaze froze on the baby wrapped in the blanket.

Egor felt the need to say something, to explain, but the words seemed to stick in his throat. The baby's cries grew louder.

'Someone abandoned it during the night outside Parliament,'

he finally blurted out. 'If I hadn't found it, it would have frozen to death.'

'Mama, who is it?' Irina's voice floated into the hallway.

'It's Egor,' called Baba Shura. Then she turned back to her guest. 'Is it a boy or a girl?'

He shrugged.

Baba Shura took the baby in her arms so that Egor could take his coat and shoes off, then they went into Irina's room together. Irina was rocking Yasya to sleep in her arms.

'Look what he's brought,' said Baba Shura, speaking in a hushed tone. 'Someone dumped it outside Parliament, apparently.'

Irina put Yasya down on the bed and covered her with a blanket. She took the baby from her mother, then placed it next to Yasya on top of the blanket and unswaddled it.

'It's a girl,' she whispered. She looked up at Egor. 'And she's hungry!'

Irina picked her up.

'Mama, get Egor something to eat, he's come straight from work.'

Baba Shura ushered him into the kitchen. The baby stopped crying. The kitchen was filled with the appetising smell of buckwheat porridge – a whole cast-iron pot of it stood on the hob.

'What if they try to find her?' asked Baba Shura. 'Maybe we should call the militia.'

Egor just sat there and didn't say anything. He was thinking about what he'd done. He should have listened to Seryoga. 'Don't do anything stupid!' he'd said . . . But Egor had decided to ignore him and take matters into his own hands. What on earth had possessed him? He hadn't even called to let Irina or her mother know!

Baba Shura stood over the hob. She was looking at the kettle, which she had only just filled with water. She was glaring at it with a resentful and exasperated expression, as though she were angry with it for taking so long to boil.

'Why did you have to go and pick her up? How are we going to manage now? She's going to be on her own with two little ones!' she cried, unable to contain her emotions any longer. 'It was already bad enough for her being a single mother to one child! But now? No husband and *two* kids?!'

'She's not a single mother!' Egor protested.

'So what would you call her, then?' Baba Shura looked angrily from the kettle, which still hadn't boiled, to Egor. 'What will people say? You need to take that poor little mite to the militia, or to an orphanage. They'll look after her, feed her and keep her warm.'

Egor didn't say a word. Aleksandra Vasilievna fell silent too. The kettle finally boiled, and a cup of coffee was placed on the table in front of Egor. He looked at the steam rising from the cup, then at the sugar bowl. He would have loved to add some sugar to his coffee and begin drinking it, but there was no spoon on the table.

Egor got up from the table without saying anything and went into Irina's room.

Baba Shura followed him.

Irina's head was bowed. She was watching the baby suckling greedily at her breast, and there was peace in her eyes.

She looked up. 'Was there a note with her name?' she asked Egor in a whisper.

He shook his head.

'We'll call her Marina then,' she said tenderly.

84

Apartment No. 10, Reitarska Street, Kiev

It was the worst night of Veronika's life. When she looked in the mirror, she felt so sorry for herself that she burst into tears. Her face was puffy and pale, her eyes were red and bloodshot and her lips were dry. Her whole body ached.

She washed her face with warm water, then dried it gently with the towel and put on her night cream.

She went back into the bedroom and sat on the edge of the bed, where Semyon was lying with three blankets over him. His face was pale with a slight yellow tinge. From the other side of the room he looked like a dead man.

Veronika wasn't looking at him from the other side of the room, though. She was right next to him. She kept pressing her ear to his cold chest, listening to the rhythmic beating of his heart as it continued to measure out the seconds and the minutes of his life. He was alive! But why was he so cold and still?

At one point Veronika was reminded of the way Darya Ivanovna's husband looked after he'd been plastinated. She even imagined Semyon sitting in the armchair facing the window, with his back to her. The idea terrified her and she felt compelled to check under the bed, in case something else was making the rhythmic pounding sound she could hear. There was nothing under there but dust, of course. Not that Veronika could see any – she knew it was there, though, because she hadn't washed the floor under the bed for at least a month.

She began to feel cold in just her dressing gown and her short nightdress, so she pulled on a pair of jeans and a jumper.

She tried to wake him by stroking him gently and talking to him, but Semyon was out cold. She could smell the river on him. The damp smell lingered on his skin, even after she'd rubbed him down with vodka.

'Is he asleep, or in some kind of trance?' Veronika's thoughts were feverish and confused. She contemplated calling an ambulance but decided instead to wait until the morning, in the hope that he would wake of his own accord.

At about 5 a.m. she made some tea and poured herself a brandy. She sat down in the kitchen and glanced involuntarily at the window-sill, where she'd left Semyon's wallet and all its contents. She picked up the photo of the blonde woman and looked at it thoughtfully.

Then suddenly the realisation hit her.

'She's the reason he tried to drown himself!' her dry lips whispered.

Her husband's night-time disappearances came flooding back to her.

She glanced out of the window at the darkness beyond. She tried to imagine herself out there, walking along the dark and deserted street, and it gave her goosebumps.

She felt lonely and vulnerable. She drank her brandy and thought about her friend Darya Ivanovna. She really wished she were here right now, sitting with her at the table. She would have known exactly what to say. But Veronika would have to wait a few hours – it wasn't fair to burden your friends with your own nocturnal problems. It wasn't as if anyone was trying to kill her or assault her . . . Nothing was happening at all really. She just had all these fears that she felt the need to explain, otherwise no one would understand her or sympathise.

When Veronika went back into the bedroom the clock said 6.30 a.m. Outside the dawn was cautiously turning the sky grey, as yet unsure of its own inevitability.

Semyon lay as she'd left him, on his back, only now his eyes were open and he was staring at the ceiling.

Veronika knelt on the bed and leaned over so her face was right in front of his. She tried desperately to catch his eye, to break his blank and unmoving stare. But Semyon didn't even seem to see her.

'Senya! Senya!' she whispered.

A vein was throbbing under the skin on his neck. Apart from that he gave no sign of life.

'What's the matter with you? What happened?' asked Veronika, searching his face with her eyes. 'Are you cold? Shall I get you a brandy?'

Without waiting for a reply or any other reaction to her words, she went into the kitchen and fetched her glass of brandy. She put her forefinger into the glass then ran it over her husband's cold lips.

She thought she felt Semyon kiss her finger, which made her smile. She looked closely at his face once again. 'He's alive!' she thought.

She held his head up and put the glass to his lips. His lips parted, and he seemed to take a sip, then he closed his eyes.

She folded the three blankets back from his chest and put her ear to it. Again she heard the beating of his heart. Slow but steady.

At 9 a.m. she called Darya Ivanovna and asked her to come as quickly as she could. She told her that something terrible had happened.

Half an hour later she was showing her friend the photograph of the blonde and the psychiatrist's certificate.

'This is serious. Very serious,' said Darya Ivanovna, after reading the certificate three or four times.

They went in to see Semyon together. Veronika thought there was an unhealthy, feverish glow on his unshaven cheeks.

'You know, this morning he looked just like your Edik,' whispered Veronika.

'Oh my God!' exclaimed Darya Ivanovna. 'I forgot to call them! I'm supposed to be picking him up this morning at eleven!'

'Are you bringing him home?' asked Veronika, sympathetically.

'Well, in a way. We're going to the cemetery,' Darya Ivanovna nodded. 'Anna and I have made our decision. We've got graves next to each other, or rather they have, Edik and Vasya. I think I'm ready to start living alone. But we need to sort your problem out first. I'll just call and ask them to hang on to him for another day.'

Darya Ivanovna also called her hairdresser and made an appointment for the following day. Then she asked Veronika to leave her alone in the kitchen for ten minutes or so. Veronika agreed gladly. She made her friend some coffee then went into the living room, sat in the armchair and began to doze off.

'I've got a plan!' Darya Ivanovna's voice suddenly woke her up.

'Huh? What?'

'Get your coat on, we're going!'

'Where?'

Darya Ivanovna waved the psychiatrist's certificate under Veronika's nose.

'We're going to see this doctor,' she said, more gently. 'He probably knows more about your Senya than you do!'

85

Apartment No. 10, Reitarska Street, Kiev

The sound of his mobile phone ringing forced Semyon to open his eyes. He lay there for several minutes without moving, just listening to the familiar melody. He couldn't feel a thing. It was as though the connection between his brain and his body had somehow been broken.

The phone stopped ringing. Semyon concentrated on the whiteness of the ceiling and the green lampshade. He thought about Volodka and remembered that he'd called him the night before to warn him that there might be another 'nocturnal wander' on the cards. It looked as though he might have been right.

The phone started ringing again and Semyon rolled over onto his side, facing the edge of the bed. He froze like that for a second, surprised that he could move after all, then sat up. Without the warmth of his blanket cocoon the cold air in the room felt like a shock. He looked for something to put on but couldn't see his trousers, or his shirt, or any of his other clothes for that matter . . .

He decided to go and get his dressing gown from the bathroom. His legs obeyed but seemed to be made of cotton wool, and he had trouble keeping his balance.

When he put it on, his towelling dressing gown seemed unusually heavy.

Semyon went into the kitchen and was surprised to see his wallet on the windowsill. He never usually took it out of his jacket. And come to think of it, where was his phone? That was the second time it had rung.

Semyon reached for his wallet. Some receipts and a few business cards fell out of it. Semyon started stuffing them back into the pockets of his wallet and suddenly realised that something was missing.

'Where's that certificate, and the photo of Alisa?' he thought.

He checked the wallet again, becoming increasingly agitated. Had Veronika been going through his pockets? Surely not. But neither the certificate nor the photograph were there . . . And again, why was his wallet in the kitchen and not in his jacket?

Semyon went out into the hallway. His jacket wasn't on the coat rack. He remembered being vaguely aware of some clothes in the bath, so he went back into the bathroom. Yes, there was his jacket! It was hanging over the side of the bath, and on closer inspection the clothing in the bath turned out to be his trousers, his shirt, his tie and his socks.

Semyon picked his jacket up – it was wet, and there was an unpleasant swampy smell coming off it.

He checked the pockets and took out his phone, some loose change and the keys to the apartment. His leather phone case was damp, but the phone itself was still working. The display showed five missed calls, all from Gennady Ilyich.

He took the digital voice recorder out of the inside breast pocket of his jacket. Thankfully it was a zip pocket, and the machine seemed to have suffered no ill effects.

'Should I listen to it?' he wondered, then shook his head. 'Later, when I feel a bit more normal.'

Semyon looked at his trousers lying in the bath. Maybe he'd

gone back down into the basement and a pipe really had burst this time.

Just then his phone rang again.

'Where have you been?' barked Gennady Ilyich. His voice seemed unnecessarily loud, and Semyon held the phone away from his ear. 'You should have picked the milk up from Hrushevsky Street by now!'

'I'm not feeling too well,' muttered Semyon. 'But I'm leaving right now – I just need to call my colleague.'

He called Volodka, who took a long time to answer.

Finally he heard a hoarse, 'Hello.'

'Volodka, is that you?'

'Ah! So you've surfaced, then?' Volodka sounded like he had a cold. 'How do you feel? How much vodka did it take to sort you out?'

'Yeah, very funny. I feel like shit. Nika's been going through my wallet – she's taken the photo of Alisa and the certificate. My clothes are all soaking wet! I don't suppose you could –'

'I'm on my way! Stay where you are. I'll be there soon.'

'The boss called about the milk . . . We have to pick up –'

'It'll keep until this evening.'

Volodka arrived forty minutes later.

'I must admit, I thought you'd look a lot worse,' he said, coming into the hallway and peering at his friend's face.

They continued their conversation in the kitchen over a cup of tea.

Coughing every now and then, Volodka described the previous night to Semyon.

When he'd finished there was a long pause. Volodka drank his tea and Semyon stared dumbly at the table, digesting what he had just heard. Eventually he looked up at his friend.

'So, you think they were trying to kill me?' he asked.

'Looks like it. Someone called you and tried to explain to you over the phone the way to the next world . . .'

Semyon's blood suddenly ran cold, as though his body were reliving its nocturnal submersion in the icy Dnieper. He shuddered then looked down at the digital voice recorder, which had been pushed to the edge of the table, towards the windowsill. He picked it up and pressed the play button.

Volodka immediately leaned closer.

At first all you could hear was rustling and crackling. That lasted for a few minutes, and then there was the sound of a mobile phone ringing, followed by Semyon's voice.

'Yes, Arkady Petrovich, I knew it was you.'

Both friends leaned even closer to the digital device. Arkady Petrovich's voice was also audible, though not so clearly.

'Play it again from the beginning,' said Volodka.

They went back to the sound of the mobile phone ringing.

'Have you told anyone else about the Embassy of the Moon?'

'No, of course not!' said Semyon's voice.

'You're being followed,' said the other voice. 'I'll help you get rid of him, and then we'll talk. I'm going to give you directions and you must follow them quickly, without looking back.'

More crackling. The sound of cars passing.

'Go down Proreznaya Street,' Arkady Petrovich's voice continued. 'You haven't left your Embassy of the Moon documents at home where someone might find them, have you?'

'No, I hid them in the cellar behind the pipes, like you said.'

'Turn left now. And hurry up!'

Semyon and Volodka listened to the recording until they heard a splash. Then Volodka nodded, and Semyon switched it off.

'Now do you understand?' Volodka asked.

Semyon didn't answer.

'They wanted to get rid of you because I was following you . . . But that doesn't really make sense . . . And who is this Arkady Petrovich? Did you recognise his voice?'

Semyon shook his head.

'You've probably got loads of nocturnal acquaintances . . .'

Semyon gave a deep sigh. 'Do you mind picking up the milk without me?' he asked, with a glance at his ailing friend.

'Aren't you going to thank me first?' Volodka wheezed. 'I nearly drowned because of you!'

'Thank you.' Semyon nodded. 'I'll never forget it.'

'No problem.' Volodka waved his hand. 'I'm off. You ought to get drunk tonight, by the way, to make sure you stay put – and besides, it'll probably make you feel better!'

86

9 May Street, Boryspil, evening

Dima got back from Kiev at around 6 p.m. He climbed down from the minibus taxi into the cool, grey twilight at Boryspil bus station.

'You smell of onions!' exclaimed Valya, looking out of the little cashier's window in the amusement arcade.

'I've given Fluffy a good send-off,' Dima said.

'Can you hang on a minute? Sonya's already here, but she's just popped out to get some cigarettes.'

Once she'd handed over to her colleague, Valya took her

husband's arm affectionately and they started walking their usual route home.

'You know, I went to see a fortune-teller today. It was really quiet, so I put the "Back Soon" sign on the door and slipped out.' Valya glanced at her husband, to gauge his reaction to this news. He'd grumbled about it last time.

Dima nodded but his expression didn't change, so Valya continued.

'I told her everything, about how there's some kind of force preventing me from going into the house . . . She told me what to do.'

'How much did you pay her?'

'Fifty hryvnas.'

'Did you tell her about the dead body as well?' Dima's voice shook nervously.

'Well, yes. You have to tell her everything or her advice won't work. I just said that the body was nothing to do with us, that it was already there when we came home . . .'

'Did you tell her where we took it?'

'No! For goodness' sake, I'm not stupid!'

They continued walking in silence for about five minutes. Dima was mentally digesting his wife's news.

'So, what did she say?' he asked eventually.

'That we have to sprinkle a child's urine in the corners of the room, and then call a priest and have the house blessed.'

'And that's it?' Dima was surprised.

'Yes.'

'And then you'll be able to go in?' Dima suddenly brightened.

'Yes.'

Dima hugged his wife. The green light on the other side of

the pedestrian crossing lit up, but he was happy just standing there.

'I'll do it tomorrow,' he promised.

'I think I should stay with your sister tonight,' said Valya, looking beseechingly into her husband's eyes. 'You don't mind, do you? It's just a bit uncomfortable in the garage . . .'

He nodded.

From the pedestrian crossing it was closer to Nadya's place than to theirs.

Dima explained to his sister that they'd had their house fumigated to get rid of the cockroaches, and as Valya was pregnant she wasn't supposed to breathe in the chemical fumes, so they'd come to her place instead. In celebration of the good news Nadya plied Valya with champagne and chocolates and showered her with kisses. After sitting with the women for half an hour, Dima made his excuses and went home. He didn't want to stay at his sister's place, particularly as Nadya's husband wasn't overly fond of him. He was a teetotal Baptist and worked in a bread-making factory, and whenever they got together, which wasn't often, there was always a certain awkwardness between them. Dima didn't know how to talk to men who didn't drink. He got embarrassed and asked inappropriate questions.

As he put his key in the lock Dima heard a creak from his neighbour's yard. Dima looked over and saw his neighbour come out onto his front porch, which was lit by a single, bare light bulb. He greeted Dima with a friendly wave.

'Can I come over to yours for a minute?' he called.

Dima froze, then shook his head. 'Sorry, we've got some building work going on,' he lied.

'Then come to the fence,' said the neighbour, coming down from his doorstep. 'I want to ask your advice on something.'

Dima went over and shook his neighbour's hand. His eyes were involuntarily drawn to the hole in the fence. His neighbour glanced at the hole too and a guilty look flitted across his face.

'You know, I put an advert up like you suggested, and someone called the very next morning,' he began. 'They reckoned they'd found my King, but wanted me to increase the reward . . .' He stopped and looked expectantly at Dima.

'How much were they after?' Dima asked absent-mindedly.

'Three hundred dollars.'

'*How* much?!'

Dima's neighbour approved of his indignant response.

'I know. That's way too much, isn't it?' he said.

'How much were you offering?'

'A hundred hryvnas.'

'That sounds about right. Your dog wasn't worth any more than that.'

'That's what I thought. It's not a particularly expensive breed, and he's too old to be worth three hundred dollars anyway. They're going to call back tomorrow and I'll tell them it's too much. What do you think?'

'Definitely don't give them any more than a hundred hryvnas,' Dima advised him. 'I'm sorry, I'm afraid I have to go now. I've got a bit more work to do,' he said, pointing at his house.

'Are you redecorating?' asked his neighbour.

'No, just a few odd jobs. I'm sanding the floor.'

As he stepped into the domestic warmth of his house, Dima remembered how he'd thrown King's body into the abandoned well.

'I wonder what sort of dog they're trying to palm off on him for three hundred dollars,' he thought with a weary smile.

He took his boots off, then went into the bedroom, switched the light on and looked closely at the wooden floor. Noticing two more pinkish spots, he washed them off with a wet cloth then rubbed the floor dry. He carried out a final inspection, and this time he was satisfied.

Dima was feeling the after-effects of his sleepless night in the garage so went to bed earlier than usual, and he was already half asleep when he heard a banging sound coming from the front yard. He was curious, but not sufficiently so to get out of bed and investigate. The following morning all was revealed: looking out of the kitchen window, Dima saw that the hole in the fence had been boarded up on his neighbour's side.

'Things are looking up!' he thought, as he put three spoonfuls of instant coffee into a mug of hot water.

87

Hrushevsky Street, Kiev

A cold and heavy rain hammered down on the ground and the naked trees, chasing everyone indoors. Egor even had the impression that there were fewer cars on Hrushevsky Street. Mariinsky Park had emptied completely, and the Communist veterans from the anti-NATO picket were holed up in their tents.

Egor wearily held an umbrella over his head. He walked to the arched entrance at the side of the park and got into his Mazda, then called Irina on his mobile phone. Her cheerful voice made Egor forget about the weather for a while. Irina told him that Yasya was sleeping and that Marina was still breastfeeding. She told him that she'd found a birthmark in Marina's armpit and that the child hadn't shown the slightest fear when she'd taken her outside and introduced her to Barsik, the next-door neighbour's dog, who had promptly tried to lick her face.

They chatted for about five minutes. The rain was beating down on the car, but it didn't interrupt their conversation at all.

Egor's shift would finish earlier that day, because he had started earlier than usual. Two of their lads had recently been fired because they'd waved their identity documents in someone's face and threatened him after an argument in a restaurant. The press had found out about it straight away, and the boss had called them all into his office in the rear right-hand wing of the Mariinsky Palace. He told them that the brawlers had been fired and warned them that until he could find replacements they would all be working flexitime.

So Egor had started working flexible shifts – from 5 p.m. to 3 a.m., or from 4 a.m. to 1 p.m., for example.

Today he would be finished by 3 p.m. The bad weather didn't bother him at all. He planned to call in at the supermarket on his way to Irina's place to pick up some groceries and something sweet for Baba Shura, to make her smile at him again.

It was still raining, but it had eased off a little.

The grey sky hung low over Kiev. It already felt like twilight.

As soon as he'd finished his shift and handed in his walkie-talkie Egor hurried to the food shop on Victory Square, where he bought some sausages, a cake, a round loaf of Darnitsky bread and some biscuits. When he was paying at the till he felt a strange, modest pride deep in his soul. He enjoyed being able to take care of Irina, the girls and Baba Shura – they were like a family to him.

He thought about this again as he waited before Vozdukhoflotsky Bridge for the traffic lights to turn green. He remembered Irina's mother asking him to take her to visit his own mother, and how upset she was about the fact that Irina didn't have a marriage stamp in her passport.

His foot moved from the brake to the accelerator, and he left the bridge behind. McDonald's loomed up on the left, and then the Central Registry Office – a dilapidated triangular building nicknamed 'The Bermuda Triangle'.

Egor saw a limousine decorated with flowers and ribbons parked outside the registry office. He moved into the right-hand lane and pulled up next to the pavement, then got out of the car and dived into the underground pedestrian crossing, holding his umbrella.

In the spacious foyer of the Central Registry Office three couples sat waiting their turn, surrounded by their witnesses and close friends and family.

'Where do you have to go to register?' Egor asked a man in a grey suit with an artificial rose in his lapel.

'Marriage or divorce?'

'Marriage.'

'Through that little door over there. That's the secretary's office. She'll tell you everything you need to know.'

Egor nodded but didn't head straight for the narrow, unassuming little door. He stood there for about ten minutes, just watching people. The next couple were summoned, and they disappeared through the ceremonial double doors as if they were being sucked into a trap.

There was something about the atmosphere there that Egor didn't like. It was either the sense of feigned submissiveness, or the presence of too many pairs of trousers ironed specially for the occasion and too many pairs of highly polished shoes together in one place.

Eventually he knocked quietly on the nondescript door and went inside. Before him sat a skinny, sharp-nosed woman of around forty, wearing glasses and a grey business suit with a knee-length skirt. Her dark fringe was cut just above her eyebrows. It was completely straight, as though it had been cut using a ruler, and you couldn't see her forehead at all.

'Is this where to register a marriage?' he asked.

'You have to fill out an application form,' the woman said.

'Um, I was just wondering, would it be possible to make an exception? Could I just bring our passports? You know, without the actual ceremony . . .'

'Why? Has your bride got something to be ashamed of? The ceremony is very important to women. You men have no idea!'

'She's breastfeeding two babies. And we can't exactly bring them here.'

'Ah, so you've already got children . . . How many?' The woman seemed interested, although Egor detected a hint of irony in her voice.

'Two,' he said.

The woman gave a heavy sigh. She moved the desk calendar towards her and started flipping through the pages. She wrote something on one of the pages then tore it off and held it out to Egor, without saying a word.

The page said *Wednesday 14th March*. At the bottom the secretary had written: 6.45 p.m., $200.

'You need to come to this office,' she said, with a long, level look at the groom-to-be, and that signalled the end of their conversation.

As soon as the Mazda emerged from the small traffic jam near the Dachnaya bus station the sky above the road cleared and the rain stopped. In fact, the Zhytomyr Highway was completely dry. Maybe it hadn't rained here at all.

Egor glanced in his rear-view mirror. There were several cars behind him, and he caught a glimpse of the grey and gloomy city on the hill, receding into the distance beneath the oppressive weight of the low, leaden sky.

88

Bekhterevsky Street, Kiev

'You want to go in together?' Inna, Pyotr Isaevich's assistant, looked in surprise at the two women standing in front of her desk.

'Yes, definitely,' confirmed the elder and larger of the two.

Inna assumed that they were mother and daughter, although there was no obvious family resemblance between them.

'I'll just go and make sure that's OK.' Inna got up from her desk.

'Take this, so he knows why we're here.' The elder woman held out a document folded in two.

When Pyotr Isaevich unfolded the paper, he was astonished to see the medical certificate he had given to Semyon.

'And there are two of them, you said?' he whispered, looking up at Inna.

She nodded.

'Are they acting aggressively?'

'They're being quite firm, but not aggressive,' said his assistant. 'But if you keep them waiting . . .'

The doctor nodded. 'Send them in, and ask them if they'd like some tea or coffee.'

Darya Ivanovna and Veronika went into the white office and both found themselves staring into the doctor's eyes. He was standing behind his desk.

'Take a seat,' he said, in a warm and gentle voice.

'Innochka, could you bring another chair in?' he called, looking at the door behind his visitors. 'People usually come in one at a time . . .'

'I know,' Veronika said agreeably, and a serene, faraway smile crossed her lips.

'Ah,' thought Pyotr Isaevich. 'It'll be easier with her.'

The other woman was frowning silently. Her expression did not bode well.

His assistant brought the extra chair in.

'Would you like tea or coffee?' she asked.

'I'll have an espresso,' Darya Ivanovna answered tersely.

'Me too, please,' said Veronika.

The doors shut behind Inna. It became surprisingly quiet in the office.

Veronika gazed intently at the white couch.

'You've come about Semyon,' said the doctor, breaking the silence.

'Yes,' replied Darya Ivanovna. 'And just so you know, he tried to kill himself last night.'

Pyotr Isaevich frowned. He looked at Veronika.

'Let me just get this straight,' he said. 'Are you his wife?'

Veronika nodded.

'And you?' The doctor turned to her companion. 'Are you his mother?'

'Of course not! I'm her friend.' She nodded at Veronika.

'And you're happy discussing your husband's problems in her presence?' asked the doctor.

'Yes,' Veronika confirmed.

'Fine,' he said calmly. 'We'll come back to his suicide attempt a bit later. First let's talk about him. Your husband is a sleepwalker. Did you know that?'

Veronika looked alarmed.

'Don't worry.' Pyotr Isaevich leaned forward a little and looked her straight in the eye. 'It's nothing to worry about. Did you think he was just going out for a walk or something?'

Veronika nodded.

'How long has it been going on?'

'Probably since the autumn. I don't remember exactly. November or December.'

'What time does he normally go to bed?'

'About eleven, unless he's tired, in which case earlier . . .'

'Does he ever stay out really late? Do the two of you ever take a stroll round the city at night, for example?'

'About fifteen years ago, before we got married –'

'Maybe after the accident?' Darya Ivanovna joined the conversation. 'Remember, Nika, you told me about it.'

'Could you tell me about it too?' asked the doctor.

Veronika sighed and began to talk, and she was surprised to feel a weight lift almost instantly from her soul. She told him about their missing daughter, about how she had begun to question herself, and about sending Semyon out to look for the child at night.

Pyotr Isaevich listened very carefully. The door opened slightly and Inna attempted to come into the office with two cups of coffee on a tray, but Pyotr Isaevich stopped her with a look and sent her back.

When Veronika reached the events of the previous night, she felt her anxiety returning. Her voice was shaking but she continued, looking directly into the doctor's eyes as though drawing support from them.

Veronika talked for about twenty minutes, and then there was silence. Pyotr Isaevich asked them to wait for about five minutes and left the room. Inna brought the tray of coffee in. She closed the door behind her as she went out.

Veronika drank her coffee and looked at the couch. Darya Ivanovna was wearing a slightly irritated expression. She glanced at her gold watch, which was too small for her chunky wrist. Then she turned to her friend and watched with surprise as Veronika placed her cup on the desk and suddenly stood up, kicked off her boots and lay back on the white couch.

'Mm, he does inspire trust,' Darya Ivanovna thought, and she looked back at the closed doors.

Pyotr Isaevich came back into the office about ten minutes later. He was not at all surprised to see Veronika lying on the couch with her eyes closed.

She raised her head slightly.

'No, stay where you are,' the doctor said to her gently. 'It's better like that. You can look up at the ceiling or close your eyes, as you wish. I'm going to ask you some questions and I'd like you to answer them, in your own time.'

She closed her eyes.

'You were in a car accident seven years ago. Is that correct?'

'Yes,' whispered Veronika.

'Were you badly injured?'

'Yes.'

'Did you have head injuries?'

'Yes.'

'Did you have a child before the accident?'

Veronika didn't answer.

'Did you think there was a child with you in the car at the time of the accident?'

'Yes,' whispered Veronika.

'Did you try to find this child?'

'Yes.'

'Did you ask your husband to go and look for the child?'

'Yes.'

'Did he go looking for the child in the dark? And return when you were already asleep?'

'Yes.'

'Did this go on for a few months, or longer?'

'Longer.'

'Did he go looking for the child later of his own accord, even when you didn't ask him? Did he himself suggest going to look for the child?'

'Yes.'

'And you stopped asking him to look for the child, because you knew he would go anyway?'

'Yes.'

'He liberated you from your obsession, by taking the burden of your anxiety onto his own shoulders. I understand that your life resumed its normal course shortly thereafter. Although you did continue seeing a psychiatrist for a while, didn't you?'

'Yes.'

'Your husband has what is known as acquired somnambulism. It is something that he developed in the process of helping you deal with your emotional issues. In other words – and please don't take this the wrong way – he started sleepwalking because of you.'

'So what about this blonde woman?' asked Darya Ivanovna.

'I don't know anything about her,' replied Pyotr Isaevich. 'There are a lot of sleepwalkers roaming the streets of Kiev at night. Sometimes they get to know one another and friendships can develop, but during the day they don't even recognise one another. They develop a specific "nocturnal" memory, which is activated only when they are sleepwalking. Semyon himself is worried about what's happening to him. That's why he asked his friend to follow him and take photos of the people he was meeting at night . . . Incidentally, you don't happen to have his friend's phone number or address, do you?'

'Volodka? No, but I can find out.'

'Please do.'

'Can he be cured?'

'Yes, with tender loving care. And it would also help if you had something else to worry about. You don't have any children, do you?'

'No. But he recently suggested we adopt a baby girl.'

'You see, he's thinking along the right lines! And now let's move on to his suicide attempt, which you mentioned earlier. It was probably linked to his sleepwalking – just an unfortunate incident. Your husband is not the suicidal type. He has the opposite psychological profile.'

'What do you mean?' asked Veronika.

'He's more likely to kill someone else than himself. But that's just theoretical, of course. Now, how to cure him . . . You know, it would be helpful if there were something to keep him awake consciously at night for six months or so. For example, if you had a baby he could get up when it needed changing, or give it a bottle. But until you do have children it would be a good idea for him to find a job that involved night shifts. Come back and see me again in a couple of days. Oh, and don't forget to let me know his friend Volodka's phone number. Just don't let your husband know that you're giving it to me.'

They went out into the reception area and stopped by Inna's desk.

'How much do we owe you?' asked Darya Ivanovna.

'A hundred hryvnas,' answered the doctor's assistant.

Darya Ivanovna placed a hundred-hryvna note on the desk. She looked at the diary, which lay open on the desk with a ballpoint pen in the centre.

'Put me down for next Tuesday, in the morning,' she said.

'Would eleven o'clock suit you?' asked Inna.

'Perfect!'

Outside the sun was shining. At the corner of Artema Street they turned left, towards Lviv Square. Veronika felt relieved of a great burden and at the same time completely drained. It was a strange, almost childlike feeling.

'I don't usually trust redheads,' said Darya Ivanovna pensively. 'But he was rather nice. Will you come to the funeral with me tomorrow?' she asked, turning to her friend.

Veronika nodded.

'By the way, you should hide the photo of that blonde somewhere safe. Just in case. I think I've seen her somewhere before . . . But put the certificate back in his wallet.'

89

Bekhterevsky Street, Kiev

Semyon went through the arch into Landscape Alley, which ran along the edge of a steep hill with a good view over Podil. You could even see the Obolon district in the distance, its tall buildings cutting into the sky. The alley was frequented by young mothers with buggies, pensioners and basically anyone else who found themselves with a little time on their hands. The noise of the traffic on Great Zhytomyr Street didn't reach this far, even though there were only two rows of old pre-revolutionary houses separating it from the alley. The air was always fresher up here, too.

It took Semyon about twenty minutes to get to Bekhterevsky Street.

'You didn't happen to meet anyone on your way here, did you?' Pyotr Isaevich asked tentatively, when Semyon came into his office.

'Like who?'

'Anyone you know?'

'No.' Semyon shook his head and sat down on the chair opposite the doctor. 'I've got a few problems,' he sighed. 'More than a few, to be honest . . .'

The psychiatrist stared at Semyon. Pyotr Isaevich's eyes that day were sharper than usual, and Semyon felt uncomfortable.

'You ought to come to me with your problems as and when they arise. But you've waited until the situation has become critical! Do you think you will learn from your mistake?'

Semyon did. He nodded.

'Good.' The doctor spread his fingers and showed them to his visitor. 'Now, I want you to copy everything I do.'

Semyon obediently spread his fingers then relaxed them, like the doctor did. They repeated the exercise together about ten times, and Semyon noticed that the doctor's expression seemed to have softened. Semyon also felt calmer.

'Right, where shall we start?' asked the doctor.

'Probably with –'

'You can tell me anything! The fewer secrets you have from me, the easier it will be for me to help you. You do need help, don't you?'

'Yes,' Semyon nodded. 'I nearly drowned.'

He proceeded to tell the doctor about his recent nocturnal activity in detail, as observed and reported on by his friend Volodka. He even told him about his membership of the Church of the Embassy of the Moon, and about the phone call that he received just before launching himself from the Metro Bridge into the icy waters of the Dnieper.

'Before you switched into "nocturnal mode" this last time, just recently, did you feel perfectly normal? Or did you notice anything different?'

'I remember being aware that I hadn't been out at night for a while,' admitted Semyon. 'That's why I called Volodka. I must have known that something was going to happen.'

'I see,' murmured Pyotr Isaevich. He paused for a moment. 'What's your relationship with your wife like at the moment?'

'Well, it *was* fine. But then she found that photo of Alisa, and the certificate saying that I wasn't responsible for my actions. I haven't seen her since. She left before I woke up this morning. We're probably going to have a massive row about it.'

'Not necessarily,' said the doctor, quite confidently. 'Clever women do their best to avoid arguments. You need to relax and forget about what happened. Try not to think about it for a while. And give your friend a break too! There's nothing inherently bad about sleepwalking. You might meet up with this woman again . . . but so what if you do? It's not worth worrying about. The main thing is not to take any documents with you – there have been several incidents recently of sleepwalkers being mugged . . .'

Semyon looked at the doctor suspiciously.

'In any case, my dear chap, sleepwalkers never die!' Pyotr Isaevich leaned forward, his eyes boring into Semyon's with a surprising, almost palpable intensity.

Semyon suddenly narrowed his eyes. Pyotr Isaevich leaned back and sat normally, shaking his head pensively. Then his whole face changed, as though he'd put on a mask.

'Now let's forget everything we've discussed,' he said, his voice clearer and more urgent. 'If you still want to cure yourself of your sleepwalking, you need to find yourself a job that involves working at night. If you work nights, then you can guarantee that you will remain in control of your actions. It's very important that you come and see me once a week, until we both agree that everything's fine.'

'What about Alisa?' asked Semyon, feeling rather confused.

'The night has many temptations,' smiled Pyotr Isaevich. 'When you give up your nocturnal life, you'll be giving up your relationship with Alisa at the same time! Why do you need to see her anyway? You've got a wife . . .'

Once he was outside, Semyon stopped and looked back at the

pale blue arched gates of the Pokrovsky Monastery. 'I bet it's beautiful here at night,' he thought.

90

9 May Street, Boryspil

Dima had a lazy start to the day. He got dressed and had a cup of coffee, then looked through the classified ads paper until he found the 'Services' section. He found what he was looking for straight away.

> Orthodox priest available to perform Christian cleansing rite in homes, apartments, dachas, cars, boats, yachts. Excellent rates. Tel. 8-044-416 86 04

Dima circled the ad twice with a pen and left the paper on the table. Then he put an empty two-litre plastic mineral water bottle in a carrier bag, put his coat on and went outside.

The morning sun had surrendered its place in the sky to dark storm clouds. The air was saturated with humidity and felt heavy.

Dima remembered the sun at the cemetery the previous day, the melodic birdsong, the peaceful atmosphere and his feeling of contentment. He wished he could rekindle that feeling of spiritual serenity right now. But the weather was depressing, and he had a tough day ahead of him.

Dima's feet led him to the kindergarten in the next street.

He went up the three concrete steps to the front door, then went inside and stopped at the beginning of a long, wide corridor. He could hear children's voices and the clattering of tableware.

He stuck his head round the first open door he came to. It was the nursery kitchen, and there were two girls in white jackets and toques pottering about by the stove.

'Where are the children?' Dima asked them.

'Which group?' asked one of the girls.

'The youngest.'

'Last door on the left.'

Dima paused in front of a door with a sign on it saying 'Snowflakes'. He opened it and saw a changing room with rows of wooden lockers on both sides, and a pair of children's boots on the floor under each one. Straight ahead, about three or four metres away, was another door. Dima pulled the door open and saw a large room and a number of two- and three-year-old children playing with various toys. A neat row of multicoloured potties stood in the left-hand corner, one of which was occupied by a little blond boy who was sitting there patiently, concentrating on the task at hand. The teacher – a girl of about twenty – was helping some of the children build a railway track on the floor.

'Can I help you?' she asked, looking up.

The children also looked up at the stranger.

'Could I have a quick word?' asked Dima quietly, nodding towards the little changing room with wooden lockers. 'I'm sorry,' he mumbled, suddenly feeling self-conscious and at a loss for words. 'Um, I need . . .'

'What do you need?' She looked directly at Dima, her green eyes sincere and obliging.

'I need some children's urine,' he blurted out eventually, holding up the carrier bag with the empty bottle in. 'For my wife . . .'

'Ah, urine therapy!' the girl said knowingly. 'Pregnant women use it to make sure the baby's healthy . . .'

She thought for a moment, then she looked into the playroom and her gaze fell on a little girl in a dark blue cardigan and thick brown tights.

'Mashenka, do you need a wee? Come on then, let's sit on the potty!'

The little girl headed quickly over to the 'toilet corner', where the blond boy was still sitting on his potty.

'Wait here,' the teacher told Dima and went back to the children, closing the changing-room door behind her.

About ten minutes later she brought the potty and its contents to Dima. Dima thanked the teacher and gave her five hryvnas. Then he grew flustered, trying to work out how to transfer the urine from the potty into the bottle. Noticing his confusion, the teacher made a cone out of a piece of coloured card and gave it to him.

'Put the end in the top of the bottle and hold it there. I'll pour it in.'

As soon as he got home, Dima sprinkled the child's urine in all four corners of the room. Then he dialled the priest's number from the classified ads paper.

'Where do you live? Boryspil?' asked the priest, in a pleasant baritone. 'In that case it'll be another fifty hryvnas for the call-out fee and transport costs. Is it just the one room, or the whole house?'

'Just one room,' said Dima.

'No, that's not right,' said the priest. 'You shouldn't sanctify one room and not the others. Why don't we do the whole house? It's not really worth my while coming all the way out to Boryspil from Kiev just for one room . . . And there's not a great difference in price.'

'How much will it be for the whole house, then?' asked Dima.

'Three hundred hryvnas.'

'Fine,' agreed Dima. 'But can you come today?'

'What's your address?'

The priest promised to be there in a couple of hours.

Instead of the rain they'd forecast the sun suddenly started shining. Dima went out onto the doorstep and looked up at the sky. Fragmented clouds scudded towards Kiev, driven by a high-altitude wind.

The sound of the telephone ringing drew him back into the house. It was the airport.

'You can come in to work tomorrow,' said his boss. 'You need to pick up your wages. But come and see me first, in the morning!'

Puzzled, Dima went over to the window, looked up at the sky again and sighed.

91

Lipovka village, Kiev region

Before ringing the doorbell Ilko Petrovich stood on the doorstep for at least a minute, studying the horseshoe nailed above the door.

'Should I tell them or not?' he asked himself. Then he shrugged.

Aleksandra Vasilievna bustled into the hallway at the sound of the bell.

'Oh, you're early!' she exclaimed when she saw the professor's familiar plump face.

'They've postponed our departmental meeting till tomorrow,'

he began. Then he stopped and thought, 'I don't have to justify myself to her!'

But Aleksandra Vasilievna didn't expect him to.

'Go on through to the kitchen. Would you like a coffee? I'll whisk it up to make it nice and frothy!'

Ilko Petrovich left his sheepskin jacket on a hook in the hall and looked down at his boots. He remembered that he was wearing new socks from the Zhytomyr sock factory – he'd bought himself ten pairs for three hryvnas each in the underground pedestrian crossing near the university metro station – so he decided to take his boots off. He looked around for a pair of guest slippers and when he couldn't find any went straight into the kitchen as he was, in his grey socks, his black suit, his white shirt and his yellow tie.

Aleksandra Vasilievna was washing a cup in the sink. The gas was on under the kettle, and an unopened jar of instant coffee stood on the table.

Ilko Petrovich thought about what she'd said: 'I'll whisk it up.' If anyone in Kiev had suggested 'whisking' him a coffee, he'd have thought them terribly uneducated. But here in this country village, spoken by this peasant woman, the phrase sounded so normal and natural! And he knew exactly what she meant: the words evoked the entire process, simple and precise. She would put two or three spoonfuls of coffee in a cup, add a spoonful or two of sugar and then dribble in some water from the kettle, to make a kind of concentrated coffee essence. Then she would start whisking this coffee essence until it frothed and turned the colour of cappuccino.

Ilko Petrovich gave a sigh. 'There's no point trying to change the way the people speak,' he thought.

A few minutes later, when the dark blue enamel kettle with its pattern of large painted daisies began snorting steam from its nose,

Aleksandra Vasilievna sprinkled some sugar and coffee into a large earthenware mug, added a trickle of water and – exactly as Petrovich had imagined – started whisking his coffee.

Ilko Petrovich suddenly remembered that she'd brewed him fresh coffee the first time he'd come. So how come he was only getting instant this time? He wasn't about to ask, though – he'd come to buy breast milk for his baby, not to study coffee-making traditions in Ukrainian villages.

'Coffee-making traditions in Ukrainian villages,' he repeated to himself. 'I ought to write that down. I could get the students to write an essay on the subject . . . Serafimchuk, at least. If I gave him the address he could come here and interview her, talk to the other villagers . . . Actually, on second thoughts that's probably not such a good idea. What if he were to find out that the professor's wet nurse lives here? They've got enough to gossip about behind my back as it is! That old professor, marrying one of his students . . . and one who was thrown off her course due to ill health, too. No, I mustn't let anyone into my private life. Especially not a smart alec like Serafimchuk!'

In fact, Ilko Petrovich rather liked the coffee that Aleksandra Vasilievna had whisked up for him, although he would never have admitted it to anyone he knew. According to his rank and status his coffee of choice should have been an espresso, or an espresso macchiato. But out here nobody cared about his status or the contents of his earthenware mug, so he permitted himself this indulgence and found his enjoyment increasing with every sip.

After placing the coffee in front of her guest Aleksandra Vasilievna had left the room. Alone in the kitchen, Ilko Petrovich was surprised to feel so at home there on just his second visit.

'How much shall I give him?' Baba Shura asked her daughter, who was sitting on the bed holding Marina.

'If he can wait a bit I'll express some fresh. One breast is completely full.' Irina touched her left breast.

'Why don't I just give him that jar from the boiler room? There's nearly a litre in there.' Aleksandra Vasilievna had lowered her voice to a whisper.

'That's yesterday's and the day before's mixed up together. What if it makes their baby ill? Just leave it in there, let it turn sour. Then I can make Yasya some curd cheese with it.'

'Well, it's up to you,' said her mother, going back into the kitchen.

'Can you wait a while? There'll be some fresh milk soon. She's just getting the baby to sleep.'

About twenty minutes later Irina herself brought the milk into the kitchen.

Ilko Petrovich stood up – it was the first time he'd met his baby son's wet nurse. He took the litre jar from her and looked around for his briefcase, but then remembered that he'd left it in the car.

Aleksandra Vasilievna opened a cloth bag for him to put the milk in.

'You can bring it back next time,' she said.

'What's your son's name?' asked Irina.

'Bogdan.'

'A fine name!' nodded Irina's mother.

Their guest placed thirty hryvnas on the kitchen table and left.

Irina watched from the kitchen window as he got into his Volga and glanced back at their house, apparently deep in thought.

As he was about to pull out onto the main road, he almost collided with a red Mazda that was turning into the lane. He slammed on the brakes, swearing under his breath, and waited until the Mazda had squeezed between his Volga and the fence before setting off again. Ilko Petrovich felt the contrast as the wheels of his car left the dirty gravel for the smooth tarmac of the main road, and from then on it was an easy drive. There was no traffic, so he didn't need to concentrate on the road and was able to focus on his own thoughts instead. Such interesting and important thoughts they were, too.

92

Apartment No. 10, Reitarska Street, Kiev

The sun spent half its time hiding behind clouds that day, and whenever it emerged the sudden brightness made Semyon screw up his eyes. In these fleeting moments he felt a rare sense of inner calm, a kind of quiet joy. He forgot all about home and Veronika, about the psychiatrist and Alisa . . . The noises in his head fell silent and he stopped worrying; he even stopped thinking. But as soon as the sun went behind another cloud the day grew darker and the anxiety would return.

It wasn't until the sun disappeared behind the city's skyline that Semyon finally acknowledged the approaching twilight and began to head home. He felt awful for putting Veronika through this. He was full of remorse – for the argument they were bound to have, and for carrying a photograph of someone other than Veronika in his wallet.

To his surprise Veronika didn't start an argument. On the

contrary. She completely nonplussed him by putting her arms round him and kissing him as soon as he stepped into the hallway, before he'd even taken his shoes off.

'Where have you been?' she asked, her voice low and intimate. 'I've missed you . . .'

Semyon panicked. He immediately assumed that there was something wrong with Veronika and that she needed to go back to her psychiatrist. But the warmth in her eyes was genuine rather than exaggerated, and her hands weren't shaking the way they had done seven years previously, when her mood could change several times in an hour.

'I went out for a walk,' replied Semyon.

'You need to rest,' said Veronika. 'Are you hungry?'

Semyon nodded.

'I've made fried mushrooms and potatoes.'

'Mushrooms? Where did you manage to find mushrooms? It's March, not September!'

'Daryushka gave me some – she's got plenty to spare. She's got whole strings of dried mushrooms hanging up in her kitchen.'

Semyon followed his wife into the kitchen. He thought about Darya Ivanovna's kitchen, where he had recently had a cup of tea, or was it coffee? He could picture the kitchen, but he didn't recall seeing any strings of dried mushrooms there. He sat down at the table, watching closely as Veronika served him some mushrooms and potatoes from the frying pan. She gave him a fork and cut him a slice of black bread, and then she sat down opposite him.

'Go ahead,' she said tenderly. 'I've already eaten.'

Semyon picked up his fork and looked down at the mushrooms. His brain was working overtime, and he couldn't think straight. A shiver of fear ran down his back. Something wasn't right . . . Her attentiveness, her show of affection – none of it made sense. Was it a normal reaction for a wife, after finding proof of her husband's infidelity, to kiss him, hug him and make him fried mushrooms and potatoes for dinner?

Semyon's suspicions made him look more closely at the mushrooms, but when mushrooms are chopped up and fried they all look the same: you can no longer tell the difference between harmless white mushrooms and fly agaric, or toadstools.

Semyon started eating some potato. He chewed slowly, cautiously analysing the taste of the food, without taking his eyes off Veronika. He was wary and nervous, like a frightened rabbit.

'Eat up!' said his wife. 'Have some mushrooms too, not just the potato!'

Semyon obediently stuck his fork in a piece of mushroom. He put it in his mouth and chewed. It tasted fine, but what would happen to him in a couple of hours' time? People die two hours after eating poisonous mushrooms! Semyon didn't know how he knew that, or in fact if it was an accurate prognosis.

'What time is it?' he asked.

'Eight o'clock already. Come on, aren't you hungry? You've had nothing to eat all day!'

Semyon nodded. He decided that after the first mouthful he had nothing to lose.

'I'm going to a funeral tomorrow morning,' said Veronika.

'Whose?' he asked cautiously.

'Edik, Darya Ivanovna's husband.'

'I thought you'd already buried him.'

'Well, he died a while ago, but we didn't actually bury him. Daryushka had him embalmed, but that didn't really work out . . .

So she's decided to bury him properly. What have you got on tomorrow?'

Semyon shrugged. 'If I'm still alive, I'll have to go to work. Volodka had to do everything without me today.'

Veronika didn't seem to have noticed what her husband had said.

'Remember that baby girl you were talking about? You know, the one you said we could adopt?' She put her head on one side and wrinkled her nose.

'Yes.'

'Go on, eat up!' She nodded at his plate. 'Well, I was thinking . . . Maybe we could give it a try . . .'

'Try adopting, you mean?' Semyon was surprised. He put his fork with an uneaten piece of mushroom back down on his plate.

'Yes,' Veronika said calmly.

'All right, I'll make a phone call,' he said, bringing the fork to his mouth. 'In an hour or so.'

They had a cup of tea, and then Semyon began to question his wife's psychiatric health again. She suddenly started talking animatedly about her childhood, for some reason. Semyon listened to her with an apprehensive expression on his face. He couldn't stop thinking about his stomach, waiting for the symptoms of poisoning – cramps or convulsions. Half an hour passed.

'They're probably just normal mushrooms,' thought Semyon, as he watched Veronika chattering away.

'You look so serious!' she said reproachfully, stopping in the middle of her story about some youthful adventure or other.

'I'll just go and make that call,' said Semyon, standing up. 'About the little girl . . .'

'OK,' said Veronika.

She stayed in the kitchen. After her husband had left the room she took a bottle of Zakarpatsky brandy and two shot glasses out of the cupboard.

Semyon called his boss.

'Gennady Ilyich! It's me, Semyon. Can you talk?'

'Yes, what is it?'

'My wife said yes!'

'To what?'

'Remember you asked about us adopting a little baby girl?'

'I remember,' the deputy answered gloomily. 'I remember all too well.'

'So?' said Semyon. 'My wife's agreed.'

'Sorry, I'm not feeling a hundred per cent at the moment. Let me send a driver for you. We'll talk when you get here.'

'What, right now?'

'Why not? He'll call you down when he gets there.'

Semyon went back into the kitchen.

He and Veronika drank some brandy.

'Spring's almost here,' said Veronika in a dreamy voice, licking the brandy from her lips.

Semyon's mobile phone rang. The deputy's driver told him he was downstairs, just outside the building. Semyon told Veronika that he was going to go and find out about the baby girl.

'Well, I'm going to bed.' Veronika kissed his cheek. 'Maybe I'll dream about her!'

The night smelled warm and damp. A light drizzle was falling. A dark blue BMW stood outside, gleaming importantly and reflecting the yellow light from the street lamp nearby.

93

Apartment No. 17, Vorovsky Street, Kiev

Darya Ivanovna's morning had started far too early. She'd hardly had any sleep that night. She couldn't get over the feeling that Edik was still sitting in the armchair facing the balcony door, with his grey stubble turning silver in the moonlight . . . She had crossed the living room to go to the bathroom several times during the night, and each time she had glanced at the armchair out of the corner of her eye.

She had obviously been thinking like this because of the funeral, which was due to take place that day. It just seemed so . . . final: the final line under her relationship with Edik. The relationship that had formed between them after his death.

By 5.30 a.m. Darya Ivanovna realised that her chances of getting back to sleep were virtually nil. The moon had disappeared completely, as though someone had flicked a switch, and the world was surprisingly quiet and dark. All of a sudden she heard an unobtrusive reproach in her head: 'Never forsake your loved ones.' It was Edik's voice.

'What am I supposed to do then?' thought Darya Ivanovna, feeling the need to explain her own decision. 'I kept him close for as long as I possibly could – at least, for as long as I was afraid to be alone. But I'm not afraid any more. He sat here in his armchair, waiting for me to learn how to live on my own . . .

And now I'm ready to face the world without him, it's time to bury him!'

The lights were on throughout the apartment. The doors of the big wardrobe were thrown open and dozens of dresses, skirts and cardigans were laid out on the bed. This abundance of apparel was not the mark of an extravagant lifestyle – Darya Ivanovna only bought the occasional new item, but she looked after her existing things so they rarely wore out.

It took her a whole hour to select a suitable mourning outfit: a calf-length black skirt and a dark blue top. She didn't have any black boots, so she chose a pair of dark brown ones with chunky heels.

Once she'd made these decisions Darya Ivanovna felt a little calmer. She sat down in the kitchen with a cup of strong coffee and a glass of *kefir* and thought about life. She thought about her husband's pharmacy and sighed with relief, glad that it had already been sold and that she no longer had anything to do with it. She thought about her friends Anna and Veronika. She recalled her visit with Veronika to the psychiatrist's office and thought fondly of the psychiatrist himself, Pyotr Isaevich. She had an appointment with him in two days' time. The prospect of seeing the ginger-haired doctor again brought a smile to Darya Ivanovna's lips.

Spent among thoughts and memories that were as simple and unreliable as a three-legged stool, the time passed quickly. The sky outside turned grey and then began to grow light.

At around 9 a.m. Darya Ivanovna called Anna and Veronika. At 9.30 a.m. the three of them got into a pre-ordered taxi and headed for the Baykov Cemetery.

At the entrance they stopped to buy four bunches of flowers and several artificial wreaths. Then the taxi driver took them right into the cemetery, almost as far as the freshly dug graves. He looked around in confusion.

'Why isn't there any music?' he asked in surprise. 'And where's everyone else?'

The women didn't reply. The eldest of the three just threw him a contemptuous look.

'Probably a suicide,' thought the taxi driver and drove off, forgetting to give Darya Ivanovna her change.

The coffins containing the men's bodies arrived about ten minutes later. Four Baykov Cemetery employees in black overalls lowered the men briskly into their graves – first Eduard, then Vasily. They gave each of the three women a handful of cold, sticky earth to throw down onto the coffins and then set to work energetically with their spades, determined to get the job over and done with as quickly as possible. Something told them not to expect a tip from the woman in the dark blue coat and brown boots, who looked like the one in charge. But in fact Darya Ivanovna slipped each of them two hundred hryvnas. So they left more respectfully, glancing back at her a couple of times in gratitude.

After decorating the graves with the flowers and wreaths the three friends walked slowly down the path towards the exit, in silence. Not one of them noticed a sinewy cat watching them from behind the monuments. The cat watched them until their path joined one of the main 'avenues' through the cemetery, then he turned and padded off in the opposite direction, stopping occasionally to look around.

94

Dima was dozing fully dressed on the sofa when the doorbell rang. The first thing he did was to check the time: 4.30 p.m. He'd been asleep for about two hours.

The sun was shining outside, and the sound of joyous birdsong was drifting in through the little top window.

'Was I expecting someone?' thought Dima. 'Ah yes! The priest!'

He got up and went into the hall.

'Father Onophrios?' he asked, looking at the bearded man who stood before him wearing jeans and a shabby canvas jacket.

'Yes,' replied the priest. 'I had a bit of trouble finding you.'

'I thought you'd be in your robes . . .'

Father Onophrios nodded at the overnight bag that stood on the doorstep by his feet. 'Is there somewhere I can get changed?'

'In the living room.' Dima indicated the door. 'Is it quite a quick procedure?'

'With God's help,' said Father Onophrios. 'Why, are you in a hurry?'

'I have to go and pick my wife up in an hour.'

'Always so much hustle and bustle,' the priest remarked calmly. 'If everyone stopped rushing about so much they would have more time for good deeds . . .'

Dima waited in the hall for five minutes then went into the living room. The priest was just putting a big cross on over his cassock.

'Could we do this room first?' asked Dima.

Ignoring his host, father Onophrios took a prayer book and a censer out of the overnight bag. He struck a match. The smell of scented smoke rose into the air, and the priest began chanting in his pleasant, monotonous baritone – it was just like being in a church. He went round all the corners, swinging his censer and intoning the requisite verse. Then he produced a piece of paper with a cross printed on it, spat on the back of it and stuck it to the wall.

'Where next?' he asked.

Dima and the priest made the rounds of the kitchen, the bedroom, the bathroom and the covered porch area along the outside of the house, even though it was not used in winter. Every time they stopped Father Onophrios read the requisite prayers, enriched the air with scented smoke and stuck printed crosses to the wall. Kitchen Fluffy emerged from his spot under the radiator when they went into the kitchen and walked over to the priest, rubbing himself up against his cassock.

'Every one of God's creatures deserves to be blessed,' said the priest, bending down to stroke the grey cat.

Once he'd finished with the house, he pulled a packet of Marlboro from his cassock and went out onto the doorstep.

'Did you have a break-in?' he asked suddenly, after lighting his cigarette.

'Attempted,' Dima nodded.

'Is that your garage?' The priest pointed at it with his cigarette.

'It is.'

'Have you got a car in there?'

'Yes.'

'It has to be sanctified!'

374

'But I've got to leave in ten minutes,' protested Dima, rationalising his reluctance to follow the priest's advice.

'With God's help we'll get it done in time. We can do the car and the garage at the same time – two for the price of one!'

Dima wasn't about to start haggling. He just took the key from the nail in the hall and led the priest to the wicket gate.

'Have you got airbags?' Father Onophrios was peering at the old foreign car.

'They didn't make them back then,' said Dima.

'In that case you need a special icon inside. It's only twenty hryvnas, but it'll protect you from accidents.'

Dima nodded. He didn't feel like having a discussion about it.

The priest walked round the car three times, and each time he bumped into Dima.

'Just go and wait outside – you're getting in the way!' he said irritably.

Dima did as he was told. He could still hear the priest's monotonous chanting.

Eventually Father Onophrios reappeared. He strode towards the wicket gate, up the steps and into the house. Dima barely managed to keep up with him.

'How much do I owe you?' he asked nervously.

'Four hundred and fifty hryvnas,' announced the priest, with an obvious sense of his own worth.

Dima paid him.

'If you ever need my services again, or if you know anyone else who does, just give me a call,' said the priest as he got changed. 'There's a discount for the second visit! And I'd be glad of the work.'

'They probably don't pay you much, do they?' ventured Dima.

'No, not much,' nodded Father Onophrios.

'I'll come with you. I need to get the minibus taxi too.'

They walked towards the *pelmeni* trailer café and got on the first minibus taxi heading past the bus station to Kiev.

Dima and the priest said goodbye warmly, then Dima got out near the amusement arcade, leaving the priest to continue his journey. He couldn't wait to tell his wife that her way home was clear, that there were no more obstacles to overcome.

95

Maryanivka village, Kiev region

'Mama, I'm getting married,' said Egor, leaning over the bed.

He looked into his mother's eyes. The local expert had managed to fix their old heater, so the house was nice and warm and the smell of smoke now went straight out into the evening sky.

Although the plastic pendant lamp didn't give off much light, Egor could see life in her eyes and a flicker of happiness too, faint yet unmistakable.

Egor remembered that his mother used to like lying with her hands on top of the blanket. She liked it when he held her hand in his.

'Her mother wants to come here, Mama, to meet you. You wouldn't mind, would you?'

He leaned closer, trying to read her eyes. He could tell the difference between 'yes' and 'no', even if her pupils remained fixed and her eyes seemed cloudy and cold.

'You wouldn't mind,' he nodded. 'Fine, Mama. Are you cold?

No. Good. I'm just going to have a little lie-down in the other room. I have to leave early again tomorrow. I'll have breakfast at Irina's and go straight from there into town. Now, try and get some sleep.'

He went out to the front yard and looked back at the house he'd grown up in. The little house seemed half the size now. It looked so small that he actually began to doubt it was the same one he'd spent his childhood in. The house couldn't have shrunk over the years! It couldn't have suddenly started leaning to one side, or sinking into the ground . . . So it must have always been like this. But how had he managed to live there and reach his full adult height? He had to bend down whenever he went into the bathroom so that he didn't bump his head. It wasn't really that surprising, though – everything looks enormous when you're a child. As you get older, you grow out of your clothes and have to get new ones, a size bigger. He'd grown out of this house too a long time ago, and when the time had come he'd left for Kiev, although he didn't exactly have anywhere there he could call home – nowhere special, nothing permanent.

His mother had always been short so it had never bothered her, and now that she no longer got out of bed her height was completely irrelevant. Being able to walk through a door without having to bend down is only an issue for those who actually move from room to room. Including Egor, all six feet of him.

The neighbour arrived at around 7 a.m. Egor's mother was still asleep. During the night Egor had got up and gone over to her bed to check her breathing, which was barely audible at the best of times but even less so at night.

'Have you got her passport?' asked Baba Sonya.

'No. What would I want with her passport?'

'We need to find it. If she dies you'll have to take it to the village council, so they can stamp it. They'll give you a hundred hryvnas towards the funeral . . . and they'll dig the grave for free!'

'You think I can't afford to bury my own mother?' Egor gave her a look of mock indignation. He didn't want to argue with this old friend of his mother's.

'You should make sure she gets what she's entitled to. They haven't done anything for her in this life, so they might as well help her out a bit on her way to the next.'

'I will,' promised Egor. 'She's got a bag somewhere in the wardrobe with all her documents in.'

'I can have a look myself, if you like.'

'Fine,' said Egor.

He went out through the gate, got into his car and started the engine. Before driving off he looked at the fence. 'I must get that painted before the summer,' he thought.

96

Gennady Ilyich's country house, Koncha-Zaspa

The sky was unusually starry for March. The driver took Semyon behind Gennady Ilyich's country house to the church. The red-brick path was lined with bollard lights, and the church itself was attractively illuminated. Its gilded cupolas twinkled majestically against the background of the star-studded indigo sky.

The driver opened one of the heavy metal gates to let Semyon through.

Gennady Ilyich was sitting on a canvas fishing stool at a table to the left of the iconostasis.

Semyon noticed several thin candles burning under an icon that was hanging on one of the white marble-clad columns.

'Ah, there you are!' cried the deputy, his voice echoing impressively round the church. 'Take a seat!'

Semyon spotted another folding stool at the opposite side of the table.

'Pour yourself a drink.' Gennady Ilyich gestured towards a brandy glass and the bottle of Martell.

The deputy was wearing a tracksuit and brand-new trainers.

'So what's the deal with your wife?' he asked.

'You know what women are like,' Semyon sighed. 'At first there was no chance, then today she brought it up again herself. Said we should give it a go . . .'

'Typical,' said Gennady Ilyich, wearily.

As Semyon's eyes gradually got used to the gloom of the church he was able to make out the individual images on the iconostasis, and he could see that the deputy's face was puffy, swollen and unhappy.

'The stupid cow,' said Gennady Ilyich. 'She had the baby then went and dumped it outside Parliament. She didn't even call security! I only just found out . . . Normally security pick them straight up and take them to the orphanage in Vyshhorod. But this time . . . I don't understand . . .' He gave a deep sigh. 'Nobody's seen it . . .'

'This "stupid cow", who is she?' Semyon asked carefully.

'Mind your own bloody business!' scowled the deputy. 'The main thing is that the baby girl's gone missing . . . And it's an important baby, with good genes . . . You know, politicians have a lot of admirers . . . But what the hell does that have to do with you?'

Semyon realised that Gennady Ilyich had already had a lot to drink. He decided just to listen, rather than ask any more questions.

'Basically, some bastard's run off with her.' Gennady Ilyich spread his hands and stared at Semyon, his eyes narrowed and purposeful now. 'If you can find her, she's yours! Someone will bring the adoption papers straight round to your place. You'll just need to change her nappies and get her milk from a milk kitchen . . . No, you won't even need to do that – someone will bring the milk to you! You just need to find her!'

'We need to talk to her,' said Semyon quietly. 'The mother . . .'

'What's the point? Oh, if you insist, fine! You can talk to her right now!' Gennady Ilyich picked his mobile phone up from the table and selected a number.

'Did I wake you, you stupid bitch?' he snarled into the phone. 'Well, I'm not bloody well sleeping! I can't sleep, and it's all your fault! I'm going to hand the phone over to someone now, OK?'

Gennady Ilyich passed his mobile to Semyon.

'Hello . . . Can you tell me what happened?' Semyon asked the woman on the other end of the line, trying to make his voice as gentle as possible.

'I wrapped her up in a blanket,' said a voice shaking with tears. 'I put her on the top step right in front of the door, where those two statues –'

'Which door?'

'The main entrance to Parliament.'

'When was this?'

'The fifth of March.'

'What time?'

'It must have been about three in the morning.'

'Did you see anyone else there?'

'I waited until the militiaman went round the corner . . . There was nobody else there.'

Semyon really wanted to know why the woman had chosen such an odd place, but the presence of the inebriated deputy prevented him asking any further questions. Before handing the phone back to his boss he looked at the display panel, hoping to memorise the number of the unfortunate mother. But the display only showed a name: Oksana. So the deputy knew the mother of the missing newborn well enough for her to be in his address book . . .

Semyon looked wearily at his boss.

'Well?' Gennady Ilyich interrupted Semyon's thoughts. 'Are you going to look for her?'

Semyon nodded.

'What are you waiting for then? Get on with it! Vasya will take you wherever you need to go.'

Semyon found Vasya the driver standing on the brick path outside the church, looking down at his feet. Everything about his demeanour indicated that he would rather have been at home, in bed.

'Back to where I picked you up?' he asked when they were already in the car.

'Yes,' said Semyon. 'But let's go via Parliament. I need to stop there for a minute.'

97

Boryspil, evening

Dima felt invigorated by the warm, humid evening air. He and Valya were walking home together. Valya was holding his right hand, and in his left hand he was carrying a linen bank bag full of fifty-kopek pieces. The weight of it was pleasantly satisfying and made him reflect philsophically on the notion that all good things are interrelated, although he knew that the same was probably true for bad things too. He was pleased that he'd managed to find both a nursery and a priest in the same day. It had made him later than usual picking up his wife from the amusement arcade, but it turned out that Valya's co-worker Sonya, the one who lived near the cemetery, was late again anyway so his wife had suggested that he go and try his luck on the slot machines while he was waiting. He went straight to the machine that he'd already won from several times, and it seemed to recognise him again. He didn't have much luck at first, but it wasn't long before he got three oranges in a row! And a trough full of shiny bronze fifty-kopek pieces! Dima knew it was wrong to gamble . . . but winning was good, wasn't it? So sometimes good things could come from bad.

'Did you sprinkle it properly, in all the corners?' Valya interrupted his philosophising.

A lorry went past, jolting loudly over the potholes in the uneven road. It was loaded with sacks of cement and gave off an unpleasant smell of building sites. Dima stepped away from the road, pulling Valya with him.

'Yes, I did. But I can do it again if you like, there's still some left in the bottle,' he said.

'You know, your sister wants to move away from here,' said his wife, after a pause.

'Really? Where to?'

'Either Canada or Saratov.'

'Why?' Dima stopped. Looking around distractedly, he spotted a newspaper kiosk that was still open.

'Well, her husband is going to try through the Baptist church in Canada, and if that doesn't work out . . . They're giving out forms here in the town.'

Valya rummaged around in her coat pocket and pulled out a piece of paper folded into four. She didn't open it.

'They're offering work and accommodation in Saratov. They haven't got enough people there for all the jobs. The accommodation is free, and they're paying at least eight hundred dollars a month. They're paying relocation expenses, too –'

'Hold on, I'm just going to buy a paper.'

He went over to the kiosk and bought a copy of the local classified ads paper, then went back to his wife.

'I'll have to think about it,' he said, taking her hand again. 'It's on the Volga, isn't it?'

'What is?' said Valya.

'Saratov.'

'Yes,' she said.

'They've probably got an airport.'

'Nadya said that a hundred people from Boryspil have already moved there, and nobody wants to come back.'

'You could get a job in an amusement arcade there,' said Dima, thinking aloud. 'You've got experience now.'

They walked the rest of the way in silence, each absorbed in their own thoughts about Saratov. Canada was such a remote and unfamiliar concept that it didn't even enter into the equation.

They stopped at the wicket gate.

'I forgot to tell you,' said Valya, slightly nervously. 'I'm supposed to go into the house without my feet touching the doorstep. That's what the fortune-teller said.'

'You mean you're supposed to jump over it or something?'

'You idiot!' Valya smiled. 'Maybe you could carry me in?'

Dima looked closely at his wife's stomach. She hadn't really started to show yet, so with her coat done up Valya didn't look at all pregnant.

Dima carried the bag of coins over to the doorstep. He opened the front door wide and went back to the wicket gate. Bending down and putting his arms around his wife just below her hips, he lifted her up and carried her like a statue towards the doorstep. He didn't notice his neighbour, who had come out into his front yard for a cigarette and was watching them with interest.

98

Lipovka village, Kiev region

That evening Egor arrived at Irina's house in a state of considerable agitation. He came in and took his boots off, then hung his leather coat up and went straight into the kitchen.

Irina followed him. She could tell that something was wrong.

'What's the matter?' she asked.

He shook his head and looked into her eyes, which were full of gentle compassion.

'At work . . . They fired my boss, and my friend Seryoga. Turns out they'd applied for Russian passports and signed contracts for work in Saratov. I was interrogated by some bloke from the Security Service. He said they'd be sending us a new boss from Lviv, from West Ukraine. "We can't trust anyone from Kiev to do the job!" he said, looking at me like I'd done something wrong. "I'm from one of the villages outside Kiev," I told him. "Same thing!" he said, so I asked him where he was from. Apparently he moved here recently from Svalyava. He was in the militia there, and now they've taken him straight into the Security Service! Maybe we should just go to Saratov? Together!'

'What are you talking about?' Irina's eyes widened with alarm. 'How would I manage there with two babies?'

'I'm joking,' Egor sighed gloomily. 'I'm not going anywhere. I had some good news for you, and I told you the bad news first. I'm sorry.'

'What's the good news?' asked Irina hesitantly.

'Well, I don't know how you feel about the idea,' he said with a shrug. 'But I'd like you to be my wife. I've already been to the registry office.'

This unexpected news took Irina's breath away: she breathed all the air out of her lungs but couldn't seem to breathe in again. She grabbed her neck with her hands then brought them to her face, to her cheeks. She couldn't take her eyes off Egor, although she looked more confused than delighted.

'Come on, let's go for a little walk. It's dry outside!' said Egor.

Irina just about managed a nod and a smile. She went into the other room and started wrapping Yasya up in a baby blanket.

Her mother stopped watching the television and came out to see what was going on. She stood in the doorway and watched her daughter.

Irina picked Yasya up carefully and gave her to Egor.

'Mama, we're going out for a walk. Can you stay with Marina?' she asked, throwing her coat over her shoulders.

'Too embarrassed to take the poor little mite outside, are you? Worried they'll ask who she belongs to?'

'Don't worry, I'll think of something,' promised Egor, keen to placate Aleksandra Vasilievna. He wanted to keep the peace, tonight of all nights. 'Everything's going to be fine. Irina and I are getting married on the fourteenth.'

On hearing this news, Irina's mother was rooted to the spot. Without looking down, she straightened her long black skirt with her hand.

'We won't be long,' whispered Irina and put her finger to her lips, looking over at baby Marina, who had turned her head towards them without opening her eyes.

Aleksandra Vasilievna started nodding and waved her hand, as if to say, 'Go on then!'

So they did.

A modest scattering of stars were twinkling in the sky. An aeroplane was flying overhead on its way to Kiev, its little lights flashing.

Yasya purred in her sleep, and then all was quiet. Irina suddenly stopped. She wanted to say something to Egor, but she couldn't find the right words, so they continued walking towards the end of the lane. They wouldn't walk right to the end of the lane, of course, because it didn't really have an 'end' – it just rejoined the main road to Kodra – but also because the cemetery was there, on the other side of the road. And the cemetery was the last place they needed to be on such a quiet and secretly happy evening.

99

Pechersk Hill, Kiev

At around 8 a.m. the following morning Semyon walked down to European Square, and from there it took him exactly eight minutes to get to Parliament. The city was buzzing in anticipation of spring. Packed minibus taxis and buses delivered fresh-faced locals and resident foreigners to work, their cheeks still rosy from sleep. Semyon felt good being up and about so early too. It was as though he'd been given a new start – such a weight had been lifted, from his chest and from his mind. He walked down the hill with a spring in his step and stopped at the militia checkpoint, near the gap in the little iron fence where the pedestrian crossing met the pavement just outside Parliament. He showed the militiaman his assistant's ID.

'Can I ask you a couple of questions?' he asked.

'Sure,' shrugged the militiaman.

'A baby girl was abandoned here, outside Parliament, on the night of the fifth of March,' said Semyon, lowering his voice. 'Do you know anything about it?'

'Nah,' drawled the militiaman. 'There's one dumped here every month. And in the winter, mainly January and February, we sometimes get two or three.'

Semyon was surprised. 'Why are there more in winter?' he asked.

'Deputies' picnics, the May Day holidays,' grinned the lad. 'Nine months later . . . you do the maths! Nature, in other words.'

Semyon nodded knowingly. Then he remembered why he was there and looked intently at the lad in the militiaman's uniform.

'So you didn't hear anything about this baby girl?'

'I wasn't on duty on the fifth of March. We're not the only security force here, you know, there's the Mariinsky Palace security too – they don't wear uniform. There's a specific protocol we have to follow whenever we find a baby – we tell the boss, and he phones the clinic . . . It's called the Goodwill Clinic, or the Good Deeds Clinic, something like that. Then they come and collect the baby. Hang on, let me just check for you.'

The militiaman raised his walkie-talkie to his mouth.

'Vitya, did we have a "cuckoo baby" the night of March fifth?'

'No, Bogdan, nothing on the fifth! There was a little boy at the end of February.'

'See?' He spread his hands. 'You could ask that lot.' He turned towards Parliament and pointed at the CCTV security control room. 'Get them to run through the film for the night you want.'

Semyon shook the militiaman's hand firmly and headed for the park. He walked as far as the barrier where the Communist veterans were maintaining their picket, then looked back at the steps up to the Parliament building. He decided to sit down for a bit on an empty bench and think about his plan of action.

Half an hour later he was talking to a militiaman sitting at the monitors in the control room. His name was Viktor. Once Viktor had been reassured that there was no political crime involved, he promised to run through the CCTV footage covering the main entrance. If he managed to find anything, he would copy the relevant frames for a couple of hundred dollars.

The day was only just beginning and Semyon was already proud of what he'd managed to achieve.

At 11 a.m. Volodka pulled up outside the milk kitchen on Hrushevsky Street and from then on they followed their usual routine: milk churns, orphanage, cup of tea in the director's office, parcel of goat's cheese for Gennady Ilyich.

By 6 p.m. Semyon had let Volodka go home and was sitting in the foyer of the Officers' Club. He was waiting for his boss, so he could give him the goat's cheese and update him on the results of his search for the newborn baby.

Gennady Ilyich was half an hour late, but he was in a good mood when he arrived. He immediately invited Semyon into the restaurant, where he ordered tea, brandy, some slices of lemon and a bar of dark chocolate.

'Today is my lucky day,' he explained. 'I've finally managed to get the Parliament café registered as a private enterprise. I know it doesn't sound like a big deal but trust me, it's worth celebrating. Now we'll have somewhere to sell our goat's cheese without having to worry about the paperwork!'

The surprise and ensuing perplexity on Semyon's face couldn't have gone unnoticed.

'It's not for business, you know, it's a matter of prestige. If I want to exert pressure on the opposition, I'll just close the café and they can go running off to the local coffee bars like cockroaches!'

This explanation amused Semyon. It would never have occurred to him that the café within Parliament could be used as a political weapon.

'So how's it going?' asked the deputy. 'Any news?'

'I'll have more information either today or tomorrow,' Semyon promised firmly.

Gennady Ilyich believed him. He raised his brandy glass.

'To success!' he smiled.

Semyon liked the brandy, and he liked his boss's mood. This was just the right time to ask a favour – he was bound to agree. Semyon knew he had a favour to ask, an idea he'd wanted to discuss, but he couldn't for the life of him think what it was. He racked his brains, trying to remember.

'So,' resumed Gennady Ilyich, after chewing and sucking a slice of lemon. 'You or some of your lads will have to spend a few days in the cheese-making workshop, to find out how much cheese they make during one shift. We'll agree the weight in kilograms, then we'll take half for the café and they can keep the rest. Is that clear?'

Semyon nodded.

'And another thing. You don't happen to know any timid, super-stitious men, do you? I've got a vacancy in the café. I need to find someone urgently.'

Semyon thought about it, and the nervous yet simultaneously slightly arrogant face of his neighbour opposite immediately came to mind.

'I do, as it happens . . .' he said. 'I'll find out whether he's interested.'

'Go ahead,' nodded Gennady Ilyich. 'It's good honest work, among the eternally ravenous political elite . . .' The deputy looked at his watch. 'Right, I've got to go.' He took a hundred-hryvna note from his wallet and placed it on the table. 'Why don't you stay here for a bit? Relax, finish your drink. I always used to have my best ideas when I was on my own in restaurants!'

Semyon watched his boss leave and sipped his brandy, waiting for his best ideas to come. But instead he remembered what he'd wanted to ask his boss about: working nights!

100

'Quiet Centre', Kiev

It was Friday, and Darya Ivanovna was in a hurry to get to her hairdresser's appointment. The salon was in a small single-storey building on Landscape Alley.

'Do you want me to give it a bit of volume, like I usually do?' asked the stylist, once her regular client had settled down in the chair in front of the mirror.

'You know, I think I fancy a bit of a change. I'm meeting someone today . . .'

'A man?' the young stylist asked in surprise.

'Yes, of course!' Darya Ivanovna looked at her indignantly.

'Oh, I'm sorry! You always look so . . . Er, how old is he?'

Darya Ivanovna thought about it.

'He's about fifteen years younger than me, and he's got a crew cut . . .'

'Blond?'

'Ginger.'

'I know.' The hairdresser gave a conspiratorial smile. 'Do you have anything maroon to wear?'

'Yes,' said her client.

'In that case let's dye it a coppery red and give you a light feather cut. It's a very contemporary look.'

'OK.'

Darya Ivanovna turned the corner into Bekhterevsky Street feeling like a different woman. Before she knew it, she was outside the front door of Pyotr Isaevich's office.

She stepped airily into the square reception area.

'Coffee, please,' she said to Inna.

The doctor was sitting at his desk, writing something. He stood up when he saw her come in.

'There's something different about you,' he said carefully.

'It's a woman's prerogative to change her appearance from time to time,' said Darya Ivanovna, smiling. She sat down opposite Pyotr Isaevich.

'Would you like some tea or coffee?'

'I've already ordered!'

Pyotr Isaevich looked into Darya Ivanovna's eyes with greater concentration.

'Is something troubling you today?' he asked. His face took on a solicitous expression, indicating a readiness to listen to his patient's problems, whatever they may be.

'I buried my husband recently,' said Darya Ivanovna, her voice light and melodic. 'And now I'm learning to live alone. But there's one thing bothering me – I keep getting the feeling that my husband's still alive, that he's somewhere nearby . . .'

Pyotr Isaevich frowned for a moment. 'But this doesn't upset you?'

She shook her head.

'He was at home for a little while after he died, sitting in his armchair. I had him plastinated . . . it's a bit like embalming. Anyway, he would spend all day sitting in his armchair and then at night he would go out! I know, it sounds crazy, doesn't it? In the morning he would be back in his chair again, only the soles of his slippers were dirty and there were footprints in the hallway and the living room . . . So then I buried him properly, in the conventional way. You know, I've thought about going to a medium and getting her to put me in touch with Edik, so I could ask him where he was going at night, and why. But I don't believe in all that rubbish. I just feel like I need to spend some time talking about him, about Edik, and he'll finally be "free" to leave . . . for good.'

'Darya Ivanovna.' The doctor clasped his hands together. 'Your husband must have been a sleepwalker. Sleepwalking can lure even the recently deceased out onto the street at night!'

'Would it be easier for you if I lay on the couch?' asked his patient.

'Yes, go ahead,' said the doctor.

So Darya Ivanovna kicked her boots off and settled down on the couch. It was incredibly comfortable. She looked up at the white ceiling until her eyes glazed over, and then she closed them.

'Tell me how you met your husband,' said Pyotr Isaevich. He spoke in a rich, velvety voice, like a stage actor.

'It was at night,' Darya Ivanovna began in a soft half-whisper. 'I was on my way home from a friend's birthday party. I was walking down Vorovsky Street, along the tram tracks where the Number 2 used to go, when a man started harassing me. He grabbed my arm and started pulling me towards the road. I'd been drinking – we'd had three bottles of champagne between three of us . . . How old was I? I must have been about nineteen. He wouldn't let go of my arm. He kept trying to pull me with him . . . I called out, and then suddenly there was the sound of footsteps in the silence. I looked round and saw a well-built young man running towards us. He was looking down at his hands, which were opening a penknife as he ran. When he reached us the man let go of me and started swearing at him. The well-built young man stabbed him in the hand and then the stomach. He cried out, and the young man grabbed my hand and shouted, 'Run!' So we did. We ran to the Haymarket, where we stopped to catch our breath. That's when he told me that his name was Edik.'

'Did he walk you home?'

'No, we went to his place. We had to tiptoe out onto the balcony, because his parents were asleep. He had a real telescope out there, and he showed me the moon and the stars. He told me that there were special secret signs written on the moon for Earth-dwellers to interpret – he used to seek them out with his telescope and copy them down. He said that whoever managed to decipher them would discover the secret to human happiness – people would live twice as long and never sleep, because they would never get tired of life . . .'

'Fascinating!' Pyotr Isaevich breathed out. 'So did you start going out together after this?'

'Yes, we went out together for five years and then we got married. In those five years he taught me all the planets and constellations, all the craters on the moon. Back then astronauts were going up into space every five minutes. But after we got married I decided I'd had enough of the universe. By then Edik had graduated from the Faculty of Medicine and become interested in pharmaceutics.'

'Your husband sounds like an interesting man,' said the doctor, filling the pause that had arisen.

There was a prolonged silence in the room. Pyotr Isaevich stood up, went over to the couch and saw that Darya Ivanovna was asleep.

He tiptoed out of the office and sat down on the sofa beneath the palm-tree wallpaper. He looked at Inna wearily.

'When she wakes up, tell her that a confidential session is two hundred hryvnas and a standard consultation is a hundred. In the meantime, I'm going out for a walk!'

Leaving his white coat on the coat rack in the reception area, Pyotr Isaevich put his grey raincoat on and went out. There wasn't a single cloud in the deep blue sky. He could hear the birds singing and the rumble of a trolleybus going past on Artema Street. He looked back at the gates of the Pokrovsky Monastery, which was inhabited by his rivals – fellow specialists in the human soul. Sometimes he felt like joining a monastery and unburdening his own soul. The monks would listen to him talk for days on end, until he'd told them everything he'd ever heard, until he had ravaged his soul, emptied it out, in order to begin his life afresh.

101

9 May Street, Boryspil

As soon as she entered the house, the first thing Valya did was to run to the kitchen and pick up her cat. She hugged his warm body to her chest.

'Oh, you've lost weight without me!' she whispered tenderly, rubbing Kitchen Fluffy's soft furry stomach. 'Let's get you something to eat!'

She started thinking about food. Putting the cat gently back down on the floor, she looked in the fridge and then in the freezer. She took out a packet of frozen pork mince.

'Dima, can you go out to the shed?' she called. 'I need a cabbage.'

Dima took the torch and went out to the shed at the back of the house. He selected a cabbage from a wooden box, removing the rotten outer leaves and testing it with his thumb for firmness. He chose the most resilient head.

'We're having stuffed cabbage leaves for dinner,' she declared.

They sat down to eat at about 9.30 p.m. Steam rose from the mound of stuffed cabbage leaves, which was generously covered in sour cream. Dima was both soothed and invigorated by the appetising smell of meat and steamed cabbage. He wasn't even upset by the fact that a hot stuffed cabbage leaf lay in a saucer on the floor for Kitchen Fluffy.

Dima poured himself a shot of home-made nettle vodka and permitted Valya a glass of brandy.

When they'd finished eating they took their dirty plates and forks to the sink, and Valya wiped the table with a dry cloth. Then she took the Saratov form from her pocket and spread it out on the table, pressing the fold flat with her hands.

'I need a pen,' she said.

Dima found a pen on the windowsill, under a pile of old classified ads papers.

Valya sat up straight, like a schoolgirl, and started filling out the form. Dima watched her in silence.

She filled in the details for both of them, writing their dates and places of birth, their current places of work and their home address in neat, painstaking handwriting. Then she stopped and looked up at her husband.

'Dima, they want to know whether we've got any relatives in Russia. Have we?'

'Well, my brother went missing over there,' he shrugged. 'I've got an aunt in Tyumen, but I don't know her address . . .'

'Let's just put "No", otherwise we might say something wrong.'

She wrote a bold 'No' in the section about relatives.

'Do we have any relatives currently living in Ukraine who are civil servants, deputies or political agents?' she asked.

'Of course not,' he said.

'What about religion and political views?'

'Write "Orthodox" and "None".'

'Are any of our relatives members of religious sects or representatives of sexual minorities?'

'Write "No"!'

'What about your sister's husband?' Valya looked nervously at Dima.

'Well, they certainly won't be stupid enough to admit it when they fill the form in themselves!'

Valya nodded and read the next question.

'Do we have any relatives in the USA, Canada, Georgia, Western Europe or the Baltic countries?'

'Write "No".'

'Oh, I'm worn out,' sighed Valya, coming to the end of the form and signing it. Dima put his signature next to hers.

'Why don't you go on to bed?' he suggested gently. 'I'm going to sit here for a bit. I've got stuff to think about . . .'

Valya left the room. The hall light went out, followed by the bedroom light.

Dima tiptoed into the living room, picked up the classified ads paper that he'd bought that evening and took it back into the kitchen.

He opened it at the 'Situations Vacant' page. He remembered his boss telling him to come into the airport. 'Well,' he thought, 'they'll just have to wait! Maybe I'll find myself something better in here to tide me over for a couple of months, and then I'll send them a postcard from the hills of Saratov!'

But the jobs in the paper were all the same, none of them very interesting: accountants prepared to work flexitime, taxi drivers, bus drivers, sales assistants in second-hand shops . . .

Dima's eyes slid slowly over the repetitious, uninspiring text, until they fell on one particular advert that genuinely surprised him, even though it wasn't of any interest to Dima himself.

Additional earnings for clergymen of all denominations. Night shift. Opportunity to obtain additional qualifications for free. Call the Church of the Embassy of the Moon on 8-096-111-333-66 to arrange an interview.

After reading the advert several times, Dima thought about Father Onophrios. He wondered whether he should let the priest know about this opportunity to earn a little bit on the side – he was obviously struggling to make ends meet.

Dima found the priest's business card. He called him and read the advert out over the phone.

The priest was interested. He asked Dima to repeat the phone number and wrote it down, thanking Dima sincerely.

Dima got under the blanket and pressed up against the warm body of his slumbering wife. Before he succumbed to the pull of sleep, he went over everything that had happened that day and sent a silent prayer of gratitude to God. He thought briefly about what he and Valya had written on the Saratov form: *Religion? Orthodox.* 'Looks like that might turn out to be the truth after all,' thought Dima, before the dark silk of sleep softly enveloped his consciousness.

102

It was a dry, calm night in Kiev, and even the change of shift was surprisingly brisk and straightforward. Egor's new boss only had one comment to make, and he made it quietly and courteously. 'When you're using your walkie-talkie, you are to speak only in Ukrainian – not in Russian or in any kind of regional dialect,' he said, smiling amicably.

Egor didn't respond. In his heart he doubted he'd be there much longer. Particularly as after three conversations with the Security Service they'd left him with the words: 'You can work until the summer then we'll review your contract. If the Russian special forces get in touch with you, let us know immediately!'

'Only two more months until the summer . . . There's no point in worrying about it until then,' he thought, glancing at a huge freight transporter loaded with new foreign cars that was heading in the opposite direction, towards Kiev.

Egor was surprised by the lack of traffic on the road to Zhytomyr. It was as though nobody had any desire to go to the west, even from Kiev. Everyone was heading into the city.

It only took twenty minutes for his Mazda to reach the turning to Makariv. The road was worse from then on, and it was another quarter of an hour before he arrived in Lipovka and pulled up outside Irina's house.

Aleksandra Vasilievna immediately started frying some potatoes with pork fat for him. She cut a few onion rings and put them on a saucer, then sprinkled them with salt. She'd been making more of an effort with her appearance over the last few days. She'd dug out three smart blouses from her linen storage bags and aired them on the line in the yard, but the distinctive smell of mothballs still lingered. There was the occasional whiff of it in the kitchen, but it was soon disguised by the more appetising aromas of fried pork fat and freshly sliced onion.

Egor and Irina ate breakfast together. Irina looked much fresher that morning. Her cheeks were glowing, her eyes were shining and she couldn't stop smiling.

Aleksandra Vasilievna joined them at the table with a cup of tea. She had been meaning to have a serious talk with them since the previous evening.

She waited until Egor had finished his fried potatoes and eaten half a plate of braised cabbage, and then she cleared her throat to get their attention.

'It's still early spring,' she said, apparently thinking aloud. 'We haven't planted anything yet. Maybe you could wait until June? The new potatoes will be ready then.'

Egor looked at her in astonishment.

'No, no, you carry on if you want to, of course . . . It'll just end up costing more. We haven't got anything to feed the guests! And there'll be plenty of them: the neighbours, everyone from the village council, the community nurse and her husband –'

'Why do we need to invite all of them?' Irina waved her hand dismissively. 'We just want to do it quietly, without a big wedding or any fuss.'

'Then how will everyone in the village know that you're no longer a single mother?'

Egor finally realised what Aleksandra Vasilievna was getting at.

'Look, why don't we have a buffet?' he suggested. 'It'll be cheaper, and it'll mean that no one will stay too long.'

'What's a buffet?' asked Irina's mother.

'Where everyone helps themselves to food and you eat standing up. They have them in the city,' explained Irina. 'So that the guests get tired more quickly and go home.'

'Only alcoholics drink standing up! And besides, where are you going to hold one of your fancy "buffets" round here?' Aleksandra Vasilievna spread her hands. 'I suppose we could always lay some tables in the yard . . . But what if it rains? And anyway, our yard isn't that nice.'

'We could do it in a café,' said Egor, finishing his cabbage. 'That's the simplest option.'

'Which café? That drinking den, you mean?' Aleksandra Vasilievna almost rose in revolt.

'I can pay them to air it out, clean it up a bit, decorate it,' said Egor, calm and confident in his role as head of the household. 'We'll be able to get thirty people in there, and that's all we need!'

'Thirty people can sit down at a table! Why do you want to make them stand up?' Irina's mother spoke up in defence of the as-yet-uninvited guests.

'You're right,' Egor surrendered. 'We'll have a sit-down meal.'

Satisfied with her victory, Aleksandra Vasilievna got up and took an open bottle of sweet Kagor wine from the little cupboard. She fetched glasses from the living room and rubbed them with a tea towel, turning the opaque glass translucent. She poured each of them half a glass.

'To harmony and love!' she said, and for the first time that morning she couldn't hold back her smile. It was a modest smile but sincere, expressing not joy but tremendous relief.

103

Independence Square, Kiev

Viktor the militiaman turned out to be a fast worker. Either that or he desperately needed the money. He called Semyon on his mobile at around 2 a.m. when he was fast asleep, pressed up against Veronika's warm body. Semyon shut himself in the kitchen to take the call and learned that Viktor had found the relevant footage and could give it to him straight away, if he liked. They arranged to meet half an hour later on Independence Square, near the main post office.

As he was getting dressed in the dark, Semyon knocked over a chair. He froze for a second. Then he noticed that Veronika had raised herself up on her elbow and was looking anxiously at him.

'I'm just popping out for half an hour. It's for work!' he whispered tenderly.

Veronika lay her head back down on the pillow. If her husband had noticed her concern, that must have meant he really was going out to work.

'Just be careful,' she murmured sleepily to Semyon, who was already putting on his socks.

The night was warm, damp and deserted. The cobblestones on Proreznaya Street gleamed in the light from the occasional street lamps. Every step Semyon took was answered by a muffled echo. He felt a surprising lightness in his legs, as though his body weighed less at night and it was easier for his legs to carry him.

Semyon recognised Viktor the militiaman immediately. He was standing in his uniform overcoat and service cap, staring intently at the tower on the top of Trade Union House, where an illuminated monitor was alternating between the time, the temperature and the address of some restaurant or other.

Two $100 notes passed through the militiaman's nimble fingers and disappeared into the right-hand pocket of his overcoat. From the left-hand pocket he produced a videotape.

'It's all on there,' he said. 'I know him. He's one of ours, from the Mariinsky security team. Egor, his name is. I can introduce you to him, if you like.'

On that note they went their separate ways, leaving behind the deserted, rainy square in front of the columns of the entrance to the main post office.

The traffic lights at the crossroads near Trade Union House were flashing orange. Several taxis went by on Khreshchatyk Street and a fire engine with its siren turned off drove past in the opposite direction, heading towards the Bessarabian Market.

Semyon walked effortlessly up Proreznaya Street, stuffing the videotape into the narrow pocket of his leather jacket on the way.

The damp air caressed his cheeks. He peered at the road. On the other side of the street a flock of youths were walking down towards Independence Square, beer bottles gleaming in their hands. They were chattering away and laughing.

Semyon listened to his body. He felt tired and couldn't wait to get back to bed. 'Good,' he thought. 'This is how you're supposed to feel at night!'

He went past the library and then past the Youth Theatre, noticing to his surprise that the doors were open and a dim light was coming from the foyer.

'Brother Seramion! We're in here!' a male voice he didn't recognise called out to him from behind.

Semyon stopped, temporarily immobilised by fear. He turned and looked back.

He was approached by a man he didn't recognise, wearing a black overcoat. The man's face was clean-shaven and there was a lump on the bridge of his nose, indicating that he usually wore glasses.

'I'm so glad you've come. Brother Vasily was saying that you were no longer with us,' he said, nodding towards the open doors of the Youth Theatre.

They went into the entrance foyer together. There was a background hum of conversation. Semyon looked around and saw a few politicians he recognised. Catching sight of Gennady Ilyich, he froze with indecision.

'Come, Brother Seramion, the doctor will be delighted to see you,' said the stranger, taking off his overcoat and giving it to a young lad.

The man led Semyon up the stairs. He knocked on some closed doors.

'Yes!' came the response from within.

Inside the room was a desk, and behind the desk sat Pyotr Isaevich Naitov, psychiatric doctor, wearing a black suit, a white shirt and a dark blue tie.

'Hey! I'm so pleased to see you!' he exclaimed, his face lighting up with a smile. There was a piece of paper on the desk. Turning it over so that the text faced down, he crossed the room and embraced Semyon.

'I knew your nocturnal self would prove to be stronger than its diurnal counterpart! I just knew it! In spite of your mistake, that ridiculous request for your friend Vladimir to follow you . . . You certainly had us all worried! But that's all in the past now. You've decided to come and join us tonight, and that means you will stay with us. Go through to the hall, I just need to make a few final changes to my speech . . . And then we'll talk, over a pre-dawn meal! Brother Grigoryan, find Brother Seramion a good seat in the hall!'

There was an interminable, impenetrable flow of well-dressed men proceeding up the staircase. The solemnity of the occasion was etched upon their faces, along with a remarkable serenity and a sense of self-assurance.

About ten minutes later the whole auditorium was full. Pyotr Isaevich took to the stage holding a microphone.

'Dear Brothers,' he said. 'Our goal is closer than ever before! We are now a force capable of taking responsibility for the future, and for this we won't need elections, or democracy, or a revolution of any colour. Five years ago my colleagues and I were of the opinion that the world was divided into psychopaths and psychiatrists. From a scientific point of view this is how it has remained, but from our humanitarian point of view the world has already changed for the better. People can now be categorised as doctors or brothers. Dear Brothers, today I present to you a council of doctors, who will work together under my authority to help you achieve social harmony and civil unity. We have all had enough of the quarrelling feuds of the psychopathic politicians who refuse to join us. Individual psychopaths confounding all the psychiatrists of the world, refusing to be cured . . . we have seen it too many times! The law of human nature is simple: we psychiatrists must work together to manage and control society's psychopaths, rather than the other way round.

By joining our community each of you has become a brother, a junior doctor committed to healing our country. We will cure Ukraine of this schizophrenia into which she has been led by the psychopathic politicians who refuse to join us . . .'

Then Pyotr Isaevich invited up onto the stage about twenty or thirty people dressed in white suits and ties. They were introduced as the council of doctors, and implementation of their recommendations was declared to be mandatory.

As Semyon watched the doctor he felt a kind of nebulous wave repeatedly trying to smother his consciousness, sending strange signals and orders from his brain. When everyone in the room stood up and began to applaud the doctor loudly and rhythmically, Semyon also found himself rising to his feet. He joined in the applause, clapping until his hands hurt, without taking his eyes off Pyotr Isaevich.

Later Gennady Ilyich took to the stage with a short speech in the name of the deputies 'who had joined them'. He announced that Parliament would soon be switching to a nocturnal working regime, which would provide them with a calmer environment in which to take rational and considered decisions.

The doctor announced an interval, and everyone got to their feet once more. Semyon rose from his seat and went out into the foyer, which was decorated with framed photographs of actors from the Youth Theatre. He glanced at the photographs and was stunned to see that the actors' photographs had been replaced with portraits of men he didn't recognise. Semyon walked over to the wall for a closer look. The first portrait he came to depicted a large-faced man with an intelligent, weary expression. The inscription underneath read:

Martyr of the Embassy of the Moon
Eduard Ivanovich Zarvazin
Pharmacologist and inventor of vitality-enhancing
medication *Invigoris*
Died November 2007

Semyon suddenly started feeling peculiar. An unwelcome, unpleasant energy seemed to be growing inside his body and inside his head, replacing the exhaustion and somnolence that were more appropriate to this late hour. He glanced all around to check that no one was watching, then made his way discreetly over to the staircase and went downstairs. He went out onto Proreznaya Street and filled his lungs with the fresh, slightly damp air.

It was so quiet outside that Semyon's head started aching, as though it missed the noise. He set off abruptly and hurried home as fast as he could.

When he reached his apartment building, Semyon was surprised to see a light on in the kitchen.

He opened the front door carefully, took his boots off in the hall and went straight into the kitchen.

Veronika was sitting at the table with a cup of tea. She was wrapped up in her husband's towelling dressing gown, which was far too big for her.

'What are you doing?' asked Semyon.

'I don't know,' she shrugged. 'I was cold . . .'

'Well, I went to pick up a videotape.' He showed her his trophy. 'For work.'

Veronika nodded.

'What's the little girl like?' she asked suddenly, and anxious little flames began to burn in her eyes.

'Another day or two and it'll all be sorted!' he promised her.

Veronika got up and went to bed.

Semyon went into the living room and put the tape into the video player.

The footage was black and white, the figures moved jerkily and their faces were blurry, but it would be easy enough to recognise them again.

A woman approached the building, carrying a baby wrapped in a blanket. She put it down on the top step in front of the main entrance and then hurried away, looking round a couple of times. Then a man in a leather coat appeared. He stopped when he got to the little bundle, then picked it up and walked off with it.

'Egor, is that you?' Semyon whispered, rewinding the videotape. 'The two of us will be having a little chat tomorrow!'

The following morning Semyon's head was still aching. He no longer wanted to have a little chat with Egor, at least not immediately. A little chat would mean having to explain things, and what would he say? Particularly after a night like the one he'd had. That the baby Egor had picked up actually belonged to him, Brother Seramion?

Semyon shuddered with fear. He had just called himself Brother Seramion!

'I need to wash it all away!' he thought feverishly, looking at his reflection in the mirror.

He got into the shower and stood under the cold water for a few minutes, then dried himself off and went into the kitchen. He made a cup of strong coffee and returned to his thoughts.

No, he had to go about it a different way, not confront the issue head-on. He had to follow him, find out where the baby was now, and then he could decide what to do.

At 10 a.m. Semyon rang Viktor the militiaman, who told him that Egor drove an old red Mazda and didn't really socialise with anyone from work but was always polite. His zone of responsibility was the area of Mariinsky Park in front of the palace. Sometimes he patrolled the other side of the palace, to the rear. Viktor didn't know anything else about him.

Semyon was convinced he'd recognise Egor in the flesh. He had a masculine face with regular features and a prominent, straight nose – Semyon had seen his profile as he leaned over the blanket-wrapped bundle.

'Where can he have taken her?' Semyon wondered. 'Surely not back to his place . . . Maybe they've got their own protocol to follow in such situations.'

He tried to imagine himself in Egor's shoes that night. What would he have done if he'd found a newborn baby on the street, wrapped in a blanket? He'd probably have called the emergency services and told them about it. Maybe that's what Egor had done. Maybe he'd already forgotten about the baby.

Semyon's thoughts were interrupted by his mobile phone ringing. It was Volodka.

'Can you wait for me? I'm going to be about ten minutes late.'

Semyon glanced at his watch – it was already 10.30 a.m.!

He went outside and took a good look around. Then he plunged into the sights, sounds and smells of the working day, into the transience and frenetic energy of urban life.

He called Volodka back and asked him to go straight to the orphanage without him.

Semyon himself went to Hrushevsky Street and walked back and forth across the square in front of Parliament. Then he took the path that led to the monument to General Vatutin, and that was when he saw Egor heading towards him. He peered intently at his face. Then they passed one another and the distance between them grew again. Semyon turned round and stood there, watching Egor walk away.

104

Apartment No. 10, Reitarska Street, Kiev

In the morning Veronika took a walk to the corner of the three cafés. She straightened the wreath on the wall then wandered into the Yaroslava café, where she ordered a Turkish coffee and two apple buns. She sat down facing the street and looked through the thick glass at the cars and the people going by.

She sat there for half an hour then went home and called Darya Ivanovna, who had caught a cold so they couldn't meet that day. After their conversation it occurred to Veronika that Darya hadn't been ill once while the late pharmacist was sitting in his armchair in her apartment, but as soon as they buried him she immediately caught a cold and developed high blood pressure and cardiac arrhythmia!

She started thinking about the pharmacist himself, and then she remembered his notebook. She sat down at the kitchen table and started leafing through it. She wasn't that interested in the sketches, but the inscriptions, which she had barely noticed last time, now intrigued her.

23 September 2006 – Dasha stupidly told her dressmaker that I was taking deliveries of 'forbidden medicines', so now she's

after something to stop her husband drinking so much. I gave her the first variant of Anti-Wimp and warned her that it wasn't exactly a cure for alcoholism but would certainly change him. It'll be interesting to see what becomes of her alcoholic!

26 September 2006 – Dasha's dressmaker came. Said it helped her husband. He's not drinking, but now he's sleeping all day and awake all night. A has gone crazy – she called during the night, threatening to go to the Security Service and confess that she stole laboratory material for me. I've got to do something about her.

28 September 2006 – A successful day! The client sent some people over with an advance of 100,000 hryvnas and an order for 300 Anti-Wimp ampoules. They're planning to take them to Germany and bring them back in officially from there, like imported goods. Because, as we all know, no one would trust anything that came from our pharmacists! No wonder they all go and get treated in other countries, even the President. Well, to hell with the lot of them!

Veronika wasn't interested in these pharmaceutical reflections. She scanned the barely legible text, seeking out her friend's name, until she eventually found an inscription worthy of her attention.

14 October 2006 – Dasha started an argument first thing this morning. I'd forgotten to turn my phone off and A called at 4 a.m. Dasha answered – I was fast asleep. A told her that she was my lover and that I'd exposed her to great danger by accepting a commission from opposition politicians. She said

that I was already a dead man but advised Dasha to leave and go into hiding. I spent half an hour trying to convince Dasha that A is insane and that everything she'd told her was rubbish. Dasha left, slamming the door. This has to stop!

'I wonder who this A is,' thought Veronika.

105

Boryspil airport
In the morning a UAZ 4x4 from the customs service of the airport stopped outside Dima's front yard.

At that moment Dima was drinking tea in the kitchen and considering his plans for the short-term future. Visiting his workplace had not featured in these plans, but Dima realised immediately that if they'd sent a car for him he didn't have a lot of choice.

He asked the driver to wait for ten minutes or so while he dug out his uniform. The right arm of his uniform jacket smelled of dog. Dima sniffed it and thought of Shamil.

'Any idea why they want to see me?' he asked the driver, once they were en route.

'I was just told to pick you up, and that's what I'm doing,' he replied with a shrug.

Dima spent the rest of the journey mentally preparing himself for an argument. It was inevitable – his boss had called him personally and asked him to come in, but Dima had chosen to ignore him. They still had his work record book and now, if his boss wanted to, he could write something in it like 'fired for gross misconduct'. He'd probably need to show his work record book in Saratov, wouldn't he? Maybe he should just burn it and say he'd lost it . . . But then he would lose all record of his length of service for pension purposes . . .

Dima gave a heavy sigh, causing the driver to glance at him with curiosity.

Dima lingered at the door to his boss's office, with a sinking feeling in the pit of his stomach. 'Well, here goes,' he sighed.

'Oh, there you are,' said his boss in a neutral voice, looking up at his visitor. 'How many days ago did I call and ask you to come in?'

'I was ill,' lied Dima. 'And my wife's pregnant . . .'

'I see,' said his boss. 'Well, take a seat.'

Dima lowered himself onto a hard chair. His eyes took in the map of Ukraine on the wall behind his boss, the portrait of the President to the right of the map and the icon in its expensive silver frame that hung to the right of the President's portrait, almost in the corner of the room.

'I bet that's a confiscated icon,' he thought.

Dima's boss had followed the direction of his gaze.

'Have you started believing in God?' he asked.

'Not exactly,' said Dima. 'Well, maybe a little . . .'

'The Chief Security Officer has been wanting to talk to you for some time now. I'm just going to let him know you're here. After you're done with him, come back and see me again, OK? And they're waiting for you in accounts as well. Apparently they've got two months' salary for you . . .'

Dima was confused. So they were paying him for his two months off? That didn't make any sense.

Meanwhile his boss made a call to someone called 'Comrade Captain' and told him that Dima was on his way.

Comrade Captain – a short man of around forty with a crew cut, wearing a pilot's uniform – was sitting in an office on the first floor.

He regarded Dima gravely. Before him on the table lay Dima's personal effects and his green work record book.

'Take a seat,' said Comrade Captain. 'So, I understand that you're coming back to work. Is that correct?'

'It looks like it,' Dima replied uncertainly.

'Well, before you do there's something we need to discuss. You may remember, at the beginning of the year we had an emergency situation. A suitcase containing a consignment of experimental medicine went missing.'

Dima stiffened. He even ducked slightly, as though a bullet had just whizzed past his head.

'Relax! We're just having a little chat. I just wanted to remind you of something. Namely, the two baggage handlers who were working on the same shift as you that day. They don't work at the airport any more, though, do they? They're both dead.'

Comrade Captain paused, with a piercing look straight into Dima's eyes.

'It's all a bit of a mystery, isn't it?' Comrade Captain continued. 'The baggage handlers are dead, but you're still alive . . . The suitcase was being transported officially, but illegally. Then there was an unofficial, but persistent investigation. They asked about you, you know, and about certain ampoules that had turned up here and there . . . Then suddenly everything went quiet, case closed, and now after two months of silence we've been instructed to destroy all documentary evidence. Everyone's supposed to forget this emergency situation ever happened, and that means you too.'

'You want me to forget about it?' Dima looked in bewilderment at the man in the pilot's uniform. 'But I . . . uh . . . can't remember anything about it anyway . . .'

'Maybe you can't remember anything about it right now, but we need to make sure that you don't *ever* remember anything about it,' said Comrade Captain, enunciating clearly and nodding to the rhythm of his words.

He took a blank form from among Dima's personal effects, pushed it towards Dima and gave him a pen.

'Fill this in and sign it!'

Dima looked down at the piece of paper.

DECLARATION

The properties of the medicinal drug Turbosclerin and all possible adverse effects that may result after taking this medicinal drug have been explained to me. I have taken the recommended dose willingly. No force or coercion was used.

_____   _____

Full name   Signature

____/____/_____

Date

'That's democracy for you! Time was, they would just have put the frighteners on you, maybe roughed you up a little, but at least there wouldn't have been any side effects to worry about! But now . . . Do you have any questions?' asked the Captain with a sigh.

'What does this medicine do?'

'It's a German drug that will make it possible to erase certain events and people from your memory when you hear certain key words. Two tablets then five minutes of hypnosis with a psychologist, and you're free to go.'

Dima panicked and glanced back at the door, his fear clearly evident.

'Calm down,' barked Comrade Captain. 'And that's an order! Three years ago you would no longer be alive. You should be grateful to the Orange Revolution. Everything's democratic now – nothing happens without the patient's consent!'

Little sparks of irony flashed in the man's eyes, and he gave a mirthless chuckle.

'What if I refuse to take the tablets?' Dima asked carefully.

Comrade Captain shook his head.

'That's not an option,' he said. 'You've got nothing to worry about. You'll just forget everything we need you to forget and then you can go and get on with your happy little life. In your little house on 9 May Street, with your wife and your cat . . .'

The man took from his desk drawer a small, plain cardboard box. He took out two tablets in a transparent cellophane wrapper. The tablets were large, about the same size as the vitamin C tablets Dima remembered from his childhood. Comrade Captain himself looked at these tablets with curiosity and suspicion. He poured a glass of water from the decanter and dropped both tablets in. The water started to foam up, and the tablets released bubbles as they dissolved.

'Fill it in, quickly,' ordered Comrade Captain, glancing at his watch. 'I've got another appointment in half an hour.'

Swallowing his saliva, Dima watched the tablets dissolve. He wrote his full name on the form, signed it and added the date. Then he picked up the glass and drank its contents in one gulp.

'Come in, Valery Petrovich,' said Comrade Captain into his telephone receiver.

The air was burning hot, the walls were melting, receding . . . The office grew wider before Dima's eyes.

Another man in a pilot's uniform came into the office. Comrade Captain stood up so that the man could sit down at his desk.

'Ampoules. Black suitcase,' the new 'pilot' began to intone monotonously, speaking slowly and distinctly. 'Baggage handlers Evgeny and Boris. Cancer medicine. Abandoned yard at number 121 9 May Street. Abandoned well. East German rug . . .'

Dima closed his eyes. He couldn't see anything anyway, apart from a kind of white mist. Pronounced in this way, slowly and distinctly, the words seemed unnecessarily loud. Each new word was spoken against the reverberating background of all the other words, and gradually it all accumulated into a defeaning roar in Dima's head. He no longer understood the meaning of the words he was hearing. He laid his head on the desk, on top of his folded arms . . .

'Wake him up in a quarter of an hour,' the psychologist told Comrade Captain.

106

Lipovka village, Kiev region

The owner of the village 'drinking den' that Egor had once popped into on his way home turned out to be the former manager of a dairy farm. She was middle-aged, with dyed blonde hair. That first time he'd turned round and walked out immediately, but today he approached it in a completely different mood. He already knew he wasn't going to like it.

'How many guests will there be?' asked the owner, all of a dither. 'And it's for tomorrow, you say? How on earth will we get everything ready in time?'

'Set the table for thirty,' answered Egor calmly, deciding to ignore the owner's emotional reaction. 'We just need to make sure the café's properly aired out, wash the windows and the floors . . . And get rid of those fish!'

She looked up at a garland of dried sea roaches hanging from the ceiling above the counter.

'I can get some of those cheap American chicken legs in Makariv,' the café owner said, planning aloud. 'What about the pork, though? That might be tricky. I'll call Byshev – if they've got any, they'll deliver it. Are you going to supply your own vodka?'

'Yes,' nodded Egor.

'Have a seat while you're waiting. I'll just work it all out.' She went back behind the counter. She got out a large calculator and found a piece of paper and a pencil. Her fingers started tapping away on the calculator buttons.

'If you bring your own vodka, then it comes to one thousand six hundred and eight hryvnas.'

'Fine,' said Egor.

'So, Thursday the fifteenth, at six o'clock?' she confirmed, her voice already different, softer.

Egor escaped from the stuffy café out into the fresh air. He wasn't due at work until the evening, so he could spend a little more time with Irina and the girls.

Aleksandra Vasilievna was not at home. Without waiting for her future son-in-law to return she had gone to make sure all the guests would be coming to tomorrow's wedding party.

After breastfeeding both babies, Irina expressed her remaining milk into a jar. When she'd finished, she sealed the jar with a plastic lid sterilised in steam from the kettle.

'Shall we go for a little walk?' suggested Egor.

'Let's wait for Mama to get back. We can't leave Marina here on her own!'

'Why do we have to leave her? Let's take her with us. Wrap both of them up! I'll take Marina, and you can take Yasya.'

They walked slowly along the roadside verge to the café – it was almost a kilometre. Egor smiled contentedly to see the café windows open and two women zealously polishing the washed glass with wads of scrunched-up newspaper, which made sharp squeaking sounds every now and then.

When they returned home an hour later Aleksandra Vasilievna still wasn't back. Egor asked Irina to find her passport, and she did.

After lunch he went into Kiev. Egor had two hours before the start of his shift, and he spent them looking round the shops. He wanted to buy Irina a present but everything he liked was too expensive, and he couldn't decide what she would like best.

In the end he bought her a gold chain and a little gold pendant in the form of a mobile phone. After all, he'd given her her first ever mobile phone!

Then he quickly returned to his car, which he'd left near the Naukova Dumka bookshop. He could have walked to the park from there – it would have taken ten minutes, no more – but Egor always felt happier when he could see his car. So he drove up to the little food shop by the arched entrance at the side of the park, left his car in its usual spot and started walking towards the

Mariinsky Palace. There were seven minutes left before the start of his shift.

107

Lipovka village, Kiev region

Fortunately, Volodka's fear that they would end up following the red Mazda all the way to Zhytomyr turned out to be unfounded. At the 33km marker, just before the service station, the Mazda turned onto a country road.

Their Niva followed it through several villages, maintaining a distance of about two hundred metres, then fields and darkness stretched out on both sides of the narrow paved road and Volodka had to lean closer to the windscreen in order to get a clearer view of the road in the diffused, close-range beams of the headlights. The Mazda's rear lights weren't much help as the road meandered like a river, twisting and turning, left and right. Three more pairs of headlights were moving behind the Niva at a respectable distance, although the cars themselves were not visible in the darkness. Both Semyon and Volodka were glad about the presence of other cars on this country road – it meant that the driver of the Mazda was less likely to notice them.

Where the road forked in Lipovka, the red Mazda turned left and began driving more slowly.

Volodka slowed down too. He waited until the car was hidden behind the bend, then he drove after it. After about three hundred metres the Mazda took another turning and began driving even more slowly and carefully. Volodka realised immediately that it was an unpaved country lane.

'Turn the lights off and wait here, I'll walk the rest of the way,' said Semyon. Volodka stopped the car and Semyon got out.

He headed down the lane and saw the Mazda parked next to a wooden fence.

Semyon walked past several houses and huts with their lights on. He had a strange feeling that he was in some kind of imaginary parallel world. He stopped and listened to the silence. Suddenly a dog barked, and the sound was immediately picked up by several other dogs.

He stood there without moving, listening to the barking and its echo. Then it stopped abruptly, as though all the village dogs had fallen silent on command.

Semyon was only about ten steps away from the Mazda when he stopped again and listened. He could already see a single-storey brick house, with the Mazda beside its fence. He could see the front porch and two or three steps leading to a wooden door. He could see the front windows, full of light.

The wicket gate was unlocked. Semyon went into the front yard and peered at the windows.

The figure of a woman appeared fleetingly in one of the windows. Semyon held his breath. A baby cried suddenly at such surprisingly close range that it made Semyon jump. Looking more keenly, he noticed that two of the little top windows were open.

'I'll have to wait,' he told himself.

He felt a growing sense of indecisiveness. The desire to wait is secretly a desire to do nothing. He already knew that.

He could hear kitchen noises – the jingling of knives and forks, the clattering of plates being set on a wooden table.

'The man of the house is getting his supper,' thought Semyon.

Now he was consumed with curiosity. What kind of supper would be served to the man of this house, after a hard day's work? He remembered the mushrooms that Veronika had prepared for him the other night. A random, jumbled selection of clips from old Soviet films flashed through his mind – image after image of men sitting at the table and women bustling about, attending to the stove, carrying steaming casserole dishes and frying pans to the table.

'It's like a different life,' he thought. 'A completely different life . . . Real life is going on out here, on this side of the window, but in there it's like something straight out of a Soviet film.'

He was struck by the unreality of everything that was happening. The unreality of this village, this lane, this house . . .

Semyon shook his head, trying to clear his own thoughts. He thought about the road to Vyshhorod – people lived out there too, in single-storey houses. But those houses looked real, contemporary even. So why did this place feel so unreal? Was it because of the darkness? Maybe it was because he'd never stopped on the road to Vyshhorod to peer through the window of a family home and witness a scene from their life.

He remembered a conversation he'd once had with Veronika. A long time ago, even before the accident, she had told him that some people she knew were selling a house in the country – for a good price too. But Semyon had refused even to contemplate it. Back then he was full of a kind of 'city-dweller's' pride. His friends used to like shouting at drivers in cars with number plates from outside Kiev, or builders coming to the city from Zakarpatya to look for work. All these out-of-towners, not used to the pace of life in Kiev, were like rabbits in the city's headlights. They were all confused and a little scared. This went on until there were too many of them to ridicule, or until Semyon no longer cared. He hadn't thought about it for a long time but now it all come flooding back, no doubt as a result of his discovery that Egor the Mariinsky Palace security guard was an out-of-towner too.

'Here, you hold her!' a woman's voice burst out through the little top window into the front yard.

'Hold on, I'm just going to feed Yasya,' answered another, younger, female voice.

Then there was the clattering of dishes again. This sound came from the window to the left of the front door, which must have been the kitchen.

Semyon pressed his shoulder up against the wall of the house. He looked down – the concrete foundations rose half a metre above ground level, making a narrow ledge at the base of the brick wall. If he stood on this ledge and held onto something he would be able to look through the window. Now he just had to find something to hold onto!

Semyon peered into the darkness and spotted a large nail sticking out of the top left-hand corner of the front door. He noticed the horseshoe nailed above the door, and an ironic, indulgent smile appeared on his face.

'Egorushka, pour yourself some tea. I won't be a minute. I just need to feed Marina again, she's crying!' called the young female voice, which reminded Semyon of Veronika.

He went up the front steps to the porch. He placed the toe of his left boot on the narrow ledge to the left of the porch, then reached for the nail with his right hand and launched his body towards the kitchen window.

Through the net curtain Semyon could see a kitchen table, a cup of tea and Egor's hand. In the far left-hand corner, a young woman appeared in the doorway. Her face was kind, but plain. She was holding a baby in a pink padded sleepsuit to her breast, and the baby's cheeks were moving rhythmically.

'Shall I mix up some formula for Yasya?' called the other female voice, from somewhere behind the young woman.

The young woman placed a hand under her opposite breast and raised it slightly, as though she were determining its weight.

'No need, Mama, I've got enough!'

She sat down on a stool opposite Egor and looked at him rather anxiously.

'But what if someone informs the militia?'

Semyon's foot suddenly started to slip from the narrow ledge. He strengthened his grip on the nail and grabbed the corner of the window frame with his left hand, which enabled him to regain his balance and find a steadier foothold with his left boot.

'You can just say it's my baby,' said a calm male voice. 'Let them think that I brought her with me when I moved in . . . And as far as the paperwork's concerned, we'll think of something . . .'

The young woman nodded obediently. An older woman came into the kitchen holding another baby, slightly larger than the first.

The young woman tenderly removed the baby from her breast, took the other little one in her left arm and gave the first to the older woman. She tucked this breast with its swollen, red nipple back into her blouse, then freed her other breast and brought the second baby to its fresh, pink nipple.

The older woman left the kitchen.

'Three is a holy number,' said Egor. 'We'll have a third baby together. When these two start running around . . .'

The woman gave a little smile.

Semyon felt the toe of his boot slipping off again. He carefully lowered one foot then the other onto the concrete slope protecting the foundations. His legs ached as though he had just been doing the splits.

He looked back at the door and at the horseshoe above it.

It was another world in there, behind that door. Egor's little family was vulnerable and fragile but full of hope. They were giving it a go against the odds, hoping for the best. Semyon knew they were totally reliant on luck, but it didn't make feel him stronger, more confident or superior to them in any way.

He'd come here looking for a baby girl who'd been abandoned outside Parliament, and he'd found her. He'd seen her with his own eyes. He'd heard her cry. But fortune wasn't smiling on him – it was smiling on Egor, who clearly wasn't the father of the first child either. Egor wasn't a shrewd, sophisticated man of the world, nor was he very good at decision-making, as was evident from his reliance on luck. Nevertheless this single-storey brick house, containing two children, two women and a Mariinsky Palace security guard, was like a complete and self-contained world, which Semyon had neither the right nor the desire to disrupt.

What was he supposed do? Knock on the door and demand that they hand over the child? No. He wasn't about to do that. He already knew the fate of this little girl. He already possessed the secret knowledge, which sooner or later he would be required to share with Gennady Ilyich and that good-for-nothing Oksana, who had abandoned her own child on the cold steps of Parliament one night in March! No, he had to think of another plan. He still wanted to enrich his family life and make his own world complete, while preserving the integrity of this other world as well. He would think of something. He'd sit right here on the doorstep of this village house and think of something, and he wouldn't leave the doorstep until he had!

Semyon felt the cold from the concrete doorstep through the fabric of his trousers. He could no longer hear the voices and noises spilling from the little kitchen window. Those sounds belonged to another world.

He sat there thinking about where to find a newborn baby girl. When the answer suddenly occurred to him, he was surprised that he hadn't thought of it before. It was so obvious: a maternity hospital! Any maternity hospital would do. He would also need a compliant and not excessively greedy obstetrician. The world was not perfect, people were not perfect, women were not perfect . . . and that was no bad thing!

'Shall I take you home?' Volodka asked Semyon, when he got back into the Niva.

'No, can you drop me off at the orphanage in Borshchahivka? I'll make my own way from there.'

Volodka gave his friend a curious look but didn't ask any questions. He just switched the engine on, turned the car round and started driving.

'Oh yeah, and one more thing,' said Semyon. 'You don't need to follow me any more at night.'

108

Striletska Street, Kiev

By late afternoon Veronika was tired of the changeable mood she'd been in all day, so she went for a walk to try and cheer herself up. She strolled along Reitarska Street to the Optika shop on the corner, then turned into Georgievsky Street. The high, white wall of the St Sophia Cathedral ran along the right-hand side of the road, and Veronika felt her spirits lift as she saw it. She approached the wall and slowed her pace, touching the rough white plaster with her fingertips. She walked as far as the old rear gates of the monastery, which had been bricked up many years ago. She always stopped here in front of the old gates. It was somewhere she came to clear her head, to forget about her troubles. There was a shallow recess in the wall where she could hide, where she could retreat from the whole world, and she did so now, pressing herself up against the wall until she felt a quiet and timorous self-confidence return.

It always surprised her how few people walked down this little road between Reitarska Street and Striletska Street, how few people even seemed to know about this secret corner of peace and quiet, hidden in the very heart of the city.

It was already starting to get dark, but Veronika's attention was so focused on the white wall that she didn't notice. It was only when a car's headlights flashed past behind her that she came to her senses and looked at her watch: 6.30 p.m. What if Semyon got home early today?

Thinking about Semyon did not make Veronika hurry home. Instead she walked as far as the point where the monastery wall ran into the courtyard of an enormous apartment building, which had been part of the monastery before the Revolution. When she reached it she turned and walked back at the same unhurried pace. She had a pensive, faraway look in her eyes.

Back on Reitarska Street she stopped outside her apartment building and looked towards the corner of the three cafés, which was always busy in the evenings. Then she looked up at the apartment windows – they were still dark. Semyon wasn't back yet.

Before going inside, she went to the corner of the three cafés and adjusted the wreath on the wall.

When she got in she called Darya to ask how she was feeling and told her that she'd been to straighten the wreath.

'Oh, is it still up there?' Darya Ivanovna asked nonchalantly. 'I'll probably take it down soon. It's been up there for quite a while now. I ought to take it to the cemetery, really.'

When she hung up Veronika looked at her watch – it was nearly 8 p.m. She decided to prepare a simple supper of spaghetti. She put a pan of water on the hob to boil and her thoughts turned to Semyon once more.

109

9 May Street, Boryspil

Valya flew into the house as though she'd been scalded. Leaving dirty footprints – it was raining outside, and she hadn't stopped to take off her boots – she went through to the living room and switched on the light. Her gaze fell on Dima, who was lying on the sofa with a towel wrapped round his head. He screwed his eyes up at the bright light.

'God, you gave me a fright!' breathed Valya, lowering herself into a chair. She pulled her boots off and threw them back into the hall. 'I waited till half past six. I thought something had happened.'

'Nothing happened,' mumbled Dima. 'I went to work. I had to pick up my wages.'

He nodded at his work record book, which was lying on the table.

'Do you want an aspirin?' asked Valya, all concerned. 'Or shall I call an ambulance?'

'No, I don't need an ambulance,' he said. 'But I wouldn't say no to an aspirin. And a shot of vodka too – that might help.'

While Valya was taking her coat off and looking for an aspirin, Dima had a sudden moment of clarity. He could recall in detail the conversations he'd had with his boss and the Chief Security Officer. He vaguely remembered a second man in a pilot's uniform, who had read out a list of words that Dima in his state of impaired consciousness was supposed to forget. To be more precise, he was supposed to forget everything related to the words.

'Ampoules, black suitcase, baggage handlers . . .' Dima could remember not only the words in their correct order, but also the voice of the hypnotist and his intonation.

Dima was frightened, because he hadn't forgotten anything. Including the main reason they'd forced him to take the tablets in the first place.

What if they realised he hadn't forgotten anything? What if they found out that the tablets didn't work?

Dima broke into a sweat.

The door opened and Valya came back into the room. She'd already changed into a dress and was holding an aspirin and a shot of home-made vodka.

'Oh, thank God you're here!' he sighed with relief. 'I feel terrible! You can't even imagine!'

'Shall I make you something to eat?'

'No, stay here for a bit. Don't leave me! Let's watch TV together!'

Valya switched the television on. The first channel was showing the news. Boring political news: various politicians at some kind of conference.

'Shall I change channels?' asked Valya.

'No, leave it,' Dima waved his hand. 'It's *Magnolia TV* after this!'

Magnolia TV started and they were both glued to the screen, fascinated by the reports of car accidents, fires, crimes and missing children.

Against the backdrop of other people's misfortune Dima forgot all about his headache.

When the programme came to an end Valya noticed that her husband had fallen asleep.

She switched the television and the light off and tiptoed out of the room.

'I should take better care of him,' she thought, looking in the fridge for something to satisfy her own evening hunger.

She put the kettle on to boil, cut a slice of bread and started making herself a sandwich with butter and sliced herring fillet mixed with finely chopped onion. She wanted something salty with her sweet tea.

110

Central Registry Office, Victory Avenue, Kiev
Even though Egor's new boss was from West Ukraine, he turned out to be a decent chap. When he found out that Egor had an appointment at the Central Registry Office he appointed a reserve security guard to replace him on the 6 p.m. shift, without making

a fuss about it. He found a replacement for his next shift too, so that Egor could have the day off.

At precisely 6.45 p.m., as stipulated by the secretary at the Central Registry Office, Egor stood in front of the same nondescript and unassuming door as before. It was the only one of its kind in the foyer. There was hardly anyone else there at that hour – no young couples, no wedding parties, just two women looking at the information about divorces on the noticeboard and a middle-aged man sitting on a chair, apparently waiting for someone.

Egor rapped on the door with the knuckle of his index finger and opened it. The secretary looked at him.

'And you are . . . ?' She glanced up at the ceiling, trying to remember.

Egor showed her the page she'd torn from her desk calendar.

'Ah, that's right. Did you bring both passports with you?'

Egor took the two passports from the inside pocket of his leather coat. She laid a blank application form on the table in front of him, and a pen.

'Here, fill this in.'

Egor glanced over the form. It was a standard application form for registering a marriage. He filled in the sections relating to the groom – himself – but when it came to Irina's details he stopped, unsure how to proceed.

'I'm sorry, but I don't know her patronymic . . . Her father's dead.'

The secretary looked at her visitor sceptically, as though she were wondering whether there might be something wrong with him.

'You've got your bride's passport, haven't you? Just copy it all down from there.'

Egor felt like a complete idiot. He copied the necessary details from the passport onto the application form, and then he signed it.

'You need to sign for her too. Just copy the signature in her passport. Then we'll pick a date!'

Irina's signature was simple and deliberate, like a child's handwriting. The opposite of Egor's.

Meanwhile the secretary flicked through the old pages of her desk calendar, into the past.

'There, put February the twelfth. Now I just need you to write a declaration . . . a couple of sentences, that's all.'

She dictated that he, Egor such-and-such, wished to register their marriage in Kiev rather than the locality specified in their residency permits on the grounds that the applicant himself was engaged in employment in Kiev at the time of submitting the application.

'Passports!' said the secretary.

She asked him to wait, then took the documents, the application and the declaration and left the room.

She was gone for about a quarter of an hour. In a strange way the silence and the close confines of this little room relaxed Egor, and he started feeling sleepy – the strain of all the emotions was clearly beginning to tell on him. Another ten minutes and he would have been fast asleep. But just then the secretary came back in, flinging the door open so energetically that the rush of air revived him.

'Congratulations,' she said, handing both passports back to him. 'I just need you to sign here as well for both yourself and your wife. And here! And here! There, now your marriage certificate is complete. We'll keep a copy here in the archives,' she said, with an expectant look at her visitor.

Egor took out two $100 bills and handed them to her.

'Leave it on the table,' said the secretary, in an offhand way. 'I hope you'll both be very happy!'

Egor had no further business in the Central Registry Office, so he left. He went outside and looked back at the brightly illuminated McDonald's nearby. Then he called Irina.

'Irina, you're my wife!' he said.

'Oh my God!' she whispered into the receiver. Her breath seemed to catch in her throat.

'She's going to cry,' thought Egor, alarmed. 'I'm already on my way home! I'll be there soon!' he promised and hung up, without waiting for her to reply.

Egor arrived in Lipovka and was about to turn into the lane where Irina lived when he almost collided head-on with a Volga, for the second time that week. The man at the wheel wore a blank, introspective look on his plump face and didn't even seem to be looking at the road.

Egor stopped and let him out onto the main road before turning the corner himself. He noticed that the gravel track had already started to dry out after the recent rain.

There was a surprise waiting for him back at the house. In the living room, where Irina slept, a table had been laid with a tablecloth. It was decorated with a vase of artificial flowers and set with glasses, forks and spoons.

'Come on then, son, show me the passports!' said Aleksandra Vasilievna, as soon as she opened the door.

Egor took his boots and coat off and gave the documents to his mother-in-law. She held them under the light in the hallway and started leafing through them, her happiness and excitement showing on her face. She found the official marriage stamp in her daughter's passport and looked at Egor gratefully.

'Why don't I hold onto your passports for a bit?' she suggested. 'We need to make sure everyone in the village sees them . . .'

Egor nodded. He went into the living room and saw Irina, who had dressed up for the occasion. He put his arms round her and kissed her. She pressed herself up against him and he felt the warmth of her breasts through his unbuttoned jacket, shirt and T-shirt.

'Come on, sit down! Mama bought a rabbit from the neighbours. She's already braised it,' she said.

There was something missing. Egor looked around and listened attentively, and then he realised: he couldn't see or hear the babies.

'Where are the girls?' he asked.

'Mama's got them in her room. They're going to sleep in there tonight. I've just fed them and I'll feed them again later, then we can settle them down,' Irina said tenderly.

It took Aleksandra Vasilievna just five minutes to finish setting the table. She put the plates out and brought in a pan of boiled potatoes and a cast-iron casserole dish containing the braised rabbit. She fetched a bottle of vodka, for which shot glasses were found in the sideboard, and the unfinished bottle of sweet Kagor wine.

Egor chose this moment to give his wife her gift. It brought tears to her eyes.

They drank the sweet Kagor first for happiness, then a shot of strong vodka each to ensure the strength of their family. This awoke their appetites. In keeping with tradition, and to remind them of the reason they were celebrating, Baba Shura cried 'gorko!' twice and the bride and groom dutifully kissed the 'bitterness' of the vodka away.

'You'll hear that plenty more tomorrow!' she said, and a joyful, tipsy flame shone in her eyes. 'Forty-four guests! Well, they might not all . . . Anyway, we'll take a bottle of champagne over to your mother first thing in the morning. Back here for lunch, and then the wedding party in the evening!'

Aleksandra Vasilievna drank more vodka than the newly-weds. Irina barely sipped hers. Every now and then she would get up and peep into her mother's room, and eventually she told them that the girls had woken up and went in to feed them. Then she poured a glass of Kagor, took a teaspoon and went to rub a little of the sweet wine on their lips.

Irina's mother starting getting her things together.

'I'm going to spend the night with a friend – we'll have a drink or two to celebrate. You two can stay here.' She nodded at Irina's small double bed, which had been attractively made up. 'The children will sleep through until the morning – so you won't be disturbed!'

She carried the dishes through to the kitchen, then put on her coat and her felt boots and came back into the room once more to kiss Egor.

'Now then, son, make sure you look after my daughter.'

The door closed behind her. Egor glanced at the dark window. They were alone together at the table.

'Shall we go to bed?' she asked tentatively.

Egor nodded.

The heat woke Egor up the following morning. The house was quiet, and Irina wasn't there. He listened carefully and heard a tender whisper coming from her mother's room – she was feeding the babies.

He looked at the electric alarm clock on the bedside table: it was 6.30 a.m. Egor's body felt heavy and languid. He thought about their night together. He remembered that Irina had gone to sleep first, and when he had finally tired of covering her back and milk-swollen breasts with kisses the slanting green lines of this same alarm clock had indicated that it was after 4 a.m. So he'd had virtually no sleep! But he still felt like jumping out of bed. He wanted to go out onto the doorstep and breathe in his fresh, new life.

He went into the bathroom first, to have a wash. He could smell Irina on his hands – a sharp, milky, sea-buckthorn smell. The sea buckthorn was from her face cream, but the sharp, milky smell was her own.

He went out onto the doorstep, and then he spotted Baba Shura out of the corner of his eye – she was sitting on a little bench under her bedroom window. She was sitting there without moving, as though she'd been there a long time.

'Aleksandra Vasilievna, don't tell me you spent the night out here!' he cried jokingly, thinking that his mother-in-law had come back from her friend's and been too embarrassed to go into the house until they got up.

'Of course I did,' she said. 'I was keeping watch over your happiness. You have to keep the happiness of the first night sacred, let nothing disturb it. Anything could happen . . . and we don't have a dog.'

'Go on inside, quickly, for goodness' sake!' Egor fussed over her.

'Only if you put some clothes on,' said Baba Shura, looking pointedly at Egor's underpants.

It was only then that he felt the refreshing chill of the concrete doorstep and the pleasantly damp touch of the morning air on his shoulders and chest.

'Egorushka! I've made you breakfast!' called Irina.

He smiled and went back into the bathroom to run a comb through his wet hair. On the other side of the door, in the hallway, Aleksandra Vasilievna was wheezing as she took her felt boots off.

It was going to be a happy day.

111

Apartment No. 10, Reitarska Street, Kiev

Three days later Semyon committed the happiest and most amoral act of his life. He was sitting in the VW Touareg belonging to Valentin the obstetrician. The doctor reached across to the back seat and picked up a baby wrapped in a warm blanket. He lifted a corner of the blanket from the tiny little face.

'She's healthy. Regular features, no hereditary conditions,' he said.

'What about the mother?' asked Semyon.

'She's a student, eighteen years old. Silly little thing. She's signed a declaration renouncing her maternal rights. I've kept the declaration, and I know where she lives. You won't have any trouble from her. Here's the birth certificate – you can fill the name in yourself.'

Semyon took $2,000 from his wallet and held it out to the doctor, who put it in the pocket of his short sheepskin jacket without counting it.

'Shall I drop you off, so that the baby doesn't get cold?' he suggested.

The journey didn't take long. The city was getting ready to sleep, and the roads were virtually empty.

'Are you sure your wife will manage?' the doctor asked, slightly concerned.

'Yes,' Semyon answered confidently.

'Call me if you have any questions.' The doctor glanced at the baby. 'And I can do a home visit if necessary. It's probably best not to call your local doctor . . .'

Semyon nodded knowingly. As he went inside he looked back and saw the doctor studying the number of his building and the name of the street.

'Oh my God!' exclaimed Veronika, coming out into the hallway at the sound of the door opening. Semyon handed her the baby, which was still wrapped in its blanket.

'Senya! Why didn't you call? Why didn't you warn me? What about a cot? And what are we going to feed it?'

'I'll pop out now and get a few bits . . . Which supermarket is still open?' he mumbled distractedly.

'The one in the Ukraine department store – that's the closest.'

Semyon hurried out onto the landing and ran down the stairs, taking them two at a time. He went outside, looked at the road and immediately saw a pair of headlights approaching. He raised his hand, and the taxi pulled up nearby.

'I need to get to the Ukraine department store. Fifty hryvnas to wait for me there, then bring me back here!' Semyon said quickly through the open window of the driver's door.

'Get in.'

The car drove round the department store and stopped at the other side, where a neon sign hung over the entrance to the supermarket.

'Right, nappies and formula milk,' Semyon muttered to himself.

It was clean and bright inside the supermarket, and almost empty. A bored shop assistant was chatting with one of the cashiers.

'Where's your formula milk for newborns?' Semyon asked, interrupting their conversation.

'I'll show you.' A girl wearing a yellow tabard led him deeper into the shop.

'Here's all the formula milk. These ones are more expensive, but better.'

'What about this one, Malysh?' asked Semyon, noticing a box with Ukrainian writing on.

'That's for people who can't afford the others.' The girl smiled.

Semyon took her advice and threw five boxes of the recommended formula milk into his basket, along with several bottles and sets of teats. Then she showed him the disposable nappies.

He was home ten minutes later. He could hear a baby crying. Veronika didn't come out to meet him in the hall – she was in the living room, trying to soothe the baby by rocking it in her arms, but this was just making the baby cry even more.

Semyon put the kettle on straight away. He took one of the boxes of formula milk and stood in the middle of the kitchen, directly under the main light, so that he could read the instructions on preparation and quantity.

Finally the baby got the milk she'd been waiting for. It might not have been authentic, but it was imported and full of vitamins.

Standing over his wife and watching her feed the baby, Semyon suddenly felt a profound but pleasant exhaustion. He knew that if he sat or lay down now he would fall asleep immediately, but he had a niggling feeling that there was something he had to do first, something important . . . Semyon racked his brains, trying to remember what it was. Yes, that was it! He had to call Gennady Ilyich. It was a bit late, but when he heard Semyon's news he was bound to forgive him.

'What's up?' The deputy's voice was surprisingly cheerful.

'I found her,' said Semyon, and at that moment he remembered the baby girl that Egor had taken. That was the one he'd found, the one he'd discovered. As for this one, he hadn't found her – he'd 'bought' her. Which one had he just told Gennady Ilyich about? Or had he meant both of them? Strictly speaking, he wasn't lying – the point was that he now had an adopted daughter. That was all. His boss could take this information however he wanted to.

'Excellent news!' Gennady Ilyich's voice grew rich and soft, like a freshly baked pastry. 'How's your wife coping?'

Semyon glanced at Veronika, who had already taken the teat out of the baby's mouth and put her finger to her lips, to let her husband know that the baby was asleep.

'Fine.' Semyon lowered his voice to a whisper. 'We still have a lot of things to get, like a cot, a buggy . . . I'm going to sort it all out tomorrow.'

'You don't need to buy any of that stuff!' said the deputy. 'I'll take care of it. It will be delivered to your place tomorrow, at around eleven. And we'll celebrate tomorrow night. OK?'

None of them got much sleep that night. As he washed and shaved in front of the bathroom mirror the following morning, Semyon looked at his puffy eyes and listened to the noise in his head – he could still hear the baby crying. He could remember getting up three or four times in the night and going to the kitchen to warm a bottle of formula milk under the hot tap, but the thought of it didn't irritate him in the slightest. He could also remember falling asleep to the sound of Veronika whispering tenderly as she fed the baby.

His watch said 8.30 a.m. Volodka would be delivering the milk to Vyshhorod alone again today, without Semyon. Semyon didn't have any commitments until the evening so he was free to enjoy the fresh morning air, which smelled of spring!

He went out and walked down to the corner of the three cafés. He glanced at the large wreath and noticed that it was hanging lopsidedly on its nail. He straightened it up and turned onto Yaroslaviv Val, heading towards the newspaper kiosk. Then he went down Ivana Franko Street and along Chapaev Street to the headquarters of the Ministry of Emergency Situations. Then he crossed Olesya Gonchara Street and ended up on Chekhov Street. He stopped near a building that seemed familiar, and then he broke into a cold sweat as he realised that it was the building where Alisa lived. He hadn't intended to come here, though – he'd just come out for a walk!

Semyon hurried back to Reitarska Street.

When he got back to the apartment Veronika and the baby were still asleep. He stood in the kitchen, looking down at the floor, and for some reason it made him think of the maternity hospital with its spotlessly clean corridors, the nurses and doctors in their snowy-white coats and the outright ban on dirty and unkempt visitors. Clean and pure and free from infection: that's how birth and childhood ought to be.

Semyon washed the kitchen floor, then the hall floor. He decided to leave the bedroom, so as not to disturb his sleeping girls.

Veronika and the baby slept until 11 a.m., when they were woken by a persistent ringing at the door. Gennady Ilyich's driver Vasya brought an enormous cardboard box into the hall.

'It's a buggy,' he said.

He asked Semyon to help him carry in all the other gifts from the deputy, which involved several trips up and down the stairs. By the time they'd finished the entire hall was full of bags and boxes. There was a pink baby bath leaning against the wall, and Semyon counted at least eight packs of disposable nappies.

Vasya left as soon as he'd dropped off the last parcel. Veronika came out into the hallway and stared at the mountain of gifts, her eyes round with surprise.

'Who's that lot from?'

'Gennady Ilyich,' said Semyon.

'That's so kind of him!' Veronika exclaimed. 'Remember what a nasty little wheeler-dealer he used to be, on Petrivka?'

'Well, I guess leopards can change their spots,' said Semyon with a grin.

The sound of crying floated into the hallway.

Veronika disappeared behind the living-room door.

Semyon slowly carried the parcels of formula milk into the kitchen and made a space for them in one of the cupboards. Then he called Volodka.

The morning outside the window was filling with sunlight. It was almost a divine obligation to go for a walk on such a beautiful day. Particularly as they now had a buggy!

Semyon unpacked it.

'Nika,' he called to his wife, 'do you fancy taking her out for a walk?'

Veronika came into the hallway again, with the baby in her arms, and saw the buggy. She didn't look too sure about the idea.

'I don't know. I think I need to work myself up to it. No one saw me pregnant . . . What are they going to think when they suddenly see me out with a buggy?'

'They will see you pregnant one day,' Semyon promised tenderly. 'If anyone asks, just say we've adopted her. Everyone's doing it these days!'

Veronika nodded. 'I'll go in a bit. I'm just going to call Daryushka first, see how she is. If she's feeling better, then maybe we could go for a walk together – it would be more fun!'

Semyon went through the bags delivered by Vasya the driver. He found about a dozen different children's blankets in one of them, and three sleepsuits in another. So it was easy enough to get the baby ready for her first outing.

Semyon carried the buggy outside, and Veronika came down holding the baby.

'Call me when you need a hand getting back up the stairs,' said Semyon. 'I'm just going to shut my eyes for a bit – I've got some work on this evening.'

As he turned back towards the main entrance he noticed Darya Ivanovna out of the corner of his eye. Dressed in a long and generously cut dark blue cashmere coat, she was hurrying across the road to meet Veronika. Her face was flushed with excitement, and there was a happy smile on her lips.

Semyon quickly shut the entrance door behind him. As he walked up to the third floor he was overcome with tiredness, a natural consequence of the events of the previous evening and his sleepless night. But it was a satisfied, contented kind of tiredness – the way a professional athlete might feel after setting a new world record.

112

Striletska Street, Kiev

'Oh, let me see her little face!' cooed Darya Ivanovna, leaning over the buggy.

Veronika carefully revealed the baby's little face and noticed how greedily her friend looked at her baby. She felt a maternal pride swelling in her chest, as though she herself had carried the baby for nine months and given birth to her.

'Listen, we haven't been to pick up the wreath yet.' Darya Ivanovna looked up at Veronika. 'Why don't we go and take it down now? Then we can drop it off at my place and go to a café. Look, she's asleep!'

They went to the corner of the three cafés and stopped in front of the wreath. Darya Ivanovna gazed at the recently installed security camera, which seemed to be focused directly on the wreath. She seemed preoccupied, apparently summoning the courage to act on her intentions.

'First she buries her husband,' thought Veronika, with a sideways glance at her friend. 'Then she takes the wreath to the cemetery. I know she's been seeing Senya's psychiatrist . . . I wonder if he put the idea in her head?'

'Right, here goes!' Darya Ivanovna exhaled decisively. She reached both hands out towards the wreath and removed it from the nail, then looked back at Veronika and said, 'Come on, let's go.'

As they walked away, Darya Ivanovna grew sad and thoughtful. She was carrying the wreath like a handbag, as though she'd forgotten all about it.

'Hey, stop right there!' cried a voice.

Veronika turned round and saw a young man running towards them.

'Don't move! Yes, I'm talking to you!' he shouted. 'Where do you think you're going with that?' he asked Darya, once he'd caught his breath. 'Who said you could take it down?'

Darya Ivanovna stared at him with total incomprehension.

'What are you talking about?'

'Why did you take that wreath down? Give it back!'

The young man was about twenty. He was clearly nervous.

'It's my wreath!' declared Darya Ivanovna calmly. 'I put it up there, and now I'm taking it down . . .'

'Right, you'd better come and see the manager. He's not going to be very happy about this,' said the lad, reaching out for the wreath.

Darya Ivanovna automatically put the hand holding the wreath behind her back.

'Why should I go and see your manager? We've already got an agreement!'

'Just come with me, please. I'm only the security guard. I was given instructions to keep an eye on things, and that's what I'm doing. I was specifically told to keep an eye on that wreath.'

Darya Ivanovna shifted her astonished gaze to Veronika, who just shrugged.

'All right then, let's go,' she said.

Veronika stayed on the corner with the buggy, and Darya Ivanovna took the wreath inside.

She was gone for about quarter of an hour. When she came out again her eyes were glassy and her face frozen, as though she'd been hypnotised or was in a state of shock.

She walked past Veronika and hung the wreath back on its nail.

'Well? What did they say?' asked Veronika, burning with curiosity.

'I'll tell you later,' replied Darya Ivanovna. 'Could you possibly walk me home? I don't feel very well.'

They walked the rest of the way in silence, much to Veronika's dismay. The only sound came from the baby in the buggy, who had woken up and begun mewling piteously.

113

9 May Street, Boryspil

That morning Valya permitted herself to lounge about in bed for half an hour longer than usual. Her co-worker at the amusement arcade, Sonya, had agreed to work two consecutive shifts. Not out of the goodness of her heart, though – she had agreed to do it for fifty hryvnas and Valya would have to work a double shift in return, but she didn't mind. She and Dima had lots to do.

They had a list of documents that they were required to submit with their completed application form for Saratov. Quite a long list, as it turned out, and they had to provide photocopies as well as originals. In addition to the standard requirements – birth certificates, school diplomas, marriage certificate, handwritten CVs – they had to submit medical certificates testifying to the absence of head lice and any chronic or infectious diseases and a separate certificate stating that they were HIV-negative.

Valya had a quick breakfast then gathered together all the documents in question. It didn't take long, because she kept all their important papers in the same place, in an old handbag in the wardrobe. Dima headed to the post office to photocopy everything, and Valya picked out Dima's smartest outfit and started ironing it.

They left the house at around 11 a.m. and by midday they were already in Kiev, standing outside a new multi-storey building on the Kharkiv Highway. Some steps led from the street down to a basement office, with a sign on the door that said 'Saratov City Trading Company'. Dima and Valya took their place at the back of a queue of about forty or fifty people.

While they were waiting Dima went to a shop nearby to get some ice cream, and then he walked to a kiosk and bought a couple of newspapers.

Finally, two hours later, it was their turn to go into the office. A middle-aged man in a grey suit sat behind a desk, with a large map of Saratov hanging on the wall behind him. There was a Russian flag hanging on the wall to the left of the map and a portrait of President Putin to the right.

Valya silently placed their documents on the table. The man put his glasses on. He started checking the photocopies against the originals, signing each one to confirm its authenticity. He added their handwritten CVs to the pile of photocopies without even reading them and barely glanced at the medical certificates.

'When you get there you'll have to undergo a full medical examination and take all the tests again,' he said, looking up at them.

Valya and Dima nodded obediently.

The man ran his hand along the folds in the documents to flatten them out and put them carefully into a new file. He tied the tapes on the outside of the file in a bow, picked up a ballpoint pen and wrote 'No. 10054' on the cover of the file next to the word 'Case'.

'You'll get an answer by post within the next two weeks,' he said, removing his glasses. 'Chances are it will be positive. You will leave three months after receiving confirmation. Transport will be provided and paid for. No more than one container of personal belongings and furniture. I would advise you not to take your piano, if you have one – musical instruments in Saratov are a third of the price they are here in Ukraine.'

'We don't have a piano,' Valya said politely, imagining for some reason that this information might improve their chances of a positive response.

'Any questions?' asked the man.

'We've got a cat, Fluffy. Can we take him with us?' Valya looked beseechingly into the man's hazel eyes.

'There is a temporary ban on exporting cats from Ukraine,' he said. 'The incidence of feline rabies here is too high. And besides, you must have heard about what's happening here in Kiev.'

'No, we haven't heard anything,' said Valya quietly, thinking about Fluffy. She'd forgotten to feed him before they left.

Before going home they went to the food shop where Dima had got the ice cream and bought a bottle of champagne to drink that evening.

Valya spent the entire journey home wondering what to cook for dinner, but as soon as they got home she was overcome with exhaustion. Even Dima noticed it and suggested they just make a couple of sandwiches and drink the champagne in the living room in front of the television.

Champagne always made Dima sleepy, but *Magnolia TV* was on

and he was determined not to miss his favourite programme. Valya went to bed but Dima remained glued to the television screen, engrossed in reports about a robbery at a branch of the Savings Bank and a fire at the Troeshchina Market. The report after the fire was about a murder. A smartly dressed man lay in a puddle of blood on a street somewhere in the centre of Kiev. His throat had been slashed.

'This case baffled investigators initially,' said the presenter. 'But a post-mortem revealed that the unknown victim, whose identity is currently being established, was in fact subjected to an attack by a feline predator, such as a tiger, a lynx or a panther. Authorities are attempting to establish whether the zoo's resident wild cats can all be accounted for. Claw marks are clearly visible on the body, and there is no doubt that the laceration identified as the cause of death was caused by an animal's incisors. This is the second time in just three weeks that a wild animal has fatally attacked a human being. The first incident, which also occurred at night, involved a drug addict who had been released on bail prior to a trial on criminal charges.'

'Laceration . . . caused by an animal's incisors,' Dima repeated thoughtfully, scratching the back of his neck. The last report had puzzled him. He was wide awake now.

He took the garage key from its nail in the hallway and went outside, feeling the warm evening air in his face. It smelled of spring.

It wasn't cold in the garage, but Dima automatically switched on his home-made heater and sat down in his favourite corner. His gaze fell on the dirty plate with traces of food still sticking to it. Scruffy had lapped the medicine up from this plate. The medicine he'd tipped out of the ampoule that two Turbosclerin tablets were supposed to have erased from his mind.

449

Thinking about the tablets unexpectedly overturned Dima's calm and pensive mood. He felt a wave of fear, physical fear, approaching. He went over to the garage doors and locked them from inside. Now Dima knew he was safe, and he began to calm down. His thoughts returned to the last report on *Magnolia* TV and the 'laceration caused by an animal's incisors'.

114

Lipovka village, Kiev region

The morning sun had turned the window of Irina and Egor's room gold. Irina was sitting on a chair, breastfeeding Marina and bathing her legs in a patch of sunlight that was streaming onto the wooden floor. Yasenka was still asleep.

Returning from the hen house, her mother went into the kitchen and put three fresh eggs on a saucer. Her emotional exhaustion had been replaced by peace of mind.

Half an hour later she made Egor fried eggs with pork fat and cut him a thick slice of white Makariv bread, spreading it thickly with butter. Her son-in-law would need his strength today! She knew that much for sure.

At about 10 a.m. all of them, including the two babies, got into the Mazda and went to visit Egor's mother. Aleksandra Vasilievna had a bottle of Soviet champagne in her handbag, taken straight from the fridge.

Egor's mother was asleep. The neighbour told them that she'd had a bad night. There were traces of foam on her lips. So they decided not to disturb her but instead to raise a glass in Egor's childhood home to both his paralysed mother and his late father. The neighbour, his mother's carer, gladly joined them for a drink.

Naturally Aleksandra Vasilievna felt a bit awkward that Egor's mother had never even met Irina, let alone approved her, but what could they do? At least tradition had been observed: they'd drunk the first bottle at the groom's house, now they were drinking the second at the bride's. The third would be shared with their guests later.

As champagne and conversation flowed, the daylight faded and evening drew near. Aleksandra Vasilievna, Egor and Irina left the house at the agreed time. The babies, fed and settled to sleep with the help of a little Kagor wine, stayed in Irina's mother's room.

Egor drove them all to the 'drinking den'. The café had been transformed for the wedding feast. Above the doorway they'd hung a traditional *rushnik* – a long, embroidered linen cloth – and different-coloured paper ribbons had been wound around the wooden columns.

Inside the café two rows of tables ran the length of the room, and there were long benches instead of chairs. The walls were also decorated with *rushnik* cloths, and plates of *zakuski* stood on the tables. Several old men and women were already sitting down, waiting for the festivities to commence. The only thing that seemed out of place was the smell of paint.

Egor gazed around the room – nothing looked as though it had been freshly painted. Everything was the same as before, only cleaner. Then suddenly he looked up at the ceiling above the counter, and his eyes fell on the garland of sea roaches that he had asked the manager to remove. It was still there, only some of the dried fish had been painted blue and some yellow.

Egor almost swore out loud but managed to restrain himself. He adjusted his suit and straightened his tie.

Groups of guests began to arrive. Aleksandra Vasilievna placed the young couple to the left of the door to receive gifts and good wishes, and she herself collected those who had already congratulated the bride and groom and led them to the table, chattering away.

Out of the corner of his eye Egor noticed that his mother-in-law was showing some of the guests the stamp from the Central Registry Office in Irina's passport. Presumably those she hadn't got round to showing the day before.

After four toasts and three cries of '*gorko!*' the festive atmosphere grew a little calmer. The guests sat at the tables drinking and enjoying the *zakuski*, and there was a lull in the general toasts. Egor exchanged a look with Irina, and both understood that they could quietly slip away.

Aleksandra Vasilievna shrugged. She didn't understand why they wanted to leave so soon but made no attempt to change their minds. She just made sure that they loaded all the bags and parcels into the car and stayed at the party on their behalf. The music got louder, and the vodka flowed freely. Egor had provided so generously that even after three more hours of drinking there was still plenty left over.

Egor and Irina looked through their wedding gifts: envelopes containing cards and money, embroidered *rushnik* cloths, knives and forks, tea sets and two horseshoes for happiness. They stood there with their arms around one another for a little while, then Egor made up the bed and Irina busied herself in her mother's room with the babies. Yasya woke up straight away, as soon as Irina nudged her little nose into her warm breast full of milk, but Marina slept on.

While Irina was feeding Yasya she rejoiced in her new-found

happiness and marvelled at the strange and topsy-turvy way life had turned out. It was no coincidence that Yasya had started to refuse formula milk in favour of Irina's own milk as soon as Egor had taken to visiting them. It used to be the other way round! She was feeding three babies now, and the milk just kept coming.

'Why don't you nail those horseshoes above the door now, underneath the other one?' suggested Irina, looking out of her mother's room. 'They'll come and check, you know. The ones who gave them to us, I mean . . . And anyway, it's good luck!'

Egor nodded.

'Egorushka, a professor from Kiev came to see us. He said that the horseshoe that's up there already is the wrong way round. The open bit is supposed to face upwards, like an earthenware jug, so that the house stays full of happiness and none of it spills out.'

Egor went and changed into a tracksuit. He'd already brought all his things, in three suitcases, from the hostel in Kiev. Then he took his electric drill, some nails and a hammer from his toolbox. He went out onto the doorstep and looked at the old horseshoe, the one he'd found outside the café where their wedding guests were currently celebrating. He turned it the right way up and and nailed the two new horseshoes they'd been given underneath it, positioning them carefully.

They embraced again, and at that moment Irina decided to admit to Egor that she was feeding another baby, little Bogdan. Her mother had warned her not to, advising her to tell the professor that she could no longer express milk for them due to a change in family circumstances. But how could she leave a baby, the son of a pale and sickly mother, without milk? 'No, Egor will understand! I'm a mother first and foremost, but also a wet nurse – that's who I am,' she thought.

It was the right decision.

'You can't stop feeding other people's babies if they're in need. And besides, if you're the one feeding them then they're not really other people's babies anyway,' said Egor, with a good-natured grin. Then he shrugged and gave her a hug and a kiss.

She could taste his good mood on his lips: they tasted of vodka and smoke, like the smell in his mother's hut.

Egor would have rather liked to press himself to Irina's breast at that moment, to feel her life-giving warmth, and she could tell.

'You go on to bed, Egorushka. I'll be right there. Let me just feed Marina first. Yasya's already asleep.'

Irina switched off the light and a blissful, inviting darkness spread all around.

115

New Ring Road, Kiev

Vasya picked Semyon up at 7 p.m. and took him to an Argentinian restaurant on the New Ring Road. The restaurant consisted of about a dozen little wooden cabins set around a large two-storey timber-framed building.

Gennady Ilyich was already installed in one of the cabins. On the solid pine table in front of him stood an open bottle of Hennessy Pure White, two brandy glasses and a saucer of lemon, orange and grapefruit slices arranged in an overlapping circle. Two fat leather-bound menus lay to one side.

'Take a seat! Have a look at the menu . . . Choose whatever you like! You're the guest of honour!'

Semyon sat down at the table. There was a faint buzzing in his head, an after-effect of his sleepless night. He could still clearly hear the sound of the baby crying, but he just smiled and opened the menu. He was mesmerised by the repetition of the word 'meat' on every line. His eyes came to rest on an entry that read 'Argentinian steak (600–700g)' and he licked his lips as he tried to imagine how big it would be, then how it would taste. It suddenly occurred to him that he hadn't had any lunch, or breakfast either for that matter. He just hadn't thought about eating at all.

'Well?' said Gennady Ilyich.

Semyon pointed at the word 'steak'.

'Excellent! You work like a man, you need to eat like one too!' grinned the deputy.

He leaned back, took the phone off the wall and started dictating their order. He broke off for a moment, waving his finger to attract Semyon's attention.

'Do you want your steak rare or well done?'

'No blood,' said Semyon.

'Well done,' the deputy said, translating his guest's request into culinary English. Then he replaced the receiver.

He poured Semyon a brandy.

'Congratulations on becoming a father!' said Gennady Ilyich, in an enthusiastic and ceremonial voice. It sounded as though he meant it too, which was something of a surprise to Semyon.

They raised their glasses. Semyon chewed on a slice of grapefruit, just to see what it would be like. He'd only ever chased brandy with lemon slices before.

'First things first,' declared Gennady Ilyich. He took a brown envelope out of his leather briefcase, which was standing on the seat next to him, and laid it on the table. 'There. That's the birth certificate. You can fill the name in yourself. And here's a credit card for expenses. Kids may be priceless, but raising them costs a fortune these days!'

'A credit card?'

'Yes. Call it a gift from her godfather! . . . Ah yes, I haven't told you the most important bit yet . . . I'm going to be the child's godfather! You didn't have any other candidates lined up, did you? I'll find a godmother too, so you don't need to worry about it. We can have the christening in my church, then it won't be far to go for the party afterwards.'

'Will Father Onophrios do the honours?' asked Semyon.

'No. That bastard left the Church and went to work for an animal rescue charity.' The deputy shook his head, clearly astonished at the clergyman's decision. 'They sent me a new one, fresh out of the spiritual academy. He's an efficient chap, and he's got a nice voice. Have you got a name for her yet, by the way?'

'Yes – Marina.'

'That's a bit unoriginal,' Gennady Ilyich frowned, but his face soon brightened. 'Well, Marina it is then! To our Marina! May she be happy, healthy and wise!'

After the second toast they both started to relax. Gennady Ilyich even yawned a couple of times. He took the phone from the wall again and declared that it was about time their meat arrived.

The first thing the waiter brought was a solid wooden board of considerable dimensions, which he placed on the table in front of Semyon. On it was a massive slab of sizzling, chargrilled T-bone steak. He set down beside it a plate of green herbs and three little dishes containing different kinds of sauce.

A moment later Gennady Ilyich's eyes lit up as he was presented with his own steak board, on which six lamb medallions were lined up in a row.

'Have you ever thought about becoming a deputy?' Gennady Ilyich asked suddenly, tearing his eyes away from his meat.

'No.' Semyon was puzzled by the question.

'Well, you should,' advised his boss. 'The early elections are being held soon, and we'll be related by then. Godfathers don't only help out their godchildren, you know. They have an obligation to help the whole family, particularly when there's a good reason to. And you and I go back a long way, don't we? We've known each other since Petrivka, since the trading days of our youth!'

'I'll think about it,' promised Semyon, without any particular enthusiasm.

'OK! But for now use your hands, not your head!' said Gennady Ilyich, and he picked up his steak knife and attacked the first medallion.

116

Apartment No. 17, Vorovsky Street, Kiev

Darya Ivanovna's alarm clock went off at 1.30 a.m. She got straight out of bed and had a shower, then went into the kitchen in her dressing gown and lit the gas ring under the kettle. She was about to make a coffee, but then she remembered the new café manager asking her not to drink any.

There was an unusually cold wind blowing outside, which was

even more surprising after the warm spring weather they'd been having lately. Apart from the sound of the wind there was silence. The city was asleep. There were no lights on in any of the buildings she walked past. The street lamps chased patches of darkness away, their glow serving only to highlight the emptiness of the night.

She could see the Radisson hotel ahead of her to the left, its facade illuminated with dozens of lights. Several Skodas decorated with the hotel's logo were parked in a neat row in front of the main entrance.

Darya Ivanovna walked as far as the corner of Yaroslaviv Val and Olesya Gonchara Street, where she stopped abruptly. There was a kind of rustling noise. She tried to hide, nervously pressing herself up against the wall of a grey building.

A crowd of rather short people streamed out onto the crossroads from the direction of Victory Square. They were discussing something energetically in a language she didn't recognise, and looking more closely Darya Ivanovna realised that they were either Vietnamese or Chinese. There were about twenty of them, maybe more, and as they reached the crossroads at the top of the hill they fell silent and looked around. Then they exchanged a couple of birdlike phrases and headed towards Lviv Square, walking right past Darya Ivanovna, who had merged with the wall.

At the corner of the three cafés Darya Ivanovna saw a pink Hummer parked against the wall to the right of the wreath. There was a low light coming from one of the café windows. She went up to the door and gave three rather timid knocks.

The door was opened by a young man wearing a suit and tie, who gave her a friendly but silent nod and motioned for her to follow him.

She found herself in the manager's office again. It was rather small, but she felt quite comfortable there. Her gaze was immediately drawn to the wall behind the new manager, where a photo of her husband Edik hung in an elegant frame. It definitely hadn't been there the day before!

The manager, a slim and reasonably attractive blond man of around forty called Nikita Lvovich, invited her to sit down opposite him. He poured some bright green liquid from a carafe into a crystal glass and handed it to her.

'It's wheatgrass juice. Very good for you,' he said, his voice soft and velvety. 'I'm so glad you came, and right on time too! Your husband Eduard was also exceptionally punctual. I didn't want to talk to you with others present, which is why I asked you to come at this hour. We don't tend to get many "customers" at night, as a rule. They're all asleep. Go ahead, drink up!' he said, looking at the crystal glass.

Darya Ivanovna sipped the wheatgrass juice. She rather liked it. The distinctive taste of the juice triggered vague sensory memories from her distant past, maybe even as far back as her childhood.

'You know, we really value everything your husband did. You might not even be aware of the important scientific research he was carrying out in our field –'

'Your field?'

'Yes,' he nodded. 'He and I were colleagues. We worked together . . .'

Darya Ivanovna looked around in confusion, wondering what her Edik could possibly have had in common with the manager of a café.

'You probably think that I'm a food industry worker, right?'

smiled Nikita Lvovich, reading his guest's mind. 'No, I'm a pharmacist. And incidentally, this is no longer a café.'

'What is it now?'

'It's going to be a private nightclub for patriotic pharmacists, and when I say "nightclub" I mean it in the literal sense. It will be frequented by pharmacists who believe, as your husband did, that our country can be cured. We just need to come up with the right medicines. I've been charged with asking you whether you would agree to become an honorary president of our club, in memory of your husband. You are very well respected within our community. You'll be able to take your wreath down in two weeks' time. By then we will be ready to replace it with a marble bas-relief in memory of your husband.'

'Honorary president?' Darya Ivanovna repeated pensively. She thought about Edik. She thought about when he was alive, and she thought about him in his more recent state – sitting in his armchair by the balcony door. So, it turned out that he'd had other secrets from her too, and they weren't all to do with women . . . 'All right,' she said.

'Thank you,' said Nikita Lvovich. 'Everyone will be delighted! And now I have a confession to make. Do you remember finding a bit of a mess at the pharmacy one night, in your husband's office?'

Darya Ivanovna thought about it. She couldn't remember any mess, but she suddenly remembered something else.

'You mean the burglary?'

'Well, I wouldn't call it that exactly. We just took what we could from the office, to keep his work from falling into the hands of the political party that paid for his last experiments. Naturally we were in a rather a hurry, so I'm afraid we didn't have time to tidy up after ourselves . . . Please accept my apologies.'

Darya Ivanovna thought about the old woman who had worked for Edik at the pharmacy for years. She'd been so frightened.

'Incidentally, we're the ones who bought the pharmacy from you.' There was a touch of pride in the blond man's voice, and Darya Ivanovna knew why: she had been paid twice as much for the pharmacy as she'd expected.

'Now, I do have one more favour to ask you,' continued Nikita Lvovich. 'Your husband must have kept some kind of archive at home – notebooks, diaries, correspondence and suchlike. Would you by any chance consider donating these records to the club? We're planning to set up a small private museum here, just for our members.'

Darya Ivanovna nodded.

Nikita Lvovich got up from behind his desk and accompanied Darya Ivanovna to the door, where he shook her hand.

'We'll be in touch soon,' he said.

On the way home Darya Ivanovna was filled with a new emotion. She discovered she liked walking the streets at night. The sleeping city didn't frighten her any more; on the contrary, it seemed like her own slumbering infant, curled up and lost in dreams. She felt only tenderness towards it. She wanted to caress it and hold it in her arms, this enormous, lovable city.

Suddenly she heard the piercing yowl of a cat from somewhere nearby, possibly from one of the neighbouring courtyards. Darya Ivanovna froze. Then just as suddenly there was silence again. A safe and welcoming silence. Darya Ivanovna went on her way, thinking about her husband Edik with tenderness and sorrow.

117

9 May Street, Boryspil

Valya fried some boiled sausage for breakfast. She put a piece in Fluffy's bowl. She didn't finish her cup of tea because she caught sight of the time and had to run to catch the minibus taxi. She would have been late if she'd walked!

Left alone, Dima reached for the latest issue of the local classified ads paper. His eyes fell on the advert that he'd circled for the recruitment of clergymen. He thought about Father Onophrios and was half tempted to give him a call, to see if they'd hired him, but then decided he couldn't be bothered. He was too comfortable sitting at the kitchen table, basking in the sun. It was so nice and relaxing just sitting there, thinking about anything and everything.

He started thinking about moving to Saratov and threw a spiteful look at Kitchen Fluffy, who was lying in his usual spot under the radiator without the faintest idea that his owners were heading off into their shiny, new future without him and that his easy life was about to come to an end. He wasn't to know that the Russians had no need for Ukrainian cats – they had enough of their own!

Dima thought about poor, dead Scruffy with a mixture of grief and gratitude. Now there was a pet to be proud of – loyal, clever and brave!

After sitting in the sun for a while, Dima decided to go to the *pelmeni* café for a double shot of vodka. Of course he could have had a drink at home, and he wouldn't have had to stop at one . . . but that wasn't very civilised. Whereas going for a drink in the *pelmeni* café meant that you were out in public, mixing with people, having conversations and answering questions. And a double vodka cost next to nothing. Maybe he would strike up a conversation with the owner of the *pelmeni* café . . . He might even tell him their secret, about moving to Saratov. The café owner would be sorry that he was losing two of his regular customers. Well, probably. If their roles were reversed Dima knew he would be sorry about it!

As it happened, there was no one in the *pelmeni* café apart from the owner. Dima drank his vodka but decided not to share their secret with the café owner. It was still a little early – they needed to receive a positive response from Saratov first, before they could start telling people.

He wandered down to the kiosk, bought three newspapers and came home.

It wasn't until he sat down at the kitchen table that he noticed the glaring headline on the front page of the *Kiev Gazette*: NEW DEVELOPMENT IN BRUTAL CENTRAL KIEV MURDER CASE.

Dima leaned over the newspaper and held his breath as he read.

The article was about a young woman who had gone into a militia station and told them that she'd been on her way home from a friend's house late at night when a smartly dressed middle-aged man had run up to her at the junction of Reitarska Street and Striletska Street. He'd grabbed her arm and pressed her against the wall with one hand – in the other hand he'd been holding a knife. She'd called out for help, and suddenly a large cat had pounced on the man. It had been too dark to see what colour the cat was, but it had sunk its teeth into the man's throat and blood had immediately started spurting from his neck. The man had let go of the woman's arm and she had managed to escape. It had taken her two days to recover from the shock of the experience, but when they showed the dead man on television she recognised him straight away!

Dima was astonished. He read the article again. Then he looked at the clock. He changed into some dark and inconspicuous clothing, put his small folding spade into a shopping bag and left the house.

An hour and a half later he was calmly walking down the main path of the Baykov Cemetery. He recognised several of the crosses and monuments. He found the area where the military commanders and Heroes of the Soviet Union were buried, and a little while later he stopped by two familiar memorial busts. He stared at the little burial hill between them. This was where he had buried Scruffy not long ago. This was where his little cat bones lay.

Dima squatted down in front of the grave. He reached out and touched the bare soil, which would be covered with grass or moss in a couple of weeks' time. Suddenly he noticed that the rear of the hill seemed to have collapsed in on itself. Dima went round to the back of Scruffy's little grave and saw a hole in it about the size of two fists. He bent down and looked inside. The shallow hole was empty.

Dima groped around inside with his hand, then sniffed his fingers. They smelled of cat. Dima stood up and looked around in confusion. His eyes fell on a saucer with the remains of a piece of raw fish, which stood on the marble gravestone of the twice Hero of the Soviet Union.

'It's Scruffy,' thought Dima. 'He saved that woman, and he's keeping the streets of Kiev safe at night! I have to find him and take him back to Boryspil, and then he's coming with me to Saratov, whatever it takes.' Dima and Scruffy – they were meant to be together.

Dima wandered around, searching for his cat among the monuments and the luxuriant vernal vegetation. But Scruffy was nowhere to be seen.

'I need to look for him at night, in the city centre,' thought Dima.

Putting the shopping bag over his shoulder, he strode cheerfully towards the exit. He had a plan of action – for today, at least. He would return to Boryspil, collect Valya from work and take her home. Later on, once Valya was asleep, Dima would write a note explaining his temporary absence and leave it on the kitchen table. Then he would take the last minibus taxi to the very centre of Kiev, where he would search the streets and courtyards for his scrawny, feral and remarkably fearless cat.

118

Apartment No. 10, Reitarska Street, Kiev
After his first night shift Semyon slept only three hours before getting out of bed again, wide awake and ready to tackle whatever the day threw at him. He was alone in the apartment. The sun was shining, and Veronika had left a note saying that she'd taken the baby for a walk. A couple of doves had settled on the window ledge, and their cooing could be heard through the little top window.

He thought about the previous night. When he and Volodka had gone to the milk kitchen to pick up the churns, the man on duty had been wearing a new uniform: orange dungarees. The streets of Kiev were busier at night than Semyon had expected. He and Volodka kept driving past groups of men striding purposefully in the same direction, as though they were all going to some kind of organised gathering.

At the orphanage they had been met by a security guard, who had wasted no time in waking up two of the older boys. The boys had carried three churns of goat's milk into the cheese-making workshop and then stood around smoking, in the absence of the director or any of the teachers. Then they had loaded five covered plastic tubs of goat's cheese into the car, each weighing several kilos.

The area around Parliament had been teeming with life, despite the late hour. It must have been the same inside: the side entrance door kept opening and shutting, letting people in and out.

Semyon's neighbour Igor had been working as senior bartender in the Parliament café for two days now and Semyon had never seen him so happy, despite the fact that his eyes were virtually stuck together with sleep. Semyon had called him on his mobile phone and he had come out to collect the cheese. After taking it inside, he had brought out two glasses of good cognac for Volodka and Semyon. The militiaman guarding the rear service entrance had also expressed his desire to sample this great and noble beverage, and Igor had gone back in again without a murmur to fetch him one.

About three minutes later four grown men had stood on the doorstep of the service entrance to Parliament under the night sky, glasses in hand. They had drunk a toast to spring, to the good things in life: 'To all the best . . . and sod the rest!'

When Volodka had been driving him home in the early hours

of the morning Semyon had started thinking about Egor. He thought about him again now, and as he did so he forgot all about the previous night.

Semyon drank a cup of strong coffee, got dressed and decided that it was time for him and Egor to meet.

He took a large carrier bag and put in two packs of disposable nappies, three boxes of formula milk and the blank registration form from the orphanage that the obstetrician had given him. Then he went outside and stopped the first taxi he saw going past.

For two hundred hryvnas the driver agreed to take him to Lipovka, then wait there and bring him back to Kiev.

On the way Semyon imagined knocking on the door of their house and being told that Egor was at work in Kiev. What would he do then? Speak to his wife? No, that would be pointless. He would just have to come back to Kiev and find Egor near the Mariinsky Palace, although it wouldn't be quite so convenient to talk there . . .

Piles of dirty snow still lay on the verges of the country road, under the pine trees that made up the roadside forest. It was warm in the car, though. The driver took his sunglasses out of the glove compartment and put them on.

They drove right up to the house. Semyon was delighted to see the red Mazda parked next to the fence. He took the carrier bag and went up the steps to the front door.

Egor opened the door, wearing black tracksuit bottoms and a T-shirt. He was unshaven and looked as though he hadn't had enough sleep.

'Are you Egor?' asked Semyon, as if he didn't already know.

'Who are you?'

'My name's Semyon. We need to talk.'

'Hang on, I'll be right there,' said Egor. He pulled the door shut as he went back into the house, leaving Semyon on the doorstep.

A few minutes later Egor came out. He had put his boots on and was wearing a black suit jacket over his T-shirt.

'What's up?' he asked. He sounded worried.

Without a word Semyon took the registration form from the orphanage out of the carrier bag. He held it out to Egor.

'Fill it in for Marina,' said Semyon, trying to make his voice sound as friendly as possible. 'You can use this form to get her a birth certificate. You might need to give them fifty bucks for witnessing it, I don't know . . .' He held the bag out to Egor. 'And this is for you as well.'

There was a moment's silence. Egor held the registration form and studied it attentively. He stared at the violet stamp. When he looked back at Semyon his eyes were full of questions.

'Maybe we could sit down somewhere for five minutes?' suggested Semyon.

Egor nodded. He gestured to Semyon to follow him into the house.

They sat down in the kitchen. They could hear women's voices and a baby crying.

Semyon looked around and felt surprisingly comfortable in the snug little kitchen.

'I was asked to find Marina,' he said. 'And I did, but I haven't told anyone. You can keep her.'

'What do I owe you?' asked Egor carefully.

'Nothing,' Semyon shrugged. 'I was told that I would be allowed to adopt her if I found her, but I found another baby to adopt. Another little girl. Her name's Marina too. So everything's worked out fine in the end. We're almost colleagues, by the way!'

'Really?' Egor was surprised.

Semyon told him about himself, about how he used to have his own security firm but now he worked for a deputy, so he spent a lot of time near Parliament.

'Maybe we could go for a coffee some time,' said Egor.

Semyon wanted to see baby Marina, so Egor brought her into the kitchen to show him.

The taxi sounded its horn on the other side of the fence.

'I'll be at work tomorrow,' Egor said to Semyon. 'Thanks for the form!'

They exchanged mobile phone numbers.

A strange feeling overcame Semyon on the way back to Kiev. He felt as though he could really trust Egor, as though he'd known him for years.

'The two of us are going to get on, I just know it,' he thought, as the car flew past the forest and the fields began. 'Maybe I could be godfather to their Marina? That would close the circle. Decent people should stick together and help each other out whenever they can.'

His mobile phone rang just as they were approaching the outskirts of the city.

'Hi, it's Egor. I forgot to ask . . . What are you doing for milk? Breast milk, I mean.'

'We're not. We're using formula for the moment.'

'You shouldn't feed a baby just on formula milk! My Irina's got plenty to spare, she'd be happy to share some with you. I'll bring some with me tomorrow. Come to the viewing area near the palace at ten tomorrow, and we can go for a coffee.'

Semyon put his mobile phone back in his jacket pocket and smiled.

119

Lipovka village, Kiev region

At around 11 a.m. Irina had just finished breastfeeding the babies when a black Mercedes 500 pulled up by their wicket gate. Aleksandra Vasilievna was the first to notice it.

'Oh my goodness!' she exclaimed, holding the curtain to one side. 'Who on earth can be coming to see us in a car like that?'

A well-dressed young woman and two young men in black leather jackets and smart black trousers got out of the Mercedes. The woman took an enormous bunch of roses from the back seat. One of the young men was holding a carrier bag, and the other took a large cardboard box from the boot of the car.

'Good heavens!' exclaimed Baba Shura. 'Who's all this from? It must be wedding gifts!'

Irina put both girls under the blanket on her bed. She went over to the mirror and adjusted her hair.

There was a knock at the door and Baba Shura hurried into the hallway, smoothing her clothes as she went.

'It's for you, Irinka!' called her mother, as Irina appeared from her room.

The young men in leather jackets put the carrier bag and the box down on the floor, nodded politely and went out onto the doorstep, closing the door behind them.

'Are you Irina Koval?' asked the woman with the flowers.

Irina nodded.

'These are for you, from all of us.' She held the flowers out to her. 'They're Colombian roses. And this is a very important letter – read it straight away, please!'

Irina gave the flowers to her mother and took the cream-coloured envelope. It was about twice the size of a normal envelope and felt pleasantly rough to the touch.

Her mother put the light on in the hall to make it easier to see. Irina opened the unsealed envelope and took out a piece of cream-coloured paper, which had been folded in two. She opened it.

Dear Ms Koval,

A recent general meeting of the closed joint-stock company Sandy Hills deemed the business practices of the former management to be unsatisfactory and unacceptable. The director, Nelly Igorievna Sarmatova, has been summarily dismissed. On behalf of the new management I would like to offer our sincere apologies for any misunderstanding that may have arisen between yourself and the former management, and as a gesture of goodwill we would like to offer you registered shares in the company. A certificate to this effect will be presented to you in due course. Looking ahead to the future, we would like to invite you to return to employment with the company. From 1 April the purchase price of breast milk will be tripled. Transport costs will be reimbursed, and your bene-fits package will include insurance, quarterly leave and paid sick leave. We would also be grateful for any new donors you might consider introducing to us; for each new donor we will be delighted to offer you a bonus of 1,000 hryvnas.

Please accept these modest gifts as a sign of our deepest respect. I hope that we will be able to re-establish a working relationship based on these new terms.

Yours sincerely,

Olga Ivanovna Blazhenyuk

When she'd finished reading Irina gave the woman a calm, benevolent look. The woman took a piece of paper from the pocket of her light-brown sheepskin jacket.

'Sign here, please, to say you've received the gifts. They're very strict about accountability now . . .'

'Is Nurse Vera still working for you?' asked Irina.

'No.' The woman sighed. 'She was killed in a car crash. All our staff are new, and young.'

When they were saying goodbye the woman in the sheepskin coat asked Irina for her mobile phone number. Just for their records.

The Mercedes left, and Irina and her mother went and sat in the kitchen. Her mother read the letter for a third time.

'You see? Finally something's changing in our country!' she said.

Irina sat and thought about the past winter, remembering the sweet porridge, Nurse Vera and Mariinsky Park. She felt a bitter-sweet nostalgia, as though it had all happened a long, long time ago.

'Vera Minyailo had a baby recently, and she's not married,' Aleksandra Vasilievna suddenly remembered. 'Why don't you go and see her? She might be interested. Then you'll get that bonus!'

Epilogue

October turned the leaves of Kiev gold. Both Marinas and Yasya had grown so much over the last six months. There was a palpable sense of stability in Semyon's and Egor's families, and throughout the country as a whole. Everything seemed to have taken a turn for the better. The two families now socialised together, and during working hours Semyon and Egor went for coffee and discussed the latest news in Ukrainian politics, from which they both tried to keep a safe distance.

A new democratic movement won the early parliamentary elections – the All-Ukrainian Embassy of the Moon Party, led by former psychiatrist Pyotr Isaevich Naitov. Darya Ivanovna Zarvazina was the third party member elected to Parliament, and Gennady Ilyich was the fifth.

At their first session the new Parliament took the decision to abolish all deputy benefits and privileges. They also switched to a nocturnal working regime, whereupon the people sighed with relief: they were happy that Parliament was now going to be working at night, when normal people were asleep.

'Have you seen what's going on back there?' asked Valya, looking up from an article about events in Ukraine in the *Saratov News*.

She and Dima were sitting in a *pelmeni* trailer café not far from Cosmonauts' Embankment. Under the table Fluffy and Scruffy were finishing off the tail of a fried sturgeon. Either the long journey or the sudden abundance of fish from the Volga had reconciled the two cats, although there was still a fundamental difference in their nocturnal habits. One of them always spent the night at home, in the kitchen of the small two-roomed apartment on Babushkin Vsvoz Street, not far from the embankment; whereas the second, Dima's favourite, spent his nights prowling the city – something to which his indulgent master did not object.

'Oh,' said Valya, putting her hands on her stomach. 'He's kicking again!'

Dima looked at his pregnant wife and smiled a faraway smile as he imagined the happy future that lay in store for them.